Black Out

Parabaloni 8

By Catherine Gruben Smith

Sola Deo Gloria

Listen to a playlist curated for this book!

ISBN: 978-1-955639-18-7

To Anna:
You already burn bright, my girl, everywhere you go faces light
with smiles. May your light always be a reflection of Christ.

Contents

"The way of the wicked is as darkness: they know not at what they stumble." (Proverbs 4:19)
"But the path of the just is as the shining light, that shineth more and more unto the perfect day." (Proverbs 4:18)

Colin Clempson sank back in the plane's seat and gave a prodigious groan. Mr. Luke, his dad's private secretary, looked up from his book. Colin noticed even the man's eyebrows were muscular.

"What would it take for you to pass my phone?" Colin demanded. The secretary didn't move. "What about lending me that novel?"

"Your mother ordered nothing but your schoolbooks," Mr. Luke said, his voice the same dead monotone Colin had always heard him use.

"But I've already finished them all," the young man complained. The secretary's eyes just went back to the page. For a moment Colin debated snatching the book. But his eyes flicked to the muscles almost bulging out of the secretary's suit coat and he thought better of it. He tried staring out the plane's little window.

The stars glowed out there. So close they seemed almost touchable. So many of them, countless hosts of brilliant balls of fire, so many lightyears away. He picked out one orb a little brighter than its fellows and wondered what its name was. How big was it? Some of those innumerable balls of fire were bigger than Earth's sun. Lots of them were bigger. So many stars. Galaxies upon galaxies, on and on and on till the human mind could no longer grasp the enormity. And here he sat, a tiny dust speck on an insignificant planet in a backwater galaxy…

Colin flung himself away from the window. He glared at the seat in front of him, desperately longing for anything except his own brain and those brilliant stars. He didn't want to hear their song. He already knew enough about his insignificance.

"Where are we going?" Colin demanded, his head snapping back to the secretary. Mr. Luke glared over his book.

"Look, I'm not the one who was caught skipping school for a whole year and got shipped off with his dad as punishment," the secretary stated. Annoyance rode it, and Colin silently congratulated himself for breaking the man out of his monotone.

"I didn't skip school, just the public part of it. I schooled myself very well, and had the best teachers anyone's ever had."

"Really."

"Socrates, Shakespeare, Newton, Plutarch–"

"Have fun convincing your mother of that," Mr. Luke broke in. Was that amusement in his voice? Huh. The secretary slapped the book closed and dropped it to his lap. "Why did you ditch school? First the private one, then the public. Why did you switch if you wouldn't stay in either?"

"Oh, the switch to public was only sort of my idea, Mom's PR person said it would look good to have me attend like 'normal people.'" Colin shrugged. The bullies in the private school had been worse than the public; until the public ones caught him off school property, anyway. He could have solved it by going to the school authorities, his dad's name would get anyone expelled, just so the school could keep the Clempson money. And get their parents fired, and the whole family run out of town. Colin hadn't chosen that solution. But he had no intention of bringing up any of that. "I got away with it for quite a while."

Mr. Luke's stare softened. Pity crossed his face, and Colin could have punched him. He knew what went through the secretary's head. *His parents didn't even notice for a full year. Do they ever notice him?* Of course they didn't. Colin refused to look away from the secretary's stare. He refused to let himself flush under his dark skin, or snap back something this man didn't deserve. But he still wanted an answer.

"So, we're on our way to…?"

"Riyadh."

"Oh. Oil business?"

"No."

"Imports?"

"No."

"Then–"

"Look, you got your answer." The secretary's tone came brusque, more than just annoyed. Uncomfortable. "Now we have twelve hours in these seats, and I am not going to pander to your conversational whims. I'm going to sit quietly and read my book and watch movies (which you are banned from doing), and you are going to shut up and read your schoolbooks–"

"I finished all of them last year."

"–or I will take you by the back of the collar and frog march you out of first class into the economy section and sit you between two fat guys. Again. Got it?" Mr. Luke stared, and Colin's hands came up acknowledging surrender. He had learned the secretary was perfectly willing to make good his threat on the first flight out of California. Mr. Luke went back to his novel. Colin slumped in his seat. Riyadh… For something Mr. Luke didn't want to talk about. But then no one ever wanted to talk to him.

No one was going to tell him what his dad was doing. Or who the stranger was who had slipped into his dad's office two weeks ago without even Mr. Luke knowing about it. Or why that stranger carried a rifle and ordered his dad around. A stranger who wore black kid gloves, kept out of full view of the windows, answered in monosyllables, and ordered the date for this weekend. Colin had rarely been scared in his fifteen years of life. But when he heard[1] his father fawning over that creep, chills had gone up Colin's spine. It had taken a lot of work to finally get his mom to notice the host of letters and phone calls from the school about her errant child, and a fair amount of skill to maneuver the conversation just right to get shipped off with his dad for "quality time with that boy."

If no one would tell him what Dad had gotten into, Colin would find out on his own.

His eyes darted two rows ahead, to the top of the first class cabin. Jackson Clempson sat relaxed, a drink by his elbow, scrolling his iPhone again. For once his dad wasn't busy with business emails, it looked like… Colin squinted and just managed to make out a headline about party balloons destroying wildlife habitats. Of course. If it wasn't business it was the Mother Earth sites.

Colin felt inclined to throw a package of plastic soda straws out the window and see what his dad did.

No. It would just give Mr. Luke more work. Colin sighed,

---

[1] He read a how-to book about spy gadgets, and was up in the oak tree trying out his new infrared scanner and listening device on his dad's office. It worked, but not enough to get the whole conversation. It worked even better on the cook, but he didn't hide as well with her, and ended up cornered in the pantry getting punched out by her boyfriend. He admitted he deserved it and returned the book to the library.

slumped farther, and tried not to think about the next twelve hours. And once they arrived he wouldn't be allowed to explore a foreign country. He had been dragged to eight different countries by now on "family vacations" his mom's PR person said they should take, and learned only that hotels everywhere were about the same. The most exciting thing was likely to be helping carry the bags. Mom usually wouldn't let him do the actual carrying, demanding "the help" did it instead. But this trip Dad had brought six large bags, and only Mr. Luke to carry them. Colin's eyes darted to his dad again. He watched one dark finger shift the screen. Woo hoo. Quality time.

But why so much luggage?

Chapter 1

Yousef crouched against the wall and watched the beamer run past. The driver didn't notice him. With the traditional hooded thobe draping his thin face, the Saudi disappeared as just another part of Riyadh. No one noticed Yousef bin Jahail Aziz. It was a gift, and a curse.

Today he would use it as a gift.

He lounged against the convention center, watching the private cars and taxis come and go. Most dropped their rich passengers and rolled on, with hotel chauffeurs behind the wheels. A Tesla drew up, and he watched three dark skinned men climb out, one hugely muscular, one a lanky teenager, and one who obviously had the money and expected everyone to act like it. The teenager took a grim satisfaction in helping with the ludicrous number of bags. Yousef idly contemplated how easy it would be to obtain a hotel jacket and drive off with a car. He would enjoy that, if he ever found a reason to take one of those beautiful machines. His family could use a little extra grocery money, and he knew where to sell a hot vehicle.

An electric van shifted smoothly through the traffic toward Yousef's side of the street. Interesting. The opulent entrance to the convention center and hotel stood across from him. He could see the golden chandeliers twinkling through the glass wall and hear snatches of the live music dancing through the lobby. Yousef's side of the street connected to the hotel by a skybridge, but people only came here after they checked in. His side held the meeting rooms, the kitchens, the boring places where people only came if they had a reason.

The van pulled off the street into the small loading dock behind Yousef. He shifted away from his wall with a smooth, bored grace and strolled up the street. No one noticed him. He shuffled slowly past the entry to the dock, nothing about him showing any interest in the place. But from under his hood he studied everything.

Eight people stepped out of the van. A group of mixed souls.

Some with dreadlocks, some with high heels. But Yousef knew the faces.

The Butwani had arrived. The originals. The ones who had been here prepping for this meeting at this convention hall in his city. Yousef felt the blood move a little faster through his veins as anger stirred inside him. Didn't Saudi Arabia have enough trouble without foreigners popping up to bring more?

One individual slid out from behind the wheel a little slower than the rest, managing to stay apart from the crowd. A medium man in a business suit, his tanned face bland and forgettable. Yousef noticed him though. The way the man moved, at the back of the group, head down, feet not quite shuffling, mouth closed… Yousef moved that way when he wanted to be in the background. Yousef stopped and leaned against the wall on the other side of the entrance to the dock. He pulled out a block of wood and his knife, dropped to a crouch, and began to whittle with a quick skill that showed his expertise. But his eyes stayed on the man in the business suit. Yousef had seen him twice before. He knew just enough to stay back and watch.

Hotel workers strode out of the door into the bay with bags. The same bags Yousef had just watched be unloaded from the back of a Tesla by a lanky teenager and bulky hired man. Five large bags, their shape strange, like nothing Yousef could identify. Parts to something, perhaps?

The man in the business suit helped sort out the luggage, quietly and competently sliding in place to be in charge without challenging anyone for it. He made sure each bag went to the right person, was carefully checked (out of view of the one camera), and loaded in the van. This man didn't belong in the background. He was the one in charge, though few around him realized it. One did, Yousef could see, a red-haired beauty with a knife in her boot. The company filed inside, chatting and easy. The man busied himself at the back of the van; waiting till everyone else had gone. The doors closed behind the last of the group and a stillness fell around the stranger. He turned back to the vehicle in the empty loading dock. Yousef noticed the van blocked the man's presence from the only camera. The man lifted the back flooring covering the spare tire. He took a small black case from inside, and ran a hand down it in a way that said it felt good to have the familiar item back with him again.

In that instant Yousef did something he had only done a few times in his life.

He prayed, earnestly and beggingly, to whatever god would hear him, beseeching the man would snap open that case. No. It wasn't really to any god. Yousef had slowly come to despise Allah as he watched his father sinking deeper into his terrorist activities, his two closest siblings driven away because of the harsh demands of the Prophet, his family torn apart. Yousef didn't put a name to the God of his prayer. But though he would not acknowledge it yet, his heartfelt pleading went to the Christian God.

The case snapped open. Yousef's knife kept moving at the same steady rate, picking away at the wood to create an intricate model of the convention center. His hood didn't shift. But he stared riveted, his forehead creased in confusion. The man in the black business suit stealthily slid the case into an inner pocket, checking to make sure no bulge gave its presence away. He strode for the building and Yousef watched him, wondering if he would ever learn what this strange development meant.

Inside that precious, hidden case lay nothing more dastardly than a pair of men's black gloves.

"I never knew there were so many names for nose shapes," Pete commented. He watched more information scroll down the screen in the Parabaloni war room, his feet comfortably propped on one of the crimson-covered chairs. He reached for his bowl of carrots on the desk. "Did you know one of them is nicknamed, 'the carrot'?" Vincent climbed off the thick rug and into a stretch. His tall form changed the light from one of the eight large windows letting in the New Mexican mountain sun, and the shadows shifted.

"Oh man, I need a break," the inventor groaned. He bent into another stretch, arching over photos splayed on the rug. Each of the photos showed a different angle of a silver egg-shaped canister. Pete tossed him a carrot and Vincent caught it in his mouth as he bent back up.

"It might be easier if you studied those pictures at a table or something," Pete said. He shifted his arm with a little grimace, testing to see how the bone healed. "Even I feel creaky after too long on the floor these days. We are getting old, Savant."

"Speak for yourself, Turtle Man," Vince grinned, and waved the carrot at the sofa situated discreetly under the tall bookshelves. "What do you say, G, are we old yet?" A soft snore drifted from the couch. Pete laughed.

"He's already indulging in the old one's desire for sleep," Pete chortled, "Gigan definitely agrees with me."

"Yeah, well, when our Frenchy naps mid-morning it usually means to watch for what he was up to during the night," Vincent grimaced. Peter's nose wrinkled and his laughter died.

"The kitchen, do you think?" the Saudi asked, studying his partner curled on the couch. The Frenchman only took up two cushions worth of space. Without his gear, it sometimes surprised Pete how small Gigan actually was. Especially knowing how lethal he could be.

"Annette?" Vincent asked the room hopefully.

"I have been directed not to report on anyone's movements last night," the Parabaloni HQ's automated voice broke over the speaker systems. "A code 24 is in place for the time slot between midnight to six a.m."

"He used a code 24?" Pete said, both his eyebrows going up. He glanced around the study a little nervously. "Maybe I'll just stay here for the rest of the morning."

"Maybe he's not after you this time," Vince suggested. "Jojo erased his rooster crow from the morning wake up call. And had some choice words to say about it, too." A grin shot across his face. "But then again he was awfully mad at you for hiding his book for three days."

"He had it coming, he kept stealing my time-travel novel while I was trying to read it. Maybe it's Jojo… but still, I shall be studious and keep researching these shadow people," Pete decided.

"Suit yourself," Vincent shrugged, and headed for the door. But he slowed and swung to a stop before he opened it, staring thoughtfully at the dark oak carved into scenes of ancient Greek history. His eyes darted to the form curled on the couch.

"You know, maybe I don't need a break as much as I thought," he commented and headed back to his pictures and broken pieces of gadget.

"Remembering a few of the words he called you when he found his mocha chocolate gone yesterday morning?" Pete asked, his crooked smile on his thin face. A carrot stuck out the side of his mouth as he kept scanning the files compiled from law enforcement agencies across the nation.

"I'm pretty sure it was just a lack of caffeine that blew over after he got to insult me for a few minutes. But I could do a little more work, maybe I'll find a breakthrough before Sim gets back with the shopping." Vincent dropped to his belly, his long legs crossed behind him, and his chin rested on his arm. He picked up one of the pictures and studied it again. A quiet half an hour ticked by in the war room, as Pete hunted for facts and Vincent and Pat turned old-fashioned photographs into hologram models the inventor could manipulate and break apart.

The soft vibration of the garage door opening in the basement below their room told them their boss had arrived. Pete and Vincent looked at each other, an inner debate raging over whether to help unload groceries. Their eyes swiveled to the Frenchman. They went back to their work. Five minutes passed as Vincent murmured to himself and Pete scanned more documents.

A sharp screech of bending metal drifted from the basement. With it came the keening outpour of a female voice in a fit of ire. The angry voice traveled toward them at a quick speed, the Arabic insults coming in a torrential outpour that felt like a swollen river overrunning its banks. The door burst open and Jojo swept in. She didn't even glance at her brother or the tall inventor on the rug. Her bare feet carried her to the couch in two bounds and her palm shot out into Gigan's spine. The Frenchman came awake with a jolt, his head snapping back as the palm strike sent him tumbling awkwardly off the couch.

"Guess how I just spent my morning?" Jojo asked, her voice quick, but sweet and soft. Pete winced. "I just died forty-seven times, in gruesome mangled ways, most of them burnt into a charred crisp."

"Flight simulator?" Gigan blinked at her, the picture of innocence. Jojo's lips pulled back in a tight smile, her dark eyes shining.

"Oh Bouncy, how good you are at pretending to know nothing," she told him gently. A couch pillow sailed into his face, then another, and another, till the couch stood stark and bony and he lay spluttering in a pile of crimson and black, one hand dramatically sticking out of the pile. Simeon strolled in and tossed a bulk supply box of energy bars to Pete. "If Simeon hadn't heard me banging on the wall, I would still be caught in the driving simulator dying in epic, terrible ways! It was bad enough to mess with the computer just enough to let me think it was me doing the crashing for the first ten times, but then to jam the door?! That was over the top, and you know it!" Gigan's head reared out of the pillows and spun toward the inventor's amused, freckled face lit by his handheld's egg-shaped hologram.

"Messing with the driving simulator?" Gigan frowned. "Vince, *mon ami,* that is not kind, to shove her confidence down just as she is beginning to learn her high speed driving!"

"Hoping I noticed the seat was adjusted for someone taller than your tiny height?" Jojo cooed. She swept one of the couch pillows off the ground and rammed it down on Gigan's head. "I did, you nasty little con artist!" Jojo shouted. "That's how I know it was you, Vincent wouldn't have been that sloppy! Dish duty, on your own, two weeks."

Jojo swept out of the room, her back straight and head high. Pete slouched into his chair, one hand over his mouth, trying not to laugh at Gigan's mixed humor and confusion at the sudden turn to his practical joke.

Vincent's hologram turned slowly in front of the inventor. The clock ticked on the mantelpiece, an old-fashioned sound to match the heavy wood furnishings and décor Simeon had chosen for this annex to his bedroom.

"Found anything?" Simeon asked, one finger flicking at the display in front of Pete. Gigan slowly climbed out of the pile of pillows and began to reassemble the couch.

"That these 'shadows' of my rescued Viking man are not documented," Pete reported. "Well, a better way to say it is that they are not caught and nothing is known of them." His fingers began to move, swiping up information. "Here are some eighty-seven cases I've found so far of inexplicable happenings. A factory explosion in Milwaukee, a murder in a West Texas airport, things that are only connected by the very ghostliness of the perpetrators. The FBI has a file devoted to the phenomenon. They sweep in without a trace, and are gone usually without even the cameras knowing. When something is caught on camera it is faceless and shadowy. It is almost as if there is some sort of cloaking mechanism at work. That is the best guess of the FBI file, some sort of high-tech jammer or cloaking device, and they are currently attempting to find a likely inventor for such a thing for the jumping off place of their investigation. Heshman[2] isn't on their list of possibilities. Andrea[3] is but they can't find her, apparently they never traced her to Italy. I did not learn more than that. No names. No starting points. No leads at all."

"It's a good start," Simeon corrected, studying the documents pulled up in front of his boy. His gaze swiveled to Vincent.

"Nothing new, sorry," the inventor reported. "It's designed to emit a constant pulse that keeps the grid down around it with remarkable efficiency, but we already knew that. On a large scale it could make it city wide. If I had to guess I'd say you're right and this is just a prototype. The real ones are probably made to

---

[2] An inventor Gigan found in a Memphis prison one time when the Frenchman was interned in deep cover to try to track down a very dangerous shipment coming to one of the inmates. Heshman is more of a mad scientist really, and he would probably be dangerous if his inventions actually worked. He has been working on a speed-of-light travel device (employing olfactory nerves and pinecone shavings) for twelve years and continually says it will be working "tomorrow." But he can be relied on to follow schematics and keep a project quiet. The Parabaloni occasionally use him to make things when Vincent doesn't have the time to do the actual fiddly work.

[3] An unscrupulous inventor the Parabaloni were obliged to chase off the Notre Dame roof and kidnap one time, who then wandered off to Italy with Gigan's evil twin brother, Grégoire. (See *Solitaire*.)

cover areas like all of Tripoli instead of just the few blocks around the lab. Also, when I say 'efficiency' I mean it can even undermine most simple faraday cages and similar failsafes people have in place to protect from normal EMPs. Which means almost all the cars would be stalled, it would knock out just about everything. Planes, of course, have the hydraulic flight option if you have to, so probably no planes dropping from the sky at least. It's oddly large for what it does. There's no compression to this gadget, it's almost like whoever made it designed it to be bigger and more intimidating than it has to be. A lot of the inside of the egg shape isn't used at all. The work seems a little familiar, but nothing distinctive enough I can pinpoint to a particular inventor. I would know more if I saw where they choose to set them up, and how they're attached. This little guy has a port on the bottom that is only full of mud from the Netherlands. Finding out what it's supposed to plug into would be my next step, but to do that we're going to have to find one already plugged in."

"Good work," Simeon praised. Vincent's eyes lingered on the hologram rotating slowly. His boss prodded him in the shoulder to make him finish his thought.

"Everyone's going to call this thing's work a blackout, and it's really a constant EMP attack!" the inventor burst out. "Can *we* at least call it what it is? It's a CEMPA."

"No," Pete broke in with a heavy frown. "'Blackout' sounds mysterious and exciting. 'CEMPA' sounds like yet another branch of government dealing with medical bills. I will not call it a CEMPA."

"Ah, come on!" Vincent complained, his arms swinging wide.

"I have to side with my partner on this one," Gigan said.

"You too?" Vince snapped at him.

"Blackout sounds so much better than CEMPA," the Frenchman shrugged.

"Thank you!" Pete said.

"Well yeah, when you say it with that attitude," Vincent pouted.

Simeon grinned and headed to finish unloading the groceries.

"Well," Pete stated, firmly closing the debate, "now that our

Frenchy's dastardly doing of the night has been uncovered, I'm going to quit the stuffy study and get some knife practicing in." He hopped up and trotted out the door, a fistful of carrots in one hand and four energy bars in his other.

"He's been doing a lot of knife practicing recently," Vincent commented. "Is there something I don't know?"

"When we were shipped to Huntsville this week and you and Sim stayed here having fun, Peter missed a mark by half an inch. It has been needling him," Gigan said.

"Excuse me, but while you two got to go track down a spy trying to undermine NASA, Patricia and I had to work twenty-four hours straight to find Luther and his band out in the forest!" Vincent objected. "You do realize that puts me as the sedentary, bored-stiff tech man for two cases in a row, and that officially gives me a bone to pick with you, boss man."

"You are not bored with tech work, my friend, just with the sedentary–"

A sharp yelp from the basement interrupted. The sound of Pete spluttering drifted up into the study. Vincent's eyebrow rose at the little Frenchman.

"Triggered when he hit a bullseye?" the inventor asked.

"If this white powder isn't flour–" Pete's voice broke off into a hoarse shout. "Hallucinogens! Frenchy, I'm going to murder you!" A smile spread over Gigan's weathered face.

"Aw, the sweet sounds of success," he sighed.

They flitted through the shadows as if made of shadows themselves. Aldrick could see them in fuzzy red and green shapes on the infrared app he had programmed on his phone. But the cameras in this power station saw nothing. They moved underneath the security, always in the blind spots, as if they had an instinctive ability to avoid the cameras' sweep. Aldrick crouched behind a coil of wires that lay forgotten in the huge building-sized room, and held his breath. His eyes stayed wide as he watched.

A large, bulky pack lay on each shadow's back. Most carried duffle bags too, bulging at the seams. Aldrick switched his phone's app to the x-ray he had painstakingly programmed, shifting positions to try and glimpse what those bags held.

Aldrick Lefebvre had an experiment in electromagnetism running in his basement at his family's Italian home, and for six months he had used the Andrea Palladio Power Station to boost his power. Usually it didn't take much work to slip in and out without security knowing. His family's smuggling business had given him many skills. And though he was fourteen he hadn't hit his growth spurt yet; he was still short and thin enough to slip through small, unguarded spaces[4]. Even so, one time a new security guard saw him. A lady, long black hair coiled in a braided bun, her eyes twinkling like Aldrick's Aunt Ginette. No, not like Ginette's mischievous attitude that didn't really bother with people other than herself. This guard laughed at the world, inviting you to join in the joke with her. It reminded Aldrick of his Uncle Guillaume. Aldrick felt her eyes fall on him, saw the way her chin lifted and mouth pursed. But she turned the other way, dropped something, and went on her rounds. Aldrick used an extendible hook to snag the item she dropped; a candy bar, with a scrawled note telling him to leave. It brought a quiet, huffing laugh to Aldrick, something that very rarely graced the young man's face. The guard probably would have had a different response if he had some of his cousins' height and build, Aldrick admitted. He left that day. But he came back when he wanted, more cautiously. She hadn't spotted him again.

But Monday when he came he saw the shadows. And he heard one murmuring about "finishing the business on Wednesday night."

Aldrick should have ignored it. He knew he should have ignored it, and he tried. But he noticed everything around him, and he liked the new nightguard, almost as much as an aunt or cousin. She walked her rounds chatting with her sister over her phone half the time. He knew the pretty young Italian held a dream to

---

[4] At least Aldrick assumed he hadn't hit his growth spurt yet. He hoped he gained at least a few more inches, though his father and Uncle Guillaume never had. His father just laughed when he caught Aldrick eyeing his taller cousins. "Smaller means we don't look threatening," Grégoire winked. "We carry our own element of surprise." Unfortunately Grégoire knows how to use it.

become a tightrope walker one day. He knew she had a date on Saturday with the man she hoped to make her husband, a Stephano Espositio... Aldrick knew that name too well, his family cursed it as one of the few detectives who could not be bought or intimidated. A good man.

Aldrick tried social media first, sending alerts to the proper authorities. Nothing came of it. Not even a "like" to show they noticed. He spent an hour pacing his little room in the Lefebvre tower, agonizing over whether to tell his Uncle Etienne, or ignore it, or take his father's pistol and go himself. If his grandmother had been there he would have asked her, but she was off visiting family in France for a month and left orders only to contact her if someone died. In the end he wrote a note for his step mom, left the pistol where it lay in its holster on Grégoire's hip as he slept off another bottle, and slipped out into the Italian night.

Now here he crouched watching these people, completely at a loss as to what to do next. What if they carried a bomb? What if they blew the place around his ears? His app couldn't identify the items inside those bags, they were parts to something unknown. Aldrick's hand dropped, letting the phone point toward the ground. His eyes strained into the darkness, trying to guess what he was seeing. The shadows reached the edge of the room near the transformers and shed their bags. Slowly, steadily, metal clinked and voices whispered and something took shape. Something silver, and large, filled with microchips and circuit boards and...he couldn't tell what it was. Not from this distance. But it stood six feet, at least. As he watched, one of the shadows stood up, reaching over his head to slip something into place.

The bags lay limp on the ground, almost empty. This thing had nearly been assembled. What was it supposed to do? Aldrick chewed his nails, staring at the scene being enacted in front of him.

The door down the room opened with a sharp creak.

The shadows near the transformers paused. Heads slowly spun to look toward the door.

Footsteps clicked on the concrete ground, quick, even, businesslike, coming toward them. Aldrick recognized the sound; the nightguard lady, headed on her rounds. Unsuspecting, unprepared for anything abnormal. Aldrick punched his phone back on infrared. He watched the red outline of one of the shadow people break away, creeping toward the sound of footsteps. They held something, but Aldrick couldn't tell what from his phone's reading. He leaned carefully around his coil.

He saw a wooden club in a burly man's fist.

Images of things he had watched weapons like that do flew into Aldrick's mind. His pale face grew paler, his stomach sick. Aldrick pulled back behind his coil and tightened his backpack. He could feel his heart pounding in his chest. But he had to do something, or that lady would never be a tightrope walker!

Chapter 2

A week before, Luther Kirl tried to bury Vincent under a burning building, and then disappeared into the woods. It took even Vince several days to track him down. His drone found Luther Kirl deep in the Vermont woods with a large group of "allies," at what appeared to be a permanent camp. Vincent managed to drop a surveillance bug on the old man while he slept. The Parabaloni had the feed running in their basement home theater, and one of them on constant duty listening to it through an earbud, in case anything useful happened. Nothing had yet.

Most of the past week Simeon kept the feed cycling in his earbud instead of detailing it to his boys. This morning as he traveled down to Las Cruces to pick up the food and listened to the miserable old man, several hypotheses clicked together into full-fledged theories. After he made it back, rescued Jojo, and checked in with the others, he headed to the darkness of the basement theater to watch Luther Kirl's feed.

The picture danced and shook as Kirl tossed on a sleeping bag on the muddy ground. A sharp expletive came from Luther and he suddenly grew still. He stared up at the rough sticks making up the ceiling of his lean-to. *A miserable old man,* Simeon thought with a frown. Luther Kirl had no one but himself to think about. Simeon knew that made life a small, sad place, filled with frustration as somehow nothing ever really made you happy. Not deep, lasting happiness. That sort can only come from looking outside of yourself. The best moments in life come from forgetting you even exist as you enjoy something else. Luther Kirl hadn't done that for years.

Simeon waited, quiet and still.

The door cracked open and Vincent slid in. He settled beside Simeon, his long legs stretched out in front of him, and his eyes went to the screen. He absently started flipping a screwdriver. Silence stretched on as Luther stared at the lean-to and the two men watched.

"How are the emails coming?" Vincent asked. Simeon shot

him a quick frown, and Vince found himself stumbling to guess what the look meant. Confusion slid through him as he tried to decide if he should be hurt by Sim not wanting to tell him about personal matters. Simeon's hands lifted and confusion mounted higher as it wasn't a shrug, or anything the inventor could name immediately.

The door to the home theater opened again and Gigan strolled in, yawning hugely. Simeon's hands dropped back to his lap so quickly it was as if he pulled a word back. Wait...Vincent's head spun, staring at the picture on the screen with new eyes, running through the past week of watching Luther and this Collective out in the woods. Surely not.

The Frenchman made it two steps, then a pair of brown hands darted through the light spilling from the open door. They wrapped around Gigan's neck, and the Frenchman jerked back with a "guk." The door snapped shut and the sounds of a sharp scuffle came from the other side. Vincent ignored it and leaned forward, his elbows going to his knees, studying Luther as the old man climbed to his feet, cursing and complaining the whole way. He slid into the cold of the woods and Vince could see his breath puff out in a cloud in front of him. Someone, a woman perhaps, turned toward Luther. The camera suddenly shifted, shaking and crackling as Luther scratched his clothing. The face fuzzed before any kind of identification could be made. The lady said something, but the crackling grew sharper and Vincent couldn't make out a single word.

A sharp smack came from outside the theater door.

"Contact!" Pete yelled with furious exultation.

"Your revenge is hardly subtle," Gigan's chuckle drifted in.

"At least you have the chance to defend yourself in an open fight, unlike your hidden skullduggery of sneaking about in the glooms," Pete snorted. Jojo stomped toward them, and Simeon suddenly slid from his chair. He pulled the door open and put a finger to his lips.

Mouths snapped closed and everyone turned toward the private theater.

A file of Parabaloni slipped in, their eyes on the screen. Luther hovered over a campfire, some sort of oatmeal substance oozing in a wooden bowl beside his elbow. Flecks of ash drifted into the bowl as they watched. Other people milled around the fire. But the camera's feed stayed focused on the flames dancing in the woodland ring. A conversation buzzed around him, and it would have been wonderful to hear it. But Luther kept scratching his shoulder, and the bug crackled. It refused to focus on any people. Pete's hands moved in the light spilling in from the open door.

"He knows about our bug," Peter signed as he stared at the scene. His eyes darted to Simeon, sitting beside Vincent again, his dog snuffling his hand. *"How long has he known?"*

"Whole time, maybe," Simeon signed.

"Do you really think he can hear us?" Gigan signed, and all eyes went to Vincent. Jojo opened her mouth, her head tipping as she pointed at the elegant hand motions fluttering about the dim room[5]. Simeon's finger shot to his mouth again, his eyes holding hers. Jojo swallowed her curiosity. She nodded and settled into her corner seat to watch.

"Rest of you, conversation. Nothing important," Simeon ordered.

"I like the Christmas presents, Vince, thank you" Gigan obeyed quickly. "Turtle Man agrees, they work nicely."

"I'm not sure I like Turtle Man," Pete said, his soft voice almost lost in the depths of his chair. "What about, 'Black Tortoise of Doom.'"

"Nope, you're the Turtle Man, dude, sorry," Vincent drawled. He drew Patricia out of his pocket and started running scans.

"There is no getting away from it now," Gigan agreed, leaning over to watch Pat work. "And your suit still smells like baked beans and smoke."

"Only to your French super-smeller," Pete said, watching as Luther stood up and stomped off into the woods. The camera swept over other human figures. But it never focused on them,

---

[5] She had only been with the Parabaloni for about seven months and there had been a lot of other things to take care of during that time. Like the Drone Wars in Nebraska, and saving the Delta Works in Holland, and other items I'm not allowed to mention. She hadn't had the opportunity to find out they used ASL for clandestine conversations, and certainly no time to learn any of the signs herself.

not long enough to get any sort of identification. Pete's hands moved again. *"It is so obvious that he knows the bug is there, how did none of us notice till now?"*

"Lion Heart has always known," Gigan signed back, his brilliant grin flashing over his face. Vincent noticed a ring around his left eye beginning to discolor and the eyelid slowly swelling. "I hope you like beans, because your suit will likely always smell of it."

"You know I like all things food," Pete shrugged.

"Our bug isn't feeding him our words," Vincent reported, his white hands easy to track even in the dimness of the theater. *"But there's a new one there, that we didn't plant, but is using the same channel as our feed. Yes, he is listening in. He can't see us. There's also something in the command center that Pat and I didn't pick up on earlier because we weren't looking for it. They have a bug sweeper. A good one."*

"How did he get the new bug and set it up to run along our channel?" Pete signed, and moved on with the conversation. "I prefer my beans not baked by cars though, the flames give it too much of a gasoline taste."

"Perhaps we should flame them with a blow torch and see what we think?" Gigan suggested as all eyes flicked to Simeon again.

"Had a visitor two days ago," Sim signed. Aurora lay across his lap, both ends of the corgi hanging off and a look of blissful happiness on her foxy face. *"Hard to notice with the shaky feed, made it hard to pinpoint. But he got it then."*

"Before or after cooking? Because we could just add artificial smoke to the pot if we chose," Pete said.

"A visitor? Contact from the outside world is interesting," Gigan signed quickly. "No, no, Turtle Man, artificial unvaryingly tastes artificial."

"So?" Pete demanded. *"We can use this."*

"Obviously," Vincent signed and grinned at him.

"Says the man who likes banana flavoring from a bottle poured over his crepes," Gigan snorted. *"How do we use it is more to the point."*

"I didn't pour, I dripped," Pete defended. *"Discuss over lunch?*

Let's go test the torch theory then."

"We're actually all home for lunch, that's a very strange anomaly for these past months!" Vincent said with a happy smile.

"I still ask, before or after cooking?" Pete demanded.

"If we do it after we will flame away all the good sauce, my friend," Gigan said.

"But we would have flaming beans in a bowl, and that would be undeniably keen," Vincent put in.

"True…" the Frenchman said, his tone suddenly thoughtful.

"Coffee," Simeon said decisively. The Parabaloni trundled out of the private theater, leaving Luther Kirl to bumble his miserable way through the woods on his own.

The drive to the hotel was too short and too opulent to be of much interest. Colin felt like he saw more people from Chicago or London than Arabia on that drive. He wondered where their driver lived in this sprawling city. The car moved under a huge gold-covered canopy and slid to a stop in front of a glass wall. There were a few traditionally clothed Arabians here. They spoke quick, lilting, strong words that seemed to dance and flow like water in a rocky river. A thin one was even barefoot, with his hood up as he crouched across the street whittling, in a pose Colin felt was straight from his copy of *Arabian Nights*.

Jackson Clempson didn't deign to wait for the driver to open his door. He slid out and strode for the foyer, still sending emails as he walked. As Colin hopped out to follow he noticed Mr. Luke move to the Tesla's trunk. The big man slid a bag strap over one shoulder and reached for another. Colin hopped over and slung the strap of his own bag over his neck. His hand darted forward and he caught the last handle before Mr. Luke could add it to the pile hanging off him. He already had enough to carry. Colin jerked the bag out with a grunt, let it land with a thump on its wheels, and trotted forward to catch up to his dad.

He missed the tiny smile that twitched at the corner of Mr. Luke's mouth as he watched the young man.

Colin pushed through the door into the foyer and turned in a slow circle as he took it all in. Three gold chandeliers sparkled from the ceiling and his feet sunk deep in the crimson rug. A fountain bubbled in the center of the huge room, as a live musician played an oud in one corner. Colin appreciated the head-nod for the local culture, a little surprised by how much he liked the soft music. The scent of cardamon and vanilla and coffee swirled in the air, and Colin fervently hoped the hot drink bar was open to all ages. He spotted his dad headed for the elevators and broke into a trot again to catch up. The wheels of his bag caught on the carpet and made it heavy to drag. The elevator doors started to close and Colin hopped through sideways, jerking the bag in behind him. It jumped forward and banged into his legs as the doors slid shut and soft elevator music took over.

Jackson glanced at the bag, then at the young man at his elbow. Annoyance shifted Jackson's face. Colin hunched a little deeper into himself and pretended it didn't matter. Mr. Luke pressed the unlabeled button at the very top of the row, to the penthouses and master suites, and slid a hotel card into the slot. The elevator started up. Jackson's eyes drifted to the gilded ceiling, as if willing it to move faster. Mr. Luke stared stonily at the wall.

They slowed to a stop and the doors slid open. Jackson stepped out and walked into the intricately tiled hallway. A glass domed ceiling stretched overhead, spilling golden sunlight around them. Colin stared up as he followed his dad, the bag's wheels clicking rhythmically over the tiles. Jackson flipped a card from his pocket, slid it in the lock, and the door sprang open, offering a glimpse of huge windows and tall ceilings and gold and pearl furnishings.

A heavy hand landed on Colin's shoulder as he started to follow, and he looked up at Mr. Luke. Was that an apology on his big face? The hand steered Colin away from the door to the next down the hall. Mr. Luke's own key card went in the lock, and the door popped open. A simple, thin room with two twin beds as the most prominent feature greeted Colin. He walked in slowly, the bag dragging behind him. A small kitchenette rested on his right, ordinary and drab. A little thrill went through him at the idea of using a counter with linoleum and not even marble. He had never done that before. His eye caught twin doors with bright sunlight spilling through them and he quickly dropped the bag, flung his own on one of the beds, and stepped out onto a balcony.

Fresh air and a cityscape that spread out to the far horizon washed over him, and Colin breathed deep. A good breeze always blew away his disappointments and troubles in life. At least for a few minutes. And this was a good breeze. Colin leaned against the railing and studied the vast city sprawling fourteen stories below him. He heard the door shut softly behind him, and felt Mr. Luke's huge presence as the big man stepped out on the balcony.

"Sorry you got stuck sharing your room," Colin said. A shrug lifted Mr. Luke's brawny shoulder. They stood in silence watching the city. "Is there a connecting door?" Mr. Luke hesitated a moment.

"Yes."

"Does Dad unlock it?"

"Yes."

"You don't seem comfortable about this conversation. I'm guessing that means it's not unlocked for me." Colin turned back to the cityscape, letting his chin drop on his arms on the simple metal railing. He could see his dad's balcony just a few feet to their left, with its gilt railing stamped in intricate designs, delicate pieces twisting in and out of each other in a work of art. Colin found himself vastly preferring his own simple metal one. Mr. Luke studied the boy staring out at the city, his young face old with a sorrow that had plagued him through his fifteen years. A frown shot across the big man's face.

A thick hand slammed into Colin and the boy stumbled, his shoulder smarting.

"Hey, what was that–" he started, but Mr. Luke's even, deep voice cut him off.

"Want to learn some karate?"

Colin stared up at the towering hulk of Mr. Luke. The man's big head tipped, asking him for a response. A slow smile spread over Colin as he rubbed his smarting shoulder.

"You're offering to teach me?"

"Yeah." Mr. Luke shrugged again. "I don't have anything else to do until the meeting tonight."

"What meeting?" Colin asked quickly. A shadow shot over Mr. Luke. His eyes darted away, a sharp frown on his face.

"You're not going. You stay here and order something from room service, ok? But I could teach you some things while we wait. If you want."

"Yeah. That would be great, thanks," Colin said, and his smile was genuinely pleased. But his mind rushed off to the one thing Mr. Luke had to do here. Who was his dad meeting?

The man in the facemask and gloves floated into his memory. Colin's skin prickled.

Chapter 3

Aldrick felt his whole body shaking with fear. But he hit the call button for the police, shoved his phone into his pocket, tightened the straps on his bag, and moved into a crouch. He could see the guard now. Sophia Ricci stepped into sight around the vast machines of the plant. She walked her rounds placidly, her flashlight sweeping the room.

The silhouette of a man rose behind her, towering in the shadows. His hand lifted, his club an unnatural shape jutting from his fist.

Aldrick darted out of his hiding place. Head down, legs pounding, he moved like a silent express train. His arms wrapped around the guard's waist in a tackle, and his shoulder slammed into her side with all the force of a mad run behind it. The two of them hit the concrete with an earth-shuddering thump. A swish of air rushed over them as the club arched from the man's fist. The guard swung the heavy flashlight at Aldrick's head, not waiting to give a warning. She had sense. Aldrick ducked the move easily[6]. The flashlight shot past him and thumped into something solid that went "crunch."

A hoarse scream came from the shadows. Sophia Ricci gasped out a muted curse and scooted over the ground like a crab. The shadows morphed into a man. His face was a strange, smushed lump that made it faceless and terrifying. He hobbled a step, his knee bent inward. He slashed down at Sophia's head with a thick wooden club, his expression murderous. Another sharper curse came from the guard. Her hand shot up with her pistol. She squeezed off two reports, each a product of hundreds of hours at the shooting range. The sound bounced off the walls and reverberated back at them. Images shot through Aldrick's

---

[6] He had years of practice dodging swings from his uncles and cousins. Most of it was good-natured roughhousing. Though there were a few who looked at Aldrick's aversion to the family business, his silent withdrawal into his gadgets, and reciprocated with hatred and hard knocks. But there were enough others in the family to duck behind, and the Maman Lefebvre of course, and it never posed much of a problem if Aldrick kept his head. His father's tantrums, now those were another matter.

mind, of murders in back alleys, sobbing, screaming victims, his father's hardened face behind the smoking gun. His hands went over his head as the noise cut through him, and he cowered.

But through his fingers he saw forms in the shadows slipping toward them. His hand shot out and wrapped around the guard's arm. She spun toward him, mouth grim, and the flashlight swung up again. Aldrick tugged, pulling her desperately toward the corner away from the huge silver egg shape gleaming in the darkness. Her eyes caught his wide, scared ones and swiveled to find what he was staring at. She picked out the forms in the darkness. Two, four, five, seven?! Sophia scrambled to her feet and moved where this pale young man in the beanie tugged her.

Aldrick dragged her toward the drainage tunnel set in the floor. He had seen the two shadows break off and head for the door. He knew their exit was already cut off, their only hope was to hunker down and wait for help. Hope for help. Pray for help, if there really was a God to pray to, like *Meme* and Uncle Guillaume insisted…Guillaume…

Aldrick shoved his hand into his bag, jerked his flathead screwdriver out, slid it in the tunnel entrance, and heaved. The grill lifted, groaning and heavy in Aldrick's skinny arms. It was a small opening, not enough for a grown man, and a five-foot drop into darkness. But as Aldrick shoved, his muscles straining, the guard managed to squeeze in. Her boots splashed into the puddle at the bottom and she stretched back up, holding the grill open for him. Aldrick wiggled in and splashed beside her. Sophia dropped to hunker against the tunnel with a gasp, her shoes slipping on the algae covering the floor. The grill snapped shut with a clang. Aldrick's hand shot through the bars and his phone's flash pierced the darkness for an instant, leaving white sparks dancing in everyone's eyes. The boy's fingers flew over his screen and the picture sailed off over continents and oceans, to land in an exiled uncle's phone. Aldrick sent two words with it, and dropped into a crouch on the floor of the tunnel.

Shadows shifted outside their grill. They never came into the light spilling from the open door. They never showed a face, or even a full form. Nausea rolled in Aldrick's insides. He sagged against the stinking wall and clutched his phone to his chest.

"Does this tunnel lead out?" Sophia asked. Her voice wavered and she paused and swallowed to get it back in order. "We need to leave now, we're sitting ducks to enemy fire." Aldrick shook his head. "What does that mean, no way out, or that we're ok here?" He spun his phone to face her. Sophia stared at words typed neatly on a note app.

The tunnel is blocked by recent rainfall. It is very dangerous to try and get out this way, almost certain to drown. I've alerted the police for help, I hope. According to my scanners these people don't have firearms.

"Your scanners?" the guard asked, and her eyes darted to the pale, skinny young man holding this cell phone like a shield in front of himself. "Who are you?"

A clang of metal slamming down on metal interrupted any reply. They spun to the grill, straining to see out. Both their eyes went to the towering silver shape in the corner of the room. Pure silver now, the outer metal casing closed down to cover the circuitry inside. Just a smooth silver egg standing five feet tall beside the transformers. It began to hum. The shadows backed away, watching it. The hum rose, turning to a whine. A soft "whoomph" ran through the room.

The lights blinked out. The huge Italian power station suddenly stilled. Air stopped blowing from the vents. The light from Aldrick's phone screen went out. He stared at it, horror rushing through him in hot tendrils, his fingers tapping the screen desperately. The gadget stared back at him, dead and lifeless. The guard listened to the silence outside their grate. With a little jolt she realized just how silent it was. No cars rushing by on the road. No motor boats speeding through the canal, or even the lagoon.

Human voices from the towns outside the Andrea Palladio began to fill the silence. Alarmed, confused, she could hear the tenor of it from even here in this stinking tunnel.

A shadow shifted outside their grate, fleeting from one patch of darkness to another. She swallowed, her hand tightening on her pistol, her body turning slowly to try to spot the shape again. They were still out there, waiting for them. Or protecting that silver egg? She could see it even in the dark. Its bright silver sheen seemed to gather whatever specks of light existed. A hum came from it, rising and falling rhythmically in a steady pulse.

"Hey kid," the guard said, leaning a little closer to the hunched ally beside her. "Are there any more of you to leap out and save the day? Because if not we are in serious trouble."

She could hear his finger tapping at the dead screen of his phone in the dark. It was his only response, except for the rising hyperventilating panic in his breathing. The shapes out there flitted and shifted, and began to clump in twos and threes. The clumps flitted toward their grill. Sophia Ricci swallowed, and realized this was up to her.

"We have to get out," she whispered. "That…thing knocked the power out. If it knocked the police's power out too they may not have received your alert, and we need to tell someone what's happening here. We're between the anvil and the hammer[7], the tunnel will have to do. If you go first I should be able to help you if it gets tough. Ok?" His fingers tapped desperately against the screen. The guard gently laid her hand over the young man's, stilling his panicked poking at the dead phone. His hand shook and felt as cold as death. "We're going to get out through the tunnel. You go first and I'll help. Ok?" Nothing moved in the darkness in front of her. Then he turned and shuffled farther into the tunnel. She slid her pistol into her holster and followed.

The steady crunch of Pete eating potato chips filled the home theater. Gigan turned the volume up to Luther Kirl's feed. The crunching grew a little louder. He spun toward the slumped form of his partner, the discolored ring around the Frenchman's eye a dark contrast to the rest of his face.

"Will you stop that?" Gigan burst out. A prolonged crunch came from Pete.

---

[7] An Italian idiom meaning what it sounds like; being stuck between two bad options. Like me yesterday when my leopard wanted to eat and I had his food, but he also wanted to eat me; either walk away and he gets hungrier and angrier, or open the feeding gate and hope he goes for his food and not my head. I may have to do something about that leopard.

"You do realize only one of us officially has to be in here checking this feed?" Vincent drawled. No one answered him. They all sat staring at the woods twisting and shaking as Luther Kirl walked under the leafy canopy, complaining under his breath about the bugs. And the cold. And the lack of any kind of comfort.

"You know, I don't think he likes it there," Pete commented. The crunch of potato chips filled the room. The feed shook in a dizzying view of the forest floor as Luther hopped on one foot, swatting wildly at a bug. Other human forms showed occasionally in the sweeping camera feed. But it always swept past, never staying on one form long enough to see them clearly. Jojo reached for a potato chip, and Pete shifted the bowl closer to her. "I'm assuming the rest of you have noticed the training equipment scattered about this place, it looks like a summer camp for mercenaries. Also, there are lots of supplies. They all seem to just be waiting."

"Perhaps hunkering down?" Gigan murmured.

"Why don't we just jump in and scoop them all up again?" Pete asked. Gigan reached over his seat for a chip. Two copper-skinned hands smacked his away, hard.

"We need information at this point, not people," Gigan answered, shaking his smarting hand. "It would remove a few bad guys from the running, but leave their plot loose in the world, whatever it is in its entirety. We need the one in charge, the one Luther said approached him."

"Hey, quiet guys," Vincent broke in, "he's bravely made the foray across the unpaved floor to the command center." A building fashioned of wood, moss, and vines appeared in the feed. It looked like a place where a black-bearded dwarf would pop out and request information about a missing faery princess. Instead an old man with a shriveled soul stalked up to it, grumbling under his breath.

"You, in charge of communications in there!" Luther shouted. The Parabaloni jerked back, and Gigan's hand flew to the volume control, twisting it down. "Inform the mysteriously elusive and inimitable Mr. Black that I've had enough of the Collective's hospitality. I'm leaving. I'll be listening to the channels if you need to find me."

"We don't inform Mr. Black of anything," someone answered from inside. "It cannot be done. But assume he already knows." An annoyed growl came from Luther and he stalked away. Tall trees, and mud-splattered piles of snow showed over the feed as Luther walked on. A deep hum invaded the air, and bumblebees bumbled into the camera. Luther gave a little yelp and started to hop and swat the bugs. For an instant the camera went wild, the crackling loud. Then Luther's swatting landed on the Parabaloni's bug. It tumbled off his clothing.

Darkness closed over the lens. A crunch sounded in the basement theater that wasn't from a potato chip. A lost signal symbol flashed over the screen.

"And once again Luther Kirl is loose on the world," Vincent drawled, his voice tired. His friends glanced at him, and the inventor found a smile sliding over him. "No, guys, I'm not slipping back into the mourning again. I'm ok, just annoyed by how much work it's going to take to track him down." He sat up, silhouetted against the light coming from the screen, and his hands moved. *"Ready, guys?"* he signed.

"Think he is ready and listening?" Pete signed back. They all spun, looking at the stocky agent watching everything from the back of the room.

"That last phrase a challenge to us," Simeon signed. Aurora snored on his foot, her legs in the air. *"He's listening. Go."* A wolfish smile broke across Gigan's face. It made even the black eye the look of a hardened warrior. He pivoted, turning back to his partner. Another potato chip crunched.

"Peter, will you stop that?" Gigan burst out, the irritation in his voice suddenly laced with despair. "We just lost our only lead, and you still sit there eating!"

"I don't think it was ever much of a lead," Pete sneered, the haughty desert dweller strong in his voice.

"Yeah, I have to agree," Vincent put in. "I'm a little disappointed in old Luther. I thought he would have known more about the main plot behind this Collective. Turns out for all his boasting, he doesn't know anything."

"Oh he knows some things," Pete broke in, his sneer strong. "Just on the fringes of the plan. It's the central parts of it, the actual important parts, he doesn't know."

"The Collective understands he is not fully committed to their cause," Gigan took up. He sounded tired, hopelessness strong in his words. Jojo found a smile twitching over her face. He was an amazing actor. "They are not going to tell him anything. For all his boasting over being able to learn anything and accomplish whatever he wishes, he has run into those he cannot manipulate. Someone with a commitment to more than just money."

"We'll find out on our own, know more than Kirl does soon," Simeon stated. "Done here."

A general stirring and conversation started up as the Parabaloni shifted out of the theater room. The bright glare of the basement's lights took over, and the double doors shut behind them. Vincent looked at Pat's screen and nodded at the others.

"Our jammer's running strong, he can't hear us unless we're in there," the inventor reported. "Think that did the trick, Sim?"

"Should have," Simeon said as he headed toward the elevator, threading his way through Vincent's stuff strewn around the basement.

"With what we know of his psyche, that little conversation should provoke him to find our information and save us the work," Gigan smiled. "Or at least start his hunt, which will make it very easy for us to keep track of him, and possibly even to feed him useful information." He broke into a trot to catch up to his boss. "It is obvious Luther thinks we do not know he is listening to us. To him it is another part of the game, as he thinks we think we are in charge when he really holds the trump. But if he doesn't think we know he knows about us listening—"

"You know you are giving me a headache?" Pete interrupted.

"You know he knows it, bro," Vincent grinned and Jojo snorted back a laugh.

"–but then what were those last few sentences about?" Gigan finished. "Why did he make such a point to tell us that particular bit of information about the mysterious Mr. Black?"

"Is that the first we've heard of a Mr. Black?" Jojo broke in.

"This isn't a mastermind from your past or something, is it?"

"This is a big world, Jo," Pete said. "There are so many people in it, masterminds from the past mostly happen in novels and movies. Usually it is new people we meet, who have never heard of us either. No, I know of no Mr. Black. Simeon?"

Silence filled the space between the Parabaloni. The elevator played the first few notes of the Star Trek theme and the door slid open. No one moved.

"Simeon?" Gigan prodded. Sim's lips pursed, his eyes on a purple stain[8] two feet from his shoes.

"Something niggling me about Holland," he said slowly. "Don't know. There's… Feel like I've met it before. But can't remember what, or where. I… Keep your phones near." He stepped into the elevator, his eyes on his feet but his expression absent, as if searching for something beyond his Teva's. Jojo noticed the stances change as the others followed him into the little glass room; they moved ready for a fight, poised to leap any direction.

"And why's that?" Vincent pushed. Simeon didn't look up, and his annoyance deepened. Vincent knew it wasn't because of the question. It was because Simeon hated still being in the educated guessing phase.

"Kirl knows too much about us. Jack[9] involved in this first business, Vincent's folks, Kirl an old acquaintance, Gigan even spied past associates. All tied together and pulling us into the plot. Coincidences happen, sometimes lots at once. But never assume it's coincidence. What if it's personal?" The idea settled around them slowly as the five stood stock still in the little glass room.

"Who would know enough about us to make it personal?" Gigan frowned.

---

[8] From an incident with a melting eggplant and a failed ray gun two years ago. Well, it didn't fail exactly, it was too powerful to be of any practical use. Not even a blow torch could get the color out of the concrete.

[9] A note for any who may not know this name. Jack Lewis Leason is a reporter who crashed the Parabaloni's first mission, and he and his wife Judy managed to help Sim and Vince foil a mass murderer from launching biological terror on the US. And last week, they had to dig Jack out of trouble when he got himself stuck in a terrorist's van in the Netherlands.

"You keep leaving business cards," Simeon shot out. "Our name known at the scene plenty of places now."

"Only for the good guys, and only our name," Gigan defended quickly.

"A name becomes a starting point, a place to look," Simeon said.

"Hey, back to Sim's point," Pete interrupted what had become a common argument. "How could it all be linked together from your past? Jack came into it on his own."

"The comments on his papers could easily have been planted," Vincent said, his brow wrinkled as he thought about it.

"And carefully crafted to give him just enough information to get curious and go to Holland," Gigan said. "Sim, if you are right—"

"Don't know!" Simeon broke in, his frustration strong. "Don't know if I'm right. Can't pinpoint where the idea came from."

"But it is worth pondering," Gigan said. "We should check in with those connected to us. The ones who will actually answer, anyway." A shadow crossed the Frenchman's face, falling into lines carved deep by the sorrows. He shook it off quickly, his head going high and his shoulders squaring. But the twinkle didn't come back into his gray eyes. "While we do that, *we* now have a name to research. Perhaps it will give you that link you lack, and be a starting point for where we go next."

"Should I chase Luther with an Amelia?" Jojo asked, a little hopefully. Drones were fun.

"He will know you are there and will do nothing useful, something misleading, or shoot her down," Gigan shrugged, and finally punched the button to take them all to the kitchen. "Don't bother yet. I still have my original question though. Simeon, why do you think Luther gave us the information he did?"

"My guess, even Kirl doesn't know how to contact this Black. Maybe no one knows who he is."

"Something like that would rankle in Luther's god-fixation like a chigger under the skin," Vincent commented. A smile crept over Vincent's face as he stepped out into the kitchen. "He wants us to find this Mr. Black for him. Shriveled old Luther needs us."

✦

"Does it show?" Colin murmured to Mr. Luke as he slid into the conference room. Mr. Luke looked at him. The movement made his white dinner jacket strain at the seams.

"No, until you keep sticking your hand over it," he muttered, a little smile twitching over his face. Colin whipped his hand away from his swollen cheek. "Next time keep your guard up when you're told." The smile left and the secretary paused. One big hand engulfed Colin's shoulder. Colin looked past him and saw a huge room in the same opulent style as the rest of this hotel, everything gold and deep reds and swirling blues and gold. Tables with white damask clothes scattered across the room, and people milled amongst them. He saw dark-skinned men in robes, olive-skinned ones in modern suits, peachy people in ratty shorts or formal wear. The hand on his shoulder gave a little squeeze and Colin looked back up at Mr. Luke.

"Listen kid, settle at the back somewhere, enjoy dinner, then go back up to the room," the secretary ordered. His face held no hint of the friendliness he had gradually adopted during their lessons this afternoon. It was expressionless, the automaton Colin had always associated with the secretary. It suddenly occurred to Colin that non-expression meant something going on behind it that Mr. Luke didn't want his employer reading. "I let you talk me into you coming to eat. But don't stick around, leave before the business of the night."

The hand left his shoulder and Mr. Luke strode into the room, threading his way through the tables to the single empty chair beside Jackson Clempson at the head table. Colin watched him for a moment, feeling surprisingly lonely. He drew in a deep breath, forced his slumped shoulders up, then walked forward with a commanding competence he didn't feel. If he had to pick his own seat, he would do it like he owned the place.

Colin carefully selected an empty chair along the wall. Three young people sat across from him at the table, in their early twenties perhaps. They seemed just ill-at-ease enough to tell him they weren't used to this kind of thing, and weren't big shots here.

The food started to come. The waiters drifted in from a

hallway near Colin's table, and theirs turned out to be a tall, thin man probably younger than Colin's dinner companions. He seemed awfully skinny, and never smiled. The steak course finally came, and Colin reached for his crystal glass. His three dinner companions chattered in Arabic, but the girl laughed as he lifted his glass to them. She lifted hers back as her dark eyes danced under her abeja. He was a little surprised by her openness, and then immediately felt like an uncultured Western snob.

Today officially confirmed he was a food snob. The sparkling water tickled his nose and tasted like someone had forgotten the main ingredients. He sat the crystal glass down, reached for his fork, and poked the overcooked minuscule steak on the oversized bed of kale. He ate it anyway, and admitted the flavor was good.

"Coffee?" a deep, sad voice asked at his elbow. Colin looked up at his waiter, black hair slicked back, hawk nose large on his brown face. Eeyore popped into Colin's mind at the man's droopy attitude and he worked hard not to chuckle. He silently wondered what it was like in the waiter's neighborhood instead of the tourist's quarter, and if they paid him enough here.

"Yes, thank you," Colin said. "And leave the pot, please." An almost-smile twitched over the waiter's thin face. He left the pot, and came back ten minutes later with a dessert cart and another pot of coffee. Colin selected three of the desserts, and grinned at the girl when she laughed at him for it. Colin kept half an eye on the main table, where his dad and Mr. Luke sat with the head honchos of this conference. Whatever it was for. There hadn't been any signs at the front welcoming the group, and no one seemed to talk about whatever mutual cause brought them together. All Colin knew was that cell phones weren't allowed out of the rooms, and Mr. Luke had looked nervous when he warned Colin to stay in tonight.

But Colin wasn't about to hide in his room now when he might get a few answers.

As he leaned back with his coffee, the lady in the chiffon dress at his dad's table stood up and headed toward the stage. Colin poured himself a another cup, relishing in the cardamon mixing with the deep bitter smell of a perfect roast, and waited to see what happened next.

The woman stepped up to the podium and favored the crowd with a bright smile.

"It is time for all but the Whites to exit the room, please." She said it so naturally, as if this was the way they started every time. An interpreter repeated it in Arabic. The three people in front of Colin stood up, still chattering. But a certain tension played in their words, and they moved awfully quickly toward the door. They left their dessert unfinished. Half the tables emptied. Even the interpreter and waiters joined the flow walking out the door.

Except Colin spotted his waiter slide into the shadows beside the door instead of exiting. Huh.

A busy hum moved around the room as people gathered their things, and chairs and people moved. Colin placed a clean fork in the basbousa, slid the baklava onto the plate, and sat it on the table for his waiter. The guy looked thin enough to enjoy finding a good snack when he cleared up later. Colin took another drink of coffee and waited. Every inch of him easy and content, as if he knew this routine. He had chosen his seat well, no lights hit him full on, and he had carefully worn his black dress shirt with his tux tonight, and selected a gray tie instead of his usual red. No one looked at him.

The soft noise of people moving stilled as the last one walked out of the huge conference room. A bang echoed as the guard slammed the door closed, and Colin jumped despite himself.

"Excellent," the lady on stage commented. "Team, please double check our requests have been taken seriously and all usual security is down." Colin blinked. A red-haired lady rose at one table near the wall, her pants suit perfectly creased.

"We made certain to dismantle the system as soon as we entered the premises," the creased lady reported. "It cannot be repaired for at least a week." Colin glanced at the corners of the room. He made out several security cameras. Each one pointed at the ground, still and lifeless.

"All cell phones and other harmful human technology are banned?" the lady on stage demanded. Colin's eyes automatically darted to his dad, across the room at the large white table. His hands lay idle on his cup of coffee, no phone in sight. "Good," the woman commented. She sat her notes in a neat pile, and favored the people in the room with a wide smile. She nodded at the red-haired lady standing near the wall. The lady hit the light switch.

Darkness fell with terrifying suddenness.

"Just so the world is dark now," the lady at the front said, her voice lilting as if it were a chant, or a tuneless song. Her voice rose. "But now, my family, we who are one with the Mother, we will bring the fire."

Flickering flames spurted into life in the corners of the room. Colin stared at dancing shapes; firelit elk, mountains, waterfalls, flying birds, all of them twisting and dancing off the people and walls. *"Magic lanterns,"* Colin's brain supplied, as he sat stock still, his eyes wider than he would have liked to admit. *"Just primitive lantern shows like they used in the 1800s. Breathe, man."* A bear slid over him and he watched it walk up the wall, shifting in the light of the flames.

"Too long the Mother has lain in the blackness under the plague of humanity," the lady chanted. "We bring the cure. Soon balance will be restored, and the plague brought to manageable numbers. We, the Collective, my brothers and sisters, will be the cure!"

The lamps adjusted again, and Colin could see the people in the room by the dancing glow. The shapes shifted and moved, almost alive.

"We have a few items to take care of tonight," the woman said, as if she stood in a normal business meeting with a clipboard in front of her. "I will go through them as quickly as possible to avoid having to guard the doors too long." Colin's eyes darted to the doors. The shifting light played over men standing at each entrance. Muscles bulged under their clothes. Most had clubs tucked in their belts. Wooden clubs, for crying out loud! "Mr. Clempson has come in person to bring the components for the Riyadh egg. And he reports the last part of the Mother Machine has been milled and fashioned in his Los Angeles plant, thank you, Mr. Clempson." Polite clapping ran around the room. Colin sat frozen as his dad stood up briefly, flashed a smile at the gathered company, and settled back in his seat. Mr. Luke sat like a stone statue beside him. "With the Mother Machine now completely manufactured, our plan can go into play. It is time, my family. We start the process of Mother Earth being renewed, as mankind is reduced back to what it should be! Abdul, please report on matters here. Is Riyadh ready?"

The man in the white flowing robe at the head table stood up, his napkin still held in one dark hand.

"We are ready," he reported. "Our inciters have been at work in the lower class, and tomorrow a mob will convene at the Royal Abdul's square. Our men will be certain to turn it from a mob into a massacre. Not only will it reduce some of the human numbers (always a welcome thing), we have also carefully planted reports that it is Afghanistan who incites the mob and opens fire on our people."

Another man stood up from the table, thinner, his suit a little ill-fitting, as if he had purchased it off a clothes rack, or borrowed it from his neighbor.

"Those planted reports will pigeon hole nicely with the 'proof' near the pipeline our team will explode tomorrow night," the man reported, his accent decidedly American. The woman's hand went up, but the man ran on quickly before she could form her question. "Of course we are sending in experts who know how to destroy the machine without spilling the oil onto the earth. We will not damage nature more than has already been done." The woman nodded and regained her smile. "It will begin a war. A long war where human will remove human from the earth, and the plague numbers will be reduced."

"Excellent," the woman took up. "It may be a smaller play than our plans in the Netherlands and Libya that were annoyingly overturned, but it will still be a good start at reducing human numbers." She turned to the creased lady.

"We have collected the bags with the components for the egg, it will be set up in time," the red-haired one reported. The podium lady glanced down at her notes again.

"Well done. I am able to report that the other eggs are ready. They will begin to deploy tomorrow, and soon we will see our work take effect across the globe!" Applause and excited cheers cut through the room. Jackson smiled, his hands coming off his cup to join in the enthusiasm. Mr. Luke sat rigid, staring at a blank space on the wall. The woman held up her hand to stop the applause, her smile strong. "Once the Mother Machine is connected, Mr. Black himself will deploy her power. If chance is kind it might be the last use of technology and hurtful machinery in years, perhaps even decades! In the same stroke the human plague will be reduced and the hated technology will be set back for years. This, my friends, is a good day for the Earth." She motioned those in the room to stand, stepped away from the microphone, and started to sing.

Colin sat frozen in his seat, his eyes wide and his mouth clamped shut. An eerie, half off-key song filled the big room. The lanterns' shapes flowed over the people and he caught fleeting glimpses of faces swaying as they sang. It was something about the earth mother, a horned goddess, north winds, starlight, and bright futures.

A chill ran down his spine.

Chapter 4

The smoke is going to be too strong!" Jojo complained. She rose on her tiptoes to peek over Gigan's shoulder into the pot. "Also the heat is too high, they will burn."

"Excuse me, but who is cooking these beans?" Gigan snorted as he spun on her, his hands going to his hips. A spoon in one hand dripped beans on his apron, while smoke curled from the acetylene torch in his other.

"I was wondering that myself," Jojo said, and sniffed. "They are burning." Gigan spun back to the pot, mumbling under his breath. Vincent strolled in, holding his open laptop, the tick-tick of the keys coming fast and thick. He paused as his nose wrinkled.

"Is something burning?" he asked. Simeon hid a smile in his cup of black coffee as Gigan shot the inventor a murderous glare.

"Only Bouncy's cooking rapport," Jojo shrugged. "It appears to be going up in flames."

"Either that, or I am on fire with talent!" Gigan countered. Flames shot from the torch and he flourished it theatrically, then bent over the pot again. Vincent settled at the table beside Simeon, plunking Rory between them.

"I can't find any rumors about a Mr. Black and the Collective," he reported. "There are plenty of 'Blacks' out there being villains. But they seem to all be something more theatrical than just a 'Mr.' and none of them fit the MO of these shadows we've been looking at."

"The fact that you can't find anything about him does fit the MO of this group," Pete commented around his fifth apple. Granola crumbs, empty yogurt packs, and fruit remains littered the counter around him. He was too busy to add much to the conversation, enjoying the strange anomaly of everyone at home and the time to replenish calories in peace. Flame whoomphed into life in the pot, licking over the top of the rim. Jojo stepped back sharply, as Gigan laughed maniacally and doused the flames with barbecue sauce.

"I'm not sure I'm going to eat that," Vincent murmured to his boss. Simeon shrugged, a little smile on his face as he watched Jojo slide in again and the two of them hover around the cooking beans. "Anything on your end?"

"Saul fine," Simeon reported. "Jonathan seeing a girl. Michelle doing well right now. Called Max, he's home watching twelve grandchildren, chaotic but happy. Haven't gotten Algy to answer yet. Daughter Alice says all's well with Algy's children, and he's in the States right now, in an apartment a few streets down from her."

"Ok, good news there at least," Vincent said, and leaned in, poking things on his laptop. The feed from a small West Texas airport security camera came up, and Vincent zoomed in on one corner. A fuzzy, pixelated form that looked vaguely human shaped came into view. He sighed and sat back. "That's the best look we can get at these shadows. Even Pat can't get a good enough picture to recreate facial details."

"What do you think they are using?" Pete asked. "And why don't we have cloaking technology to fuzz our faces yet, Savant?"

"That would be really keen!" Vincent agreed, suddenly eager. "Hey boss man, think we can keep one of these people to try and wring their secret from them?"

"A cloaking device would be very handy in our line of work, I approve of this idea," Gigan nodded. He stood on his tiptoes to get a better look inside the bubbling pot. "But I am rather surprised they have it before we do."

"Our inventor has been a little busy recently," Jojo defended their friend. "It's hard to have proper ideas when rushing around saving the whole world."

"We've only saved the world three times last year that I'm aware of," Pete mumbled around banana, "the rest of our missions have been saving smaller areas. Just lots and lots of smaller areas."

"What sort of device do you think these shadows are using, Vince?" Gigan asked. "I find it telling and a little scary that we have not heard even a rumor of such technology."

"I don't know…" Vincent said slowly, leaning in and staring at the pixelated figure of a murderer. "The distance makes it hard to tell anything, this person must have known where the security camera was. Maybe there's something like our jammers, set on a channel that interferes with the video feed? Or maybe…" A hand ran through his hair and his mouth fell open as his genius started to work. Gigan suddenly noticed Simeon; the old agent's mouth twitched in amusement as he sipped his coffee and listened to this conversation. He guessed something they didn't. As usual. A bubble popped, spraying barbecue sauce up toward Gigan's face. The Frenchman sent another bout of flames into the pot and plunked the torch on the counter.

"All right people, we are all here and no one is being drowned or blown up or even shot at," he started.

"What a strange morning," Pete cut in. Gigan ignored him.

"It is time to decide where to start in this business. We can track down Luther, or let him run his course and see where it takes him. But now we know of this mysterious Mr. Black. It would seem he is the one in charge of the situation. If he has been the plotter behind what we have found so far, what do we know about him and his plans?"

"He is fond of flooding," Jojo put in.

"And exploding things," Pete added.

"Planner," Simeon stated.

"Enough to use two different parts of the world and leverage politics to start war," Vincent finished Simeon's thoughts.

"And good at using people, we see from Luther and whoever setup that cyber attack on Holland," Jojo added.

"Nasty and subtle enough to hide a plot under a plot," Gigan said. "We know from the comments Peter overheard from my old associates (and just Greg and Abassi Si's involvement) it has tie-ins with New Age environmentalism. However, all of Mr. Black's plots seem to tend mainly toward dealing death."

"That's what Luther hinted at too," Vincent said, his nose wrinkling in disgust.

"Yes, a group set on bringing death for their cause. To prove a point, or actually a part of their cause, do you think?" Pete asked.

"Does it matter?" Vincent growled, flinging himself back in his chair and glaring at his laptop. "I hate dealing with that kind. The destruction they leave in their wake while we track them down is…" His voice trailed off and no one took it up again. They stayed still, scenes replaying inside them they wished with all their being they could forget. Jojo silently sat the sauce on the counter and waited, letting them have the moment; and guiltily grateful again she wasn't out on the full-fledged missions. Vincent drew in a breath and forced his moodiness away with an effort. "But, we managed to stop the bloodbath in Libya, keep the Maeslant from destruction, stop whatever virus they were trying to let loose, keep another war from breaking out, and thanks to Sim's efficiency, even caught their plot within a plot. So we've done pretty well so far."

"I think we are on top of the game," Gigan nodded. He saw Simeon's forehead wrinkle at the comment and mentally sighed. Fine, so maybe they weren't on top yet. "But we must not discount Sim's thoughts about this also being a personal attack. Can anyone think of the next strike point for this Black?"

"Dude, Sean!" Vincent groaned.

"Elaborate please?" Gigan demanded.

"He's helping people, doing exactly what this Mr. Black doesn't want! Sean is using the Tolliver accounts so well he's gathered a whole office full of people to help him with the details." A flush of anger rushed over his freckles. Pete's eyebrows went up in surprise at their inventor. "They're a charity, for gosh sakes, a darned good one, taking the messes we find out there and making the world a safer place. Did I tell you there are no more orphans in the Osheana's place? It's closed down because all those kids have a home now. All of them! They're helping people all over the… Oh shucks. That's exactly what these shadows *don't* want. Everything Sean is doing is against Mr. Black's core values, as we understand it. I would bet my watch he's a target."

"The Osheana's closed?" Pete said. Vincent suddenly realized his work family stared at him with hungry eyes. He sank back, his anger gone. A wide smile spread over his face.

"Yeah, Pete. I haven't had much time where we're all together to tell you about it. Every one of those kids we carried there, broken and bleeding and hopeless, have new homes now. Real homes. Sean is smart and savvy and found people who know what they're doing to vet prospective families, and they give preference to Christian couples. Sim, I told him not to discount singles if they were real and just wanted to help. Guys, we're stopping things from getting worse, and that's awesome, and we do a really good job at it. And now Sean is coming behind us and making the world better than we found it when we swept in."

Silence tingled in the kitchen as the Parabaloni just stared, seeing so much more than the walls and floor. Jojo turned the burner to low under the beans, her own mind running over more pictures of destruction and death than she realized she had garnered in her months running with this crowd.

"Can I visit your charity after we're done?" Pete asked, his voice tight and a little wet. A sniffle came from Gigan. Then he burst into a laugh, delight bubbling from it and filling the kitchen.

"I will be beside you, Peter, as soon as we can break free!" he said, his face shining. He clapped a hand on Vincent's shoulder. "This is the news we needed, my brother, the perfect coupling to combat this Mr. Black and his cronies. They aim to destroy humanity, as they elevate nature herself making her the real owner of this planet. But Sean knows the creeds by heart, bless him, and knows humans are gardeners, not plagues. Through Sean's work, nature herself is renewed as sin's destruction is taken head on and beaten back! The Dominion Mandate in full force, yoked to the Golden Rule, and taken into all the world in action. God bless that big Irishman, eh Peter?"

"Yes?" Pete blinked at him and Vincent laughed.

"We have to stop Black," Simeon firmly brought them back to their current point. He poured another cup of coffee and the steam curled around his face as it tumbled into his cup. "Sean's cleanup work is wonderful news. But we need to stop *this* mess before it gets worse. Think Black's got the next move. We don't know where he'll strike, but need to be ready. Vince, call Sean, warn him to skedaddle whenever he gets the call. Try to talk him into a safe house."

"He's too engaged in his work for that, but I'll try," Vincent said, and pulled out his phone to reach the Irishman. Sean answered on the second ring, and Vincent breathed again.

"Listen dude, we're worried you might be on a bad guy's hit list. I know some really good safe houses— What?... Yes, Sean, you usually have to leave your normal routine to go to a safe house... How sure are we?" Vincent looked at Simeon, and got a stare back. The inventor made a face at his unhelpful big boss[10] and settled in for a long argument.

The lights came on again. Colin sat and blinked in the sudden glare. The woman blew out her lantern and walked off the stage. The hum of conversations coursed through the room, as chairs were pushed back and people began to make their way toward the exits. It was all suddenly so normal, so freakishly ordinary, Colin felt his nervousness climbing into panic. He leaned back, forcing himself to breathe evenly. His eyes fell on his dad pacing toward the door back into the main hotel. His expression held more than his usual bored look. He wore an excited smile, his eyes bright. He looked animated. Colin had never seen him like that. He kept his eyes on his dad until Jackson Clempson walked out of the room. Steadily, people filed out the doors, taking the hum of conversation off with them into the hotel. Someone switched the lights off.

Colin sat stone still in his chair. The only illumination came from the sky bridge lights flowing in from the hallway. The shadows lay deep around him as he stared at the coffee in the carafe. He blinked once, long and slow, as his brain tried to catch up to what he just heard.

He had to tell someone! The cameras were down, no one had

---

[10] Gigan took over the official title of boss, and then Simeon's retirement turned into only a semi-retirement, and the team found themselves fumbling for the proper names. It evolved into Gigan as the "boss man" when the others really needed an answer or wanted to complain. Sim became the "big boss," while they referred to their real Team Leader as the "Big Boss." (Yes, in conversation they say, "Capital Bs Big Boss." Vincent once won a very important chess match because his teammates started praying, and the "Capital Bs" thing confused the opponent so much he lost his concentration.)

seen it through security surveillance, and everyone in that room had been in on the plot. Even his dad. Even Mr. Luke! Colin was the only one who could report it.

But who could he tell? Did the local police even speak English? *How* could he tell? His phone was still confiscated by Mr. Luke. And that lady had said all the modern means of outside communication, and especially proof of what he had heard, were turned off. Who would believe him? A fifteen year old gangly American kid babbling about lanterns and eggs and exploding pipelines and the culling of the human race… Oh man, this was crazy, he had to have heard this wrong, or it was an elaborate joke, or–

Or it was real and he was the only one who knew about it.

Colin's fist clenched. His eyes darted to the hallway leading to the sky bridge and the lobby. Daylight had dimmed and deepened into dusk. It would be smart to change out of his tailored suit before he ventured out on the streets of a big city he didn't know at night looking for someone to help stop a crazy group of earth-loving egg-planters gone evil… This was crazy. Really crazy.

Colin took a deep breath. He felt it echo in a hollowness inside himself; the feeling had come and gone this year as he spent his time alone with his books. Old books, most of them, written by authors who believed in a Being bigger than themselves. It had helped wake a longing for someone more powerful than himself, who could deal with things like this. A dad who actually listened would be nice. Someone to pray to Who was actually in charge would be even nicer. A blond-headed inventor under a greenhouse roof popped into Colin's mind again for the hundredth time. His mom had forced Jackson and Colin into that socialite gathering a couple weeks ago. And he had sat at the same table with Vincent Tolliver and heard him talk about his God who filled holes and gave all humanity purpose and beauty. Something had resonated deep in Colin as he listened to that brief exchange. Maybe he could find Someone to pray to…

If he didn't end up knifed in a Riyadh back street somewhere. Perhaps he could just ask the concierge? *"Excuse me, but could you call the police for me? I just heard of a master plot to start a war with a neighboring country and explode one of your pipelines tomorrow. Oh, and there was something about egg planting."* What would he get back? A raised eyebrow with a, *"Perhaps they're trying to grow a chicken?"* He squeezed his hair, trying to think.

A hand tapped his shoulder.

Colin started to his feet, swallowing a yelp as his chair overturned. His hand closed over the only thing near enough to grab and he hefted the coffee carafe, ready to swing. A strong, olive skinned hand snatched it away.

"Stop that, you'll spill perfectly good coffee," his waiter complained. Colin's racing heartbeat slowed a little as he watched the tall young man set the carafe on the table. The waiter pulled a prepaid phone out of his pocket. Colin stared at it numbly. He had never seen a phone with actual buttons. The waiter handed him a torn scrap of paper, numbers scrawled over it.

"You have to dial it just as I have written, or it will not reach the American number," the man's deep voice wrapped around him as Colin numbly accepted the phone.

"What? Who?" Colin stammered. He realized his hands were shaking. The waiter gave him a look Colin had seen older brothers give their younger siblings at school when the younger ones were being little idiots. He felt himself shrinking in size.

"You want to report that meeting to someone who can help, right?" the waiter said. He tapped the scrap of paper in Colin's hand. "Call that number, tell them what you heard. But do not," the man's finger moved, poking Colin in the chest, "*do not* let anyone in this hotel hear you making the call. Anyone, got it?"

"Got it," Colin swallowed.

"Oh, by the way, your dad is about to leave so make it quick if you want to catch your flight home."

"Wait, what?" Colin gaped. "Why is he leaving so quick? How do you know my dad?"

"I know things," the waiter shrugged. He picked up the coffee and the plate of extra desserts and turned toward the hallway again. But he paused and looked back at Colin. A smile shot over his face, twisting his features into a puckish, Elvin humor that made his dark eyes dance and lifted goosebumps on Colin's arms. Thoughts of genies of the desert shot through the young man, and he suddenly remembered not all of them were nice.

"I think they'll like you." The man turned and strode into the hallway.

"Wait, what? Who?" Colin gasped after him, like a broken record. But his waiter had been swallowed by the hallway, lost in the depths of this hotel. Colin stepped back from the yawning hole of the hallway, clutching the phone in one hand, a small scrap of paper in the other, and trying to clutch his sanity. He leaned against the wall, his eyes shooting around the room to make sure he was alone in this big place.

The shadows lay deeper now, and what light drifted from the open doors leading out to the skybridge was artificial. But he was still alone in this huge room. Colin punched in the number.

"Look, Sean, I know we don't know a lot about this situation yet, but aren't you the one who complains about–" Vincent drooped in his chair, and flung one hand up. "Ok, you stubborn Irishman, you won't leave your work, and you don't want to freak your people out with a private guard until we're a little more sure of our facts, I get it. For complaining about the tension in our full Parabaloni job you're ridiculous… Fine, just watch your back. We'll contact you when we know more." He tossed the phone on the table and regarded the company. "Stubborn Irishman."

"We didn't really expect him to back down," Gigan said. "He complains about what we do, but he is brave, and a good man who will require a good reason to leave his work."

The ticking clock, Pete's apple crunching, and the bubbling of the pot took over the kitchen. Gigan picked up his bottle of sauce.

"How much barbeque sauce do you plan to put in there?" Jojo demanded, staring into the pot. She stepped back quickly as the torch shoved over the rim.

A bright hymn in Arabic broke into the kitchen as Pete's phone rang. Everyone turned and stared at him. No one ever called Pete. The Saudi sat frozen, his latest apple still in his mouth. The ringtone danced around the kitchen, melding with the bubbling beans. His hand moved slowly as he pulled out his phone and studied the number. His brow furrowed, his mouth turning into a hard line. But he swept the gruesome remains of the fruit bowl's contents away, sat the phone on the table, and punched it on speaker.

"Hello," he said, his tone a challenge.

"I was told to call you," a young voice broke over the instrument. It came low and shaky. "Listen, there's a creepy group gathered in Riyadh and I sat in on their meeting. They said they've planned a mob around a royal square, and they're going to open fire there on their own to make sure it becomes a massacre, and then they're going to blow up a pipeline, and blame all of it on Afghanistan to start a war. They say it will cull the human plague, and other creepy stuff like that, and I'm freaking out, really, really freaking out. Then there was something about planting eggs that I didn't really understand, and my dad manufactured–" The voice broke off into a sharp intake of air. "Apparently he made some kind of a mother machine for them, and it's all ready to be 'deployed,' and I don't know what to do!"

"Where are you?" Pete demanded.

"The Royal Fasa Hotel and Convention Center," the voice rattled off. It came a little stronger. "In the conference room, everyone just walked out."

"'Just walked out?'" Pete said, his voice ringing with urgency. "You should not be making this call there."

"It's ok, my waiter already warned me to make sure I'm alone."

"Name," Pete demanded.

"He didn't give me a name–"

"Yours." Pete silently filled in the name of the waiter and felt his stomach clenching. The number of people in Riyadh who knew his number boiled down to one. A prayer for Yousef flew toward heaven's throne as he laid his brother in Christ's arms again.

"Oh, uh, Colin Clempson."

"What about this 'they,' did they have a name?"

"She said 'the Collective' when she first started talking. Listen, can you help? They brought in their own security for this conference, and cell phones aren't even allowed in the hotel while they're here, and I have to go, I need to find my dad because he's leaving already and– Wait, why did he bring so much luggage if he's leaving right away? He carried something here, for them. What did he bring?"

"Colin, listen to me," Pete broke in. He could hear the tone change, the sudden shock of realization. The sudden stealing of a pair of nerves, young enough to take risks that experience would think twice about. "We will take care of it. Don't go poking into things, just do what you're supposed to be doing. If your dad is leaving, get on the plane with him. You got the information where it needs to be. Leave it there now, got it?"

A harsh, deep voice broke over the phone, too far away to make out the actual words. Static crackled and through it a sharp exclamation came from Colin. The line went dead. Silence filled the kitchen as the beans bubbled.

The Frenchman whipped his apron off as Pete started shoving energy bars into his pocket and Vincent reached for his laptop sleeve. Simeon's mug clinked onto the kitchen table.

"I'm not going." Every eye turned to the stocky agent with the dog splayed over his feet. "Need Algy to answer first. You four take care of it." Gigan let an ill-tempered scowl wrinkle his face for an instant. Then he snapped into his commanding mode and swept toward the door.

"Perry, ten minutes," Gigan ordered.

Aldrick's arms and legs pumped, forcing him through the water. It pressed into him, black and cold, squeezing the air from his lungs and making them burn. The tunnel narrowed. Aldrick pushed off the concrete sides, and squirmed like a worm. He had no more room for a full swimmer's kick. His feet moved like a baby trying to imitate a swimmer's motion as his hands scrabbled for a purchase to heave himself higher. His hands hit slick, smooth algae. He scrabbled and squirmed, unable to move any higher. Stuck.

White sparks danced in front of his eyes as his lungs burned like acid boiled inside them.

A hand shoved his foot and Aldrick shot forward. His flailing fingers found an iron rung protruding from a wall. He heaved, jerking himself forward with all the desperation of a drowning man.

His head broke the surface. Air rushed over him, bringing the sounds of splashing and his own choking gasps. Aldrick hung onto the rung and gasped and choked for three seconds. Then he brought his bare foot up, hooked it in the rung, and flipped backward with a gymnast's agility. The noise cut off, enclosed in the heavy bubbling of the dirty rain water. His hand brushed thrashing fingers. The guard gripped his wrist like a vice and pulled, squirming past him. Aldrick flipped his thin body, squeezing past her as she treaded water at the top of this tunnel. His head broke the surface again and he gasped and choked, working his foot out of the rung. He tapped the iron rungs, hoping she understood through their hacking gasps. Sophia Ricci gripped the rungs and started to climb, her long black hair dripping behind her with a steady kerplop. As her breathing regulated again, she began to register more than just the burning need for air. The sounds from above drifted in.

The endless movement of water in the lagoon. Voices, loud and scared. Nothing else. No car horns blaring. No motor boats roaring through the water. No steady humming from the power station. No music pouring from pleasure boat's speakers. Her hand closed on the top rung. She reached up to find the cover to the tunnel, and ponderously pushed it open. Sophia scrambled out onto the dirty ground outside the station, panting and dripping. The salty breeze, carrying the stink of Venice and people, blew into her as she stood up. Sophia looked at a world stopped in its tracks.

The cars on Via dei Cantieri stood still, nose to bumper. Their owners sat staring blankly in front of them, or milled among the growing crowd drifting from Moranzani and Fusina, nervous and aimless. She could just see the lagoon, packed with pleasure boats, as always. But most of them lay still in the water, rocking gently. Only the sailboats still shifted past, like birds with white wings glistening in the dark night.

And it was a very dark night. There were no lights where they stood on the mainland to pierce through the darkness and pick out the Queen of the Adriatic. Nothing could be seen of Venice, usually so romantic and lovely, like a fairytale island in the midst of the water. Now it was only a blob of darkness. Everything lay still and dark.

The young man tugged her wet sleeve, and Sophia spun. He stood hunched beside her, and one thin finger pointed. The entrance to the Power Station lay about half a mile to their right, seeming bright with its blue paint as it rose into the night sky.

Black shadows slid from the door to slip into the moonlight. The shadows headed their way.

Perry sped over the clouds and the sun gradually sank. Vincent swiveled in his pilot's chair, watching as the scene slowly darkened and the stars began to appear. Dots of beautiful white light, incomprehensible miles away. Their massive size dared a tiny speck of dust on a tiny insignificant planet to think of itself as important. But Vincent knew Who made those balls of flaming white light. And he knew that God thought enough of humanity to create each person special, and to send His Son to this tiny insignificant speck of a planet to save His own. The stars blazed above Perry. And each one called the inventor to remember how small his inventions were, and how big his God was. How little each individual computer chip and circuit mattered, and how much each human soul meant in the eyes of their Creator.

The copilot's chair gave a little squeak as Gigan dropped into it, his laptop under his arm. Vincent flashed him a smile and went back to staring out at the night sky. Gigan started to work on files[11], and the tick-tick of his keys wrapped around the two men.

---

[11] The Parabaloni had always kept a certain amount of case files, for clients, or to remember details they might need to refer to later. But this past year, as more scenarios called them, and the team found themselves split up more often to handle it all, they took to putting each case in their own online database. That way details could be accessed by all members, and things that might come back to either haunt or bless the team could be rehashed if needed. (Such as the time in Romania, when

A question shot out from the Frenchman every so often, clarifying points. Vincent added details on the four missions they had finished this past week, and watched the facts adding up. After two hours Gigan sighed and closed his laptop. The two men just sat, tired and still, their minds reworking scenarios despite themselves. Wondering if some of those cases added up with this Mr. Black, and what they were headed to now. But they watched the stars too, and gradually the peace slid through their souls into the silence. It stretched into a quarter of an hour, then a half.

"You're thinking of something," Vincent finally broke it softly. "Care to share?"

"A poem Simeon told us many missions ago," Gigan answered. His eyes were half closed as he lay back in his seat, his legs crossed on the instrument panel and his hands comfortably behind his head. "And yet with neither love nor hate, / Those stars like some snow-white / Minerva's snow-white marble eyes / Without the gift of sight.[12]'"

The words spun around the cockpit in his French accent. Vincent nodded slowly, watching the innumerable points of light as the plane slowly changed hemispheres. Only human souls had the gift of love and hate.

"You know, I think I met that Colin kid at Miss Eve's shindig," Vincent commented. "A clean cut African-American, probably mid-teens, quiet and…worn maybe, like he was tired of making it on his own. Of course that was my own guessing, he didn't tell me anything. What I noticed could have just been him up too late playing video games. Do you think he's all right?"

"No idea. We will pray so, and we will be there well before morning."

Silence fell gently around the two like a soft blanket as their

---

Vincent was on his own, running from a gang of cheese smugglers, and ran into a hulking figure who beamed at him with only eight teeth in his mouth and started babbling about owing a favor. Vincent accessed the files on his watch and scanned enough to find the guy's name and the incident two weeks earlier with Gigan and the rice blights and the sumo wrestlers, and called in the favor. The sumos stopped the gang, and the cheese was safely returned; after Vince extracted the chip with vital information from the pilfered parmesan wheel.)

[12] Robert Frost's "Stars"

eyes turned back to the burning balls of white light. Gigan's eyes closed the rest of the way. Another quarter of an hour slid past as Vincent watched the plane and contemplated cloaking mechanisms, and Gigan napped.

The Frenchman's phone vibrated in his pocket. He swept it out before the movement stilled and looked at the message. His feet came down and banged on the cockpit floor, his face hardening like a stone house with windows on fire. His fingers flew over the keyboard, as he started to mutter in French. He stared at the screen, tense and waiting. His mutters rose to furious shouts as his face flamed.

Chapter 5

The hotel staff's voice was loud and angry as he lectured at Colin, and the man was in no mood to give the phone back. Colin fluttered a hand in a half-hearted apology, and managed to dart away before the security man got to the "where's your parents?" part of the harangue. He trotted across the sky bridge back to the main hotel, stepped into the elevator and hit the unlabeled button, slipping the card Mr. Luke had handed him into the slot. The doors slid slowly shut, and the elevator rose. Calming eastern music drifted into its golden interior. His head hummed with the elevator and he felt his muscles tensing. He forced himself to swallow and bounced on his toes, loosening up his joints. He couldn't show how freaked out he was to Dad. Or Mr. Luke. The karate lesson had been great, but he couldn't trust his life to a guy just because he had been nice for one afternoon. Colin didn't kid himself, anyone who talked about culling the human herd like that lady would be perfectly fine with slitting a fifteen-year-old snooper's throat. He had to move carefully.

The elevator dinged, the door slid open, and Colin strolled out. The glass dome arching over his head twinkled with stars and his head went back as he stared at them. These were different stars than he was used to. It was as if he had walked off the plane into a whole new world. A world where his only companions turned out to be monsters, and even the heavens mocked him with their unfriendly strangeness. He swallowed, a difficult thing past the lump in his throat, and stuck his key on the lock pad to Mr. Luke's room.

The door jerked open. Colin's key card, suddenly finding the lock gone, slammed into Mr. Luke's white shirt front as the big man stood in the doorway. He glowered at Colin, his anger almost palpable.

"Uh. Hi?" Colin tried.

"Where have you been?" Mr. Luke growled.

"I found good coffee," Colin said, and managed a beautifully happy smile. "They have really good coffee here. Why, what's up?" Mr. Luke shifted a fraction and Colin pushed past him into the room. He glanced around quickly. The roller carry-on still lay on the bed where he had tossed it. His own bag and Mr. Luke's overnight bag hung from the big man's shoulder.

"We're leaving. Your dad is not happy about the delay you've caused."

"What? Leaving already, we just got here," Colin said, his surprise perfect.

"He's already taken the car to the airport, but I told him I would stay and find you. Now come on, let's go!"

"Ok, ok," Colin complained, letting the sassy teenager drift into the words. He grabbed the handle of the roller bag and pulled it toward himself.

"Not that one," Mr. Luke said quickly. But his eyes snapped and Colin could almost swear shame flitted over his face as he looked away.

"Why, what's in it?" he asked, and decided his only course was to play up the impulsive, slightly idiotic teenager. As he spoke his fingers went to the zipper and he slid it open.

"Stop!" Mr. Luke barked, his voice loud and angry. He leapt forward as the word ripped from him and his hand gripped Colin's wrist, jerking it away from the bag. Colin staggered back, trying not to yelp at the pain of Mr. Luke's grip.

Something white and something shiny metal gleamed at them through the open zipper. Mr. Luke's face worked as he stared at the bag, too many thoughts coursing behind it for Colin to guess what went on inside him. The secretary dropped to his knees and reached for the zipper. His big fingers eclipsed it and he pulled it the rest of the way open. Colin leaned over Mr. Luke's shoulder, staring at the contents of the carry-on bag. A rectangular metal box encased something, a screen display set at the top. Colored wires stuck out of the top of it and reached into something that looked like a white putty. The white putty filled the rest of the bag.

"What is it?" Colin whispered.

"Explosives," Mr. Luke whispered back. One hand went to his face and ran down it, stopping over his mouth. He knelt and stared at the bag. Colin stood rigid behind him. Did he run? Did he run with the bag? Did he punch a button and explode this thing before the Collective could use it? What did you do when you were stuck in a hotel room with a bomber and a bomb half a world away from home?!

Mr. Luke spun on one knee to face Colin, and the young man stepped back sharply, his hand searching behind him for the lamp on the end table. Not much of a weapon, but anything he could grab...

"I didn't know," Mr. Luke said. His voice shook. Colin might have imagined it, but grief seemed to lace it. "I didn't know what he was bringing, or how much this Collective was planning, I swear to you, I didn't know! I had to keep this job, my dad and sister are both disabled and– till tonight I hadn't heard anything about their plan to start wars and cut back the human race, I thought it was just some normal wacky environmentalists, I thought maybe we had been delivering them cases of money or even just flyers. I...I didn't know."

Colin studied his lined face, his trembling hands, the way his eyes pleaded with a young almost stranger to believe in his ignorance. His fingers peeled away from the lamp.

"Normal wacky environmentalists?" he asked. A sharp, short laugh barked from Mr. Luke.

"Ok, poor choice of words," he murmured.

"What do we do with it?" Colin asked, his gaze going back to the bag. The putty looked like the clay his teacher made him use in art class last year. It looked so innocent. His eyes snapped back to Mr. Luke's and he found his shoulders squaring. "We can't just leave it for them."

"No, we can't," Mr. Luke agreed. His voice was quiet, his shoulders slumped.

"And what about the other bags? What's in those? Ok, ok, let's think about this for a minute." Colin sucked in a breath, his eyes bright as he stared at the carry-on. "You go get the other bags, we'll barricade ourselves in here, and call the police. Once they get here, we'll turn the stuff over to them, and hope it doesn't get used on America or anything nasty like that."

"Saudi Arabia is our ally, haven't you been doing your

geography?"

"Ok, fine, that's a good thing, it will work out better for us that way," Colin said, and swept up the phone off the nightstand. "Hello?" He pulled it away and stared at it as if it were an alien artifact. "Isn't it supposed to have a number I can touch for information or something?" Mr. Luke plucked it from his hand and put it to his ear.

"Dead," he reported and dropped it back on the receiver. "And they confiscated all our cells when we walked in."

"Right. Paper airplane message off the balcony?"

"The odds of that actually making it to the police are...haven't you been doing your math?"

"I'm trying not to freak out here and come up with some kind of a plan, all right?!" Colin exploded, bouncing on his toes.

A knock rang on their door. Their heads swiveled slowly, staring at it. The sound came again, a delicate, patient sound. Colin dove for the bag, zipped it back up, and shoved it between the twin beds out of sight of the door.

"What?" Mr. Luke barked.

"Maid service," a female voice almost cooed. No hint of an eastern accent laced that word. The two men looked at each other, alarm on both their faces. Mr. Luke shoved the bag at Colin, grabbed the young man's shoulder, and propelled him toward the connecting door to the suite.

"They want this. Get it out," he hissed in Colin's ear. "The other bags have already been claimed, get this one out of the hotel."

"But–" Colin squeaked. He found himself shoved through into the suite, the bag banging into his long legs. Black paint gilded with elegant swirls and patterns stared back at him as the door softly closed. A lock clicked from the other side.

"Come in," Mr. Luke growled, muffled by the door. "Don't forget the fresh towels."

A sharp bang shot through the suite as the door into Mr. Luke's room crashed open. Colin jumped a foot. A crash shattered the quiet, glass tinkling as something heavy thumped into the wall. Colin scuttled toward the door to the hall, the bag clicking over the swirls of marble making up the floor, his breath bursting from him in panicked spurts. More thumps came from the connecting room, soft and thick, and he recognized it from his brief lesson with Mr. Luke this afternoon; blows hitting human bone and skin and muscles. Except this was the real thing, not a lesson. Another crash came as the second nightstand went over, and Colin felt his panic climbing higher. The silence of the fighters was absolutely terrifying.

His fingers wrapped around the gold doorknob and Colin eased it open. He cracked the door and stuck one eye to the sliver, staring out at the hall. He didn't see anyone. He pulled the door open, jerked the bag into his arms, and ran. Colin's converse tennis shoes pounded over the marble, and he silently thanked the fates he had forgotten to bring his dress shoes. The elevator dinged softly as he punched the button and he cringed at the sound. The doors slid slowly open. He darted through the crack as soon as the bag could fit, and jammed his thumb into the "close doors" button, again and again, quietly begging it to move faster. The doors closed. The elevator began to shift smoothly down. Colin suddenly realized how heavy the bag was. He eased it to the floor with an effort, ran a hand through his hair, straightened his vest and tie, cleared his throat and lifted his chin.

When this door opened to the lobby, he had to be completely in charge. He doubted this Collective would rush him openly in the lobby, even with the whole pack of them here. It was up to him to march through without giving anyone the chance to stop him.

What happened after that… Colin could feel sweat trickling down his spine.

Somehow he had to keep this bag away from these people.

Simeon sat still at his desk. The team had flown off hours ago, and the quiet pressed in around him. Aurora gave a soft groan in her sleep and rolled to her back, her legs sticking straight out and her lips flopping away from her teeth. The clock ticked rhythmically on the oak mantelpiece. A piece of wood popped as it settled deeper into the fire. Simeon clicked through the online sites again, looking for anything else useful. His eye lingered on an advertisement that definitely didn't come from a local paper; their goading Luther Kirl was showing fruit. His mouse shifted to pull up the other tab he kept checking, a harmless looking description of an antique greeting card display in Memphis, Tennessee. He reached up and pulled the laptop closed with a quick annoyed movement and leaned back in his chair. Simeon didn't move. He sat still staring at his phone lying silent on the desk.

Algy still didn't answer.

A few hours of not noticing a call was normal. Even twenty-four hours, perhaps. But with Algy stateside and a little bored trying to live a "normal" life, this silence was not normal. Alice hadn't seen him for two days.

Simeon swept up a drawing pad and pencil and started to doodle. A greeting card with an old-fashioned Edwardian couple on it spun from the pencil. A faceless black shadow formed, hovering over a chessboard.

Mr. Black knew about Colin Clempson's call. This is his sort of game, elaborate plots that drew his enemies into his play, while he called all the shots. It amused him to pull in Luther Kirl, a man with as big a god fixation as Black's own, only to prove Mr. Black was the real god pulling even Kirl's strings. This Riyadh business had Black written on it. Simeon let his boys rush off to stop whatever plot Black planned for them. They were good, and could handle it.

But Mr. Black would be upping the game now. The chessboard shifted to a new page, with silver eggs and rifles and TNT as the pieces. They had found his clues, even his hidden egg at the Maeslant, and set him in the last round. This round would be more intense, more tricky. Something nasty would be left *here* for them, something they might have stopped if they didn't rush off to save a situation across the world. The question was, where and what, and how best to get ahead of this man instead of constantly dancing to his tune? The faceless, formless shadow reappeared on his notes, a flute sticking out the corner that ought to have a mouth.

In the end they had to get ahead of him, and do it in a quick, clean sweep. They had to get to know this Mr. Black and how he worked, and that took time. And they had to do it while chasing at his heels putting out the fires he set for them. The shadow moved to a new page, flitting ahead while fires blazed behind him and a white horse charged between the flames. So where would this particular game piece be laid?

A globe swept from his pencil onto the paper. Another sketch of an Edwardian greeting card joined it. Beside that a quick sketch of a thin-faced, shriveled old man flew from his pencil.

Luther Kirl might be the key to getting ahead. A quick sketch of a barracks set within a high stone wall, with mountains rising behind it, flew over the pad of paper. A Viking peered over the parapet. Beside it an old fashioned newspaper advertisement flew onto the page. Simeon flipped his phone on and quickly tapped in a number. Kalifa[13] answered on the first ring.

"We have only two cells open right now," he stated, his cultured voice coming fast and stressed in his native Arabic, "I hope you're not calling with more than that."

"Actually wondering if I can take one away," Simeon said.

"Really?" Kalifa asked, and Simeon smiled at the hope riding the word.

"Algy being gone taking a toll?" Simeon asked.

"When is he coming back?" Kalifa snapped, and Simeon laughed.

"Start training someone to help. Not sure he is coming back. At least not to stay. Realized grandkids are nice and he's getting old."

"Wonderful." Kalifa breathed out a long breath, letting some

---

[13] A note for those who don't remember this name. Kalifa is a would-be-Jihadist, dropped at Algy's door by the Parabaloni, and since claimed by Christ and turned jailor-evangelist. He and Algy run a compound in the Caucus mountains where people of interest (such as others like Kalifa) are left to keep them out of trouble and teach them Christ's truth. It's a unique place partially because the internment duration and what happens to the inmates afterwards is entirely in Algy and Kalifa's hands. They tend to take "likely prospects" (those already showing at least a vague inclination to listen to the gospel), and so often the inmates become changed from the inside out and simply released into the fold of Christ for more...normal discipleship. Sometimes, the compound becomes a half-way point before real internment in a place better equipped to keep nasty people out of harm's way.

of the stress out. When he spoke again the anxiety had dissipated. "I am glad he has found his family. He has much to give them, and he should have that time. What can I do for you, Mr. Lee?"

"Wondering about the last one we brought."

"Peter's Viking man? Arnulf Jones does actually have Norse blood running through him. He is coming along nicely. He is even asking the right sort of questions."

"Think we could trust him on a job?"

"Do I think he would rush off and bomb a building, or do I think he would disappear and not be heard from again?" Kalifa tried to clarify. Simeon stayed quiet, and on his end Kalifa grinned. Mr. Lee could say so much with silence. Kalifa answered both questions. "No, I do not think he is the bombing type, he seems genuinely concerned his actions caused damage to 'ordinary people.' I do not have a definitive answer on the last question."

"In your opinion?"

"I think he would prefer to earn his money, if the job did not kill him. Quite possibly he would even stay in contact to learn more of what he searches for."

"Good. Sending a plane ticket and instructions for him."

The red-haired she-devil struck out with a straight kick to Luke's middle. He caught her leg and twisted, a sharp kiai breaking from him. The big goon rushed him from behind, and Luke dropped the she-devil to spin toward the goon, his arm shooting out in a straight punch to the enemy's kidney. The big goon knocked it aside with an outward block and kept rushing. Luke spun to the side with lightning agility and the big goon rushed straight into the skinny goon. Both slammed into the wall with a deafening thunk. The basement rang with it, the wall shivering under the blow. Luke didn't let himself consider what the guests might think about the strange thuds and crashes that had moved steadily through their hotel for a quarter of an hour. He brushed the blood away from his cut eyebrow and took up a front stance, slowly shifting his footwork to spin in a circle, looking for the she-devil.

The two goons gained their feet. The big goon cracked his neck, his face murderous. Luke drew in a breath and forced his tense muscles to relax, regaining his focus with an effort.

"All together, boys," the she-devil said, her lilting voice carrying her enjoyment of this whole situation. Luke followed the sound of her voice and found her in the shadows just across from him. She held a knife. Luke's face hardened, knowing he could not survive this. But he readied his stance again and focused on the she-devil. He would take her out before they killed him. He would not let this one out on the streets after Colin.

A mindless yell burst from the goons and they rushed him. He could see the fury rippling over their faces in the fluorescent lighting spilling from the basement ceiling. The she-devil darted forward with the grace of a dancer, her knife flipping to an underhand hold, her eyes focusing on his leg, picking out where his artery would be easiest to cut. Luke roared another kiai, leaping toward the lady.

A sharp, metallic "thwack" rang through the basement. It came again in almost the same second, and both goons dropped in their tracks. They bounced on the concrete ground once and lay still. Something moved behind the she-devil, and she spun, a snarl flickering over her lips.

A metal bar smashed into the side of her head. She crumpled like a black-clothed doll and lay still.

Luke felt himself tensing, his leg automatically going back as he regained his stance, his eyes searching the shadows for the new threat. A man stepped toward him. The hood of his black robe lay draped over his face, hiding all but a few strands of straight black hair and the end of a sharp nose. A metal bar rested on his shoulder. Fresh blood stained the end.

"There are more of these pipes in the corner," he said in good English, his voice deep and mournful. "Why are you still fighting bare handed like a dad-blamed idiot?" Luke blinked at him. The figure gave a long-suffering sigh and gestured toward the stairs. "You had better go now before the head man comes hunting for you. The kid is headed toward the royal square."

"The royal square, where is that?" Luke burst out.

"Really? Saving your hide isn't enough is it, no of course not, it's never enough. Do one thing and everyone expects you to finish the job and save everything, and never even considers you might be needed somewhere else. And never any thanks, either." A picture of Eeyore projected itself into Luke's mind at the mournful complaints, and he fought back a hysterical laugh. He could almost feel the figure glaring at him under the hood. Luke tried to look humble as he brushed away the blood dripping into his eye. He felt humble right now. "Go out the front, turn left, two blocks, turn right, go four blocks, right two, left one, you're there."

The figure melted away. Luke blinked, and spun in a tight circle, but he couldn't see anyone. No one but the three crumpled forms bleeding on the concrete ground. He ran for the stairs, repeating the directions in his mind and pressing a bunched piece of his ripped suitcoat to the cut on his head.

As the door to the first floor clanged behind Luke, a figure in the dark corner shifted. A pistol glinted in the florescent lighting, held in hands encased in black kid gloves. The black-clad fingers screwed a silencer onto the barrel with a slow relish. He had watched the easterner slip out a window to the loading bay. His minions lay still. The big annoying fighter ran toward the other annoyance and the square. He was confident no one even knew he existed. The figure slid the pistol into his jacket pocket and began to walk up the stairs, his steps measured and neat. The door closed softly behind the figure as he went on his business.

Yousef watched through the basement window as the head Butwani, the stranger with the black gloves, strolled out after Luke. Yousef let himself groan. He stood up, leaned the iron bar against the wall, and headed for the valet station. These amateurs, they could never save a situation on their own!

Chapter 6

Jojo and Pete sat in Perry's living area, lit by their laptops and the moon's glow spraying through the windows. Vincent and Gigan stayed in the cockpit, but Pete and Jojo didn't feel inclined to join them. The sibling's eyes focused hungrily on the screens. Neither spoke as the plane sped over the ocean. Scenes from security cameras cycled steadily over Jojo's screen as Pete scanned reports from Riyadh authorities. The siblings didn't have to speak. Both knew the silent prayers for Yousef speeding heavenward, and the hopes intertwined in each begging word.

Jojo sat up suddenly. Pete shot from his loveseat to sit beside her on the couch, his eyes on her screen. She rewound the tape for him.

The opulent façade of the Royal Fassa Hotel stared at them from the angle of a security camera mounted across the street. Dusky light played with the forms moving outside the hotel, making it hard to get a clear focus on anyone. A young man with a sharp nose and a lugubrious frown stepped up to a red Tesla as it stopped at the curb. He wore the livery of a hotel-employed valet and the picture was grainy and indistinct in the dusk; but Pete and Jojo would have known him if he wore a banana suit. The driver tossed Yousef the key to the Tesla and strolled into the hotel as the young man slid into the car.

For an instant Yousef's dark eyes looked directly at the security camera. He smiled, a sly, puckish look with the humor of a prankster enjoying his own joke. Jojo felt her stomach tighten at that familiar, wonderful, terrifying look from her brother.

The car sped off. Jojo's fingers flew over her screen, tracking it through whatever cameras she could find. Pete did the same on his own, but he had more practice than his younger sister. He slapped her shoulder. She looked at his screen, and saw the world outside a baker's in the tourist quarter, the time stamp only three minutes from the earlier scene. A young man, perhaps fifteen, ran down the sidewalk. A three-piece tailored suit set off his chiseled features very nicely. But they could see the fear in the whites of his eyes even through the grainy light of the camera's lens. A gray carry-on bag dragged behind him as he ran. With a little squinting, Pete made out the shapes of a Riyadh gang farther down the street giving chase. The kid had good reason to be afraid.

A flash of red came from the corner and a Tesla screeched into the street on two wheels. The kid jerked toward the apparition.

In the instant he jerked toward the car, a muzzle flash came from a dark alley behind him. The boy doubled over, one arm going to his side. His knuckles grew pale as they tightened on the bag's handle. As if it were more important than the fact a bullet just grazed his side.

The red Tesla screeched between the young man and the alley. The passenger door flew open, a calloused, brown hand shot out and wrapped around the kid's arm. The hand jerked the young man and the bag into the car, and they could see a large dark-skinned man leaning over the backseat, steadying the teenager. For a moment the brown hand formed a C. Then the Tesla spun into a small side street and was lost to sight. Jojo started to track the Tesla again, but paused, her eyes on her older brother. Peter's finger went to his screen and he leaned forward, staring unblinking at the corner.

A figure moved in the alley where the shot had come from. Indistinct, a shadow, hardly anything but movement. But for a moment, he caught a glimpse of a pair of hands reloading a pistol; they were encased in gentleman's black gloves.

Gigan's voice rose to a sudden babble of French in the cockpit. Anger and fear underlay the words. Pete and Jojo looked at each other. Pete's lips pursed. But he sank back and kept cycling through camera feeds, aware he would hear of the happenings after the Frenchman calmed down and formed a plan. Jojo looked at Pete and hesitated. Maybe Gigan needed to report to Simeon before it was common knowledge. Jojo sank back against the cushions beside Pete and they kept cycling through the digital world of Riyadh, looking for their brother.

"Care to share the excitement?" Vincent broke through his French buddy's tirade. Gigan spun his phone to face the inventor. His face was haggard and pale, his gray eyes tight. Vincent noticed Gigan tap his watch, requesting Simeon come online.

A picture was opened in the texts, the scene in sharp relief from a flash dispelling the darkness. Blurry figures in dark clothes, their faces turned from the camera. But one figure stood out in grisly clarity. A man lay dead on his back, knee bent as if broken from blunt trauma. Two bullet wounds still bled. A wooden club had spilled from his hand onto the concrete ground. A silver egg loomed in the background of the scene, still and immense, brooding over the subjects. Two words lay typed under the photo.

Help Uncle!

Vincent's eyes flew to the sender's name. He remembered the skinny kid in Paris taking apart his Amelia on Perry's couch, glued to the gadgets and screens, never meeting anyone's eye... Gigan's reply already lay under the words.

On my way, two hours out.

A terrifying red notification lay under the simple sentence; "Not Delivered."

"I am taking this mission, Simeon," Gigan stated, his voice clipped. "I am assuming you can take over remotely for the Riyadh task."

"Pat tells me the photo is from the Andrea Palladio Power Station, in Moranzani, near Venice," Vincent said. Gigan flung himself on the instruments and began to change Perry's flight pattern, pointing the plane's nose toward Italy. "Did the folks move from where we dropped them? Or is Aldrick just off on an adventure?"

"I don't know," Gigan growled through clenched teeth. "All I know is I am too far away."

"Moved last year," Simeon said over the speaker system.

"And you know because..." Gigan growled.

"Your sister's Instagram account very active, can find out anything on social media. Check it occasionally in case."

"In case of moments like this, when I am needed, and *still two hours out!*" Gigan's fist pulled back in a lightning punch and slammed down against the control board. He flung himself back in his chair, drew in a deep breath, and controlled himself with an effort. "Simeon, you hate smart phones and light-spraying gadgetry, what are you doing checking social media accounts?"

"Have a tablet," Simeon said defensively, and Vincent snorted[14]. "Check for when it's needed." The men in the cockpit supplied the unspoken words; *Because he takes care of Pete and Gigan. He knows they need that connection to their families, but it hurts too much for them to keep checking. So he does it for them in order to offer updates.* Gigan's shoulders slumped a little farther and the angry smolder in his eyes dimmed. Vincent wondered why the big boss had stayed back when he knew they were headed toward hard family matters. It wasn't like Sim. Which meant there was something awfully important they had missed back in the States.

"What else did you learn?" Gigan asked, his voice tired. Silence expanded from the speaker. Vince and Gigan could feel the apology and sorrow in it.

"Moved for the family business," Simeon said. Gigan's jaw tightened. A muscle on it jumped. "And your twin's taken to the bottle." Gigan's eyes closed. His fist pulled back again. Vincent shoved his roll of paper towels[15] under his buddy's hand before it smashed into the metal. Gigan punched it four times, then watched the crumpled roll fall to the cockpit floor with a smoldering eye.

"My knuckles appreciate it, but it is not as satisfying," he growled.

---

[14] Simeon's "tablet" is a kindle fire that by now takes twenty-five minutes to load if turned off. But he declares he likes the familiar, and refuses to let Vincent give him an updated model. It gives the inventor goosebumps every time he sees Simeon waiting for it to load a page.

[15] Vince always keeps a roll in his cockpit, because he still never remembers to secure his Dr. Peppers when he turns the plane into a roll for the sheer enjoyment. And Pete continually trails food into the cockpit, and the partners' roughhousing inevitably squishes it. They also come in handy for those rare moments when a girl in hysterics is hiding in the cockpit and they have to keep her quiet to hide her from the fuming sheiks outside the plane.

"Hold tight, buddy, we'll get you there and you can punch the people who need it," Vincent said. He dropped a hand on Gigan's tight shoulder and squeezed. "God's got him, G. God's already there." The Frenchman's shoulders sagged, his head bowed. He nodded and dropped back to his chair again. He spun in little half circles, chewing one mustache.

"It is almost on the way to Riyadh," he said, "so at least it shouldn't interrupt that mission too much."

"Right, they can drop us off on the way," Vincent nodded.

"'Us?'" Gigan snapped. "I don't recall requesting a—"

"You're too deep in this with family involved, you need another along," Vincent interrupted, "and something tells me Petey would prefer not to skip out on a Riyadh case with a probable Yousef connection." Gigan opened his mouth to protest, his eyes still smoldering, but Simeon broke in.

"He goes." No one argued with that kind of Simeon order. Gigan's mouth snapped shut.

"Besides, there's an egg thing there. Maybe I can come up with a way to break the pulse," Vincent added. "I would bet you anything the power's out all over that area of Italy already. And right now I don't know how to bring it back. We can't do anything but prepare for it."

"We must assume none of our trackers or scanners will be functioning," Gigan said. "How do we find our target?"

"That's right! We can't use a quick weapons scan, or even an Amelia to find out where the baddies are grouped," Vincent frowned. "We can't assume they'll still be at the plant after two hours. How do we find him?" Silence fell as the two agents wracked their brains, their brows furrowed. On the other end of the watch channel, Simeon rolled his eyes.

"Use your own scanners," he said.

"What?" they chorused. At another time their syncopated surprise would have made Gigan laugh.

"Tracked people for years before any of your fancy gadgets. You have brains. Use them."

"Just…like that?" Vincent blinked. Gigan pulled out his phone and quickly navigated to the maps, pulling up Venice and the power station on the mainland. His anger dissipated as he found a way to apply the time.

"We know he was here when the text came in. Since he is asking me for help, we must assume he is not going home for aid. I wonder why?" the Frenchman's voice died away, and he chewed silently on his mustache as he glowered at his boots.

"So where would he go?" Vincent broke in. Gigan snapped back into looking at the map.

"Live on the coast of the lagoon," Simeon supplied. "Miss Ginette often posts pictures of sailing and rowboats."

"We will assume he takes to the water then," Gigan said, studying his phone. "The closest waterway is here, the Navigilio del Brenta. It leads deeper into the mainland, or out into the lagoon. The channel is narrow, hemmed in by houses and concrete, and if you are being chased you want options."

"So he heads to the open lagoon," Vincent nodded. "More maneuverable and probably more familiar too, everyone sails there. Then what?" Silence fell. It drifted into a tense five minutes as Gigan shifted his map helplessly here and there, and Vincent's brow stayed furrowed.

"I don't know," Gigan burst out. "Ordinarily I would order an Amelia ahead of us to check out the area and scan for problems, and we would find him in under two minutes! What do you do without that?" Simeon resolutely held back a sigh and resisted the urge to just stick his finger on the map and point out the likeliest places. They needed to do this on their own.

"What do you know about your nephew?" he prompted. *A struggling youth,* Gigan's brain fired off the answer, *who hates watching the evil, and whose father keeps pushing and pushing him to join it, till Aldrick has become practically non-verbal in his withdrawal into his gadgets.* None of that was helpful. Simeon's voice went on, flowing into Gigan's frustrated panic and channeling his thoughts. "Texted you occasionally since Italy. Where would he think to go? Where would he feel safe?"

"Aldrick is a smart one," Gigan started. "And he doesn't trust easily. He is especially wary of strangers, in any guise... He would not go to the police. He would not bother to avoid crowds, he knows a crowd is a good place for a single person to hide. He would assume he was on his own in this, and try to disappear. He always tries to disappear. The best place to vanish alone, at night, in a small boat, and where the enemy would not dare to be... Venice. He is going to the city proper, where tourists flock in droves every day, and the nights stay almost as busy. The enemy would have no reason to be there, as they are busy on the mainland, and their work is already done; knocking out the Andrea Palladio knocks out Venice too."

"So we know he's in his boat, and he's freaked out, and he's headed to Venice from the Navigilio del Brenta," Vincent broke in, looking over Gigan's head to see the map. "Where's the best place to disappear? I'd stay in the boat as something I know instead of hopping out on the first landfall, and take the next canal that opens."

"That puts him here," Gigan pointed. He zoomed in a little closer, his voice soft and thoughtful as he studied it. "There is a church almost as soon as you enter the canal. A Catholic, 1500s beauty."

"Is that a likely spot?" Vincent asked.

"The few conversations I've had with Aldrick have shown me a young man who wants Christianity to be true, and most days even considers himself a Christian. Someone seeking like that, whose *Meme* takes him to mass whenever she can, would see a church of that sort as a sign. That's where we start."

"We should probably skirt the area, at least at first, and come in on a high glide," Vincent added. "I bet you anything the air space above Venice knocks out our electrics and Pete will have to handle Perry manually. Hey Sim, you think we can land with the water skis and still take off? Petey's become a good enough pilot for it."

"Air drop," Gigan ordered, his voice snapping. "Into the lagoon, quickest method and most accurate for the area."

"Dude, we'll land on someone's fishing boat," Vincent grinned. Gigan didn't smile back.

"Then we will have transportation too."

Aldrick darted across the road and ran. He leapt the fence to the green field running beside the Via dei Cantieri. His toes dug into the damp earth and he sprinted toward the nearest canal, the Navigilio del Brenta. Sophia hesitated by the road, her eyes darting to the people milling amongst the stalled cars, their hands flinging up in dramatic gestures as their words spilled quickly and helplessly into the night. She sprinted to catch up to the thin young man. She couldn't let him rush off on his own. What if these shadows followed him?

The guard thundered up beside Aldrick, and he glanced over to see her pistol in her hands, her face hard. A tick beside his left eye jerked rhythmically. He looked away from the gun. The shadows slid over the road behind them, moving between the cars in the darkest parts, wherever it was devoid of people. No one noticed them. They glided through the night, moving as if the darkness closed around them and propelled them forward.

"I can't get a good shot," Sophia said. She shoved her pistol back in her holster and concentrated on catching up to the kid again. He was fast. "Shouldn't we be running toward town?" He just leaned harder into his race. Sophia had to work hard to keep up, and didn't have the breath to spare for conversation. The young man suddenly made it to the edge of the canal. He leapt off the concrete side, and Sophia's heels dug into the damp earth, staring over the edge.

Aldrick's shoes plunked down in the little boat the family kept for outings and small side missions for which it was useful not to leave tire tracks or the memory of your face in a taxi driver's mind. His fingers flew to the bowline and he quickly undid the knot binding them to the little iron ring. His boot came up and shoved off the concrete side of the canal, and the boat shifted into the water, sending ripples dancing with moonlight. He looked up at Sophia.

"We should go the other way, where other people are!" she panted. Aldrick's face shifted, and she read a story of complete contempt and utter distrust of *people*[16]. Sophia suddenly felt

---

[16] Aldrick knew the crowd mentality too well. If something bad went down and one person stood near, he would probably try to intervene. If something bad went down

small, as if her twenty-four years had only shown her a tiny, safe portion of the world. She dropped into the boat.

Aldrick shoved off, pushing an oar against the bank to drive them further into the Navigilio del Brenta. He tossed the oar to Sophia and reached for the small sail lying in the bottom of the boat. In a minute and a half he had the mast locked tight and the black sail spread into the night.

A breeze caught them, drawn by the cool water and carried along the concrete walls making up the canal. It filled the sail and Aldrick leaned against the ropes, shifting them with practiced skill. The night lay deep enough around them the canal wasn't busy. But people always ranged in this corner of the world, at all hours. Stalled boats littered the canal like human-made islands, drifting in the breeze as their owners stared at their dead cell phones and blinked stupidly at their silent engines.

Behind them human-shaped shadows dropped over the edge of the canal into a sleek sailing boat. They threw the boat's mooring line off and shot toward the little rowboat.

"They're coming after us," Sophia reported, holding the oar out of the water. "Aim for Moranzani or Fusina, we need to go to the police with this." Aldrick tugged a rope and leaned and they shot through the open locks connecting one side of the canal to the Conca di Moranzani. He dared a look over his shoulder. The sailboat drew closer quickly. His eyes turned back to the canal, his jaw tight. The police were slow and ponderous in these little cities, used to filling out forms for tourists over lost items. Tonight whatever poor soul had night duty would be preoccupied with people rushing in demanding they do something about the blackout, and those crowding the door asking for news the police didn't have.

And then there was the danger of being recognized. "That's Gregoir Lefebvre's boy. What's he doing out this late at night?

---

and ten people stood near, they might look at each other and intervene. If something bad went down, and a hundred people stood near, they would all look away and pretend it was someone else's problem to deal with, and no one would do anything. Aldrick's father was smart enough to use it well, as the hamster smuggler learned to his pain, and others that Aldrick tried with all his young heart not to think about when the night closed around his bed.

Well now we know who caused this problem!" Aldrick's eye ticked again. No police.

Aldrick briefly considered the sprawling, leaky old tower on the lagoon shore, overflowing with Lefebvres bristling with weapons. He glanced at Sophia's uniform, the guard badge shiny and bright. And he remembered her boyfriend's name, the man she hoped to marry, the police detective. A good man, smart and brave, who didn't take bribes or listen to threats. Aldrick knew the hatred that flew from his family when that name was mentioned. No. They needed to disappear.

He leaned back against the lines, tightening the sail to try to catch whatever breeze they could. The little boat pushed past a stalled motor boat, sprayed water up the sides of the canal onto the streets of Fusina, and shot out into the lagoon. A muted curse came from Sophia and she moved to stand and get at the sail. The boat rocked dangerously and she sank back.

The breeze died into a soft caress. Aldrick's frown tightened. He shifted the lines, working the sail to catch as much of the breeze as he could. Water splashed as Sophia tried to work the oars. She didn't seem to even know what an oarlock was. Aldrick paused to slip the two oars into the slot for her. As he spun back to the sail his gaze automatically went to the sky.

With the lights dead the stars shone with a brilliance he had never seen in his whole urban life. He picked out Orion and followed his belt to Taurus, dazzled by how many lights twinkled above him. Unfathomable miles away, huge fiery balls and whole swirling galaxies of colors and phenomenal power. So many of them! There were so many, many stars to be seen when the human lights went out. And here he was, a tiny speck on a minuscule planet in a lesser galaxy... Did it really matter if they made it to Venice?

Sophia's mind stayed on their immediate situation, and her eyes went to the entry to the canal, a few yards behind them. The sailboat drifted from its mouth, and its sail dropped almost lifeless. Dark forms stood on its deck, watching them. The moonlight shone strong, and she could see all but their faces; those seemed indistinct, shadowy, formless, and terrifying. Goosebumps rose as she stared at the creepy people. Two of them held rifles.

"Look out!" Sophia shouted, her pistol snapping up.

Rifle shots echoed over the lagoon as the shadows fired on the small boat. Aldrick dropped to huddle against the bulwark, his arms over his head as bullets whizzed past him. Two splintered through the boat's keel, spurting water into the night. Aldrick gasped and grabbed for the lines again. Someone back in Fusina screamed at the gunshots on the eerily quiet night. Sophia's pistol barked beside his ear and Aldrick shuddered, his breath coming in gasps. But he pulled the lines, shifting them with an expert's skill into the wind and winching them tight. They had one small advantage over a sailboat on a night like this. He threw himself at the oars and bent to the work. His muscles strained, and he did his best not to think about how much better and quicker his cousins were at this. Even his girl cousins. Mostly he tried not to think about how easy a target he made sitting upright in the boat, churning up white foam on either side of him, as if to say, "shoot here."

"I thought you said they didn't have firearms?" Sophia growled, her pistol still raised as she tried to aim it in the shaking boat.

These must be new shadows, Aldrick thought, and for a moment his finger itched for his phone, and even his mouth worked to say the words. But his throat grew dry and thick, and the words died inside him. He felt like crying for his dead phone.

Aldrick's strokes were not as powerful as some of his cousins. But they were sure and steady and he knew how to use them. The little boat shifted smoothly and quickly through the lagoon. They shot between two stalled fishing boats, their outboard motors lifted from the water, their owners crouching and looking wildly around them for the shooters. Stranded and lost without a phone to call for help, without the ability to fix the power on their boats.

Water bubbled steadily through the holes gouged in the keel.

Aldrick grunted at Sophia and his head nodded at the bucket lying against the gunwales. She glanced at him, but kept staring at the sailboat, drifting slowly, slowly after them. The water sloshed over her boots. He grunted again, more urgently. She glanced back, her brow knit.

"Bail," Aldrick said. His voice came small and hoarse, unused to being used. He nodded at the bucket again. She looked down, took in the bubbling water lapping at her shoes, and her eyes grew wide. Sophia shoved her pistol back in her holster, snatched the bucket and bailed. *At least she knows how to do that,* Aldrick thought as he dug the oars into the water and strained to draw them back again. He aimed toward the closest landfall he thought these shadows would not dare to wander, not with the hordes of tourists flocking the whole island all day long. They could hunker down in some of the tiny side streets and wait for morning. Or maybe that text made it through and he would come... Aldrick didn't let himself hope, turning his mind quickly to find the best spot to hide for a few hours.

Surely Venice would be safe.

Chapter 7

Luther Kirl brooded at his desk. His current abode, a flat in a London high rise, stood high enough to shut out the noise of humanity pressing through the streets. Not even a clock ticked. Absolute silence rested in his modern office, accentuating his solitariness and offering no interruption to his black thoughts.

Most of the revolving thoughts involved Vincent Lee Tolliver and his team of agents, and a mysterious figure in a black oval mask.

No one else in his life had managed to squirm out of Luther's nets. He could pull the strings of the world. Bring down kingdoms and lift up diplomats with the power of his money and connections. But these few humans stayed out of his grasp. It niggled in his mind like buzzing flies around a drowsy figure's head at night. He should be able to control everything. Annoyance churned in him. As the days turned since Vincent Tolliver made a fool of him with that stupid hologram and stolen helicopter, the annoyance hardened to hatred.

Using the Parabaloni for his own means (proving he could control even them), and then bringing the team down, became an obsession.

The first thing he would use them for was to rid himself of the other buzzing fly. The man calling himself Mr. Black still evaded all Luther's attempts at bribery, or even identification. Luther had worked with this Mr. Black for a year now, amusing himself by following the man's leads and granting requests. It had been fun at first. But by now, as they neared the man's goal... Luther still didn't even know Black's real name. That drove deep and burned harder even than Vincent's work.

Luther growled something under his breath and leaned forward in his desk chair. This ergonomic design didn't squeak, and he almost missed the sound. His hand flipped the switch to the Parabaloni's feed. Nothing. Not even static. He had found a way to listen in on them, and was certain they didn't know. But then the blasted people had run off and left their headquarters! Maybe he should find better sound technicians and geeks to try again.

"Mr. Kirl?" the secretary's perfect country English accent curled over the speaker system, breaking the silence. He flipped her communication channel open.

"What?" he barked.

"A man here to see you. He doesn't have an appointment," she reported, and Luther's mouth opened to tell her to send the man off with a very rude comment. "He says he is here about your advertisement." Luther's mouth snapped shut. His eyes brightened. He only had one advertisement out right now, and it couldn't be found in the local newspaper.

"Send him in," he snapped, and flipped the channel closed. Luther quickly tucked his extendable knife up his sleeve, cracked his drawer open so he could reach his pistol, and waited. The door opened and a burly man strode in. His long blond hair hung over a pair of shoulders that looked as wide and muscular as a bull. But his clear blue eyes shifted nervously around the office. He stopped just inside the door and stood still, staring at Luther.

"I want to see the money first," the man said. His voice shook. Luther smiled. He sat his foot on the briefcase under his desk, and pushed. It slid across the room and rested against the man's boot. He knelt down, unsnapped it with shaking fingers, and lifted the lid. Luther could see the shine in his eyes as they widened.

"If you prefer pounds instead of American, I can make the change," Luther said. "But I assume you know walking out of here is contingent on my deeming your information worth my money. I presume you have what I requested?" The man's tongue flicked out, running over his dry lips.

"I don't know Mr. Black's name. No one does. Privately I don't think he has one. But I do know a little of why he's doing this. His motive. I think it would give you a starting place to find out more." The man's mouth snapped closed and he stayed crouching beside the open briefcase, watching the shriveled old man behind the desk. Luther spun his chair in a half circle. His guest couldn't see the old man's finger flicking the screen in his desk drawer; scrolling information. The chair moved in another tight half circle as Luther's sharp old eyes never left his caller.

"Arnulf Jones, isn't it?" he said. The big man started in shock. Luther cackled at his reaction. "I remember the people I hire, Jones, if I let them be near me. You were one of the ones who disappeared in Holland. But now you're back." His cackle died and his voice dropped into icy seriousness. "What happened?"

"Those people who swept in and ruined it all threw me in the back of their plane," Jones growled. No hesitation. Either the truth, or a carefully prepared answer. "They wanted to know things about you. I didn't tell them anything."

"Nothing?" Kirl asked. Jones shrugged, and a little wily smile curved over his face.

"Well, just enough they thought I didn't know anything and kicked me out."

"And now you're here."

"I like money."

"Don't we all." Kirl's teeth flashed for an instant, then he dropped back to staring. His chair swiveled in another half circle. "What else can you do, Jones? Besides get caught by those trying to ruin my plans, and turn almost informant, and then show up for more money?"

"I was a good bodyguard," Jones said, a little surly defensiveness creeping in. Luther cackled again.

"You gained a masters in videography, before deciding your martial arts sideline was more fun," Luther stated. Jones just stared at him, his mouth a little open. "I could use that knowledge." The chair kept moving in tight half circles. It stopped abruptly as Luther made his choice. His dark eyes burned bright at Jones and his teeth bared in what seemed almost an animal's snarl instead of a human's grin.

"Tell me about Mr. Black."

The Tesla rolled through the opulent Riyadh streets. Classical music drifted from the speakers. Colin concentrated on the music, on the comfort of the seat, on being off the streets with the bag still intact.

He did his best not to think about the gang chasing him. Mr. Luke showed up just as they caught up to him, and sent Colin pounding off again with the bag. But the gang still followed. Turns out a big city isn't the best place for a teenager in a suit with a nice shiny carry on bag to wander at night. Go figure. Mostly he tried not to think about that sudden shot from the alley as he ran, and the fire burning in his side. At least he wasn't bleeding on the car seat anymore. His eyes darted to the side, to this unexplained waiter who turned up in a Tesla and jerked him and Mr. Luke inside. As he watched, the young man's finger flicked the turn signal. The car began to click rhythmically and they turned into the airport. Colin listened to Mr. Luke stirring in the backseat, relieved to finally be here. Their car pulled smoothly up to the loading curb.

Colin's eyes focused on a figure leaning against the wall of the airport. He was only medium sized, dressed in simple black slacks and a leather hoody, his hands behind his back. But the man stared at their car. He looked familiar. A soft hum went through Colin's head as his memory projected that man's face at an out of the way table in the creepy meeting tonight. Luke hopped out, relief and stress fighting on his big face. Colin's eyes darted to the secretary. Did he not see the creepy guy in black leaning there waiting for them? The young man's mind rushed back to long before tonight, and the masked stranger who slipped into his dad's office; Mr. Luke hadn't seen him either. How much *didn't* Mr. Luke know about what was happening? The secretary reached for Colin's door. The young man darted a glance at the guy in the black, just waiting for the bag to get out of the car. He focused on Mr. Luke, and shook his head.

"No. This bag full of explosives isn't safe here, and I can't abandon it," Colin said. Luke just stared. "I'm ok, the bleeding's stopped, there's a first aid kit with plenty of antibiotics in this car. I'll reclaim my phone from the hotel after the weirdos have left and I've gotten rid of the bag. I have my ID and passport, the concierge will know the phone's mine. I can get to my apple wallet then and buy a ticket home." Luke just stared, his features inscrutable. Yousef's head bobbed gently to Bach, his eyes half closed as he enjoyed the speaker system. "It's ok. Your family needs you. I've got this." Luke's hand darted for the door handle again. Colin slammed the lock down and rolled the window up to just a crack. "You're causing a scene, man. Go!"

"I can't just leave you here with this," Luke said, his voice coming out strangled. His eyes darted to his watch, then toward the airport, then back to Colin.

"Did you make the call?" the waiter broke in. Colin could only see the tip of his nose for the darkness of his hood. His waiter stayed an inscrutable enigma.

"Yes. The guy said they would take care of it," Colin reported. The waiter's head dropped back to relax against the seat.

"Then the situation will be taken care of. None of you are needed," he said.

"I'm not leaving this bag!" Colin growled through clenched teeth. His arm tightened around it, his face pale under his dark skin. Despite himself his voice shook. "My dad brought it, ok, he was trying to explode people! *People!* And start a war to kill thousands, my dad, I can't just walk away from that and pretend I'm not a part of it! I have to see it through." His eyes shot up and latched onto Luke's. "You're the only one who can keep Dad monitored. Go, keep your job and be the inside man for whoever it is coming to save the situation."

"I can't just–" Luke started again, his voice hoarse. The man in the black hoody turned toward them, ever so slightly.

"Go!" Colin shouted.

"Ok, you don't have to scream at me," the waiter complained, and pushed the car into gear. The handle ripped from Mr. Luke's grasp as the Tesla leapt into the sea of airport traffic. Colin watched in the rear-view mirror as Mr. Luke stumbled forward at the force of losing his hold, his mouth half open. He spun in a tight circle and one hand ran through his hair. An agonized glance went back to the red car, then he started to run. Toward the airport.

The man in the hoody stayed leaning against the wall. But his icy blue eyes never left the red car, till the distance cut them off.

A polite knock on the door drifted to the Hector Lopez's dinner table. Paula huffed, sat her fork down on her plate, and sent her teenage son a long-suffering look. His friends always came at dinner, and had appetites even bigger than their attitudes. And grocery money after Christmas was always tight. But Hector Junior shrugged at her, even looking up from his smart phone to meet her gaze. The knock came again, a little louder. Hector stood up and headed for the door. It had snowed last night, and now that the sun was down in the New Mexican mountains even salesmen shouldn't be left outside in the winter cold. Hector pulled the door open and found himself blinking at a stocky silver-haired man in a tailored wool coat.

"Want to buy your Corvette," the man said.

"My Sting Ray?" Hector yelped. A pang cut through him at the thought of his precious classic car lovingly tucked away in its private garage. "I built that from scraps pieced together from places all over the world, and it took me nearly twenty years! You can't just buy twenty years of someone's life!" He started to swing the door shut. The man's thick boot slammed into the floor, stopping the door. Hector found himself staring at a stack of money as thick as the family *Biblia* resting on the coffee table.

"Might be able to let you buy it back later this month. Depends," the man's rich voice wove around Hector like a spell as he stared transfixed at the cash. He had never even seen that much cash in this digitalized world. A fluffy dog head poked out of a pile of snow near Hector's garage, tall fox-like ears twitching. She sneezed out snow, then leapt out in a long bodied arch to land in the next snow drift.

"Depends on what?" Hector found himself asking. A shrug lifted the man's broad shoulders.

"On how lucky your Sting Ray is."

Water sloshed against Aldrick's calf. He gritted his teeth as he drew the boat another stroke through the lagoon. The extra water made it heavy and ungainly to row. But they had still managed to outdistance the stalled sailing boat. He couldn't even see it as he rounded the point with Venice just on his right. The night lay dark and quiet in the ancient city. Aldrick pulled at the oars again, ignoring the first landfall. It was a jut of land turned into a parking lot, too open for Aldrick's peace of mind, not familiar enough to him. Sophia's bucket sloshed as she bailed, her breath coming in pants and puffs as she worked to keep them afloat.

A canal opened, leading into the city. Aldrick shifted his hold and tugged their rowboat around to face it. He pulled into the canal, the water from their wake sloshing into the bricks making up the aquatic street. Ancient villas stretched up beside them, constantly kissed by the water from the lagoon, and the familiar stench of Venice wrapped around them. Aldrick felt the oars scrape against the bricks of the canal, and knew he couldn't row far here. It was designed for poling thin gondolas, not rowing fat little boats.

Their rowboat sloshed deeper into the city, and the towering stone edifice of a church looked down on them. Gold glinted on arches and finials pointing up to the star-studded heavens. A monument to a God who cared if two insignificant people made it to Venice. Peace seemed to radiate from the beautiful old church. Aldrick's heart leapt out toward the building, and his mind sent a pleading prayer for help to the God of his Uncle Guillaume. He lifted an oar and let the boat drift forward to thunk into the canal. Sophia's hands slapped onto the street and she vaulted out of the boat with a splash and a thankful curse. Aldrick followed her, his backpack still tight against his back, his pale face white as paper under his black beanie. He jogged for the church door. Sophia caught a glint of metal in his hand.

"Are those lockpicks?" she asked, her voice sharp and loud in the quiet night. Aldrick shot her a glare. A flood of words boiled up inside him, about how important it was to get out of sight, and how little breaking into a church for sanctuary mattered in the scheme of things. But his cell lay dead in his pocket, he couldn't type them on his note app. The words smoldered inside him, dying before they reached his hot throat. Sophia held up her hands and took a step back. "You know what, that's ok. I made sure you got out of their sight, and I'm really grateful you knocked me out of the way of that club. Thank you, kid. Now I'm going to go try to find someone to tell that there's a giant silver egg pulsing in the Andrea Palladio, and attempt not to get arrested for breaking into a sacred historic structure." She stopped backing suddenly and her face worked with something. She darted forward and wrapped the skinny kid in her arms, giving him a quick squeeze. "Thank you. Get home safe! In the mouth of the wolf, kid.[17]" Sophia darted away and trotted up the darkened street.

Aldrick watched her go, his arms hanging limp by his side.

The lifeboat gave a little "blorp" and sank under the gentle waves of the canal. The mast slowly dropped as he watched it. Aldrick winced, trying to think of a way to explain that one to Uncle Bappy. He would not be pleased his nephew had lost another boat.

He gave a mental shake and spun toward the church. The enemy sailboat moved slowly, but the breeze would freshen, and it would come. He had to be off the streets when they arrived. Aldrick stole around the back of the church, searching for a side door. At least this blackout meant he didn't have to worry about security systems. He quickly slid his picks into the lock, tweaked the tumblers, and slipped into the darkened church, closing the door softly behind him. He found himself encased in darkness. The smells of musty wood, old paint, and stale incense hung heavy in the air. Aldrick breathed deep. He swung his backpack around and dug inside for his flashlight. He clicked it on and a dim red light just managed to pick out his shoes[18]. Aldrick swung his bag back up, and shuffled farther into the church.

Outside, three black figures filed onto the street. They stepped to the edge of the canal and watched as the top of the mast with the black sail tipped and disappeared beneath the waters. Three heads lifted, listening to the quiet night. One pointed up the street deeper into Venice, toward the sound of boots jogging. Another pointed at the beautiful white church standing

---

[17]"In the mouth of the wolf" is the Italian equivalent of "break a leg," because apparently there is a superstation in Italy that if you wish someone good luck the opposite will happen. *"In bocca al lupo"* is how you say it in Italian, and I think we all agree it sounds better like that. The traditional response is, *"Crepi il lupo,"* "May the wolf die."

[18] He had learned from several instances of trying to sneak past his father's room that one didn't use bright white flashlights, and even penlights could be too bright on a dark night. He carefully adapted his flashlight with a red filter taped over the top. It helped for stargazing too, something he quite enjoyed.

sentry over the waterway, where a dull red light could barely be seen through a windowpane.

A quiet debate raged as Aldrick shuffled his way through the dark sanctuary, and Sophia Ricci ran down the ancient cobblestone streets. Three heads turned toward the church. Mr. Black had only given orders about the boy. They would ignore the guard.

Chapter 8

A grin spread over Mario Gorgonzoles's red face as his sail-boat, *Silent Beauty*, swept up beside another stranded motor-boat. The night's breeze had freshened quite nicely, perfect for a good sail. He relished the sound of his keel spraying water up the boat, of his sail flapping as he pulled athwart the wind. And the silence of what was usually a roaring, obnoxious motor; tonight it would not interrupt his quiet sailing.

"Ahoy, Flavio," Mario called, not bothering to hide his glee. A muttered greeting came from Flavio and his son, Marco. They shuffled on their deck with hands in their pockets, glaring from under their fishing caps. "Come, I will ferry you to the mainland. The coast guard has stated they will collect the stranded *motor-boats* in time."

Flavio and Marco climbed aboard the *Silent Beauty*, swallowing their pride as best as they could, and lent a hand with the sail. The ship turned into the wind and they began to beat in toward the mainland. Mario just managed to hold back his delighted chuckles.

Two black shapes rushed out of the night. Huge, winged things, like monstrous bats. The wind whistled through the pointed wings, outspread and enormous, eclipsing even the stars. White water sprayed from tails touching the lagoon. A cry ripped from Marco. They just glimpsed the apparition, and the two fig-ures swept up to the *Silent Beauty*. Black boots clumped onto her deck as they landed. Figures with armored vests, utility belts, black masks hiding their faces, wings spread out behind them. Their hands went to their chests and unclipped the wings in a movement so swift and synchronized it seemed inhuman. The wings swept off, carried by the sea breeze into the night. The short one swept a dull black pistol up as he thundered over the deck and pointed it at Mario's face. Mario's hands shot above his head and his eyes crossed as he tried to stare at the barrel nearly pressing into his nose.

"Venice, now!" the apparition spat at him, anger deepening it to a growl.

"You could have just said, 'please,'" the tall one complained in English.

"We need speed," the short one growled. The pistol never wavered.

"Venice," Mario stuttered, and reached for the lines.

The Tesla turned the corner and Colin lost sight of Mr. Luke. And the creepy guy in black. He sank back, refusing to admit the fear tightening his chest as the car carried him steadily deeper into the unknown. He glanced at the driver beside him, forcing his muscles to relax and his tone to be casual.

"You have good taste in music," Colin commented. The waiter acknowledged it with an elegant bow of the head. "What's your name?" He sat silent, weaving through traffic, working their way out of the airport. Colin looked out his window, resigning himself to knowing his ally as The Waiter.

"You may call me Alean," Yousef decided to answer.

Colin spun around, looking at his driver. The man pushed his hood back, letting it fall to his shoulders. He looked at Colin, his face drooping with a melancholy that didn't match his bright black eyes. Colin felt as if there was a challenge in that name. As if daring the young man to make something of it.

"Ay-lean," Colin tried it carefully. "Thanks." The challenge left as the man's shoulders slumped a fraction and he turned back to the road. Colin's eyes closed for a moment, hoping it would help the pounding in his brain go away. It didn't. "I know it's crazy cliché to ask it, but I kind of have to. Where are we going? I mean, where do you take a bomb you really don't want to blow up?"

"We'll let them handle it," Yousef said easily. He spun the car out of the airport and onto a small road. "I know a spot for you to lay low while you wait."

"I told the man on the phone I was at the hotel."

"They'll find you," Yousef shrugged. Silence fell in the car. But Colin stared at the dashboard and let just a little of the *"How?!"* that wanted to burst from him be seen in his expression. Yousef glanced at him and answered it. "I smiled at the security camera when I swiped this car." Silence fell again, thick and heavy.

"That's it?" Colin burst out.

"I erased myself from the security tape afterwards, of course. But I left enough time for them to find it."

"You're kidding, right?"

The black eyes shot him that same "don't be an idiot little brother" look this Alean had given him at the hotel, and Colin knew he wasn't kidding. He turned back to his window and blinked at the road. Three streets rolled under their tires as the Bach switched for a lilting Schubert.

"How many little brothers do you have?" Colin asked.

"What?" Yousef blinked, startled out of his lugubrious calm by the question.

"It's a lot, I can tell, you know how to take over and protect and make me feel like an idiot, all with only actually saying a few words."

A laugh broke from Yousef, deep and long, as he let himself enjoy Colin's assessment. But he didn't answer the question. The car drove on, and Colin let the quiet linger. He leaned back, his head pounding and a steady ache pulsing in his side. Street lights and lit store fronts flashed past the window as Yousef drove farther into town. The opulence started to fade. Dirt began to invade the scene, splashing up the cracked sidewalks onto stores with no English explaining the goods inside. Colin looked at the Arabic scrawled across the fronts of the shopping malls and felt small and stupid. He knew so little about anything but his own country.

The car sped up. The streets began to go by too fast for Colin to get a good look at them. They revved into a repair garage and pulled to a stop over the pit. The garage door rattled as a worker pulled it shut behind them, cutting off the outside.

Men began to appear outside the car. They milled in a slow circle, grease-stained and dirty, looking the fancy machine up and down. Yousef's hood lay back over his face, carefully keeping his features in shadow. Colin swallowed hard and checked to make sure his door was still locked. Yousef stepped out into the garage.

"*Aleankabut!*" someone called in a deep voice. He sounded amused, as if the name were a joke. Colin looked quickly for the speaker and found a man in a robe, past middle age, his paunch showing strong, and his arms out in welcome. "It is a beautiful car you have brought me. This is for me, isn't it?"

"All for you," Yousef smiled. But an edge cut through it, carrying sarcasm and a deeper meaning Colin didn't understand. The man laughed.

"It will fetch a good price, and removing the identification does not take too much from such cars. I think I can spare you a decent fee." The man's twinkling eyes landed on Colin, studying him appraisingly. "Is that for me?"

"No."

"I thought not. If you had wanted me to take care of that package, *Aleankabut,* you would have aimed better."

For the fortieth time that day Colin found it hard to swallow through his constricted throat and tightening chest. The man turned toward a room set off the garage and disappeared. Yousef spun back to the car and leaned in at his open door.

"Out," he ordered. Colin grabbed the first aid kit with trembling fingers and pushed his way out of the car with the bag. He tried a shaky smile at the men around him. They stared back unblinking, unmoving. The paunchy man scuffled out of his office and moved to Yousef. He handed him a wad of bills that made even Colin's eyebrows go up. Yousef shoved it inside his robe and strode for the exit. Colin trotted after him, hurrying to get close to his ally again.

Yousef walked out the door, spun to the left, and took two more long steps. It carried them out of the light of the garage door into the deep shadows cast by the building. He spun on one heel and paused, looking Colin up and down.

"Dirty, blood stained, and still upright. You'll do," he commented. Yousef started to walk again. Colin fell in behind, trying to tell himself he wasn't dizzy and his side didn't burn and his head didn't feel like a world of pain about to fall off onto the sidewalk. His eyes went up to the dark sky, silently searching for something familiar.

The few stars that broke through the manmade glow of this city of millions were as strange and foreign to Colin as the Arabic scrawled over the storefronts. Nothing but huge glowing balls that would disintegrate a tiny speck like him. The darkness of the heavens pressed down on him like a weight. He turned his eyes back to the cracked sidewalk.

For two streets the bag clicked behind them and Colin hoped he wasn't swaying on his feet. A few people along their route glanced at them and then hurried on their way. Colin watched one couple break into a trot across the road and disappear down the street.

"Why is everyone in a hurry?" he asked nervously.

"Curfew is near," Yousef answered. "Shut up." Colin shut up. They turned another corner and Colin blinked at a brightly lit, opulent, clean street with storefronts that obviously catered to the tourists. Yousef walked up to a store with garish neon declaring it sold crepes. The place huddled dark and empty. He unlocked the door with the twist of his wrist and pushed through. Colin stepped in and inhaled deeply. It smelled heavenly.

"Gosh I wish it were open," he murmured. Yousef pulled open the display refrigerator and gathered an armful of prepackaged cold crepes and iced coffee. He strode for the back room. The bag clicked over the tiles as Colin followed.

"Shouldn't we leave some money or something?" Colin asked fuzzily. One of Yousef's shoulders rose in a shrug as he walked past the sinks and ovens of the kitchen.

"I have a card that entails me to a lifetime of free crepes," Yousef answered.

"Golly. I want a card like that, how did you get it?" Colin leaned over a stainless steel counter as he followed his guide, and saw his own face staring back at him; gaunt, reddened eyes heavy with pain, stress lines etched across his forehead… He looked away.

"Eh," Yousef shrugged in a way that meant he wasn't impressed by the reason the card was gifted. He pushed through the back door, stepped across a dank alley, and flicked his key in the lock of a metal door set in a metal wall that towered high into the night sky. Colin followed him into black darkness, too tired and numb to wonder if he was about to be knifed and left to rot.

Yousef closed the door softly behind them, and Colin drew to a stop. He stood still and tense in complete darkness, gripping the bag's handle and trying to convince his pounding brain to think. Yousef's footsteps thumped over the concrete ground to a corner of the room. A click came, and a lamp flipped on. Its light spread enough to show Colin an empty warehouse. No, not quite empty. Where the lamp stood rested a packing crate, a pile of fabric in the vague shape of a pallet, and what was probably wood shavings scattered over the ground. And Yousef. He flipped his hood off and stared. Colin walked forward stiffly till he made it to the blankets and crates.

"Here's your spot," Yousef said. He sat the crepes beside the blankets and strode for the door.

"Hold on, I..." Colin's voice drifted off into nothing. A hand fluttered up from Yousef as he walked.

"Sleep, relax. They will find you." The door closed behind him. Colin blinked at the huge empty room, his hand sweaty on the bag and his side pumping fire into his veins.

"But who are 'they'?" he murmured into the dark.

Chapter 9

The light spun across the floor again. These shadowy people had been searching for Aldrick for hours, they just wouldn't give up! Aldrick hunched beneath the table and tried not to breathe. Again. It felt like a lifetime he had been playing cat and mouse with the bearers of those lights. How long had it been? One hour? Two?

The light was all he could see of them. Two faceless beams of light moved with tiny rustling noises through the still church. They murmured occasionally when they met in the aisles, or after sweeping a hallway. So far Aldrick had learned they spoke English (one in an American accent, one northern European), the exits were guarded, they knew he was here, and they were out to kill.

The light played under the table, moving slowly around the opposite corner from Aldrick. He rose to his feet, pressing himself against the underside of the table. The light turned to the floor and he moved, the white beam creeping past the toes of his tennis shoes. Aldrick felt his breath strangle. But he kept shifting, silent, smooth, and quick, his backpack a millimeter from brushing the top of the table. He made it into the portion of darkness the light had already swept. It shifted up, over the back wall, then to the corner he had just left.

The light moved on. Aldrick sagged. His head dropped to his knees and he drew in slow, steady breaths, keenly aware of even that sound in the still air. He sat back and eased his legs out, slumping to let his heavy backpack rest on the ground. Aldrick's exhausted eyes flitted to a beam of moonlight filtering through the high windows of this church. The beam played over a Titian painting on the upper wall. Vibrant colors filled the gilded frame; an angel hovering over the world, tall and powerful and ethereal while humanity stared up at him, firmly stuck to the dark earth. If only help like that could come to him! *Meme's* angel figurines she kept around the kitchen swept through his mind and doubt crept in. Her delicate little figurines with the sweet faces didn't seem much like the type who rained death on Sodom and Go-morrah, or caused humans to fall just by appearing... But maybe the God who made the angels that the Bible described would be willing to notice a tiny speck of humanity hiding under a table. Aldrick had no one else to turn to. A prayer slid from him, hesitant and almost unwilling, unsure he really wanted to speak to the Maker of the angels. *Oh God, get me home!*

A light hit him in the face. For a single wild heartbeat Aldrick frantically realized he should have specified his *earthly* home. Then his feet shoved off the hardwood floors and he sprinted into the darkness. The light followed him, tracking his movements with a silence and expertise that chilled his spine. Aldrick's feet found the stairs and he ran. A soft pop came from the sanctuary. His backpack ripped, and a ping of metal rang as the bullet hit his toolbox. He ducked his head with a gasp. Aldrick was suddenly acutely thankful for his small frame; a little scrunching meant his backpack could cover about all but his legs. Each wooden step seemed like a shortcut to heaven as he flew higher into the church. Past the Titian paintings on the gilded wall. Past the windows overlooking the rooftops of Venetian villas.

Another pop, rip, and a crunch came as something in his bag stopped a bullet. A gurgling whimper slid from Aldrick. The stairs turned, and he spun out of sight of the sanctuary into the old belfry. He pounded up the last steps and strong armed the trapdoor. It thumped heavily as it flew open and Aldrick squirmed out.

Cool, humid air wrapped around him, carrying the stench of Venice and the far reaching sea. Red rooftops stretched away in the darkness like terracotta hills, punctuated by the main clock tower rising in a glorious spire. Tonight no lights reflected off the canals like a fairytale scene. The city lay deep and black, like a nightmare from the real faery tales *Meme* used to scare Aldrick and his cousins with during sleepovers. Suddenly the terracotta tiles of the rooftops looked like the scales of a host of slumbering serpents, just waiting to wake and roil and eat him alive. Aldrick slammed the trapdoor home and crouched on top of it, breathing in panicked gasps. He heard footsteps pounding up the polished wood to his tower. A door to the street level creaked as it slid open. Too late to try to slip off by the roof, someone was down there on the ground watching!

He looked around wildly, searching for something heavier than his ninety-two pounds to drop onto this door. The old bell stood stark and monstrous in the darkness above his head. It would serve well, if he could cut it down.

Someone slammed into the trapdoor. Aldrick jolted and clamped his teeth. He didn't want to die. Not yet, he had too many experiments going on in his basement! And his last words to his father would haunt him forever.

The trapdoor jolted again, harder, and Aldrick clung to the edge to keep on top of it. *Please, God, I know there's no reason for You to notice me, but please, send help!* he begged, with every ounce of desperation in his bones.

The trapdoor banged, sending him perpendicular to the world for an instant. Aldrick shoved his legs into the ground and drove it down again. It thunked on something with a watermelon thump and slammed closed.

"Please..." Aldrick whispered into the darkness, his voice hoarse.

A muted, furious yell came from below him and the trapdoor flung open. Aldrick slammed into the belfry's decorative iron railing. A figure in black clothing leapt at him. A boot smashed into the young man's throat. He hit the ground, spine bent over his backpack, his windpipe closed. He gagged and slammed a fist into the boot. It felt like punching a rock. The figure above him leaned in, the foot pressing harder against his throat. He could see the man's eyes past his black knit mask, bright, shining pinpricks surrounded by blank blackness. Aldrick felt his body failing him. His arms slapped uselessly against the boot, his blows growing feebler. His fading vision focused on the big bell, glimmering in the bit of moonlight escaping through the clouds.

The Maker of that moon failed him; just like almost everyone else. Aldrick's eyes closed, despair wrapping around his pounding heart and squeezing it. His struggles stopped, and he lay still, one hand pressed against the black boot.

Something pinged on the metal railing above Aldrick's head.

The boot shifted. The young man's eyes fluttered open. A figure, fuzzy and indistinct in Aldrick's failing vision, vaulted over the railing. Black mask, plated vest, one boot on the metal rail, the other striking out into the enemy's chest.

Definitely not an angel in a white robe blasting lightning at the ungodly.

The kick landed with a solid thud. The boot jerked away from Aldrick's throat. He rolled to his side coughing and retching. Hammer like blows rained on the other side of the belfry. Aldrick lifted his eyes in time to catch a palm strike slamming into the black enemy hard enough it lifted him off his feet. But the man spun in midair, and his hand landed on the bell. A muted clang came from the cast metal, as the black glove slammed into it. Then the enemy pushed off, launching into the masked rescuer with a double ax kick.

A series of lightning blows thudded and smacked in the dark night. They were too quick for Aldrick to catch as the two men spun and ducked and kicked and jumped. Their gloves and boots blurred as they danced around the ancient belfry, towering over venetian villas. Aldrick staggered to his knees and crouched against the railing, his vision still fuzzy and swimming. But he could see enough to watch the masked one shove a pistol onto the black enemy's chest and pull the trigger. The bad guy kept moving, somehow the bullet didn't penetrate. The moon drifted from behind a cloud, and Aldrick thought he spotted judo, karate, sucker-punches, Krav Maga, even a few moves that seemed like capercaillie. The enemy didn't give his rescuer the chance to use that pistol again. Aldrick knew enough about martial arts to recognize two masters, even through his hacking gasps.

The men circled and struck, silent except for a few grunts and their huffing breaths. The enemy moved quicker, harder, frustration getting to him as he couldn't get past the rescuer. Aldrick controlled his own body enough to realize his rescuer didn't just circle; he was moving the enemy deliberately toward the railing. The young man reached for his backpack, mentally running through the contents, trying to think of anything he could use as a weapon to turn the tide for his rescuer. Maybe a monkey wrench to the enemy's ankle?

The black one stepped into a shaft of moonlight at the edge of the belfry. A soft thud came and Aldrick thought he saw something sparkle for an instant in the moonlight near the back of the man's neck. The enemy arched, then crumpled silently forward. His forehead slammed into the bell on his way down. A deep throated "dong" rang through the darkness, prolonged and deafening in the still night. The black one thudded into the ground and lay as limp as the fishes in the village market. The rescuer jerked his black mask off and spun toward the boy.

Aldrick saw perfect mustaches under bright gray eyes, concern almost radiating from his rescuer's weathered face. A soft sob slid from Aldrick. Uncle Guillaume bounded over and pulled him into a hug that hurt the young man's gasping lungs. But Aldrick wouldn't have traded that hurt for any gold in the world. His arms shot around his uncle's neck. For that moment he let himself pretend he was four again, instead of his grown-up fourteen.

An angel in a plated vest and mustaches! God heard after all. Relief washed through Aldrick, and it stemmed from more than just being alive.

"Come, let's get you home," his uncle said, his voice wet. He tightened his hold on his nephew, sat on the rail, pivoted, and dropped over the edge. Aldrick's arms jerked tighter around his uncle as cool air rushed over him, stinging his skin at their speed. Gigan's boots rammed into the cobblestones, and Aldrick felt his toes touch the street. He pulled away, coughing through his bruised throat, a headache starting to pound behind his forehead. And trying to get a good look at Uncle Guillaume without seeming too obvious about it as he watched him pull the grapple free and begin to rewind it at a furious speed. He looked older. Older than two years should have made him at a normal aging speed. And he had an impressive black eye. What astounding adventure had given him that injury?

A tall figure strolled out of the dark, and Aldrick startled back, his pack hitting the church.

"All taken care of, Gigan," the man drawled, and Aldrick's

tight shoulders relaxed. He knew the voice from two years ago. A little thrill of excitement went through him, and he was glad of the dark. He knew his cheeks would be flushed with excitement at seeing the BIGG2 again in the flesh. What a brain for machines and computers that man had! "The guards are out cold, two people, one a gal. Nothing in their pockets except a change of clothes that isn't black, nothing remarkable that I saw. Do we take one with us for information?"

"It would slow us down too much," Gigan barked. His hand landed on Aldrick's shoulder and he stalked up the street, his eyes sweeping everything. "Are you all right for a jog, little thinker?" Aldrick nodded. Gigan broke into a quick jog, moving up the canal toward the lagoon. Aldrick pulled out his cell phone and tapped the screen with a desperate hope. It stayed black and dim. His face worked, his eyes in a near panic. But he cleared his throat and drew in a deep breath.

"There's…" he started, his voice barely carrying over the sound of their boots on the street. It faded and he felt like screaming at the world in frustration. A white pad of paper dangled in front of his eyes, and Aldrick blinked, his steps automatically slowing.

"Here, dude," Vincent said behind them. Aldrick's awe climbed higher at the total calm in the inventor's manner. He might have been on a moonlight stroll with a girl on his arm for the way he acted. "I can't believe I'm saying it, but old ways will work just as well. Oh shoot, I don't have a pen. I mean, who carries a pen these days?"

"Then why do you have paper, Savant?" Gigan murmured.

"Simeon left it behind when we stopped at *Las Delicias* after church for Mexican food, and I thought, 'Oh hey, I can pull it out later and show him he actually forgot something.'"

"I expect he thought the waiter needed it, considering the man forgot our orders twice," Gigan commented. He stepped to the side of the street, jimmied a trinket seller's cart open, and snatched a gaudy pen colored with cartoon-style Venetian scenes. He stopped and blinked at the cart, suddenly remembering he couldn't access the seller's account and transfer the exorbitant tourist-trap price.

"Um. Either of you have any cash on you?" he asked. Vincent chuckled and grabbed the pen. He scrawled the name of the cart on a page, stuffed it in his pocket to send the money later, and handed the pad and pen to Aldrick. The boy stared at them for a moment as if trying to remember how to use the foreign instruments. He started to scrawl over the pad as Gigan started them moving.

A night guard from the power station was with me. She ran off into the streets a few hours ago to find someone to report to. Did she make it? Can you find out? And do you know how we kill the egg?

"You're going home!" Gigan burst out. Aldrick pulled away, his mouth drawing into a tight line as he glared. Gigan drew to a stop at the top of the canal and pinched the bridge of his nose, his eyes closing.

"We don't know how to kill the egg yet," Vincent supplied as his buddy gathered himself. Gigan started the group off again, briskly walking along the street facing the lagoon, scanning the area for a likely boat to commandeer[19]. "But that's one reason I'm here. If we can do it quick, we can just send up an Amelia drone with the guard's description and track her down. It depends on how much trouble that egg is going to give us. I couldn't bring many tools with me on this little venture, speed getting to you was our main goal."

Aldrick's face lit up and he gave a little bounce as he spun. His eyes flew to Vincent's for an instant in his eagerness. He twisted around again in almost the same moment, his head hunched into his shoulders like a skinny turtle trying to disappear. But the pen scrawled across the paper again. Vincent silently wondered if autism played a part, or just natural shyness pushed gradually deeper and deeper by mishandling at school

---

[19]The local sailboat out helping those stranded with their fancy motors* hadn't stuck around waiting for their return.

* Two months later the owner of the *Silent Beauty* had to swallow his pride when his own ship hit a whale, broke the mast, and he had to be rescued by Flavio in his motorboat.

and a roaring, outgoing family.

"There," Gigan snapped. He broke into a jog and leapt into a trim little sailboat moored to a jetty. It tipped and dirty water sloshed over his boots. Obviously not a boat in the best of condition. But if it would sail, it would do. Aldrick pushed the notepaper into Vincent's hands and leapt over the side, reaching for the lines to help shake out the sail with his uncle. The inventor swiped a k-bar absently through the mooring rope as he hopped into the boat with a wet slosh, his eyes on the paper.

I've been poking at electromagnetism in my basement, that's why I've been at the AP station. I have tools if you want to use them. Just avoid Dad and the others, you can slip in through the window if you're quiet. Andrea is pretty cool, I think she would help if we asked.

A lot went into that little note. Vincent quietly handed it to Gigan as his long leg shoved off the jetty, pushing them into the lagoon. He smiled at Aldrick, and then remembered not to do that as the kid ducked back, turtling like a pro.

"Let's go get a good look at this egg first," Vince said. "We can decide what comes next after that."

Arnulf Jones climbed into the small loft bed in his minuscule little apartment in a ratty part of London. He lay there and listened to the blaring party music drifting up from two floors below him. It just kept going. And there was no depth to the music's lyrics, nothing but air trying to fill... to fill what? A bony eastern warrior leaning against a counter in a crowded garage and coldly telling Jones how much trouble he had almost caused floated back into his memory. Other scenes, from trouble he *had* caused followed on its heels, just like it did every time. And his soul, so long covered by just living day-by-day without much thought, slowly cracked open like a yawning chasm trying to swallow him whole. Over and over again, every time he grew still, the same memories butted in, and the crack grew just a little wider.

But recently, conversations with Kalifa started to cut through the vicious cycle. Just as he had begun to think enough to realize he needed filled by more than what he had, Jones started to hear about One who took the past, present, and future and did what He wanted. Forgive, set free, and grant a purpose… Was it just bologna? Or was it too good to be true?

Luther Kirl thought he could do what he wanted.

A grimace cut over Jones at the memory of his employer. Hate-filled, horrible old man. Well, his sort of employer. He should probably check in with his real employers. Jones opened the window above his head and heaved himself out with a quick, smooth move. The bustle of London buzzed around him. The air hung thick with cold humidity, and the stench of the Thames, millions of humans, and the Indian restaurant across the street. His big hands gripped the stonework and he skimmed to the roof without even glancing at the eight stories below him. He crouched on the eave above a window and surveyed the dark sky above him. Only gray clouds, threatening more drizzle.

Could there really be Someone past all that?

A rain drop hit him on the nose and Jones sighed and pulled his phone out. He punched the number to his new boss and put the phone to his ear.

"Yes," the rich tones of his contact said from the other end. Nothing else. Jones silently wondered what his name was, and if he was connected with the bony warrior who had chased him over the Maeslant.

"Checking in," Jones said, and just stopped a strange desire to call this person "sir." Weird. Jones hadn't called someone sir in his entire life. "I'm hired, like you wanted. But as a videographer not a bodyguard. I told him what you gave me about Mr. Black. Kirl seemed to accept it. Right now I just wait around, but I'm on the payroll and he says he wants me for something soon. He asked my advice on purchasing cameras, and he wants very impressive military grade spy cams."

"Let on why yet?"

"No," Jones said. An interested grunt came from the other end. Nothing else was offered. Jones spoke again, a little hopefully. "Any orders?"

"No. Check in when you know something new. Erase your call

logs[20]."

"What? Oh, right." Jones waited another moment. The other end was suspiciously quiet. He pulled his phone away and looked at it. A blank black screen stared back at him, his contact had hung up. Jones sighed, erased his call log, and slid the phone back in his pocket. His gaze turned back to the impenetrable sky.

---

[20] Simeon has three numbers preprogrammed in his phone, and they're restaurants. He has solved too many cases by what he found on a person's personal device, whether tracking down people they knew, or events marked in calendars, or old texts, or search engine histories... It's a little scary, honestly, when he started pointing how much you can glean about a person if you know where to look. All the Parabaloni clear their phone's memories with almost obsessive regularity.

Chapter 10

The Andrea Palladio rose into the night like a piece of sky very bad at camouflage. Bright blue paint almost gleamed in the darkness. Gigan, Vince, and Aldrick stole closer, skirting around the people who milled and complained and gesticulated with the southern heat running through their veins. Most turned their eyes on the power station and glared. The team stayed low and moved in the deepest patches of darkness, using every ditch and tree shadow they found. Aldrick, glued to his uncle's side, found himself in awe of their skill. No one saw them, even with the whole countryside focused on the power station. He found himself thinking of the shadowy enemy slipping through the dark chasing him. Had they been using the same skills? No, that was silly. No one was as good as Uncle Guillaume.

Vincent flitted up to the metal wall and cupped his hands in front of him. Gigan darted from the cover of a little gnarled olive tree. His boot touched his friend's hands, and he vaulted over the fence like a black lightning streak, his pistol out and ready. The metal pistol didn't gleam, Aldrick noticed. Its matte black metal, carefully unpolished, seemed almost invisible in the dark night. He noticed Vincent staring at him. Aldrick swallowed. He tightened the straps of his backpack and ran forward. His foot landed in Vincent's cupped hands, and the inventor heaved. Aldrick practically flew over the fence, eyes wide in surprise, his arms flapping like a chicken as he tried to regain his balance.

A wiry, iron strong arm caught him and lowered him silently to the ground. Vincent gripped the top of the seven-foot fence and heaved himself over with a single arm, his legs held tight like a gymnast's, toes pointed as he flew over with perfect ease. He landed cat-like beside Gigan, his eyes sweeping the area.

"No one visible," Gigan murmured to him. Vincent nodded and flitted off to scope out the left side of the yard. "Stay behind me, thinker. Confound it, I miss my scanners." Aldrick obeyed as they began to steal closer to the towering building. They made for the back door closest to the transformers, sweeping their half of the area with swift thoroughness.

The Frenchman paused, suddenly statue-like as he stared at a bump ahead on the ground. Aldrick rammed into his shoulder and staggered back a step. Gigan moved again, his feet shuffling over the ground in the quick way of a soldier on his guard, his pistol pulled up and ready. He reached a still form, and Aldrick made out its general shape. Not a cast off part of the machinery, as he had first thought. Well, not the station's machinery.

He saw a policeman's uniform, ripped and bloodstained, the hat mercifully pulled over the face. Young, male, already stiff… Aldrick's eye ticked. He rubbed it as he looked at his feet.

Gigan forced his eyes from the crumpled form of the young policeman; more blood, more trauma, more sorrow poured into the dark world. He had found so much of it, for what felt like so, so long… He focused with an effort on the trail left by the murdered man's attackers. Faint, but he could still see the scuffed ground where at least five of them had turned back into the station after their murder. Anger boiled in him. Another one snuffed out, sent hurtling into eternity. This poor soul young enough he had to be new at this job, stuck on night duty, then hammered by demands to know why the station broke down. Gigan could picture him trudging toward the door, grumping and calling out insults at the power station, hoping to find someone to answer his questions. Then the sudden terror of a black enemy pouring from the door. No way to signal for help. Nothing but a voice to yell for those who couldn't hear him over their own complaining. He didn't even carry a weapon. He probably left it back at his station, with no idea he was headed toward an enemy. And they had killed him with blunt instruments and knives.

Gigan began to mentally curse his weakness in giving in to Aldrick. He should have sent the boy home instead of bringing him here. Too late now.

Gigan stole toward the door again, his steps silent, his pistol held ready. Every sense felt over-exerted, as if he could have heard a fly sneeze a mile away. He longed for his scanners and sensors. Without them he had no idea what to expect. As he drew closer, he realized the black rectangle was an open cavity, beckoning, inviting like a spider to his web. They left the door open.

A steady pulsing drifted through the open door. Gigan glanced at Vincent. Floyd lay ready, crooked in the inventor's arm, the MP7's black skin carefully keeping it invisible. A semi-automatic was a good choice for the one on watch, where a quick spray of bullets could solve certain problems that might arise. The inventor should be the watchman. But Gigan had brought Aldrick along… Vince lifted his gun with a raised eyebrow. Gigan nodded at his buddy. Vincent dove through the door in a tight roll, aiming for the side to keep out of the light from the door. Gigan moved in the same second, shifting smoothly in front of Aldrick and slipping them both in at the left, using Vincent's movements as a cloak for their own. Aldrick saw their guns switch owners in the same blur of movement, as they tossed the weapons through the shadows. Then his backpack pressed against the metal wall and his eyes strained to see through the darkness past his uncle.

The silver egg gleamed deeper in the blackness. Vince froze in a crouch, studying it. The metal seemed to suck the light from around it and hold it for its own. An evil light, a megalomaniac light, something screaming "me, all me, look here!" Distracting him from the area around the egg.

Vincent's focus snapped back to his immediate surroundings. A whisper of movement shifted the air behind his head. He dropped to his belly and rolled. Vincent's ribs hit feet and he shot to a crouch. The side of his hand slammed into his attacker's knee. The crack of the blow seemed louder than a gunshot in that silence. A sharp intake of breath gave Vince the position of the enemy's head. He came up like a spring, one fist in an upward strike, his whole body behind the move. The blow smashed into skin and bone, and he felt the head snap back.

Something else moved behind him. Vincent spun, his long leg out in a sweeping kick, trying to guess how many roamed this darkness.

Two huge, muscled hands clamped over his sweeping ankle. A grip stronger than he could fight twisted his foot. Vincent spun with the move. He hopped off the ground and his arms went to his chest, accepting the momentum instead of letting it twist his leg out of the socket. As he spun, he drew his knee in sharply. It propelled the rest of him toward his attacker. His free foot kicked hard into a stomach, and one arm groped blindly for a neck. He found a nose and took it. Vincent's fingers squeezed and twisted, and a rough voice yelled in pain. The huge hands dropped his ankle. Instead they rammed like a driving piston on his ribs.

Vincent slammed into the floor with a shuddering bang.

Pete caught the little bell above the door as he spun into the Crepe Shop. The bell didn't ding merrily. He let it go and stole forward. His boots hardly made a sound as his hands wrapped around his pistol and his eyes swept every inch of the darkened restaurant. His scanners showed nothing living inside this shop. But he had learned to still be cautious. Especially with someone like Yousef, an expert at leaving practical jokes and traps in his wake.

Jojo walked in behind him and drew a deep breath, relishing the familiar smells[21]. She headed for the display refrigerator, unsure whether to savor finding herself in the familiar store again, or weep for days gone that could not be regained. She chose to be excited over the idea of delicious crepes and pulled open the refrigerator.

Pete swept through the kitchen, every sense alert, ducking to look under stainless steel work stations and carefully checking the skylight before crossing underneath it. He saw nothing in the spotless restaurant, no sign of anything out of place, no hint of anyone having passed this way. No clues from Yousef. Peter drew up beside the door, his back pressed against the metal, listening. No sounds reached him from the alley. His watch

---

[21] Back in his brief days as a Saudi anti-terrorist man, Mu'tasim Aziz (Peter's name before his conversion) happened to walk past the opulent Crepe Shop in the tourist quarter just as a jealous rival (who had tried to start a sardine store and failed) enacted a violent armed robbery. Mu'tasim burst in through the window and managed to roust the robbers, getting clipped in the arm by a bullet along the way. The grateful owner gave him a card entitling him and whoever he brought with him to free crepes and coffee for life. He, Jojo, and Yousef used it often, usually as a reward for having survived one of their many adventures.

reported only emptiness. He eased the catch down. A minuscule click told him it stood ready. Pete spun, his shoulder hitting the door, his pistol up and ready for anything.

An empty back alley greeted him. He shuffled to the door leading into their warehouse[22]. His eyes raked the walls making up this alley and skimmed over the edge of the roofs to make sure he didn't miss anything. Cold from the metal warehouse door seeped into him as he pressed his ear against it, listening and silently picking the lock open. His scanner finally reported a living human inside. 'Seffy? Peter silently hoped, another prayer rushing from him to his Father.

He could hear a soft sound from inside. A whisper of a voice. A muted groan?

Pete pulled out his flashlight, holding it far enough away from his body to confuse any possible shooters trying to pinpoint his position. He turned the knob and spun inside, clicking the light on and focusing the beam where his scanner pinpointed the threat.

A pile of old sheets and blankets lay in the corner, beside a rusty old lamp and a leaning card table. The young man he and Jojo had watched Yousef pull into the Tesla staggered to his feet as the light hit him. Alarm almost radiated from his chiseled features as his hands shot up, fluttering just a little to show he held no weapon. A blood-stained bandage pressed against his right side. Pete could see the young man's Adam's apple bob as he swallowed hard. The flashlight beam shifted away, running quickly over the rest of the big room. It lit on nothing but dirt and a few odds and ends of debris. The air smelled faintly of fish. No Yousef. A wash of heavy weariness suddenly cut into Pete. It felt so long that he had been fighting without a break, all he asked was one break, maybe a little conversation with his brother– He stopped that line of though abruptly as unhelpful, pushed it out,

---

[22] Yousef discovered the abandoned* warehouse eight years ago. It had become the headquarters and hideout of the mischievous Aziz children, and usually where they carried their crepes after an adventure.

*It used to house sardines, and still carried a fishy smell. But after the sardine business failed, a heartbroken owner never ventured near it again.

and focused on the work.

The beam lit up the young man again. He flinched, his hands still up. He had moved. Sidled a little left. In front of a carry on bag resting innocently on its wheels. Pete's eyes focused on the bag. The kid's Adam's apple bobbed again.

"Look, if I'm trespassing I apologize," he said, his accent decidedly American. Probably Californian, and definitely the same that made the call to Pete. "I'm not from here, I didn't know I'm not allowed in this place." His lips thinned, his voice growing frustrated. "And I don't know why I'm bothering, you probably can't even understand me."

"Are you alone?" Pete asked, his soft voice carrying in the quiet. The young man's eyebrows went up at the perfect English.

"Um, yeah, just me."

"For how long?"

"My waiter brought me here and left again, I don't know how long ago. I think it's been hours." A wince cut across his face, as his right arm flinched. Peter quickly shoved his anxiety over Yousef away and stepped forward, reaching for his bag strapped to his back. The kid watched him warily, but he didn't shrink away.

"Colin, we are who you called," Pete said, pulling his doctor's kit out. His hand brushed his watch. "You may lower your arms." The young man lowered his hands. Jojo stepped through the door and closed it softly behind her. Colin stared at her, his face emotionless, carefully hiding his surprised confusion.

"Hello," Jojo smiled at him. "Aren't the blankets dreadfully scratchy? I never could get the boys to throw them away."

"They are still perfectly fine blankets, even with a few holes," Pete explained, and shrugged at Colin, inviting him into the conversation. "These women folk, always insisting on their own way." Colin's broad shoulders drooped, he blinked rapidly, and suddenly looked like a scared kid trying to cope with a crazy situation as his defensiveness dropped away. Pete quickly got him settled on the blankets and started to clean his wound. Jojo handed Pete two of the crepe containers and plopped on the blanket across from Colin, popping hers open and taking a sip of the coffee. She pushed another container toward him.

"Bullet passed through tissue and exited cleanly," Pete reported. "Bleeding already contained. Did you fix this?"

"I read a book on first aid earlier this year," Colin nodded, his voice distant. His eyes darted to the two people. "Aren't you even going to ask who shot me?"

"Do you know?" Pete asked."

"Well…" Colin blinked. "No. I guess I don't. It came—"

"—Out of a dark alley, yes, we saw that part." Jojo put in as Pete worked and the young man stared at them with growing wonder. "And we know who your waiter is and generally how he operates."

"What we need to know is more about this 'Collective,' and what happened after you hung up. What's with the bag?" Peter demanded.

"My dad brought six bags with us when we flew from California," Colin said. His voice shook over the word 'dad,' and he stopped and swallowed. He steadied himself and the story poured out, factual and even, up to the point where he unzipped the bag and they discovered the contents. Colin paused, watching the faces around him. Jojo took another sip of coffee, relishing the heat. "Isn't the part with plastic explosives where you're supposed to gasp or curse or something?"

"We see a lot of this kind of thing," Pete mumbled around crepe. "Then what?"

"Mr. Luke turned out to be an ok guy. He insisted he didn't know about it, and I believe him. We knew we couldn't just leave it there. So then someone knocked on the door saying it was maid service, but we both knew it wasn't (she didn't even try to use Arabic or an accent), and Mr. Luke shoved me into the connecting room with the bag and told me to get out. I did. I guess they didn't want to cause a scene in the hotel, or maybe they didn't recognize the bag right away, I don't know, I just walked out the front door. But my phone had been confiscated, so I couldn't find the police, or speak the language, or even figure out which route to walk to keep in the good part of town." Over their earpieces, the Aziz heard Simeon's long-suffering sigh. Pete and

Jojo carefully didn't laugh over the big boss's reaction. "Pretty soon I noticed people in the alley noticing me. I mean, big city, me still in my suit, nice new bag… Anyway, I got jumped, managed to get out, got jumped again, then Mr. Luke showed up with his extensive martial arts training and sent me off at a run. That's when the shot came from the alley. I don't think it was the muggers."

"I think you're right," Pete said simply. A half smile twisted Peter's face and his eyes dropped to the scuffed watch on his wrist. "I always said a woodworking stall was too tame for you. I'm glad you found your niche finally as a waiter." Colin looked up at him, his face confused.

"Oh I've already found a better deal in car salesmanship," a deep, lugubrious voice came from the shadows to their left. A tall man in a black thobe stepped forward, stopping where the light barely touched him. His hood stayed up, and the shadows seemed to keep him as their own. Simeon, watching over Pete's feed, noticed a shiver run over Colin.

Jojo shot forward with a squeal and threw her arms around him. Yousef's hood flew back at the onslaught as he swayed awkwardly into the light, revealing a long face, straight dark hair framing features that Simeon could have picked out as Pete's brother from a crowd of a hundred. Surprise creased Yousef's face. Then his arms came up and he squeezed her back, his eyes closing as emotion scored his face for that instant; a brief quick move before pushing her away, his expression dropping into a morose melancholy. The way the lines on his face melded into place told Simeon the young man lived hidden behind that expression. Peter didn't move, stiff and awkward.

"It's good to see you, 'Sef," he burst out, his half smile strong. Something twitched over Yousef's face. Nervousness? An answering smile? Pete handed a crepe container to his brother and turned back to place the last item neatly in the doctor's kit. "Now, what about this situation? We have a pipeline to keep from being blown, and a square full of people to save, and a war to stop. Again. How much time do we have, Colin?"

"They said 'tomorrow,'" Colin answered. "Nothing more. I

guess it is kind of already tomorrow."

"The mob shooting will be this evening," Pete said. "They have to wait till enough people are gathered to make opening fire worth it."

Yousef spoke from the shadows, a grim relish lacing his words.

"Leave that part to me."

Vincent's eyes closed. In one smooth movement he spun to his back, aimed Gigan's pistol, and fired. The bullet hit the giant on the cheek. The brief flash from the muzzle lit the world for a millisecond. It gleamed in Aldrick's wide terrified eyes, and shot through the eyeballs of fourteen attackers to make white specks dance in their vision. Every one of them spun toward the flash, smug, exultant. That muzzle flash pinpointed the threat, making him a sitting duck. None of them realized someone else saw them in that brief flash.

"Gorgon," Gigan snapped through the darkness. Heads spun, suddenly aware of the second figure against the wall.

The giant toppled with a huge thud. Vincent let himself stay in the man's trajectory. The weight felt like a rhinoceros smashing into his body[23].

As the thud echoed through the room, Floyd spoke in the French agent's arms. Fire danced on his barrel in a staccato burst. Gigan emptied the clip and clicked another home as he shifted him and Aldrick to a different position with silent, lightning speed. He froze again listening to the room, Floyd ready. He could hear Aldrick breathing in little hyperventilating gasps behind him. The sharp thuds of bodies hitting the concrete ground drifted from the dark; all fourteen accounted for. A muffled grunt came from where Vincent lay. Gigan stood for a full minute just listening. Another sharper grunt came from Vincent and he hefted the giant off. No other sound stirred the Andrea Palladio.

Gigan reached into his pocket and pulled out his solar flashlight. He held it overhand, ready to smash it into any threat's face,

---

[23] And Vince would know, after that business in Mbita on the shores of Lake Victoria.

and clicked it on. The beam hit a sweaty, panting Vincent slowly sitting up beside a hulking giant of a man. It swept on, quick, competent, driving into every shadow immediately pertinent to their position. The shadows fled from him, empty. He let the light play over the ground. Fourteen figures in black lay still on the concrete. Their faces were a deformed, hazy, lump, as if they were monsters modeled poorly from clay. The Frenchman took a quick step toward the nearest one and knelt beside him. His light played over the cloaking mechanism.

"Is that..." Vincent murmured, disbelief in his tone. A guffaw burst from Gigan, bubbling through the dark.

"Woman's pantyhose!" Gigan crowed. "Just ordinary hose pulled over their faces, as a two-bit thief might do to knock over a gas station!" He remembered their conversation in the kitchen and Simeon's amusement about their thoughts on this "cloaking mechanism." The Frenchman's laughter burst out again.

"Stay in the cameras' blind spots, work hard on camouflage, use the surroundings, and any accidental sighting muddled by the hose... Yeah, I've got to admit it works," Vincent commented reluctantly. Annoyance flooded his tone. "But, man, I was hoping for something really cool!" Gigan tossed Floyd back to the inventor, still chuckling. Vince caught it with one hand as he stood up. He dropped the MP7 into his holster and headed for the egg. "I have another complaint, boss man. Every time you pull a Gorgon on me you wait till I have an elephant as a shield."

"A lighter shield would mean less cover," Gigan shrugged, but his smile came through the words as he followed his friend.

"You could at least help get the hulking bad guy off!" Vincent's beam clicked on and played over the silver egg. "And now I've got his blood all over me."

"Ah, poor fellow, forget your change of clothes?" Gigan grinned behind his light.

"Only you care about the shirt," Vince snorted. "It got on my tools and it's sticky." A soft whimper came from by the door. Gigan moved back to his nephew in two bounds. His flashlight beam lit on wide eyes sweeping wildly over the bodies around the room. Gigan's hand landed on Aldrick's shoulder and he spun the light till the beam shone on both their faces.

"Look at me, Aldrick," he ordered. The boy turned away, trying to squirm from Gigan's grasp, his breath still coming in sharp pants. "Aldrick, look at me!" The pale face spun around and focused on his uncle, his expression hard and betrayed. "They aren't dead." A spasm of hope shot over Aldrick's face. "We didn't kill them, I am not Grégoire. It is not our place to be judges and executioners. I will not leave them free to murder again, but we hand them to the law alive when we can. *That* is my job. When it is possible, I give them to the law of their countries, and it gives them more time to repent. God made them just as He made me, and the bad guys have souls that will last forever. I have killed, Aldrick. And in my line of work I will have to again, often. But it is not murder, it is always only in defense of those who would be murdered without my intervention. Do you understand?"

"Bullets...?" Aldrick's whisper met the dark and was swallowed, almost before even his uncle could hear it. But Gigan understood. He flipped his pistol around and pulled out the clip. He handed it to Aldrick, keeping the light steady for him to study the clear polymer knock-out bullets inside, the liquid agent swirling inside the case.

"I keep a pistol with live ammo on me too. But I was reminded on the church tonight that even firearms fail sometimes, when the enemy is prepared with very good gear." His brow furrowed and Gigan's eyes darted to the people lying huddled on the ground. "Most do not even know that brand of bulletproof vest exists, and very few can afford it..."

"Guys, I know you're both pretty into the whole philosophy and ethics side of things," Vincent drawled, "but could we maybe save the explanations till after we're done and in a safe spot? I could use your light, G." Gigan took the clip back, gave Aldrick a friendly slap on the shoulder and bounded toward his buddy.

"What are we dealing with, *mon ami?*" he demanded.

"A bigger version of the one Sim found–"

"No, I thought it was merely something laid by a giant metal chicken."

"–but this one's plugged in. And no wise cracks about that, it's an important point even if it doesn't seem like it right away. It's what it's plugged into that's important." Vincent's hands came into the light. His finger ran along the hairline crack circling the egg, marking where it could be broken open. Then his light moved, shifting over wires and clamps that disappeared underneath the egg. "Help me tip it. But gentle, don't drop it!" he ordered. The inventor pushed against the egg and Gigan found the silver pressing into his arms. The weight was intense. His boots bit into the concrete as he pushed back, his muscles straining. Two hands landed below his, and Aldrick leaned against the egg, adding his thin strength. Gigan smiled in the dark, and hoped his nephew could see it.

"Yeah, that's what I thought," Vince said. "Let it down nice and easy, fellas." Gigan and Aldrick pushed and a sharp grunt came from Vincent as he tried to catch it. "Easy!" he gasped, "I said easy!" A gentle clunk came, then a sharp breath from Vincent. Gigan's light swiveled and focused on his friend. Vincent's light spun to illumine the Lefebvres. "So, as it's set up now, it's connected to the main infrastructure of this section of Italy. We try to break it open, blow it up, anything like that, and it fries everything. Fries it as in melting the wires and starting fires all over this section of the country. That's not fixable damage. Of course it could all be rebuilt, wires re-laid, all the things. But if we let it fry the infrastructure it would take months, maybe even years, to fix."

"Cut the wires connecting the egg," Gigan said with a shrug that said it was obvious. A frown cut over his face, his forehead furrowing. "But no, that is too easy a solution for this mastermind playing with us in the shadows. He would make it seem so simple, then cause something dreadful to happen because we missed a tiny thing he left behind."

"Yep, you got the game figured out. We could cut the first one, maybe two, but it's too fast and the egg would bypass the cut ones and still send its lightning rays into the country."

"Lightning rays?" Gigan asked, one eyebrow going up.

"Ok so I was trying to use imagery," Vincent said, his voice quick and annoyed, "every time I tell you what I really see you and Pete yell, 'Queen's English, Savant!' and I get tired of it."

"Fine," Gigan chuckled, "I'll take the lightning rays. Do you think you could make a method of cutting the wires that keeps it from lightninging?"

"'Lightninging,' really? Anyway, yeah, I'm pretty sure I could make a clamp to intercept the signal before the egg could fry anything. Yo, Aldrick, do you have—"

"Excuse me for interrupting," Gigan broke in, "but I believe I hear people." Two lights clicked off and silence fell around them. The egg pulsed in the quiet. Outside, voices murmured and shouted, and the noise grew steadily closer.

Gigan grabbed the pad of paper from Aldrick and the gaudy pen flew over it as Vincent pulled out a roll of duct tape. Aldrick's heart leapt as he recognized the lead voice.

Sophia Ricci marched into the Andrea Palladio with the little band who had formed after hearing her story. The missing policeman's father marched beside her. Stephano Espositio, her detective boyfriend, walked on her other side. His bright eyes took in everything and one hand hovered near his pistol. They had managed to collect a few old fashioned actual flame lanterns and solar-powered flashlights. The glow they cast fell on a pile of black clothed people lying unnaturally still by the transformers. A silver egg stood near them, pulsing rhythmically. A hush fell over the crowd. Sophia broke into a trot and knelt beside a giant of a man splayed on his back, his nose bleeding onto his black clothes. She plucked off a piece of paper duct taped to the body.

"He is breathing," Stephano said above her. "All of them are. What does the note say?" Sophia handed him a note in English, French, and very poor Italian.

These are the bad guys. They murdered the policeman outside the back door. DO NOT TOUCH THE EGG.

Stephano dropped the note and raced for the door. The policeman's father followed him, his face working with dread. Sophia spun to her feet and studied the four white papers fluttering on the silver egg, the duct tape a darker silver in contrast to it.

DO NOT TOUCH! It is booby trapped. We are working on a solution and should have it settled by daylight.

The little band of citizens huddled together and looked at each other, unsure what to make of this oddity. A cry came from outside the back door. Grief and horror mixing in a wordless wail. Several swallowed hard, and the lantern's light shook. Stephano strode back in, his face a storm of anger. As he reached Sophia, his eyes caught a reflection in his flashlight's beam. He bent down and picked up a clear casing in the shape of a bullet. Taped to it lay a simple gray business card; an MP7 and pistol lay crossed over an open Bible, with a single word typed underneath. Stephano's eyes widened, and Sophia saw him overwhelmed for the first time.

"What?" she demanded, snatching the card. *Parabaloni...* it meant nothing to her.

"You are sure of your description of this boy?" Stephano demanded.

"Yes, you recognized him from what I told you, I could tell, but you didn't say anything. Who is he?"

"Your mysterious ally is Grégoire Lefebvre's son and heir," Stephano said. Backs stiffened in their little band of citizens. Anger invaded their confusion, murmurs and dark curses spewing from them. They could still hear the weeping drifting from outside. The silver egg pulsed over it all. In the shadows by the front door, Aldrick hunched, his arms going around his chest, his eyes dropping to his feet. Gigan's hand stayed on his shoulder, propelling him along as he and Vince glided toward the exit. "I thought I knew what this was about, or at least those responsible for it. But this..." Stephano tapped the card in Sophia's hand, and then held up his flashlight beam to shine through the empty casing of the bullet. His voice changed, coming with awe and excitement. "This alters the situation. I know the name of the Parabaloni. They are legends among the lawkeepers and militaries, spoken of in whispers. The stories of what they have done to right the world are so fantastic only half are believed. We will not touch the egg, and we will wait. At least until morning."

A little smile flitted under Gigan's mustaches as he slid out the door and into the night. Good, they had bought a little time. He looked up at the tall form of his friend darting for the wall.

It was up to Vincent to beat the clock and outthink the enemy.

Gigan's job would be to keep him alive when the Lefebvres found visitors tonight.

Chapter 11

The others looked at Yousef. He stood tall, his hands in his thobe's sleeves, a sly smile creasing his face. It wasn't a friendly smile. A thousand things shot through Pete's mind at that moment. But he found only one thing coming out of his mouth.

"You're taller than me, you fustilarian[24]!"

"I've been taller than you for years, 'Tassy," Yousef said, his shoulders squaring and his head going up.

"I bet I can still do more push-ups than either of you," Jojo shot out.

"I can beat you at push-ups, and you know it," Pete said defensively.

"Since when," Yousef sneered, the twinkle in his eyes betraying his enjoyment at needling his big brother.

A video of Simeon behind the wheel of a car projected from Pete's watch. The stocky spy gave a discrete cough and stared at the three siblings, with an obvious "snap out of it," look. Yousef and Colin both stared in stiff shock at the apparition. Pete pulled a speaker from his jacket pocket and tossed it on the card table. The projection switched to the speaker as the table wobbled dangerously.

"My big boss," Pete introduced.

"Mr. Aziz, you want the mob mission?" Simeon's voice sounded as natural as if he were in the room as it drifted from the speaker. His southern tones made Colin think of long mustaches and impossibly brave cavalry charges.

"My friends and I can handle the situation at the square," Yousef said, obviously trying to recover his austere gravity. Pete and Jojo's eyes narrowed and her mouth formed unspoken words; *What friends?* Colin got the confused idea Yousef wanted to stick his tongue out at them. The teenager's ears started to hum and he rubbed his aching head. "I can stop the massacre, dismiss the mob, and regain the papers they wish to plant for the frame-up. I have a network at my fingertips that makes that

---

[24] A low personage, a scoundrel.

situation easy to handle."

"The pipeline," Colin said, "what about that? If you handle the square but they manage to blow the pipeline and plant those papers saying it was Afghanistan, that could still cause a war."

"One incident may not be enough to cause a war," Pete said. "But we will deal with that."

"How?" Colin and Yousef both burst out.

"You probably already did," Simeon stated. They all looked back at the speaker. "The bag. That's their bomb."

"But they'll just make another one," Colin said.

"It's not easy to find that much explosive that quickly," Pete said, "or to make a bomb you can control within ten hours. It should be fairly simple to track them down through their scrambling to regain what you took."

"What about a bomb you can't control? A gas pipeline would already burn pretty well," Colin said, then stiffened, his face intense as he thought. "But no, you're right... At the meeting, the guy reporting about the pipeline assured the speaker they knew how to blow it so it wouldn't leak oil everywhere and harm... mother nature, I think he said."

"We need a full report on that meeting soon," Pete stated as he handed Yousef a coffee cup. "But now—"

"Didn't bring the kid one," Simeon interrupted, his tone aggrieved. Everyone paused and blinked at the speaker. A half smile twitched over Pete's face.

"Oh, um, I'm fine—" Colin stammered, fumbling for some sort of understanding of this situation that kept swirling into the unexpected. Pete interrupted again.

"Fine," he said, quick and businesslike, "Jojo, you go gain Colin a coffee, Yousef and I will watch your back."

"I don't need watched like a sick puppy—" Jojo started as she trotted for the door, but both her brothers interrupted with hoots of incredulity, that ran off into reminders of the troubles they had dug her out of. Their words ran over each other and dropped into a blur of Arabic. The metal door closed behind Pete and silence fell in the big warehouse. Colin sat still, staring at the door. He spun to the speaker.

"Siblings?" he ventured, trying desperately to get a handle on all this.

"Yes," Simeon answered. "Need a few minutes alone." Colin nodded, evenly, easily, as if everything was just fine. He leaned back against the wall, just a little too relaxed to actually be relaxed.

"Mr. Clempson, tell me about your father." Simeon watched the young man through the camera on the side of the speaker. He saw him stiffen, and his expression harden.

"What do you need?" he dodged.

"Think he meant for this Collective to take things this far, or is he out of his depth?" Simeon asked, offering him a direction for this conversation.

"He brought them a bomb, and looked so excited as he left the meeting, I haven't..." Colin's shoulders slumped. "I have never seen him excited like that. Yes, he means this Collective to deal their damage. Why are these people doing it? They do realize their plan means killing people, right? Lots and lots of people whose only crime is that they exist?"

"They realize," Simeon said. "Not hard for most if they have a cause. Elimination is just numbers if you don't know the ones dying."

"But someone knows every one of those numbers! They have family, and friends, and hobbies, and jobs, and favorite foods, and... How could a human be ok with just killing off other humans?" Colin looked as if he might be sick, Simeon could see the paleness beneath his skin. That would be very hard to fake. The kid might be a good actor, but this seemed a genuine reaction to the situation. Good, that's what he needed to know. Simeon moved the conversation back to its original course.

"There's more you didn't say." Shoot, how had he known even just over the speaker system? Colin's lips tightened. But he answered it.

"I think my dad's also out of his depth. He is excited about this Collective's goal but– A stranger slipped into his office last month. I didn't see enough except to know it wasn't a regular, they were intending to get in and out unseen, and they had this weird black mask on. I only caught a glimpse, but it was almost like a hockey mask, or one of those death masks the old English kings would use. Just an oval with slits for eyes and mouth. I was watching from outside through an upstairs window, I couldn't hear much, but Dad looked…scared. He booked this trip with Mr. Luke right after the stranger disappeared."

"That why you managed to get taken along?" Simeon asked on a hunch. The young man's eyes snapped to the speaker, his lips a thin line. Simeon couldn't read his expression. Colin didn't deny it. Silence stretched into a long minute.

"Um, so, I know I'm not used to this sort of thing," Colin burst out, "but with a war and explosions and murders to stop, should they be taking this long to catch up and get a coffee?"

"They need a few minutes," Simeon repeated. "Mr. Clempson, I am not going to be available soon."

"Off to rescue someone where you are?" Colin asked, still fishing to get a grip on these people.

"Stay here, rest," Simeon didn't answer. "Jojo will stick near and keep you and the bag safe."

"I'm not going to just sit on the sidelines–" Colin started, staggering to his feet. He stumbled, one hand going to his side, the other to his head.

"Blood loss, lack of sleep," Simeon stated. "Rest. We'll need you later."

"No! I have to see this through, I'm not going to–" He broke off in shocked horror as a "poof" came from the speaker and a gray cloud mushroomed from the top of it. The cloud spread in an instant, too quick for Colin to get out of its range. It filled his nostrils and he staggered back, hacking. His feet caught in the scratchy blankets. Then his vision blurred. He slowly folded on himself. The scratchy, dirt-smelling material met his cheek, and for an instant annoyance filled Colin; he had tried to keep most of himself from the germs teeming in these ancient blankets. Then everything went black.

No swift chatter in Arabic filled the Crepe Shop kitchen. The Azizes gathered near the coffee dispenser, the tallest a little apart from the other two.

"I've missed you," Jojo said. "Thank you for helping me get out."

"Who says I did?" Yousef challenged.

"How are the others?" Pete asked, quick and stiff.

"Alive, growing," Yousef said, his natural melancholy strong. "Om grows out, while Da merely grows mean."

"Is it very bad, for the littles, and you?" Jojo asked, her voice soft. Yousef paused, and Pete noticed his shoulders drop a fraction.

"Most are too young to remember him before," Yousef rumbled. "And they know now to stay out of his way. No, it is not too bad."

"And you?" Pete asked.

"I am Yousef, I go and come as I please," the young man shrugged. Evading the question.

"Come with us," Jojo burst out. "We could be a threesome again against the world!"

"You always have a home with us," Pete stated, the words sincere. But his eyes dropped, as if he knew something Jojo didn't about this offer.

"I am needed here," Yousef answered, suddenly harsh and stiff. "Do not ask me."

The lights blinked off. Air stopped moving through the vents, and the quiet hum of the percolator and refrigerator motor suddenly died. A strange silence fell around the three dark blotches of the Aziz. No traffic, no blaring music… Jojo turned and filled a to-go cup with the dark, black Arabic coffee before it started to cool.

"You don't seem surprised by this," Yousef murmured.

"We see a lot of this kind of thing in my line of work," Pete said. He grimaced and his eyes flew to his silent watch. "We have work to do." He still stood, stiff and agitated. His lips parted to say something.

"We need to move," Yousef stated. Unemotional. No expression showing on his face. Pete's shoulders slumped. But he swept on to business.

"Jojo, mind playing guard to the suitcase?"

"All right," she agreed. "I will stay with Colin and get him to tell me about that meeting."

"Yousef," Pete said, "someone will be at the Farsee Fountain every two hours, starting at 0600 this morning. Check in, or we will assume you are not handling the mob, and do it ourselves." His half smile crossed his face. "And this is where my boss would disappear, off to save the world again."

"Does he do that often?" Yousef rumbled.

"All the time," Pete nodded. "It's not invisibility spray either, I've checked his pockets. I never thought I'd meet someone better than you at disappearing, but he has you licked."

"He's shorter," Yousef said defensively. Jojo snorted back a tight laugh. The siblings stood awkwardly silent for another four seconds. Then Yousef faded into the blackness toward the door. Pete and Jojo murmured goodbyes and the party broke away, each headed for their jobs.

✦

The world swam slowly back into focus to Colin. It came in shapes and colors that fuzzed and moved. He sat up slowly, a groan echoing deep inside his brain. He slumped against the wall and the ground under him tangled in his feet. He let his eyes close and counted to fifteen in a slow, measured beat, keeping time by the pounding behind his skull. When he opened them again he saw his legs twisted inside dirty, scratchy blankets, and a dim old lamp barely giving out enough light to illumine his corner. Beyond it was only a vast empty room, unnervingly dark, that smelled like old fish.

The young Middle Eastern woman sat in the single chair beside the leaning coffee table, watching him. Her hijab lay limp on her shoulders and her glossy black hair wound in a braided bun around the back of her head. It made her look somehow more terrifying, like an assassin in disguise, or an angry schoolmarm.

He gassed me! pierced through Colin's buzzing mind. But the words that slid from his mouth came milder. "I didn't want sleep!" The woman held an aspirin bottle out to him.

"You needed sleep. And you were giddy and overwhelmed

and not feeling reasonable," she said. "You were out for about two hours."

"Two hours!" Colin yelped. His hand clamped onto his head and his eyes closed as the headache flared. He reached for the aspirin bottle.

"We haven't missed the fun," she soothed. "Now it's time to get to the fountain to check in. Take it with you, we need to go." She strode for the door and Colin scrambled to his feet obediently. But he saw her pause as she reached the metal door and one hand balled into a fist. She pulled the hijab back over her black hair and adjusted it so only the oval of her face showed. She threw a look over her shoulder at him that smoldered, as though daring him to make a comment. Colin, wiser than many men twice his age, played stupid and pretended he didn't notice anything. Jojo swept out and he followed her into the early morning.

Colin stepped into a town trying to cope with a whole new living situation. Pedestrians walked in the middle of the streets, and voices rose in strange strong languages, as Riyadh woke up stalled by the loss of power. Colin saw dark-eyed women behind their veils, trying to keep the children out of the streets, as the cold night air of the desert reigned inside houses. Men gathered in groups, loudly gesticulating, strong voices lilting in ways that made it hard to even interpret the mood. Restaurants stood open, advertising sales, trying to counteract some of the backlash of their failed cooling systems. As they strode down the street, Colin could glimpse inside the shops and restaurants and saw cashiers in tears and angry people in long lines, as no one could figure out how to pay with the power down.

And three different robberies happening on side streets. Some people were happy to take advantage of downed security systems with no way to quickly contact law enforcement.

And the quiet. Yes, people complained and children yelled in the excitement of the adventure, and a few cashiers lost it and started yelling at the queue in front of them. But no cars poured through the city. The powerlines didn't hum and buzz. No phones sprayed YouTube videos into the morning sunlight. The TVs inside restaurants hung black and silent. Even the refrigerators sat like useless hunks of metal instead of churning out ice and humming as they sucked power from the wall sockets. Colin had never realized just how much the world changed without the gadgets.

He found himself envisioning a world where the grid stayed down. No communication except from hand-to-hand. No proper refrigeration. No good transportation. Golly, no fresh water as things were designed right now, which meant terrible sanitation. Man, without power they would be back to ancient times with blunderbusses and the Pony Express and furs!

Spices rose from back kitchens and market stalls, and Colin's spine went a little straighter. This past year found him constantly hungry, as he gained four inches and two shoe sizes. And here it all smelled like an adventure. A shiver ran over him and he slumped again, sidling a little closer to this competent lady striding ahead of him. He was already enmeshed in an adventure, one more serious and deadly than he ever thought he would wander into. His side pulsed again as he remembered it, and his eyes went to the carry-on bag clicking rhythmically as it rolled behind the lady.

"How far is this fountain?" Colin asked.

"The team will manage, you do not have to worry about the bag and the rest of this situation," the lady answered. Colin blinked, surprised to find her answering everything swirling in his brain, not the actual question. She spun to walk backwards so she could look up at him. "Stop hinting and trying to get me to answer what you actually want me to tell you, and just ask the real question. A good con man learns how to turn it off, that's as important as learning how to work your natural skill."

"Uh..."

"My name is Jojo, the bugs will get in if you let your mouth hang open like that, and let's speed up, we need to catch that engine."

Colin's mouth snapped shut. She started to trot and he automatically loped at her heels, his thoughts pounding like his headache. Did he play people all the time? Sometimes, yeah, but all the time? Possibilities spun inside him, not all of them nice, and it took him another block to pinpoint the noise Jojo meant. An engine roared somewhere ahead of them. It blasted into the quiet morning like a monster from another world. Colin could hear it grind and complain as the gears changed. Jojo picked it up to a run, the bag vibrating and jumping as it rolled behind her.

An ancient truck rolled out of a side street. Its main color seemed to be rust. As it turned into the road Colin could see it vibrating. Something metal jiggled off it and bounced into the road. Men jammed the pickup bed, some in their traditional thobes, others in business suits or jeans. None of them looked pleased. A man with a face like worn leather sat at the wheel, his thin frame straining as he laboriously tugged on the wheel. He grinned as the truck turned toward them, his whole face taken up with an expression of exultation.

"Now you turn it back on," Jojo said, and Colin's eyes flicked to her. "We need to buy that truck and get everyone off it."

"Does he speak English?" Colin asked, looking back at the man.

"Does he have to?" Jojo discreetly pushed a wad of bills into his hand, enough even Colin stared at it. Simeon always insisted they travel with cash. A two-by-four section of precious floor space in Perry's garage was turned over to a box[25] with cash from the most frequently visited countries. Gigan, Vince, and Jojo[26] had complained at the space it took before; but not after today, when nothing but actual physical bills worked. "You are good enough to make this talk for you."

"Why me?" Colin asked, uncomfortably eyeing the weathered

---

[25] No, not a safe or even a lockbox, just an ordinary metal storage box. I thought that oddly un-smart of the Parabaloni too until I met Perry and realized he *is* a safe, and then walked into their garage and noticed all the other things around the box. Anyone who tries to steal cash from people who stock their garage with that kind of weaponry and destruction-dealing-devices is indeed an idiot, and will not get far.

[26] Not Pete. He is constantly purchasing food items as he goes, and it's easiest to just shove a wad of cash in someone's hands and keep moving. (Like that time in Tripoli when he wanted the whole tray of sweetbreads while being chased by evil agents in a jeep. He took the tray too, and it came in handy against the onion-scented goons a few streets later.)

old man in his traditional thobe and turban.

"Because it would look really weird for a woman to do it here, it's already weird enough for me to be out with just you, now go." She pushed him forward, and watched as Colin's shoulders squared and he straightened to his full six feet. His finger discreetly counted how many bills he held as he smiled and stepped into the street, waving at the truck. Jojo watched him start a wordless conversation with the truck driver as she did her best to be invisible on the sidewalk with the bag. He didn't pull out the whole wad of bills. He started with a quarter of it, and watched the expression on the truck driver's face. He only added two more bills before the deal closed and he moved to the people in the back, apology almost dripping from him. She could see their shoulders slumping as they recognized what was coming and faced the long walk wherever they needed to go.

Colin Clempson really was a natural.

Chapter 12

Gigan flitted past the ground floor windows. He could hear slurred conversation and laughter two flights above him, mixing with complaints about the blackout and unusable smart phones; several of the younger set had obviously never gone to bed. Occasionally an older voice shouted at them to quiet down, but it only brought more laughter. An ordinary night at the Lefebvres. Gigan paused at the huge bay windows in the breakfast nook. On one side the land fell away to the lagoon, and he watched white-capped waves moving and sparkling in the moonlight. His eyes shifted to the other windows, raking the open ground leading toward Fussina.

Only a few dots of light showed people out there. The dots danced and shifted, firelight gleaming through the dark. It hearkened back to older times and harder methods of living. These shadows wanted to make that a normality, culling any who could not survive harsher extremes. Gigan idly wondered if any of them had grandmothers they bumped off in the night. He fervently wished his *Maman* hadn't chosen this month for her trip back home.

He moved silently through the darkness and glided down the basement stairs. The scent of damp mold and stale air engulfed him as he moved deeper. A flashlight beam bobbed and danced and he could hear Vincent still mumbling things he didn't understand.

"How goes it?" Gigan asked.

"It'd go better if we had a third person to hold this darned light steady!" Vincent complained. His voice came muffled around the flashlight handle stuck in his teeth as he and Aldrick manipulated wires and cords into a clamp.

Footsteps thumped on the stairs to the upper stories, above their heads. Heavy and slow, as if the person dragged themselves down. The light caught Aldrick's pale face. He stared at the basement door, his eyes shining with alarm. Gigan spun on his heel and darted silently toward the ground floor. Vincent saw Aldrick's mouth open, his expression haunted as he watched his uncle disappear. But no words came, his mouth closed, and he turned back to the wires. Vince spit the flashlight onto the work-bench.

"It's ok, dude. Gigan will handle it without hurting your dad. Well, without hurting him much, anyway," Vincent added, and it made a smile twitch over the boy's face. "Just keep praying we can get this gizmo right, don't move your thumb, and see if you can get that micro screwdriver a little closer to me..."

The moon shone through the windows with a silver brilliance as Gigan slid out of the stairwell and pressed himself against the wall. A silhouette of a man moved in the kitchen. He flipped the light switch up and down as he cursed with impressive creativity. Gigan recognized his twin's voice. But it came hoarse and slurred. He recognized that too, from the last ten years of their father's life. He stole closer till he stood just behind his brother. Gigan tapped Grégoire on the shoulder. The smuggler spun, agile and quick, the movements of a predator on the alert.

Gigan's right hook smashed into his jaw. Grégoire spun again in a neat semi-circle and crashed into the wall.

"That's for letting yourself turn to drink, you complete and rotten idiot!" Gigan barked. "You know what it does to a man, better than most, and you know we are susceptible! What are you doing letting yourself walk openly into such an imbecilic–"

A lightning strike at his midriff cut him off. Gigan blocked the blow with his arm, and stepped in. He caught Grégoire's next strike with his forearm and shoved forward, pinning his brother against the flower wallpaper. Grégoire's head shot out and caught Gigan between the eyes. The smuggler brought his heel up into Gigan's knee, destroying his solid stance, and jerked free. The two spun out, circling each other like lions in a territorial squab-ble.

"You know better than to come here," Grégoire growled. "Now I understand why Aldrick did not sleep in his bed, why he has been out all night, and turned off the tracking on his phone! It is not enough that you betray and destroy your own family and exile us all from our homeland. Now you return to make my own son hate me!" Gigan barely checked his first reply before it escaped; *You've done that with no help from me.*

"Aldrick is in the basement with a friend of mine, sorting out this blackout business," Gigan answered quickly. He knew Grégoire wouldn't wait long before starting the fight again. "Long before he called me in he became involved in much tonight. But he has been brave and smart, and he's done well. You should be proud of him. After, of course, taxing him with leaving without telling anyone and getting into the mess in the first place."

"Don't tell me about my own son!" Grégoire screamed. He charged, grabbing an iron candlestick off the counter and swinging it at his brother's head. Gigan twisted, snapped his arm around Grégoire's neck, and jerked him into a headlock, judo striking the wrist holding the makeshift weapon. Gigan stopped facing the bay windows. He stood unblinking as he stared into the moonlit yard.

Shadows flitted over the damp ground.

The candlestick rattled onto the ground, bouncing across the kitchen floor as Grégoire hissed in pain. His elbow smashed back into Gigan's gut. His twin only drew his arm tighter around Grégoire's neck.

"Stop and listen to me!" Gigan snapped. "People are sneaking closer to the house, they murdered a man with blunt instruments and knives two hours ago!" The struggles suddenly stopped. Gigan loosened his hold and pushed a hand into Grégoire's back, shoving him out of striking distance. "Look, out the window. Do you see the shadows? They are the ones who caused this blackout, and it is more than just a loss of electricity that will be restored in the morning, believe me. They're a worldwide domination sort, and they're after Aldy. (And me and my work brother, but that's less important right now.) I don't know enough to guess what their attack will be like, but I'm not happy about their numbers."

"I see seven," Grégoire said. His voice came clear and alert, none of the earlier hoarse slur scarring it.

"Ten," Gigan corrected. "And that is just from this window's vantage point." He choked back the order that came naturally to him, closed his mouth, and waited. Grégoire stood silent and motionless for eight long seconds watching the shadows draw closer. He pivoted on his heel and his gray eyes met his twin's.

"Stop bouncing on your toes, we have time," he growled. "I will rouse the family. You keep watch and see if you can gain a better count. And keep them from getting access to the house!"

"Well duh," Gigan muttered under his breath. But as he darted to the back windows (always staying out of view of anyone outside) a thankful prayer blew heavenward. Grégoire wasn't currently out to shoot him in the head. Hopefully. He forced a deep breath into his lungs, making them unconstrict, and gave his twin to the Lord again. The prayer felt automatic and cold. He had prayed it so often, begging and pleading. And yet here he was, again… Gigan shoved away the thoughts as unhealthy and unhelpful and focused on his work.

Another eight shadows stole through the darkness toward the back of the house. Gigan longed for his scanners, wondering how many he missed in the dark. They were good at using the land and keeping out of sight. He reached the back door and slipped up beside it, rising on his tiptoes to peer out the little window.

A shadow neared the door. Medium height and bulk, something in his hand Gigan couldn't quite make out. The Frenchman silently unlocked the door. He pulled his lubricator from his utility belt and oiled the hinges quickly. The shadow hesitated, glancing over his shoulder. Gigan pulled the door open, shot out, wrapped an arm around the person's middle and neck, and dragged them inside. His foot closed the door softly as the shadow made "guck" noises and clawed at his attacker's arm. Gigan rotated his wrist so his pistol shoved against the stranger's temple. The struggling suddenly stilled. Hose covered his face, smashing his features into an unrecognizable lump. The humor of that FBI file devoted to the "cloaking phenomenon" hit Gigan, and a laugh burst from the Frenchman.

Footsteps, quiet French cursing, and squeaking old floorboards echoed above their heads. He swallowed his humor with a sudden snap that he hoped made this bad guy assume he was unhinged, and pushed his gun barrel closer.

"How many of you are outside this house?" Gigan demanded,

choosing English. He loosened his hold around the man's neck a fraction. A sharp breath sucked into the shadow. Nothing else came from him. Gigan pressed his pistol harder into the man's temple. He felt a tremble run through him, but the man gave no other response. The agent tried the same question in Italian. No response came from this heavy breather in his grasp.

A flood of Lefebvres poured into the room. The ridiculously handsome Ettienne led the pack with a swagger, his face livid as he focused on Gigan. Then he noticed the shadow in his big brother's arms; all his boiling anger turned on the enemy, and Ettienne's shotgun jerked up. Gigan spun his pistol to this stranger's neckline and pulled his trigger[27]. A sharp pop rang even over the noise of the feet and hissed voices, and the shadow suddenly went limp. Ettienne's finger left the trigger. But his shotgun swung straight at Gigan's face. With one hand the Parabaloni let go of the shadow, plucked the gun from Ettienne's grasp, and shoved it through Clarice's strap behind his back. At the same instant he swung his pistol up and stepped into the move. Ettienne's mad rush suddenly stilled as he found his gun gone and his forehead pressed against the warm metal of a freshly-fired pistol barrel. The shadow crumpled to the floor and lay in a heap. The crowd grew suddenly still and quiet. Eyes darted from the frozen Ettienne, to Gigan's unemotional professionalism, to the still black form on the ground.

"We have other enemies right now," Grégoire stated from the back of the crowd. The worried faces spun to him. "Guillaume-Theophile, I assume this blackout means no scanners will work?" A shiver ran down Gigan's spine at hearing his real name from that familiar voice. Years worth of memories flooded him, and he couldn't decide if the shiver came from pleasure, sorrow, or fear. He pushed it all quickly away and focused on the work.

"Nothing more advanced than paper or open flame will

---

[27] Even a plunger bullet can do serious damage when fired pointblank at a temple. Aim at the cervical bone along the neckline and it will leave a mark, and probably powder burns, maybe even break the skin and scar. But it leaves them alive. Aim at a rhinoceros anywhere. And don't use plunger bullets on a rhino, it just makes them mad. Really mad.

function just now," he said. His boot tapped the shadow lying still beside him. "Grégoire, this enemy holds an unlit torch."

"He was planning on setting fire to the house?" Grégoire asked, staring at the ancient tool.

"No, he wanted it to light cigarettes. What do you think?" Gigan snapped. He swallowed it, reminding himself his twin hadn't been at his best when he found him a few minutes ago. "We know these people favor what one might call 'earthy' methods. Torching something fits their MO."

"Don't let them come any closer," Grégoire ordered. Weapons bristled around the room, and the people quickly fanned out throughout the house. "Ettienne, take charge in the kitchen, that is where most of them are approaching." Ettienne gave Gigan a murderous glare. The Parabaloni pulled the shotgun out and handed it back; the barrel facing Ettienne. A snarl rippled over the young man's face. But he snatched it and ran from the room, headed for the kitchen. The sharp reports of gunfire rang from the house. The twins stood still. They stared at each other, the black shadow lying between them. Gigan tried to think of something to say. He felt empty, as if even his words had dried up and disappeared in the fire of hatred spewing from his family. He had prayed so long for some change, even a small ray of light for his family, so long.

He reached for Clarice, and turned to the window. Seven shots spun from her barrel, and five seconds later Gigan let her drop back on her strap. He turned to trot toward the basement, his work here done.

"Don't bother him," he ordered Grégoire as he trotted past, one gloved finger flicking at the man lying huddled on the ground. "I'll want him later."

Gunfire echoed through the old house, and Gigan picked out the sounds of four different guns from the stories above him. He wondered idly what the towns would make of the commotion. The door was closed as he reached it, and Gigan quietly blessed Vincent's foresight. It wouldn't do for some of these hotheads to realize a stranger was in the basement. He opened it and slid in, closing the door behind him.

A clang rang on the metal door as a bullet ricocheted off, clipping the concrete wall and spraying chips onto Gigan's cheek.

"Stop, it's me, good grief!" Gigan blurted out, freezing at the top of the stairs.

"Give me that," Vincent said in exasperation.

"Hey, that's my pistol!" a female voice said in high outrage. A flashlight beam shown on Gigan's face. He let his tired eyes close until he felt it shift away. "How was I to know it wasn't one of the family out to kill you, or these other things out to kill Aldy?"

"Can I come down now?" Gigan asked.

"Yo, Gigan, I think we've got it done!" Vincent answered. "Andrea[28] trotted down and we finally had our third person to handle the light–"

"Yes, let the woman just handle the flashlight–" Andrea complained, but Vincent ignored her and rolled on.

"–and now this should work to cut the egg off. Then we can do whatever we want to with the egg itself, see how it ticks and make it stop, all that good stuff," Vincent said with a sunny grin. Gigan eyed the twisted clamp bristling with wires and what looked like knife blades.

"It looks like a gnarled ancient porcupine with a broken spine," he commented. Aldrick's huffing, quiet laugh came from the darkness by the bench. Gigan felt his emptiness invaded by a deep gratitude. He had been able to come for his nephew tonight. Aldrick still lived to laugh in the darkness.

"Yeah, well I'm not sure I realized just how hard it is to work exclusively without programming of any kind. We had to fit a lot of bulky things in here," Vincent said, staring at the thing in his hand. He turned to Andrea. The scientist held the light, an annoyed scowl on her pretty face, her black hair tumbling down her cotton pajamas. "Do you think you and Aldrick can make more?"

"Exactly like that unwieldy ugly thing?" she demanded.

---

[28] Another note for those who may not remember these names (there's a lot of names swirling during this particular job, I know). Andrea is a crooked scientist the Parabaloni both foiled and worked with in an earlier case dealing with the Lefebvres and a ton of mosquito drones. When that job was finished, Andrea and Grégoire (Gigan's evil twin) hit it off enough she decided to stick around and see what happened next. By now, during this job, she is officially Aldrick's step-mom.

"Because I can do so much better than that rattletrap."

"Great, do it," Vincent grinned at her. "More tonight would be great, I have a feeling we're going to need them soon. These people get around with their eggs."

"About that…" Andrea commented, suddenly hesitant. She gave a shake, like a terrier coming out of a stream. "Oh what the heck, you know what I do."

"Great. What did you do?" Vince asked warily.

"I designed the eggs."

"For reals?" Vincent commented. Aldrick leaned around him and stared at her. "Dudette, that's some nice piece of gadgetry."

"You don't have to sound so surprised," Andrea snapped. But Gigan saw her usual smugness come back, and knew she was pleased by the comment. "And before you ask, no, I don't know who wanted them, and I didn't know what they were going to do with them, and I certainly didn't suspect it to be used here. All I got was the order (very carefully anonymous and untraceable) and the money. It was good money. I assumed someone wanted it for a single city. Maybe for a robbery spree. It would be very handy for that."

"Don't give Grégoire any ideas," Gigan murmured.

"Do you still have the plans for me?" Vincent asked.

"No, go make your own egg," Andrea complained. Aldrick grinned and flicked a paper pellet at her. "Fine, I'll help you this time because these creeps used it in my hometown and are after Aldy. But I still can't give you the orders. Part of the deal was that I delete them after I sent the schematics, and then erase those too."

"That's not suspicious or anything," Vincent drawled.

"Oh stop it, that's not so strange for the clientele I work with."

"She is a mad scientist," Gigan shrugged.

"I am not mad! Well, only sometimes and usually because of Ginnette."

Aldrick's huffing laughter came again.

"Ok, Andrea," Vincent tried a different way, "why is there so much space unused in these hulking gadgets? I saw the one at the power station here and it's enormous for what it does."

"I don't know," she shrugged. "I designed it to the specs the client ordered, I didn't ask why. Don't be so demanding. When I said I would help I didn't say I'd dance to your tune."

"Ok, fine," Vincent sighed. "Can you please use your inside knowledge and smarts and get us a better version of this clamp thing to cut off the egg? Gigan, you ready to go deliver it?"

"Almost. Aldrick, no, you're not coming," Gigan said. A sharp protest came from the boy, a cry that started as a word and cut off. "You are needed here to show Andrea exactly what to do as she came in at the end of the process, and it is dangerous enough even being here. Besides, you should not have run away tonight without telling your father and you know it." A sullen huff came from Aldrick. He flung himself into his chair and pulled his beanie over his eyes. Gigan's mouth opened to tell him to stop with the attitude and then closed again with a troubled expression. He wasn't his father. How far could he go before he overstepped into territory that rightly belonged to Grégoire? His shoulders slumped as he spun back toward the stairs and headed for the door. He heard Andrea begin to demand things from Aldrick, smoothly taking over. Sliding smoothly into the place Aldy's uncle just left behind. Vincent poked Gigan in the shoulder blade and the Frenchman blinked rapidly, coming back to the situation. He forced his shuffle into a trot as he headed to the stairs.

Vincent's solid presence moved behind him. He could hear the well-known measured tread, even smell the workbench grease and the annoying lemon shampoo Vince favored. A comforting sensation of *home* rolled into Gigan, flowing from the sunny, kind inventor solidly at his back. Unless they changed substantially, he could never come back to the Lefebvres. They would not let him. But Vince and the others were family by now, a second one added to his birth family. Gigan never felt more grateful for it than at that moment, trotting up the darkened stairs of the old Italian tower villa. It scattered his tired depression and put a little of his usual bounce back into his step. His eyes went out the window and the abnormal darkness of the night fell around him.

It was time for the Parabaloni to take control.

But the thought of that black clad enemy in the mud room teased him, begging for attention. Gigan gave in. He spun to Vincent as they ghosted out the side door.

"Are you all right with a lone infiltration, Vince?" he murmured. His mustaches bristled with a wolfish smile. "I have a secondary infiltration to make."

Chapter 13

The truck jerked and bounced, stalling and revving in abnormal patterns as it made its way toward the fountain. Jojo ground her teeth together and tried not to shout at this kid. The truck jerked, snapping her neck back. It stalled again.

"You have to put the clutch in before you try to change gears," she said.

"I know, all right!" Colin burst out in exasperation. His dark eyes spun to hers, his strong jaw locked and highly annoyed. "Why can't you do this again?"

"Women don't drive in Saudi Arabia. I shouldn't even be in the truck with you so shut up and get us moving again or–"

A man in a black robe and turban stepped up to the truck cab and Jojo came as close to cursing as she ever had. The Mutaween already prowled the streets, even with a citywide blackout and the sun's rays just barely glinting off the roofs. The man's truncheon swung back and forth on his wrist and he glared over his bristling mustache and beard.

"What are you doing out together?" he snapped in Arabic, every word laced with an angry suspicion.

"He is my cousin," Jojo answered him, her eyes down demurely. She suddenly felt naked without her veil, and hated herself for the feeling. "We were caught when the blackout hit, and now that the curfew is lifting we are trying to reach home. I am afraid he isn't used to driving."

"You should not be out together." The man eyed Colin with fury in his black brows, and the truncheon moved to his fist. "Why are you silent, why do you let the woman answer for you?" Jojo decided she wasn't in the mood for diplomacy. She brought the muzzle of her little pistol out of her sleeve and fired. The bullet hit the man on the nose. His eyes glazed and he tipped forward onto Colin's lap. The young man gave an "eep," and his hands shoved into the Mutaween's shoulders. He tipped backward and hit the ground with a sharp crack. Colin cringed, his head ducking toward his shoulders.

"Go already!" Jojo snapped. Colin pushed the clutch in,

shoved the stick to first with both hands and let it out carefully. The truck jerked forward. The engine revved and he pulled the stick back to second with a grunt.

"Was that a policeman you just shot?" he asked, a squeak in his voice.

"Not a real one, only a religious type. So what were you doing in Riyadh?"

"I got in trouble and my mom made my dad take me on his business trip," he said, his face creased in concentration as he focused on driving around stalled cars.

"What did you do?"

"Really?" he snapped, his eyes darting to her. Jojo shrugged, no apology in her expression. Right now was a good time to ask Colin questions, he was distracted and annoyed enough by driving stick that his guard was down. He wasn't weighing every word before giving the "right" answer.

"I think I can promise it couldn't rival the trouble my brothers and I got into growing up. I am curious, and the more we know of you the better we're able to work together."

"I notice you say 'of you' without volunteering much about yourself," Colin said. "All right, fine, I skipped school for a year and my mom finally realized it."

"A whole year?" Jojo blinked.

"It's not like I skipped school*ing*, I had the best tutors in the world! Dante, and Plato, Shakespeare, and even some Saxons when I felt like it. I was keeping up just fine."

"Good for you," Jojo said. "But I'm sorry it took your parents a full year to notice." The truck jolted violently as Colin's face suddenly went stoic and emotionless. He wasn't used to people just saying things like that. They usually tried to pretend they didn't notice while giving him pitying looks and false cheeriness. "Yousef is who he is partially because no one ever noticed him except Peter and I. Don't let it define you, Colin. Their choices are their own, how you stand before God is what's important."

"Subtlety isn't your thing, is it?" Colin asked, and Jojo shrugged.

"I can be subtle when I need to. But we never know how much

time we're given with a person. Too often we don't say something, and then we have all of life to regret it. Look, there's the fountain, pull onto the side of the street, right there."

Colin dragged on the wheel. The effort of pulling the old truck inside the parking place strained his strength after this crazy weekend. He took his foot off the pedals with a grateful gasp as they rolled into the cracked lines of the parking spot, and the truck stalled again. Jojo grabbed the hand brake and pulled as they kept rolling. The truck came to a stop with a screech of old dirty brakes and she rolled her neck painfully.

"When I get a car, it's going to have power steering. I never knew that was optional!" Colin commented. Jojo laughed and eyed the cracked fountain in the plain concrete square. The ornate stone looked broken and depressing without the pump sending water cascading over it. The water lay stagnate and sad in the cistern, not the bubbly thing she was used to.

Did they wait here? All she really knew was that Peter hadn't come back, and that meant it was her job to make this hour's check-in with Yousef. She silently prayed nothing had happened to her big brother. Well, nothing more dangerous than he usually ended up with. She stared at the entrance to the fountain. Her hand rested on the bag as Colin slumped over the steering wheel. No one stood in the square yet, they should go unnoticed here for a few more minutes. Except for the fact they had just roared in with the only engine in what seemed the whole city.

Yousef stepped out of the street across from them, his hood casting all but his hook nose into deep shadow. He sank back into the darkness of the street again. A stab of horrible homesickness cut through Jojo; Mu'tasim didn't stand in the sun waving at him to stop playing games he should leave well-enough-alone, as she remembered seeing them in so many rescues and adventures of the old days. Suddenly all she wanted was to be alone for a good cry.

"He disappeared again. What does that mean?" Colin asked.

"It means he is taking care of it and we wait," Jojo said automatically. Wait...her eyes dropped to her hands. It was all she could do, wait. God alone could touch Yousef. Jesus was the only one Who could step in and change her family. Jojo sat still and put it in His hands again. Those hands, scarred through love for her, upholder of all the stars in their brilliance and billions, could save a few more wayward souls. Jojo laid her family on Him, and let it go. That was the hard part. To let it go, and turn her mind and energies to serving where Jesus had her now.

Yousef stepped out again and waved them away in a quick, annoyed movement. Colin turned the key in the rusted ignition, and grimaced as he reached for the stick again. Jojo picked up his coffee cup, sitting forgotten in the ancient cup holder, and started giving directions for the airport where they had parked Perry. Their plane would be a good spot to wait.

Pete leaned over the handlebars of his borrowed bike, urging it to move faster. The cool desert morning wrapped around him and made his own sweat feel cold against his skin. He reached the end of the hill and the cracked road flattened. Dirty storefronts lined the street in an uninterrupted line, metal gates pulled down over most of them and locked tight. No cars lined the street as he pedaled on through the dark. These people timed their egg-filtration well, curfew kept the streets mostly clear of stalled cars. A breathless chuckle slid from Pete as his legs pumped him up another hill. "Egg-filtration," he would have to bring that one up to Gigan just to annoy him with its utter stupidity. Pete topped the hill and leaned over the handlebars again. The air swirled around him and hit his hard black backpack like a wind aid. He could see the cracks at the bottom of this hill if he concentrated. Dawn threatened the night's dark. Good, he should be just in time.

Masala's store lay in a black heap ahead of him. Peter hadn't known it existed when he lived here. His SEF team hadn't known about it either, he could swear to that. But Simeon Lee knew it well enough he had a loyalty shopping card.

Pete coasted down the hill and gently applied the brakes. The innocuous façade of the machine shop gleamed in the graying light. Dirt and grease crawled up its sides and he could smell the old metal. No one in the neighborhood gave it a second glance, he knew, it was just Masala's shop in the line with all the others.

But at 6:35 exactly, Akbar Masala would unbar the door to his basement. And down under the innocuous machine shop lay the best supplies one could obtain in Arabia for making bombs. Actually Simeon preferred Masala's camel hair fuses to any he had come across, and for that it could be argued the best stocked store in the world. Pete hopped off his bike and leaned it against a grocer's across the street. He levered up the board trying to block a broken window, grabbed a handful of pine nuts, and munched as he watched Masala's. Usually this street would already be spilling out its people. The baker should have been here hours ago, getting his fresh stock ready. This grocer usually opened about now.

But everything lay still and quiet. Abnormally, freakishly quiet. It was the cars, Pete realized. This blackout circumvented the cars' usual failsafe, the normal traffic of a big city just wasn't happening. And without the constant lines of metal machines it seemed like a dead town.

A slight movement came from the minuscule alley beside Masala's. Peter frowned, his eighth handful of nuts partway to his mouth. He stuck a bill in the pine nuts to pay for his breakfast, let the board fall back in place, and strolled toward the storefront. The movement could just be a stray cat. But he didn't feel like taking any chances with these shadows they dealt with. If this Mr. Black was one of the elite few who knew of Masala's well stocked store he could regain what Colin managed to remove in a single stop. And maybe the cloaking devices this Collective carried worked for the human eye as well as the surveillance feeds. Man, they really needed some of those gadgets.

Pete ignored the official front door of the machine shop and shifted silently into the alley, keeping on the balls of his feet, his pistol out in his hands. He spied a jagged crack scarring the basement window. A frown cut over Pete, hardening his face. He leapt over the window to keep the light pattern inside from changing, landing lightly on his toes to keep the noise down. The dirty blue door to the basement was closed and locked. Peter picked it open and turned the knob. He gently raised his pistol, said a quick prayer, and darted through into the stairwell.

The door at the bottom was unbarred, and open. Masala would not have left it open.

His steps stayed silent as he took the darkened stairs three at a time. But the light and air flow would have changed when he opened the upstairs door, if anyone paid attention in the basement, they knew he was coming. He ducked low as he reached the stair's end, and shot to the left, shoving himself behind a shelf of fuse caps. His gaze darted around the store, taking in the situation.

Masala lay on the ground in the center of the metal shelves. Very dead. The blood still flowed. Masala opened one minute early today. Which meant, Pete was one minute late. The store owner had probably relied on a stupid smart phone to tell him the time, and had estimated wrong without it. Pete pulled his eyes away from the grizzly pile of what used to be a man, remembering the hissing laugh that came through Masala's yellowed teeth the last time Simeon ordered more fuses.

Pete's sweeping gaze stopped, riveted. A patch of shadows near the back of the store stood out in deeper black.

A figure. Just standing, stock still. Staring through the shelves at Pete. The Saudi silently cursed this blackout; none of his night vision gadgets worked, even his watch scanners couldn't track him. The figure moved. Smooth, competent, fully aware he was being watched. Peter could see him in an outline as he shifted out of the deepest shadows. A man in black slacks, a black leather hoodie, and kid-gloves over his hands. An oval facemask with rectangles for eyeholes covered all but two ice-blue eyes. A pistol glinted in one glove, pointed straight at Peter's heart. Pete's pistol pointed unwavering at the stranger's facemask.

The abnormal silence of the morning closed in on the store. The two men stayed as still as the body lying between them. Pete studied the stranger, noting the black curl spilling over his mask and the suppleness of his bearing. He marked him as not actually old, maybe near Gigan's age. A bag lay at the man's feet. Explosives and fuses filled it, piling out the top. Enough to take out the pipeline, and another target on his way. Pete could not allow the man to leave with that bag.

"What now?" the bomber asked, his voice even. Almost strangely even.

"We could both toss the weapons?" Pete suggested.

"I hardly think that's wise. You would just slide your knife from your sleeve, Pete. Oh yes, I know your name. You don't think Mu'tasim fits you any more." Subtly implying it did still fit; trying to unsettle, to get him off balance. The man took another step to the left.

"You do realize how unattractive and stupid that facemask is, don't you?" Pete asked, honestly curious why this man picked it. He stepped left too, keeping this murderer the same distance away from him. The black shelves cut between them, and the only sight they had came interspersed with explosives, detonator caps, casings, fuses smelling distinctly of camel.

"Should I care what it looks like?" the even voice asked. Ah, that sort. "Some of your pretty sisters across town might care. Your *Om* knows how to wear an outfit, almost as well as she fails to work with people." Pete felt his bile rising. The facemask tipped to the side, slowly, almost gently, as the man studied Pete's reaction. The figure's finger tightened on his trigger.

Pete's shoulder rammed into his shelf. Seven feet of black metal tipped toward the figure's corner. Red fuse caps fell like plastic hail. Pete shot down the line of shelves. A bullet ricocheted just behind him, and through it he classified his opponent as highly trained and quick to adjust. That type would wear bullet proof armor under his clothing, and would not be easy to take out.

A bullet slammed into his back, right between his shoulder blades. Pete staggered at the force, feeling his vest strain, trying to contain the damage. He flung himself into the shadow this stranger had started from, and came to rest in a crouch in the deep well of blackness. His spine and neck ached. If he didn't have a vest, he would be dead. If he used a lesser brand of vest, he would probably be paralyzed. This man played for keeps.

A flutter of movement drew Pete's eyes to the counter. He just managed to see a black boot disappear behind the thick wood. Peter slid his Sam mask[29] over his head and shifted carefully, trying to get to a position for a good shot at this creep.

A bullet pinged off the wall an inch from his forehead. Pete's nose wrinkled and he stopped moving. The stranger couldn't get a good shot at him until he moved. Who was this man in the shadows? The shadow himself, perhaps? Or a righthand man? If he could just learn more…

"The other customers here know not to bite the hand that makes the fuses," Pete said. "Why kill Masala?"

"Do you still not know my reason?" the voice asked. This was Mr. Black himself then. Pete pinpointed him from the voice, and waited. "Perhaps I am culling the herd." He moved, shifting to the far side of the counter. Where he could get a good shot.

The figure darted into a kneel, his head and gun coming into sight over the top of the counter.

Pete anticipated it. A shot squeezed from his pistol, then he went into a roll. His bullet hit the mask in the center of this man's forehead and ricocheted off with a sharp "ping." Pete rolled into the shelves again. Four bullets rang off the metal shelves around him, showering sparks. Each shot came closer to Pete, as the man honed his aim, even while the Saudi moved. This opponent was good. Too good? Simeon's main rule of spyhood rang in Peter's mind. *"When in a dangerous place finish the objective, get out, get safe, then think about the next step."* Don't focus on the stranger. Focus on the bag. He couldn't let that leave this shop.

Pete's feet jammed into the wall and his shoulders shoved into a shelf. Bomb ingredients showered onto the concrete floor. No grunt or yelp came from the shadow to give away his new position, darn it. He was too good for that. Pete shoved ear plugs[30] under his mask and sprang to his feet under a window, his back against the wall.

---

[29] A knit mask made up of bullet proof fabric, with more conventional bullet proof glass in place for the eye-section. One of their more useful gadgets. In Mumbai they found out it also works to keep cobra fangs from penetrating.

[30] Usually, the Sam mask does it for him. It has automatic noise cancelation that kicks in whenever certain decibel levels (such as gunshots and explosions and rhinoceroses bellowing in your ear) happen around it. But of course during blackouts, that feature doesn't work.

A lit fuse burned in his hand.

Light from the window over Pete's head played through the shop. The creep crouched beside Masala's body, his pistol still out, caught in mid run. For that instant they froze, like a painting locked in time. Pete saw no fear in his enemy's icy blue eyes. Not even a tightening of his muscles to show any normal terror of death.

Pete flung his fuse.

It landed in the bag hanging from the man's shoulder. The pack of fuses caught immediately, and a bright yellow flame licked at the man's hoodie. The bag dropped from his shoulder and he dove headfirst into the cracked window. It shattered, spraying glass onto the sparking flames. Pete shot out the window above his head and darted forward. He aimed for nothing except distance, striving to get as far as he could from the shop.

The heat force hit him first. It felt like a burning wall fell on him. He slammed into the street face first, and the force pressed into his back, holding him down. The noise came next. A furious clap of thunder that slid right through his body and shook every organ with its volume. Yellow light danced over him as the fireball took hold of the shopping mall. The pressing force lifted as the explosion moved into devouring flames. Pete let himself groan as he pushed himself to his feet. He staggered two steps, unsteady with the ringing in his head and the strain on his sore muscles. But his eyes focused on the bicycle, still leaning unexploded against the grocer's.

Pete dashed for it. He needed to get out of this area. He needed to think.

No. He needed to take out these people.

Where would this Mr. Black go next? Pete had to find their hub, the place Black would think of as the most important. Peter's eyes went to the darkened streetlights and the stranded cars lining the side of the road. His lips tightened and he spun his bike toward the central Riyadh power station. It was time to do some culling of his own.

He glanced at his watch and his frown tightened. He had only told Jojo to make one stop at the square. In ordinary life he would just send her a quick text. Or even skip the square altogether and send that text to Yousef. Confound this stupid power outage! The solitude of being cut off from communication that usually hung at his fingertips cut into Pete. In the same instant his eyes flew to the houses and stores flashing past, and he knew fellow humans lived there, just a shout away if a stranger desperately needed help. He was cut off from phone contact, but suddenly vividly aware of the local humanity that he usually didn't give a thought.

Pete's lips pursed a little tighter, he forced himself to focus, and sped up, his legs pumping against the pedals. And distances... he was remembering how long it took to get places with just a bike, and it wasn't all pleasant memories. But then his mind flew to the last time he actually needed a bike, and a dirty motel room in the Caucus mountains, and a blond-haired messy stranger who had stepped in and changed his world. And now here he was again. A bike his only mode of transportation, with the familiar smells of Riyadh whipping into him in the wind; spices, humanity, the dirty breeze, old exhaust, even some camel scent. It seemed almost as if he had come full circle. But in that instant, when he should have been overwhelmed by the constricting sorrow of all he couldn't return to and the destructive weight of still fighting in a world more broken than before, what he felt most were the arms of his Father. God enfolded him in that circle. Always there, always protecting, always breathing out His love. Pete felt it in a still peace in his soul. In the verses that told him he was on the right path, pleasing his Savior by doing good. In the upholding hand that got him past the weariness of yet another sleepless night and demanding physical day. A smile curled over Pete. He drew in a deep breath laden with the scent of memories, and let himself stand tall on the pedals as he sped through the morning.

Through the storm of memories and emotions, he chose to focus on his solid Anchor. On the One thing that never changed. It granted him the ability to focus on his work, again. Always so much work.

He had to get this done. The square first, then the power station. Pete pushed his thoughts aside, let his tired brain go blank, and concentrated on speed.

The top of the fence showed in a dim gray light as Vincent slid over it. He landed with a quiet thud in the Andrea Palladio and stole quickly behind a small storage building. He could hear voices arguing in Italian over the definition of "daylight." Apparently the whole party had decided to wait up.

The dead policeman was gone. Vincent skirted around the stained concrete and sidled up to the door. These people didn't keep very good watch, someone should have noticed him. But then every Italian loves a good argument, the man on guard probably just couldn't resist. Vincent slipped inside and into the darkness, eyeing the company gathered in the pool of lantern light.

Three concerned citizens stood arguing with what Vincent's trained eye put down as a high-ranking detective. One of them had a fire axe on his shoulder. The citizens said daylight meant "the first rays of dawn" and they should attack the egg to get their power back, while the detective argued daylight meant "when you could actually see things clearly." Four other people lay on the ground, obviously wishing they were back home in their own beds. The woman Aldrick had recognized sat near the egg, a little bored the inventor guessed from her posture. She sat up straighter and turned toward the door. Noticed the light shift at his entrance perhaps? He was long gone, of course, but at least she had noticed. Vincent rolled up the edges of his Sam mask so it was just a beanie, strolled to the egg and carefully, gently, started to attach his current cutter. Not too bad as a name… Ceecee, perhaps? Or Ceril? No, this hunk of wires and metal wasn't a Ceril.

A sharp cry came from the woman. She spun on one knee, and her pistol leapt up to point at him.

The cold barrel of a machine pistol touched her chin. Sophia froze, her lungs heaving. She definitely hadn't reckoned on a reach as long as this stranger boasted. Silence fell so suddenly it rang like a bell. The company stared wide-eyed at the tall, supple stranger in black, kneeling in the shadow of the egg they were supposed to be guarding. The detective never looked away from the barrel resting gently on the woman's chin.

"Now let's not be hasty," the inventor drawled. American cowboys paraded through Sophia Ricci's mind at the voice, and she felt a little of her panic calm. He stumbled through the same phrase in Italian and then shrugged, a sheepish smile coming over his face. He chose the detective as the leader and focused on him. "I'm really bad at pronouncing other languages, do you know English?"

"Yes," the detective said, his accent thick. "Stephano Esposi-tio, head detective, Italian branch, etc. Please remove your gun from Sophia's face. Then we'll talk." Vincent's green eyes flicked down to Sophia's. Again she recognized a sun-browned cowboy of the open plains, one of the strong men with twinkling humor.

"You ok with a draw?" he asked. "We both put them away. Ready?" He pointed his barrel at the ceiling and sat back, watching her. Sophia drew in a tight breath as relief made her head sing, and carefully lowered her pistol muzzle. "Excellent. Ok, I'm the dude who helped write those notes, about not touching the egg till daylight." He slid Floyd back into his holster and leaned over the cords snaking from under the egg again. "Without this weird looking doolymahickus clamped over the cords, the egg will fry your infrastructure. Give me just another second… There. That should do the trick. Let's find out, shall we?" He gained his feet and his hand shot out, palm flattened. It smacked into the silver egg. It tipped and rocked back and forth.

The instant the silver casing rocked back to the ground, a bright white spark fizzed along the thick cords. The white spark hit the current cutter and blazed into a white ball. For a moment it lit up the ten faces of the people in the room as they stared at it. Then the light died and the rhythmic pulse of the silver egg took over the room again. Sophia realized she could see the outlines of the big machines in the gray light of early morning. And she could see a grin slowly spread over the inventor's freckled face.

"Yay, it worked," he commented. Vincent slipped his Sam mask the rest of the way off and shoved it in a pocket as he straightened slowly and stared at the egg. One hand ran through his fluffy hair, and his green eyes took on an absent expression. He pulled a screwdriver out of his pocket and flipped it like a gunfighter about to head out for a showdown. "Now, Mr. Eggy, let's see what you have in your insides."

Pete coasted up to the plain square on his borrowed bike and leaned it up against a wall. He leaned against the wall too for a moment, blowing hard, his legs stinging. It had been a while since he had to bike fast and far. He hadn't had time to do it for fun in…it must be a full year. Pete pushed his sweaty hair out of his eyes and stepped up to the Farsee Fountain. He stared at the stagnate water in the dirty old pool. Cracked concrete curled into a crumbled fountain, the swirls dry and pitiful as the pump lay silent. He could see how old and tattered and sad this piece was with the power gone. His eyes dropped back to the pool. All the water would grow like that soon. Stagnate and undrinkable.

"Tell us you are here, or we will handle the square ourselves," he said, still staring at the water.

"This is a dumb arrangement," Yousef complained from an alleyway, and Pete's half smile twisted over his face. "How am I to get anything done if I have to be here every two hours?"

"Fine, we can make it three hours," Pete said. He heard shoes scrape dirty concrete and tightened. "Don't leave yet, 'Seffy!" The noise stopped, and Pete suddenly found himself at a loss to go on. He thought of Gigan and Vincent, and knew he would just say what he felt to them. But he trusted his team with his life as a part of how he earned his paycheck, and with that went a trust that ran deeper than just life… But right here stood his flesh and blood brother. He would choose to be open. Only if he led the way could he expect openness from Yousef. "I wish I could take the family burden off you. It wasn't supposed to be yours to bear, I never meant for you to have to be the others' protector. I know it is a hard task, with the little ones' lives in the balance, and Father certainly no help. It should be his task, I know. But it has always fallen on us, and now it is yours alone and I cannot fix it and it breaks me to know you cannot just leave. Yousef, I pray for you every day, and it usually turns to this; that Jesus will be yours and help you to bear what I cannot. It was not my Jesus that forced us away from you, Yousef! You must know that. The real Jesus calls us all and loves even His enemies." Nothing came from the alley. Pete wondered if his brother was still there. "Listen, Yousef, there are those who will not appreciate the business you run at night."

"How do you know what I do?" Yousef snarled.

"It is my job to know things," Pete told the fountain. He had seen the signs in the security footage he and Jojo watched as they trailed the Tesla, in the way Colin reacted to Yousef's presence, in the mannerisms his brother adopted. And the things Pete's watch had reported in Yousef's pockets before the blackout. "You have made good inroads into the underbelly, and I wish you well. But there are those who do not like competition. They will strike at the family to destroy you. It will happen soon, especially if the win is yours this evening at the square."

"You do not know all things, oh wise one," Yousef sneered. Soft footsteps ran down the alley, disappearing into the city. Pete sighed and turned back to his bike. The fact that was his only comeback meant Yousef ran scared, and the warning came as news to him. He hadn't considered the backlash. Great, more to deal with. There were still some hours between now and the evening attack on the square at least. Peter mounted his bike again, checked his watch, grimaced, and pushed off in a rush.

Gigan stole through the tall grass, zig-zagging irregularly and offering silent imprecations on his family's shooting. A bullet, embedded in the heel of his boot, tickled his foot as he ran and it rankled him. They knew he and Vince had stepped out the door, and still kept shooting. Thank goodness he was out of range now.

Two shadows moved steadily ahead of him, always shifting into the deeper pools of blackness. The black clothes of the man Gigan had pulled into the Lefebvre laundry room lay loose on the French agent, it wasn't the best of fits. But it should work to mask him as he drew closer to the two shadows. The hose pulled over his face smushed his features together and smelled of garlic. He began to wish he had swapped places with Vincent just because of the uncomfortable facemask. Gigan made certain his tall friend got through the Lefebvres shooting range, past the routed enemy, and on his way to the Andrea Palladio before he slipped off for his own morning mission. A part of him nagged, saying he should have stayed with his buddy till the egg job was done… But these shadows tried to kill Aldrick. They tried to set fire to the family house. And besides, Vince was a good agent, a very good agent, he really didn't need to be babysat.

The shadows in front of him disappeared. Gigan stayed at the same pace, the same irregular movements that kept him in the deepest shadows as he moved. But inside his heart began to beat a little faster. Where had they gone? It took exceptional skill to disappear so thoroughly in a place as packed with humanity as the mainland near Venice.

The ground rose steadily in front of him, a gentle slope with tall green salt grass whispering in the breeze. Voices drifted faintly to him and Gigan slowed, his eyes roving the area. Gray daylight penetrated slowly, enough he could make out the grass, and a small trail of smoke drifting out of the top of the hill. As he reached the top, Gigan found it dropped in a ragged circle that created a hollow, deep enough to hide anyone from sight. The smoke twisted into the sky from a campfire. He could see the flicker of its faint light as he gently poked his face over the edge. Twelve people sat there, the firelight dancing over their black clothes and weirdly featureless faces. A shudder ran over Gigan. It looked like blank putty, as if their individual souls had been wiped clean with their facial features. He had to remind himself it was just the hose smushing their faces. One removed the hose, and his ordinary features sprang to their proper dimensions. Others followed his move, till they sat without the face covering. Gigan memorized features as he tried to hear the words, and missed his gadgets again. A video recording would be so very useful. The conversation came in English, accented from different countries. The snatches he heard seemed to be general small talk like, "The smoke is in my eyes," and "It's nice to have that mask off." Suddenly the voices came stronger. Counting. They were counting their number, deciding if they needed to go back to hunt for another.

"Tollimé ran behind us. He ought to be here by now," a deep voice grunted. Gigan slid his legs over the edge of the hollow and dropped into the camp. "There he is. Is that the last?"

"I made sure Irene returned to the mother before I left her," a small female reported, her voice devoid of any emotion. But Gigan could see the reddened eyes and knew the unemotional voice lied. The Lefebvres could shoot well when they needed to, they had missed him on purpose. (Well, he chose to assume the miss had been purposeful.) He knew four shadows lay dead in the grass outside their house. These others would have followed if they hadn't retreated so quickly. Gigan slumped in the back of the hollow, where the night's darkness stayed unpierced by the light, and waited.

"Agate is still out," a thickset male growled, hunched over the fire. An uncomfortable silence fell. The firelight danced and popped, and slowly the dawn light crept over the top of the hollow. Gigan eyed it, estimating how much time he had before someone got a clear look at "Tollimé."

"Is it true Agate is Mr. Black's second in command?" a skinny shadow piped up.

"Be careful talking about Mr. Black," another murmured, looking over her shoulder. "He could be nearby listening. And he doesn't like to be talked about."

"He doesn't like to be known," the hunched one grumbled. "No one really knows anything about our leader except that he wears black kid-gloves when he's out on business." His spine straightened, his shoulders squaring as he gesticulated angrily. "Any of us could die in this plot he has going, and do we know what it really is? Six months we trained with him, and I still don't even know his main plan!"

"We know it is the first big step to resetting civilization, and erasing the imbalance of human numbers overrunning the earth," a woman said, her voice firm, her shoulders squared as she glared at the growler. "It is a goal worth dying for."

"A death like that might bring you back as something very grand," the small lady said, her eyes very far away. "A butterfly, or a horse that's wild and free. Or maybe even…" Her eyes traveled up to the unrivaled stars, brilliant even as the sky turned from black to a dim gray. Pity stirred Gigan as he watched her. The woman's one hope for her dead friend lay in the theory of reincarnation, wrong on so many levels. How could she look up at those brilliant stars, in their millions and billions, and think it all came by the chance of nature? God sang in those stars. He blasted His presence in a billion balls of brilliant light that danced without misstep year after year after year. Every human soul who looked at those stars felt the awe of their Maker. Yet this woman could twist it to a longing to be among them, to *be* a ball of brilliant fire someday. That was no hope. That was a desperate longing for hope twisting inside her and looking for something to grasp.

"A death like that leaves you dead," the hunched one snapped. Gigan could see his eyes glowing in the firelight and knew the fear there. "Does anyone know what Mr. Black plans?" Eyes looked away, shadows shifting uncomfortably.

"He was with the party heading to Riyadh," the skinny one said, and heads spun his direction. "Alf caught a glimpse of the gloves and told me."

"He always attends the meetings," the strong woman said.

"So what's Agate doing?" the skinny one demanded. "We already finished here. This portion of Italy will be cut off, and the gates will be down for the water to sweep in and out. What else needs done?"

"We had a witness," the woman said, reluctance in her voice. Gigan could see the forms stiffening, pulling back from each other, not meeting each others' eyes. He knew exactly what ran through them. That sentence brought the past twelve hours back to their minds with clarity, and with it their twenty-one companions brought down in the Andrea Palladio, Venice, and outside the Lefebvre tower.

The tower.

The reality of these people's plan suddenly rushed through him. This Agate would still be there. The shadows were a distraction, to let that one, that second in command, sneak closer and get to Aldrick. What would he do! What method did he favor? Torching? A quick bullet? A dart from a blowgun? A snake under the bed? Terror crawled up Gigan's throat and he sat rigid, his eyes bright. His hand stole into the belt strapped around his middle. He pulled air into his lungs, clamped his mouth closed, and flung a gas pellet into the fire.

A cloud of white puffed into the hollow. Sharp gasps and soft thuds filled the area. Gigan shot forward. He took a precious three seconds to tuck a Gideon's New Testament into the small woman's pocket. Then he chinned over the top of the hollow and took off at a sprint. Around him the gray light of first dawn changed the landscape into eerie, half-real shapes looming in the dark. Gigan's eyes went to the stars, slowly fading to the day, and his mind flew to their Maker. Oh dear Jesus, let him be on time!

Chapter 15

White sunlight covered the tower and sparkled off the water of the lagoon. The pile of old masonry sprawled over the grass and rose into four stories of red bricks, with crenellations crumbling and uneven at the top. Gigan scanned the place with his eyes, his trained mind looking for anything out of place, anywhere an assassin would go to work. In the night he hadn't realized how much of it was actually castle stone. Torching this place would do little harm, just burn some of the supports and the kitchen roof. The shadows had been sent as a front, nothing more.

Lights blazed to life inside the building. A rap album blared from the third story, loud and obscene for the sole purpose of being obnoxious. Gigan's watch and scanners flared back to life and he felt his smart phone vibrating as it reset. His hand flew to his watch, selecting the weapons and bomb scanner and setting it off incendiary. His face hardened, his eyes tight. His run picked up to a dash.

Inside the tower, Ettienne shifted his shotgun on the scratched kitchen table. He stared at the lone figure dashing over the grass, and his face held a dark hate. For Ettienne, all their troubles swirled around this one brother and his ideology. Guillaume-Theophile represented a different world of beliefs and lifestyle, one that had destroyed Ettienne's. Just seeing him sent rage flaring into the young man. He never connected the reaction as a response to his conscience that never quite died due to his mother's determined prodding and churching. Ettienne didn't make it a habit to think about things. He felt, and he acted.

His shotgun rose, slowly, still hesitantly, and he secured it against his shoulder. The barrel slid out the window, careful not to disturb the broken pane. Ettienne focused on the bare head above those perfectly trimmed mustaches.

Grégoire's hand landed on the barrel and jerked the shotgun away. Ettienne started to his feet with a series of oaths spilling from him, his face livid as he towered over his older brother. Grégoire just stared at him, his gray eyes contemptuous. The fury melted into a scowl, and Ettienne slunk away toward the stairs. Grégoire spun to the window, thinking hard. Why was Guillaume rushing back alone? He stepped outside through the kitchen door, the fresh morning air rolling over him and blowing away some of the sick headache from his hangover.

Gigan leapt for the stonework.

Grégoire gaped stupidly as Gigan scurried up the stones of the tower without any gear, moving faster than a lizard. Three stories sped under him as he darted upward. On his way past the third story, he reached into the open window and threw the speaker out. It crashed to the stones by Grégoire's feet and shattered into four pieces. The morning grew suddenly peaceful again.

Through the birdsong and gentle breeze, Gigan heard two things. A fuse burst to life at the top of the tower. And a gun cocked just above him, on the other side of the tower's crenellations. There wasn't time for a good dodge, not if he was to reach that fuse. His fingers dug into the crack and he heaved himself upward, his legs held tight together, straight and even. A pistol shot echoed off the stones. He felt the bullet rip through his arm and he lost his hold at the flaring pain. But he had already made his move, and kept it from being a deadly wound. Gigan shot up the last story and his toes hooked between a crenellation. He pulled himself up with a quick acrobatic twist, every muscle in his body straining. He vaguely heard Grégoire shouting something, but had no energy to register if his brother gathered help or more enemies. Gigan's good arm caught the edge and he rolled onto the tower top, his wounded arm clutched to his chest. Blood soaked into his shirt. He could feel his head beginning to sing, his body weakening at the shock and blood loss. He pushed it all to the back of his consciousness.

A massive bomb lay just beside him. He saw the distinctive red of Semtex. Secondary explosive, thank heaven, not first. Gigan flung Vincent's Benito over it, his hand shaking hard. The bomb cap melted over the components, darkening automatically as it sensed the early sunlight. No knowing how this one would detonate, but "at dawn's first light" seemed like these people's style; Gigan was profoundly grateful Vince knew enough to fore-stall it. The lasers embedded in the Benito sparkled under the skin, sensing the initiator and jamming the switch.

Thank God, he was on time. Vince's bomb cap had only failed twice in his long experience with it. And even then it kept the worst of the explosion contained.

He let out his breath in a gasp and fought his way to one knee. A scrape of metal on stone came from behind him, faint but def-inite. Gigan snapped Clarice up, and a bullet spun from her barrel, the report echoing off the stones around him. The bullet went straight into the barrel of a pistol peeking over the crenellation. A sharp bang sounded like a deeper echo to Clarice's shot. A puff of smoke and flames and metal shrapnel burst as the pistol ex-ploded. An arm flailed up over the edge of the tower. Gigan pulled Clarice around. But blood dripped on his good hand, and his grip slipped. His mini sniper clattered to the ground.

Before Gigan could grab her again, a man heaved himself over the tower top. He rolled to his feet in the same move and kept coming. He wasn't clothed in black. Dark gray, rippling and flow-ing with lighter shades, curled around him. It covered all but two dark eyes that bored into Gigan, blazing with the light of a fanatic. Gigan's hand dropped for his pistol. Agate's leg shot out in a front kick. The toe of his boot caught Gigan's knuckles with a force that numbed his fingers and sent his pistol clattering across the tower top. The Frenchman's arm shot out and wrapped around Agate's ankle. He sprang to his feet, keeping the leg tucked under his arm. Agate staggered, pushed off balance. But he rammed forward, jerking his leg out of Gigan's grasp and coming in close.

The Frenchman didn't take the bait to fall back. His good arm came up in a blur and the heel of his hand smashed home under Agate's chin. The man's head snapped back, and he felt the crack of it down to his toes. Gigan's wounded arm moved automati-cally. His fist rammed into Agate's midriff, sending pain rocketing through both men. Agate fell to his knees, breathing in gasps, and folded over himself. Gigan kneed him in the face.

The trapdoor flew up and Grégoire came out in a rush, his pistol raised and ready, four other Lefebvres in his wake.

They came just in time to see Gigan's last lightning, ruthless move. A huge man in twisting gray tumbled back limp and unconscious on the stones. Blood splattered over the tower top. A shiver ran over Gigan as his left arm curled to his chest again, and Grégoire knew most of the blood wasn't from the stranger's broken nose.

Grégoire's eye fell on the bomb. His whole body went cold. He stood there staring at it, his knees locked as images of flying masonry and mangled bodies and burning buried basements went through his mind.

"Do you have someone who knows how to disarm it?" Guillaume-Theophile's voice broke into his twin's chilled stupor. The voice came strained, and Grégoire looked at him. Gigan gripped a bandage with his teeth and pulled it tight around his bleeding arm. Red soaked through it almost immediately.

"No," he found himself murmuring stupidly. His brain felt numb. He suddenly savagely wished their *Maman* hadn't chosen this month for a trip home to France.

"It's all cool, I've got it," an American drawled, and Grégoire spun, his pistol snapping up. Guillaume's tall, blond-headed friend chinned over the edge of the tower and hopped to his feet. Apparently these people spurned stairs. Grégoire couldn't help thinking the Lefebvres standing huddled near the trapdoor looked like a gaggle of hens in the presence of a great heron. And not just in stature, he felt with a stab, as the stranger stepped up to Guillaume and quickly took over the doctoring. A new wad of bandages and some sort of clotting agent came from his capacious pockets. Grégoire dully comprehended the salve bottle looked well used. "Letting yourself be shot on the first stop of a mission, really G? I knew you needed me along, but this…" He finished with a long-suffering sigh as he smothered the clotting agent over the bullet wound and watched to make sure it worked.

"This isn't the first stop, it's technically my sixth," Gigan said with dignity. It broke into a hiss as Vince drew the new bandage tight.

"How are you counting?" Vincent laughed. He plopped down next to the bomb, studied the readings on the Benito, and pulled a handful of tools from a cargo pocket. Gigan settled with his back to the stones near his friend. He started listing his stops here while Vincent argued that Italy itself made one stop. He dismantled the bomb with quick precision as he talked, and both of them ignored the Lefebvres. The gaggle of hens slipped back inside, murmuring things about telling the rest of the family it was safe, and breakfast being ready. Grégoire stood there. His twin looked tired and bloody, and he huddled near his partner, as if for warmth. Or protection. He recognized the brotherhood in the interplay of the two, the inside jokes and teases that only they understood. It twisted around them in a mesh that held them close and shut everyone else out. Vincent started to slip the explosives into his tattered shoulder bag, his work done. Grégoire still stood, silent and unsure what he felt. The bright green eyes of the inventor caught his and he found himself held by them.

"We need whatever current cutters Andrea and Aldrick have managed to turn out," he said. Grégoire nodded and flung himself down the ladder.

Vincent watched him go. A sort of anti-Gigan, silent and dark and moody... The inventor turned back to packing the explosives and didn't look at his buddy hunched against the stones. This was a time to let him take the lead. Sorrow seemed to seep off the old masonry and into Vincent's bones, sapping his strength and sending a crinkle around his eyes that wasn't from a sunny grin. Why did everything have to be so sad? So much grief. Even the best things, like family. And when the best things broke they carried a mourning that never truly left. He sure knew that truth. And he had found it all over the world, for so long. It felt like a ceaseless ocean of death and destruction and the sorrow it brought with it. Situation after situation. Again, and again, and again... Vince let his mind go numb. Birdsong and sunshine drifted over the ancient building. A speedboat roared by in the lagoon, and car horns blared from the road. Pat kept vibrating in his pocket, furious she had been shut down. Vincent missed the quiet.

"It is already numbing his brain," Gigan murmured. Weary sorrow dripped from his voice, and Vince didn't have to ask what he meant. Various phrases of consolation and false hope rose to his tongue. But none of them seemed right. He moved to the wall beside his buddy, dropped an arm over his shoulders, and drew him into a hug. Gigan huddled into him. That, more than any words in the world, told Vincent how broken his heart and spirit were by this visit. A sharp sniffle broke from the Frenchman.

"That detective and Aldrick's guard lady are taking care of the baddies you left in the hollow. I'll toss this one at them," he said. "We're done here, Gigan. Let's go find Pete."

Pete rolled through the second-story window and landed silently inside the power station. A deep "whoomph" pulsed through the air. Every second it came again, gently beating like a strange rhythmic heart. Pete glided up to the door and slid out onto a catwalk running along the edge of the building. Black forms moved up both staircases. It seemed the enemy had seen him enter. The metal stairs made no sound under their feet, and each face seemed terrifyingly similar, blank and featureless, as if it was just mounds of putty rolled and placed on a body. Pete leaned forward, and looked over the edge. Shadows milled on the ground, shifting in the darkness below.

A silver egg shape sat in one corner. It shone, as if it sucked in the few strands of light drifting in the high windows.

Pete stood still on the catwalk, watching these people slip up the stairs and calculating. He had come a little more prepared for what he would find than in Tripoli. He could handle this crowd if he played it smart. But how did he want to handle it? His main goal here was to draw out Black again, to try to corner the mastermind... If the sounds of a fight drew him here too early Pete might end up in trouble. Mr. Black was good. The shadows swarmed closer, and Pete watched, and made his choice. Take out his henchpeople. Then make noise to try and draw out Mr. Black.

The first one moved onto the catwalk. Pete slid his air filter over his mouth and stood tense, glancing back and forth between one group and the other. The second group stepped off the stairs onto the catwalk.

In one lightning move, Pete clipped an S hook to the railing and leapt over the edge. The rope retracted with a sharp zipping sound and Pete fell toward the main floor. He flung a gas grenade and it smashed onto the concrete rushing toward his feet. A white cloud billowed into the air engulfing the Saudi. His boots touched the ground and whiteness swirled around him. He heard the soft thumps of falling bodies. A black figure toppled toward Pete, and he spun backward out of the way. A thickset man slammed into the concrete just in front of Pete's army boots.

The white cloud began to dissipate, and dirty sunlight crept back. The silver of the egg gleamed through the dimness. Bodies splayed on the ground around it in a grizzly show of a failed guard.

A soft whine zipped past his ear. A whisper of sound on the concrete behind him gave Pete the trajectory of the projectile, and his eyes went back up to the catwalk. The enemy on the stairs had avoided the gas. Four figures now stood ranged along the railing, spaced far enough to make it hard to take them out together, blowguns trained on the area beneath them. Pete leapt over a fallen shadow and darted under the catwalk's metal. Black figures flowed down the stairs after him. He didn't have a second gas grenade[31], gunfire signaled trouble to anyone outside, and the moment he pulled his rifle they would go to ground and become hidden enemies in the shadows. Peter eyed the eight people stepping off the stairs. They moved toward him, using the machines in this power plant as cover. They didn't seem to be interested in taking him out from a distance. A beam of sunlight sparkled on a knife blade from a lady shadow on his right. A red curl tumbled from her mask and played down her shoulder. A sharp clunk came from the other side as a bulky shadow's club hit the metal of a machine. It would seem these people favored old fashioned, nastier weapons.

---

[31] After an accidental detonation in Brazil he woke up covered in tarantulas, with herons trying to eat the gargantuan bugs off him. It took him two days and three trips over highly dangerous rivers to find the trail of the diamond counterfeiters again. He balked at the idea of carrying gas grenades. If the mission demands it he never carries more than one very carefully packed.

Pete shifted toward his left, his weight centered, ready to move any direction. To the four people watching him come closer, he looked like a dancer, with Death lurking in his shadow. The bulky woman in the lead hefted her club, iron studs sticking from it in every direction. She didn't rush him. They stayed grouped, fanning out just enough to draw Pete into the center of their semi-circle. He didn't take the bait.

Wait, was that hose pulled over their face? Sudden understanding of the cloaking device used by these shadows shot through Pete and he burst out laughing. His soft laughter filled the space between the enemy as he slid toward them. Icy fear slid into his targets.

Pete darted forward like a black lightning strike, and the heel of his boot landed on the lady's hip in a snap kick. She went down, but her club struck out at him. Fast, skilled, the movement of someone used to using the weapon to deal damage, not just carry for show. Pete bent backward like grass in a high wind. His hands planted on the ground, and as the club passed over him he kicked up. One foot slammed into a short guy's head. The other hit an open palm, as a supple shadow struck back at him. The enemy's hand closed, trying to trap his foot. Pete shoved off the ground, pulling in and twisting in the same movement. As he twisted, his foot struck out at the short guy. It caught him in the kidney, and sent him to the ground in a writhing heap, out of the fight. Pete's hand flattened and he struck out at the lady as she pulled her club into a backswing. The flat of his hand hit her neck. She went limp, her club banged into the ground, and she folded.

But the thin man wasn't going to be taken so easily. He darted forward with the easy grace of a martial arts master.

Peter decided he had taken out enough. If Mr. Black got interested, so be it. His plunger bullets could reach through the ridiculous material pulled over these people's faces.

A sharp rattle of automatic fire split the quiet of the power station as Pete held down the trigger to his new M16 rifle. Fire danced on the end of her barrel, bright in the dimness of the huge room. The thin man and his small companion tumbled to the ground. The rifle's barrel spun, and three of the other four creeping up on him tumbled. A frown crossed Pete's face as the knife wielder dove behind a machine. He whipped his backpack up over his head and spun out to where he could see the catwalk above him. He heard the "tick tick" of darts hitting the hard pack and ricocheting off, but his rifle already spoke. Four seconds and eleven of his enemies lay in silent black heaps with the egg's honor guard.

But the Knife Lady still wandered out there. Anyone who voluntarily chose a knife as their primary weapon in a hand-to-hand fight was a dangerous character. There was no predicting what else she might carry on her person.

And if Mr. Black came, Pete might not know until it was too late.

The old highway stretched away in front of the classic corvette, winter trees swaying in the breeze. The rising sun hit the sharp, sporty outline of the car and glinted off the red paint. A John Denver song drifted from the radio. A dog nose shoved out the crack in the passenger window every few miles, snuffling the wind. The trees hugged the road and stretched high into the sky, blocking out all other views. A certain sense of home brooded in the thick Southern trees for Simeon, sending his earliest memories parading through him.

It seemed out of place to be tying Algy to this corner of the world.

A green sign came into view as he topped another hill. Only two more hours to Memphis. Good.

His watch vibrated and Simeon glanced at it. Vince and Gigan were back online. Excellent. He pushed the pedal down and the engine revved, cutting over the asphalt at speeds not really legal. Aurora gave a happy little growl and snuck her nose out of the crack in the window again. Sixty more miles sped under the tires of the classic car, and Simeon silently praised Hector's automotive skills. He tapped his watch's buttons in a cadence asking for Vincent to come online, and slid the mini earbud in his ear.

"Hey Sim," Vincent's voice broke over the instrument. He sounded tired, and a little depressed. Worn, Simeon amended, and a frown cut over him. A plane's engine roared in the background of the call.

"Made it out?" Simeon asked.

"Yeah, G and I are on our way to Riyadh to meet up with the others. We snagged a Learjet 45 at the local airport, and I forgot how slow normal planes go compare to Perry. But we're getting there. We brought the Italian egg along to dissect and see what we can learn. I haven't decided what to call it."

"Egbert," Simeon supplied. A laugh broke from Vincent, and Simeon felt justified in his corniness.

"Thanks, Sim, I needed that," the inventor chuckled.

"Rough?" Simeon asked, concern dripping from the word.

"Oh, the work wasn't bad. I made us a couple of gadgets for the Egberts, I put the specifications up on our site[32]."

"Good job," Simeon praised. "Send them to Heshman?"

"Sure..." Vincent said his voice absent. "There, done. He's got the schematics with a request to get it done ASAP. I'm assuming that means you're expecting trouble wherever you're headed."

"Always expecting trouble. Anything else to report?"

"Gigan got to punch some people and yell at his twin. I think that helped a little. But he's depressed and tired and I can't blame him. He's asleep right now, pretty deep due to some blood loss, he got winged by an assassin on the Lef– his family's roof." A deep sigh flew from the inventor. "Sim, this old world is just...sad."

"Oh the sorrow of the world," Simeon said softly, quoting a Jojo phrase.

"Yeah. It all breaks so easily!" Vincent burst out. "We work so hard, and then everything we do is just so...fragile, so quick to get destroyed."

"Good things are fragile. But the good we see around us is very good, Vince. We work hard to preserve the small pieces we can, and it makes a difference. And the best in life can't be

---

[32] I accessed the Parabaloni site once and found a crepe recipe and a picture of Aurora and Abir being cute alongside a report dealing with gruesome guerrilla warfare in Columbian red zones. It's that kind of a site.

completely broken. Hurts for Gigan to go home because his family is still his. Pete and Jojo rushed to Riyadh because their brother is still a brother that needs them, and their love doesn't waver. Even death doesn't take away the good that came from the living. Don't let the dark blot out the light. It might be a tiny dot in a vast field of black. But the darker the night, the brighter that dot burns."

The roar of the engine drifted over the feed, and Simeon just let Vincent think. He wished he could be there to see his face.

"You're always right," Vincent murmured. A sniffle hung behind the words.

"Not always," Simeon said softly, and hundreds of failures paraded through his mind. "But God's big enough to catch what we miss and carry all the broken pieces. He even takes those pieces and makes beauty."

"Like a mosaic," Vincent sniffed.

"Or a kaleidoscope," Simeon agreed, a little smile crinkling his brown eyes. "Pray, Vince. Always."

"Yeah. Thanks Sim." A sharp sniff came from him. Then his voice came stronger, more like his normal self. "We're about four hours out still, I can only press this jalopy so fast. Where are you? Your white horse isn't prancing around New Mexico anymore."

"Headed to Memphis."

"Huh, actually stopping at Heshman's. I'm assuming that means Algy still hasn't answered. But isn't he in some little town in Tennessee?"

"Been living in Northhaven."

"But you're headed to Memphis..."

"Using my own tracking skills," Simeon supplied. "Pete and Jojo found the Clempson kid and their brother. Got a little catching up, maybe. Kid has a bag full of explosives."

"A small bag?"

"No."

"Great."

"Not on a timer, inert."

"That is actually great."

"Vince, watch your backs, double check your areas. This is a nasty creep playing god, likes to leave surprises."

"Any other advice?"

"Might try Little Abdullah."

"Oh yeah, good thought." A long yawn broke over the speaker. "Well, this thing has a decent autopilot. I'm going to catch a light nap. Keep in touch, Sim."

"Will when I can. Vince, good job being their support."

"Yeah," Vincent murmured. He silently wondered again why Simeon wasn't here doing that. Vincent opened his mouth to ask what he had missed. But Simeon's voice came first, and it was laced with a tension that meant it took an effort to broach the subject.

"Vince? Headed to Iowa Friday. To take Susie out."

Several replies flew through Vincent's mind, the first one a tease about being careful using the phrase "take out" in their line of work. But it was swallowed in a smile. He felt that smile too, deep inside him.

"It's about time," he said. A sharp, short laugh burst from Simeon. "Do I get to meet her this trip, or should I wait till later?"

"Want to?"

"Whenever it's right. I figure I'll have plenty of time in the future to meet the lady," Vincent said.

"Take it you're all right with my moving it forward."

"Dude, if you approve her she must be pretty great. And I've always liked the sound of it."

"Of what?"

"Sim and Sue. You'll have an easy time monogramming your towels, but a difficult time figuring out whose S is whose."

"Joker," Simeon commented, and Vincent smiled in the plane cruising toward Arabia. His natural grin smoothed the lines off his freckled face.

"That leaves me in a conundrum about a wedding present though. I've promised G and Pete their own private planes so they can take their bride wherever they want. But you and your complaints about height, maybe a reliable pilot you can take along? Though where I'll buy one you approve of–"

"Oh stop," Simeon broke in. "Push too hard, you'll make me

regret telling you about Friday."

"All right, all right," Vincent grinned. "But you know you would tell me anyway. You promised."

"I would," Simeon said, and let it carry enough melancholy regret, he made his boy laugh again. "Fly safe," he ordered, and signed off.

The sun rose a little higher, and Simeon watched it chase the shadows away. But there would always be some that stayed hidden, behind trees, and even under beautiful shiny things like good cars. A frown cut over Simeon as he pushed the pedal down a little harder.

This job ate away at even the hardiest of souls. Finding out about his parents on top of the rest of the work was finally pushing Vince too hard. Their inventor needed a way to get some real time off. They all did.

Chapter 16

Jojo laboriously turned the last key in the last hidden lock on Perry's outer wall. The metal dug into her hand, and she tried not to grunt too loudly. Colin stood watching with what seemed to be a permanent blank look, attempting to hide his bewildered surprise. The key clicked, finally, and the door popped open an eighth of an inch. Jojo pulled her k-bar out of her boot and levered on the oval door. It stuck. She hoped Pete took care of this blackout soon and Perry could go back to his bad jokes as she worked her blade under the metal catch and tried to flip it open.

The airport was weirdly deserted. With the air traffic comms down and the electrical systems cut off, no one flew in or out of Riyadh. Everyone had just gone home. Those who hadn't already been home when the blackout hit, anyway.

Home. Jojo barely held back a sigh. So close… She wanted to see them, to walk the old streets, and laugh with her siblings, and gain all the news, and feel her mother's arms around her! But now her father knew she was with Peter. He knew she was a Christian. Getting caught and murdered would not help the little ones. She couldn't go home.

Colin wondered why she swept her hand over her eyes like that. A part of him inside twisted and his hand twitched to lay it on her shoulder and tell her it would all be ok. He rubbed his hand and looked away. How did he know it would all be ok? The billions of stars from his flight down here blazed in his memory and a shiver ran down his spine. This universe was so vast, and their tiny little lives so small and short and tangled. His throat tightened and he couldn't say it would be ok. Jojo levered on the knife and the door cracked open an inch. She grunted as she pushed. Colin reached for the crack in the door and wedged his fingers into it. This he could help with.

A sharp heave from the tall kid, and the door swung open with a protesting creak.

"Man, this thing ever get oiled?" Colin asked through gritted teeth as he forced it open the rest of the way.

"It's not supposed to be done manually," Jojo said. She

hopped up in the body of the plane and Colin watched her pluck her head covering off with an impatient huff and fling it into the corner of – was that a living room? Colin heaved himself inside and looked around. He had been in private planes before. But as he shuffled into a kitchen with espresso stains on the counter and a cat food bowl half shoved under the sink he knew this didn't even come close to that kind of classification. His eye ran over the leather furniture going-to-shabby, and an open door with a glimpse of a comforter wadded up on a bunk. This was a home. But for whom?

The roar of an engine broke into the strange silence of the morning. It moved over them, growing lower and louder. Colin crossed to a window as Jojo headed for the small kitchenette. She pulled out four mugs, Colin noticed. A jet plane touched down on one of the many empty runways in the dead airport. It slowed quickly, but kept taxiing. It headed straight for them, and Colin couldn't help wondering if it would run into this plane home. If it tried, this place would probably man its own cybernetic strike force and blast it off the earth. Colin spun to the young woman in the kitchen staring at coffee grounds with a smolder in her eye that said she would rather do her own grinding with her teeth today.

"I'm just going to ask it," he burst out, "who are you people?"

"We are an elite team sent in to fix broken things," Jojo said.

"Not enough people in the world to do that," Colin muttered under his breath as he turned back to the window. Her eyes blazed into his back.

"Things will be fixed," Jojo snapped. Colin spun back to her, his lip between his teeth; he hadn't meant his comment to be heard. "The heaven and earth will be made new, the curse will be reversed, and all will be a perfect paradise where God and man walk together. And that's a future reality as real as the floor you're standing on right now, Colin. What we do is bring a tiny glimpse of that to a world still breaking from the curse of pain and sin. Good people make a difference. It may be a small one in the face of bad odds, but we can make a difference. Don't let the sorrow of the world overrun your hope. If you love Jesus, that hope is as real and firm as the sorrow, and it will win."

"You're so sure of all that," Colin commented. His dark eyes studied her and he let his curiosity show. But nothing else. She couldn't guess what went on inside him.

French complaints rattled through the dry air, and both their attention went to the open door. A short wiry form heaved himself up. His mustaches bristled, and one arm lay strapped against his chest in a sling.

"Why is this door open?" he snapped. "Jojo, you are in Riyadh, deadened though it may be you still can't just enjoy the fresh breeze—"

"Oh shush, Bouncy," Jojo sighed, suddenly simply horribly tired. "We just got here, I saw you landing. Your worry is sweet, but give me some credit for not being stupid."

"All right, sorry," Gigan said, his hand going up in apology. She pushed a mug of iced coffee into it, and Gigan's expression shifted to delighted relief. He took a sip and the stress lines seemed to melt and his tight shoulders slumped. As the stress that bristled his mustaches left, everything drooped into an exhausted grief. It seemed an integral part of him. Her French buddy looked ten years older than when she met him seven months ago. Oh, the sorrow of the world… Jojo grew very still.

"What do you want, Gigan?" she asked softly. It wasn't a demand. It came as a real question, her eyes distant as she stared at the wall and saw something that wasn't there.

"A refill," Gigan murmured around his mug. "I hope there's more. And thank you." He spun on one heel and Colin suddenly found icy gray eyes staring into his own. "Bouncy" did not fit this man. "We have a heavy egg in the plane. Would you be willing to lend a hand, as I only have one right now?"

"Sure," Colin murmured and followed the little Frenchman toward the door.

Jojo stayed stock still by the coffee pot. A refill. That didn't help. Well, it only helped temporarily.

Everything but Jesus was temporary.

That fact shot through her like a lightning bolt, and mingled with the truths she had just spoken to Colin. They rammed into the soul-breaking sorrow of being so close and unable to go home, till the sorrow burnt in the blaze of the Son. She *could* go home; if she recanted and came back to Allah and was a good Muslim. But that wasn't what she wanted, bile rose at just the thought of it.

She wanted Jesus.

He held everything she really wanted in the palms of His scarred hands, and nothing could pluck her from His grasp. As she stood beside the overworked coffee machine Jojo remembered it again. Everything but that central, blazing fact of Jesus holding her fast burnt away. Human love changed with death, or disagreements, or even just time. Jesus never changed. Righting the world remained a beautiful goal, but she couldn't even start to help people without bringing Jesus with her.

Jojo Aziz smiled through her tears as the familiar Riyadh sun poured into her temporary home. She knew what she wanted. And He was more than enough. Jojo swiped a hand over her eyes and headed to open the garage door for the fellows, her head high. She knew what she wanted. And she knew she was needed today, right here, right now. Take it step by step. She could figure out where her happy place existed while she worked, right here and right now.

Colin hopped out onto the asphalt after the Frenchman and walked toward the small plane. What on earth was a heavy egg? The pilot's door shoved open and Colin paused mid step as the tall Vincent Lee Tolliver unfolded himself from the pilot's seat. He gave a smile as he leaned against the plane and regarded the young man.

"Hi again," Vincent said. Colin couldn't think of a thing to answer. But his face broke into a brilliant smile. What were the odds?

Jojo's little speech clicked in place with Vincent's comments at the socialite gathering last month, like gears churning together in perfect unity. The odds were actually pretty good. Only someone with a faith in something bigger would be willing to step out and try to make a difference in the face of the darkness that seemed to overwhelm at every turn in this old world. And how many people in America actually believed like *that* anymore? Believed strong enough to live it, pour their time and money and energy into changing things…

Could *he* actually help? The stars blazed in his memory and a part of him whispered, "What's the point?" But another part, like a new seedling slowly unfurling as dawn breaks, whispered, "There might actually be a point to everything."

The small plane's loading doors swung open and Colin stepped back just in time to keep it from smacking him in the face. A gleaming silver casing in the shape of an egg lay on its side.

"That looks really heavy," Colin heard himself comment as his brain buzzed with new ideas.

"Yep," Vincent nodded. "You get that side."

Simeon coasted past the old fashioned house set in the pretty garden. Dormant rose bushes climbed up a trellis set over a patio filled with tables and chairs and winter ice. Bushes marked out a maze behind the two story cottage, and Simeon eyed it speculatively. He went around the block once, turned into a side street, and parked the corvette convertible in front of an art studio. He let Aurora out to sniff a tree, and studied the scene. He couldn't see any enemies or obvious traps at that two story house. But there were no people there either.

Of course, a display of antique English greeting cards would hardly draw a large crowd in a town like Memphis. But this was a one weekend only display, before it moved on to the next city. Simeon had nearly missed the connecting link. Tucked away in the description of the display was the name of the main artist, Penelope Bentley; Algy's wife's grandmother. Algy didn't care about such things. But his wife Elene had. He would come, for her sake.

Coincidence to have *that* display so close to where Algy lived? Yes. But one subtle enough Algy wouldn't be suspicious. Just subtle and deadly enough for a man like Mr. Black.

Simeon whistled Aurora to heel and walked up the street. The corgi trotted happily beside him. No one watched him that he could tell.

A pair of middle aged women stepped out of a cupcake shop as he stopped at the corner, and began to gush over Aurora. Simeon moved a finger telling Rora she could go. The dog leapt off, bouncing all over them, her tail nub wiggling like something with a life by itself. The ladies didn't have the right muscle tone to be fighters, or the type of clothing that could hide a decent weapon. Simeon only partially paid attention to their little shrieks and laughs as the corgi shed all over their shoes and tried to eat their to-go boxes. Instead he used the time to study the building. They walked off toward their cars and Simeon called Rora to heel again. She leapt to obey, licking the last of the frosting off her black lips.

"Mercenary," Simeon told her. The foxy ears flicked back and she grinned at him, her tongue hanging out. Simeon shook his head and walked across the street. The awning over the patio cast a shadow over him as his eyes swept everything. His shoes crunched on the gravel path as Aurora padded beside him. Simeon froze in mid step, staring at the path. The dog stopped so suddenly she sank back on her haunches. She completed the move, plopping on her backside as she waited.

A line bulged across the path. Just a small hump running under the gravel. Another lay two feet in front of it, and one more a foot after that. Perfect to catch different gates, almost assuring one of the humps would be brushed by someone walking this path.

"Stay," Simeon told his dog. She dropped obediently to her belly and stared at her master. Simeon gauged his distance, shifted his weight, and leapt. He landed beyond the three hidden trip wires, not trusting the spaces in between. It would be just like Black to lay decoys and put pressure plates in between the wires to catch those who thought they were smart.

He was close enough to see in the windows now. Antique furnishings sat tastefully strewn about a living room, set off by salmon-colored wallpaper cut through with golden diamond shapes. Algernon Fitzkin sat cross-legged in the center of the floor. Very still. Three trip wires wrapped around him in a tight tornado of black lines. A pair of black gentleman's gloves acted as a very thorough gag. Algy's eyes seared into Simeon's through the windowpane. The Englishman blinked, rapidly, then slowly, rapid again, nothing moving except his eyelids. Simeon followed the morse easily.

Attic.

He gave Algy a nod to say he understood, motioned Aurora to stay still, and leapt for the bricks on the old cottage. He scaled it in three seconds, and carefully, slowly pushed the round antique window open. It spun on a pole embedded in the center, and Simeon slid through and dropped in a crouch on the old wood of the attic. It creaked and groaned under him. His little pistol glinted in the clean light as he swept the triangular room. No dust cloud spurted up around him. Someone used this place, recently.

Nothing moved. His watch showed no living things up here.

But a pile of TNT sat in the corner. A pile that reached nearly to his chest.

A simple timer was shoved into the pile, and three black wires ran into it. Simeon made a quick, thorough sweep of the rest of the place, making sure there were no more surprises. Then he bolted for the pile and his wire cutters sprung into his hands. The lines were taut inside the timer. Whoever placed this trap had gambled with his own life. And been very, very certain of Algy's ability to remain perfectly still[33]. Simeon gently pinched the timer and drew it from the stack centimeter by centimeter. Sweat trickled down his spine as he reached for the wires with his cutters and prayed his dog obeyed. This would make a crater in the garden if it went off. There wouldn't even be a trace of him and Algy for his boys to track. Simeon pinched the first wire and squeezed, being oh so careful to keep the trigger still. The wire sprung in two, the long end curling on itself like a demented cross between a ribbon and a snake. Simeon reached for the second and a sharp

---

[33] He has been taken for a statue on many occasions, and people all over the world have found him the most dangerous piece of art they ever met. Once he was accepted as a bush for three days before erupting in leaves and branches and bullets. The German spies he surprised could never face another bush without a shudder.

twang was muffled by the old wood of this cottage. He breathed out slowly, evenly, keeping his muscles from tightening as he reached for the third. It sprang back and coiled around the other two. Simeon let himself puff out a breath of relief. He still held the timer with a gentle touch, keeping it absolutely still.

"Done. Rora, inside!" Simeon called, and heard the sound of his dog leaping up and springing across the gravel to find her way in. If Algy couldn't hear him from up here, he would see the dog run by and know he was safe to move. Sim very gently began to unpack the pile of TNT with one hand as he held the timer still with his other.

Mr. Black would not be satisfied with one activation method.

As he worked, Simeon analyzed what he saw. The timer was set to go off in two hours and twelve minutes. A random time? Or was something coupled with that? Mr. Black liked to have things play off of other things in his games. But this stack of TNT piled haphazardly felt random, like the similar stack in the lab in Libya. Precision and planning didn't reign here, just an unholy delight in destruction.

Glass crashed and tinkled downstairs, coupled with a sharp huff from Aurora. She chose to make a way in today. He could hear her claws clicking over the wooden floors as she trotted into the living room. Simeon gently pulled off eight more sticks of explosives and laid them neatly in his own pile. Algy's hoarse voice echoed up from downstairs in a series of strong words and conversation with the dog. Simeon pulled off twelve more sticks, and found the second trigger. A simple stick wired to the timer. If he had pulled it out of the pile, the whole thing would have ignited. He flipped his wire cutters, sent up a quick prayer for Vincent and the others, and started to snip. In twenty seconds he had it all deactivated, and as inert as a pile of explosives could be. He headed down the old fashioned stairs.

The wood on the landing let out a squeal. Aurora gave a chewing alarm bark and barreled toward him. She rounded the corner to the stairs with every hair raised and a thick growl. Then she saw her man. Her ears slicked back and she took the rest of the stairs in three bounds, her rear wiggling like crazy. She gave his hand a quick lick then bounded back to the ground level and spun to him with the hair-trigger reflexes of a cattle dog, staring with a "hurry up already" expression. Simeon tried not to sigh over how young she felt and how creaky he was and just walked into the living room. Algy looked up at him, and Simeon knew he at least felt more alive than his friend right now.

"Rora is good at taking out a gag, but she still needs work on 'find the wire cutters,'" Algy croaked.

"I'll add it to her training," Simeon said. He knelt on the ground beside him and started to use the wire cutters again. "Who?"

Algy's head drooped and his haggard face gained more lines. A tingle ran through Simeon; it seemed he would actually find some answers today.

Chapter 17

Pete let his rifle dangle on its shoulder strap and switched his pistol clip for live bullets. He couldn't count on a sneaky person like this Knife Lady to offer him a shot with bare skin for his plunger bullets. He pulled his Sam mask tighter over his head and padded toward the machine Knife Lady had ducked behind. His senses strained to catch any sign of her. A sound, a smell, a telltale movement...

The steady "whoomph, whoomph" pulsed from the egg. Pete had to force his eyes not to wander toward the silver. It captivated with its shiny menace.

A whisper of sound, of air moving at a high velocity, swept toward him. Pete dropped to one knee, his heart pounding. A heavy blow glanced off the top of his mask, and Pete's head sang. A flash of metal twinkled in the light as a throwing knife skidded into the floor. He swept his bag in front of him and rushed in the direction the blade had come from. A sharp "ping" rang as a knife glanced off the edge of his pack and slashed his shirt. But then Pete made it into view of the Knife Lady's cover.

Adeela, his pistol, spoke with a deafening bang, invading the steady pulse of the egg. Knife Lady flung herself backward at the same instant. He saw his bullet clip her shoulder and heard a sharp gasp from behind the machine. Pete shuffled forward, his pistol held steadily in front of him, ready to fire. He spun around the machine.

Empty space greeted him. Nothing but shadows between two hulking transformers. Pete's eyes flicked to his left. Darkness seeped from a sort of aisle created by giant coils of extra cables. A single drop of bright red blood gleamed on the first of those coils. Pete moved inside, shifting in a silent professional shuffle, every sense straining.

This wasn't a hunted versus hunter situation. They both hunted here.

Pete spun around the first of the two giant coils, his pistol ready. A whisper of movement came from his right. Pete flung himself backward, as his pistol swiveled toward the area. A knife blade slammed into his throat with a force that sent stars sparking behind his eyelids and brought a gagging cough from him. But the Sam met his vest seamlessly, and the blade didn't penetrate.

His pistol flashed in the same instant the knife blade hit, and for a moment the world lit around Pete with the muzzle flash. He saw a red curl flutter three coils in front of him.

Pete dashed forward, holstering his pistol and shifting silently into the deeper shadows to his left. He shot past the area, not into it. He couldn't be predictable to this kind of enemy. He crouched, staring at the area he had seen the curl. Was that movement just beyond it? Yes. She had slipped out, and waited one coil ahead of him. Pete watched as the faintest silhouette of a head with long wavy hair leaned into the aisle created by the giant coils, looking for him. Pete slid his knife from the sheath on his arm.

Her head snapped toward him. Pete swung his pack in front of his face. His knife snapped out of his hand. A sharp thwack hit his pack, and a sharper ping of metal against metal came from the aisle in front of him. Pete whipped his pack down and darted forward. His knife lay on the ground, another blade under it. The woman had knocked his away with one of her own. She had serious skill.

Pete darted out of the aisle back into the main room, Adeela in his left hand, his knife held loose and ready to snap off in his right. His gaze swept the area. Fresh air and sunlight cut through the scene and he spun toward the door out.

He just spotted the tail of a red curl disappearing as the door swung closed. Pete darted forward, praying he wouldn't be too late to tell where she went to ground, dreading a cat-and-mouse with a knife thrower in the massive grounds of this power plant complex. The noise of a squeaky wheel reached him. Pete stood to the side and looked out the window set in the door. A slim woman with luscious red curls tumbling down her back rode swiftly off on Pete's bicycle. She headed toward the main road. She kept riding, never turning to show her face. The set to her shoulders and the speed she moved didn't seem worried, more like...contented. As if she had done what she meant to. Pete turned slowly and looked around the building.

Black figures littered it like fallen logs. The hose pulled over their heads made them seem like creepy uniform automatons, as if their personalities had been wiped away. He glanced out the window again. Knife Lady was doll sized now, turning onto the main road into Riyadh. He watched her pick up the pace, her hair a fiery streak behind her. She still never looked back. Surely she wouldn't bomb the place with her companions here. Pete spun to look up at the catwalk.

"Surely she would not bomb the place with so many of their own here," he said.

"Oh, she would," Gigan answered, strolling out onto the metal catwalk. His arm lay in a sling strapped against his chest. "They seem to delight in death, in removing more of the human plague. But she would not, I think, blow it with that egg there." He stirred a fallen man's arm with his toe and watched it thunk back down. The man's blowgun rolled off the catwalk and tumbled to the concrete ground of the lower story. Gigan leaned on the railing and swept the room with his gaze. "I do not think you need my help this time."

"The Black Tortoise of Doom feels justified for the fiasco in Tripoli."

"You are the Black Turtle Man, there is no doom involved, and it wasn't a fiasco because the Bird Man swept in just in time."

"Meh, should have been twenty minutes earlier and saved me a few bullet wounds."

"I can give you some fresh ones if you like."

"I'm good, thanks. Actually, I was hoping to have someone else offer to shoot me."

"I can call Jojo," Gigan suggested as he started to walk down the stairs.

"*Dummkopf,* listen. Mr. Black is here in Riyadh, I came up against him in Masala's bomb shop. He murdered Masala. He seems…" Pete's face wrinkled as if he were trying to put something into words. "…very good at what he does. I hoped to draw him out by coming here and making trouble, to try and learn more, or maybe even catch him. But he did not come. And the best of the lot, a red-haired Knife Lady, just stole my stolen bike and pedaled away."

"Borrowed."

"What?"

"We do not steal, you know that, we borrow and do our best to return."

"Gigan, we have a silver egg still 'whoomphing,' a lady running away from this place, twenty-three bad guys who will wake in roughly forty minutes, a murderer on the hunt for us, and some nasty plot to unearth and stop. I am not concerned about returning a bike to someone who had a perfectly good car sitting in their driveway. Put your handmaiden of philosophy away, and let's get on with it!"

"Ethics, not philosophy," Gigan muttered under his breath, as he stomped down the stairs and moved toward the egg. He spun on one leg, and waggled a finger at his partner. "It matters. Especially when more important things are going on around you, it matters whether you care enough to be good in even the small things." Pete threw his arms up in dramatic despair.

"Fine, I did not steal it. I will replace the bike when I can!"

"You know you remember the address you took it from."

"All right, all right, just blow up the egg and let's get on with it." He didn't say what they both knew; Gigan's extra sensitiveness to the commands meant his family troubles paraded through the Frenchman's mind. Pete's eyes went to his buddy's wounded arm and he wondered who had fired the bullet. His mind flew to his father, and uncles, and a few of his aunts, the plenty of people in his own life who wouldn't be joking about shooting him. Pete's shoulders slumped. He stepped over fallen shadows and followed Gigan toward the egg. The Frenchman knelt near the strand of wires running from the egg and took a clamp out of his pocket.

"Peter, this Black and his Collective are the nasty sort who like to hide surprises," Gigan ordered, "make a sweep while I set up the deactivation device on this thing. I hope."

"The Bird Man is not so sure of himself, I see," Pete commented as he pulled his pack around. A knife blade stuck out of the backpack's seam, a perfect shot at the only place it might penetrate. He would have to get it repaired after this case. Pete stared at the blade. "Does it seem—"

"Yes, it is odd she aimed *for* the pack. Dust it for fingerprints."

"They would not be hers," Pete said as he carefully wrapped the knife handle, wrenched it free, tucked it in his pack, and reached for his lights.

"It will not be hers, but I do think it will be interesting," Gigan agreed as he carefully clipped the coupler over the wires. Pete clicked on his UV, infrared, and LED lights and started to sweep the room.

"Gross," he murmured, as he did every time he started a sweep with his lights. A smile flitted over Gigan's face at the familiar reaction from his partner. He shoved his shoulder into the egg, making it rock. Sparks shot from it through the cords and cut off in a sharp burst of fire at the clamp. He pulled the second gadget Vincent had given him from his pocket and stuck it on the silver; a concave disc with a simple switch. It fused to the egg's metal as it touched it. Gigan didn't flip the switch. He stepped back and studied the egg whoomphing in the dim light. It didn't just sit there. It loomed. Menacing, as if it sneered at everything not as shiny and smooth and perfect as its oval.

"Gigan?" Peter said, his tone suddenly hard. The Frenchman spun. A simple golfer's cap hung from Pete's hand. A tingle ran down Gigan's spine.

"Left by a worker, do you think?" Gigan asked. "It would not have been one of these shadows, they are obviously determined to be uniform."

"We are in Saudi Arabia, Gigan, this is not normal attire. And while there are foreigners, there's no reason one of them would have been here. The plaid pattern isn't random, I've seen it somewhere..." Pete's eyes closed and Gigan knew he sorted through facts filed away in his mind, small things he never thought would be needed. His eyes popped open and they shone. "Sean."

Gigan's finger shot out and hit the switch on the disc adhered to the silver egg. The "whoomph" grew deeper, then died into silence. Gigan jerked his phone out of his pocket, staring mesmerized at the screen as it slowly rebooted. Finally the phone sprayed light and it was ready. Pete winced. The white backlight felt surprisingly bright and obnoxious after the hours without screens. Gigan quickly connected the phone to the Tolliver satellites that worked nearly anywhere in the world, and hit Sean's number. His ears sang and he begged God to let the big Irishman answer the phone.

"You want a camera for each of these people," Jones told his employer. A frown crossed his face as he watched Luther Kirl keep spinning his chair in half-circles; his employer didn't seem to be listening. Luther Kirl gave a little huff of annoyance, like a five-year-old told he was wrong, and looked up with a glare. Jones just kept checking over the camera, refusing to think about how easy it would be for this man to shoot him in the belly and pay people to cover it up. "You don't use just one shot on a live filming, you have different shots so you can switch to the camera where the action is when needed."

"That is one reason you're here, you know," Luther said, a little petulant. "You will understand the actions of men of action and be able to track it."

"Sure, I know how men fight. But I'm still concerned about the sound."

"It isn't your job to be... Oh fine, that is actually your job," Luther said. His mood changed with the sudden flip that Jones found extremely unnerving, and the old man cackled like a rooster. "Fine, fine, you will have your four cameras for the four Parabaloni. You are sure you can make this work in the dark?"

"Yes, these have excellent night visibility." Jones smiled, his big hands gentle as they ran over the camera, as if it were a favorite dog. "But the sound from so high up—"

"We can't get closer, I keep telling you!"

"But why?" Jones blurted out. "You've told me you want this to be a good show, whatever this is. Why are we using practically satellites and spy cameras?"

"You can do it, can't you?"

"I can pull in enough with these you'll be able to see what goes on, and I can probably even catch expressions and moods. But all of that is just pantomime without the sound."

"Fine, I will call in a technician to do something about the sound," Luther grimaced.

"Can I practice with this one?" Jones asked quickly, and Luther cackled again. He made a shooing motion toward the door.

"Go play with your toy, Jones. But remember if you get caught as a peeping tom, I'm not bailing you out, and if you break it you're paying for it!"

Jones actually grinned at the old man. He hefted the camera onto his shoulder and headed out to see what he could spot with it in Hyde Park.

And report to his real employer. Spy cameras for four pairs of bolognas in a fight, set in an undefined location for an undefined time… Jones had at least a small tidbit to report. He just wished he understood it!

Chapter 18

The last wire around Algy's arms sprang free. Simeon pulled a thermos from his pack and poured a stream into the lid. The scent of thick, sugary English Breakfast tea filled the living room, and a short laugh broke from Algy.

"Of course you even came with tea," he commented, and took it from his old friend. He lifted the lid in a salute. "Cheers, mate. And thank you." A quiet moment passed as Simeon didn't interrupt Algy's enjoyment of good tea after a rough night, and just finished clipping the wires. The last one sprang back and Algy carefully stretched his legs. He held out the lid for a second cup and Simeon obliged as he helped him to the couch. He noticed Algy's hand shook and reached for his package of nuts and jerky.

Two minutes, four cups, and some protein later, the two sat still on the pretty pink settee. Algy stared at his empty cup. Simeon didn't push. Aurora rammed her nose into Algy's hand in an impatient demand to be petted. The Englishman sighed, scratched her ear, and sat up.

"I can feel you not pushing," Algy said.

"So?" Simeon pushed, one hand flaring in a demand.

"Always so gentle and patient with your friends, until that curiosity of yours creeps in," Algy said, a smile flitting over his face. It disappeared. "Yes, I knew the voice. He didn't so much confess it, as... Oh, I'll start at the beginning, when I first found him. You never met him, you were in deep cover in Croatia during that phase of life."

"Good times," Simeon murmured. He had come back to the West fourteen years ago. The memory of why he flew West fluttered into his brain, and Simeon sat still, coaxing it back. All of it back. A dark night, with storm clouds and pouring rain and an even, unemotional voice... He remembered now, Algy had just handed him the key. One more violent hunt in a lifetime of violent hunts. This Mr. Black had a longer beginning than he suspected. A sharp sigh blew from Algy, he sat up, and launched into it. His thick British fit neatly in the elegant setting and antique greeting cards. But the story hardly matched the scene.

"We were in Germany at the time, in self-exile hiding from Bruno and his East End thugs. I ended up in the local bobbie's station due to getting some judo practice on a shop-lifter and questions from the constabulary, you know how it goes. There was a young man there in a holding cell because no one knew what to do with him. Bloodied, but not with his own, without much more than a blanket someone had tossed him. Apparently he had wandered out of the Black Woods and into the backstreets a few days before, and that morning the gangs had found him. He left four dead before the bobbies intervened. He said his name was 'John,' he was sixteen, and no, he wasn't cold. Nothing else. Blast it, Aimie[34], I should have known right then, with his intense stare and unemotional voice, I should have known better..."

"You took him home," Simeon prodded.

"Yes. Alice had just gotten married, we were a bit bored and missing young things company, and he just looked so... lost. He was very keen to learn what I could teach him. We spent most of the days out walking the towns and woods, and I poured my knowledge into him. It was like filling a dry sponge. He taught me a thing or two about stealth and wood-craft, too. He never called me anything but 'Sir,' and he never gave much of a response at all to Elene when she tried to spoil him. He didn't want to live in the house with us, he usually slipped out to a lean-to he built in the backwoods of our little

---

[34] A note for any who don't recognize this name. When Algy met Simeon, he wasn't a Simeon. At that time Sim worked under the name Aimerie Carmicheal, and was one of the best "up and coming" singers in London, in both the operatic and pop music crowd. That phase of life ended, and Simeon Lee became his real name*. But Algy still prefers Aimerie, or Aimie for short.

*Yes, that's actually his real name, he has an authentic birth certificate for it. No one cares the dates on his certificate and the day he celebrates his birthday don't quite match, so it's official.

property. He never told me his story. And every time I called him 'John' it felt like using an alias. The only time I saw him smile was during munitions classes." A deep sigh flew from Algy again. "I should have known better and stopped the teaching. A part of me did, I even mentioned it to Elene once or twice. But you draw close to someone you train. When you spend that one-on-one time with them every day, it's as if a part of yourself goes to them. As if you are creating an extension of yourself, something more than just you, and to toss him out on his ear..." Simeon's mind flew back to a night last month, when his three young men fought over the rules to a board game while Jojo's feet stuck off the edge of the couch waiting for them to finally shut up and play.

"I get it," was all he offered. But the tone came soft and gentle, and Algy knew he did get it. "What happened?" Algy stared at the ground, his tone the voice of someone wishing he didn't have to remember.

"After a year, 'John' slipped into our room in the middle of the night. He had kerosene and matches and a hatchet, and every intention of bashing my and Elene's faces in and burning the house down to remove the evidence he had ever been there. I know that was his intention because he told us so when I leapt at him and flipped on the light. Aimie, one of my main regrets in life is having given another monster the tools to break the world. Because I gave him everything I knew."

"Didn't give him everything," Simeon objected. "You and Elene lived for years."

"Well yes, there is that," Algy agreed. Hints of relief flowed in his tone. His friend didn't blame him, or even seem particularly concerned. "But it was one more reason we were hiding in the caucuses all those years. Aimie, he is a rotter to the core. With God in charge I can't say he is irredeemable, because our heavenly Father can do anything. But Elene did all that can be humanly done. You know how she was."

"Yes," Simeon agreed softly, remembering the second night he had met Algy's young wife. She had walked away from the party she was hosting, picked the lock on his door, and burst in as he curled on the guest bed sobbing his lungs out over the picture of a baby in someone else's arms. There had been no hesitation in Elene Fitzkin, no English embarrassment over a show of emotion, no worry over propriety. She knelt beside him and sang a lullaby about gentle, gospel love. He hadn't believed the message then. But it still calmed his wild sorrow and gave him back the sanity he had been losing before she came in. She had even coaxed the whole story out of him, something only one other person in his life managed when he didn't want to give it. Elene Fitzkin had always known just what was needed, and gave it with all her heart.

And yet this 'John' still tried to bash her head in with a hatchet.

"Algy, sometimes love isn't enough," Simeon said. "He would have learned without you. With you, he at least got the gospel with his training."

"I did give him that," Algy said quietly.

"This time?"

"Oh this time, as I'm sure you already know since you showed up with wire cutters and hot tea, I walked right into his arms with this silly little greeting card display. *Greeting cards*, Aimie, and I fell for it!"

"You came for Elene," Simeon soothed, and tipped his head to say go on.

"I don't have anything useful for you, I'm sorry. I got conked and came back around already nicely wrapped. I didn't see him. Well, no more than a hand. And the only comments he made were about you. He told me you *might* come. And something about how if you didn't it would all be your fault."

"Exact?"

"'It's so easy. If your good Mr. Lee doesn't come, he can watch the fun on the news, before even that falls victim. And he can know it's all his fault.' Nice chipper fellow, that. All right, break it to me, what's he been up to?"

The lights blinked off. Algy's eyes flicked to the bay window and noted all the store windows were just as dark. They watched the cars outside this antique house slowly slide to a stop. A confused murmur drifted through the panes as drivers stepped from the stalled cars. Algy held out the lid again. Steam drifted from the stream of dark liquid as Simeon filled it.

"I did meet him," Simeon commented.

"After he finished here?"

"No, fourteen years ago."

Both Algy's eyebrows went up.

"Came back from Croatia when I did because I got a tip someone was sniffing around Germany for you. Didn't know where you went to ground, so couldn't warn you, and came back to deal with it myself. Dealt with it, forgot it. The time afterward of just hiking and relaxing at the ski lodge is what stuck in my mind. Two whole weeks of peace without any kind of job to do is much more memorable in our kind of life."

"It is. And we deliberately try to forget the violence and remember the peace," Algy nodded slowly. "It's a survival technique built into us, I think. But now you have remembered. So how did you deal with this sniffer?"

"Took some doing, but I found him. Sort of. Tracked him down late, outside Munster. Light was failing. A storm rolled in, violent cold rain. We had a conversation out there as we hunted."

"Not the wild goats, I assume?" Algy murmured. "Let's hear it, mate, take me back with you[35]." Simeon's eyes closed and Algy watched him returning to the scene in his mind.

---

[35] Simeon's best friends (and the children at church) know his knack for storytelling. It stems from his avid reading and his poetic soul, and he has the power to transport those he chooses into his own places and memories. Saul and Algy used it many times to recreate scenes and help them solve especially tough cases. Vince stumbled on it by accident one time when in the Middle East and a roach crawled over Sim, and a simple question from Vince sent the whole tale bubbling out. Max, his little nurse friend, used it to learn what the nightmares stemmed from and help Sim come out of it. But Max always told the rest of us never to ask for what he learned. Vincent agrees.

The rain drowned the scent of the Black Woods. Every breath drew in freezing water droplets as the icy rain pounded into his trench coat. Nothing could keep it out, and the ice clung to his skin, wrapping around him as tight as the darkness of the night. The dark fell inky and complete. No lights from the small town broke into it, nothing but black night filled with the roar of the rain. A clap of lightning cut the sky in two and dazzled his eyes, and the thunder rolled with it.

A figure stood six feet in front of him.

A young man, medium, ordinary, muscles honed and in good condition. Stiff and straight, as indifferent to the icy rain pounding into his black hair as a marble statue. But his eyes… Those burned.

The lightning died and blackness filled the world.

"Why are you looking for Fitzkin?" Simeon called over the rain. A voice drifted from the dark. Unnaturally steady, worse than the automated tones that came from the hated computers and AI Simeon's colleagues flocked to; this was still human.

"He burns too bright." The voice stole closer. Simeon moved with it, his feet sliding silently backward over the wet grass.

"What's that mean?"

"He's so sure his goodness will fix it all." The voice came again, and it moved with Simeon. Staying just a few feet away, always in front of him. "He doesn't know the dark always wins."

A bolt of lightning lit the scene again, jagged and white, cutting the dark to shreds. The figure stood four feet in front of him. Those blue eyes burned into Simeon's. The light glinted off something metal peeking from the stranger's sleeve. Darkness closed again.

"Nature just called your bluff," Simeon said. "The dark is deep. But even in the night, light cuts in." He slid quickly four steps to the right, his little pistol sliding into his hand.

"Just a quick flash, then it dies." The voice came from right in front of him, now three feet away. "Everything dies. Everything can be killed. I know you, Aimie, you burn too. But I am lord of the dark, I break and it will not be made again. The whole world will know my work. And it's so easy."

'Let's see how easy you find me,' Simeon thought. But he said it by movement. The stocky agent shot forward. The stranger pulled a metal pipe from his sleeve and slashed at Simeon's head with quick arrogance. Simeon spun into the blow, caught the man's arm under his, and used his enemy's own bones and sinews to flip him on his head. The iron pipe sailed away into the rain and thumped harmlessly into the sodden grass. Then the pummeling began. The stranger knew how to fight. But he didn't have Simeon's experience, speed, or strength. It took ten minutes for it to turn to a running battle, with the stranger retreating toward the black blob of the woods looming in the darkness.

The rain pounded harder. Every breath sucked in icy water particles, and it blinded the senses. Simeon waded through churning mud, deaf to all but the howling wind and pounding water, wrapped in the dark night. This stranger could ambush him easily if the man stopped and used his head. And the ice clung to Simeon's skin[36]. He began to think fond thoughts of the ski lodge where his tattered duffle bag lay waiting for him on a warm bed. He had played long enough with this creep. His eyes sought the sky as he slid his little pistol into his hands again.

For the thousandth time he felt the desire tug at his atheistic heart to pray to the God of the weather. All he needed was light for one good shot. If only he could believe Algy and Max's God could really be good...

Something loomed in the dark to his right, and a vague sense of movement coupled with it. Simeon shifted his trajectory and charged, his thick shoulders squared, and his senses searching through the downpour.

A shaft of lightning cut through the sky. Iron girders holding up a powerline glinted in the flash. The black clothes of this stranger stood out in stark contrast as he clung to the bars ten feet over

---

[36] Simeon doesn't like the cold. It started in his formative years, being locked outside his foster family's house during a particularly harsh Virginia winter. A stint in Antarctica constantly battling frostbite, hunting for evil agents and searching for a new element hidden in the ice, added to it. Only the penguins sitting on his toes saved his foot.

Simeon's head, staring at his ruthless hunter.

"Death is so easy to bring," the stranger stated. The lifeless voice barely carried over the roaring rain. His hand moved, darting for something in his black coat. The lightning died, swallowed by a deafening clap of thunder. Simeon's pistol spoke. The flash lit the night in front of his eyes, as the gunshot melded with the thunder.

The soft thud of a body hitting the mud came from four feet in front of him. Mud splattered up onto Simeon's coat from the man's fall.

"Don't announce your shot before you take it," Simeon murmured into the night. He slid his pistol back in his pocket, turned his back on the night, and trudged off toward the ski lodge and his warm bed.

Silence spread in the living room, deep and full as the lights stayed dark.

"Lovely," Algy burst out. "I don't suppose you came back to see if he was dead?" Simeon shrugged.

"Wasn't concerned about saving souls then, but still knew life is precious. I chose not to make sure."

"You gave him a generous chance, that paid off for him it seems," Algy said. His hands flew up, one running through his hair in an exasperated movement. "'Lord of the dark,' honestly?"

"Going with Mr. Black now."

"That suits him much better. I take it he resents that you won, and he's been plotting revenge for the past fourteen years."

"Not sure it's just revenge..." Simeon said slowly. The two of them watched the street outside as the silence expanded around them. More drivers stepped out of their stalled cars, and the murmur from outside grew from confused to angry.

"I didn't think a blackout would take out the transportation too. Don't most cars act as faraday cages or something?" Algy commented.

"This one more of an EMP that just keeps attacking. Takes

out normal precautions." Simeon stood up and screwed the lid back on the empty thermos. "Come on. Have two hours to stop it here."

"Stop what?" Algy asked and watched Aurora spring up and trot two inches behind her master's ankles.

Simeon shrugged.

"Lovely," Algy murmured again. He stood up to follow and groaned.

Sean O'Leary's phone burst into a merry Irish jig. Gigan's photo (Clarice resting on one shoulder, his lips twisted in his teasing smile that sent his gray eyes twinkling) sprang up on his screen. Sean hoped it wasn't the "one phone call" from a Parabaloni arrested in some stinking hole in the Andes or something, he already had enough to do today. He swept up the phone and slid the call open.

"Sean, O'Leary," he told it.

"Get out," the bouncy Frenchman ordered. Only he didn't sound bouncy right now. He sounded scared.

"Anywhere in particular?" Sean asked. But he rose from his desk and was at his office door in two strides.

"Somewhere near you is a threat ready to go off," Gigan's voice came strained and fast, and that scared Sean more even than his words. He could hear the soft voice of the thin one saying something. "Probably a bomb." Sean's heart started to hiccup. But as the Irishman stepped through his door, none of his employees could tell the tingling going on inside him.

"Don't hang up," he murmured to the phone. Then his voice boomed through the offices of Tolliver Charities, Inc, reaching through closed doors and into every corner. "All right people, everyone out! Hang up the phones and skip it, I've just been informed there's a gas leak somewhere." Groans and complaints came from this blatant lie. Sean repeated it unabashedly, ushering people out with a firm, calm efficiency. The last things he wanted were panics or heroics. He swept little Nadia, the two-year-old who often visited her father at work, into his arms and moved with the family out the door. "Stop complaining about taking a half day, you strange people, and go party at the zoo or something!" he ordered the crowd in the parking lot. He handed Nadia to her mother, murmured something about making sure everyone had gone, and stepped back inside.

The door closed behind him, and he could feel the solitude close in. He could also feel his heart thundering inside him. Oh why didn't he work for some old millionaire who played golf?! His finger shook as he pushed the speaker on.

"Gigan, I have everyone out. Where is this bomb and how do I stop it?" he told his phone.

"Get out!" the Frenchman snapped, fury in the tone. Sean's jaw tightened as his voice came clipped and rushed.

"Look, our building backs up against an eight-story office building that's filled right now, and a launderers packed full on the other side. Even if I ran in and pulled the fire alarms, someone is going to get caught in this blast if I don't stop it. And also I have contact information for Christians and front line workers here that it's not safe to save online, and if I lose those I would lose them, and they might lose their lives. Stop arguing and talk to me!"

"I don't have time to access cameras, and Vince isn't here to do something clever," Gigan said, silently cursing Vincent's money man in round Shakespearian terms. Sean's reasoning and bravery were both sound; but that didn't make it any easier for Gigan and Pete, grouped tense and helpless, half a world away. "I can't remotely access your smartphone and run scans!"

"You are a scanner," Sean stated. He hit the button for video chat and started to stroll through his building. His pulse sang in his ears and it was not easy to go slowly. He prayed he wouldn't burst a blood vessel or have a heart attack before he could stop this threat. "What do you see?"

Half a world away the two Parabaloni saw unconscious

shadows fallen around a silent egg, a shaft of light from a dusty window making its silver almost glow. Gigan pulled the phone from his ear and stared at it as Pete stepped closer and looked over his shoulder. A notification popped up on the screen. Gigan punched it, trying to swallow all the words he wanted to say about the Irishman's national stubbornness. The picture came in skipping and fuzzy, then began to clear. They saw neat offices and a desk covered in scrawled papers. A phone off the hook and a box of old magazines. A wilting vine that Pete automatically noted needed magnesium in the soil, a ceiling fan that squeaked, and an overworked coffee pot.

"Is it something that ticks?" Sean asked, and it came out in almost a squeak. He cleared his throat self-consciously.

"No, Sean, most bombs don't tick," Gigan said, his teeth grinding together. "Just get out."

"Where is most likely?" Sean asked, and moved the phone as slowly and smoothly as he could manage.

"Is that a courtyard?" Gigan asked suddenly, squinting as he tried to make out what was through the sliding glass doors. Sean bounded across his office and flung open the door. He took a step onto the gravel walkway and stopped, his jaw dropping. He suddenly didn't need Gigan to tell him where to find the bomb.

Eight white rectangles of what looked like modeling clay stuck to the wall under each window facing the courtyard. Whoever had placed them managed to keep it just below the bushes, so you didn't see them unless you actively walked out into the courtyard. Red digital numbers counted down on a timer above each.

As he stood there gaping, the numbers shifted smoothly to forty. Then thirty-nine.

"Cut yellow!" Gigan and Pete shouted. The words came hoarse, almost a scream. Sean's brain registered the blue and yellow wires sticking into the top of the white putty. His hand dropped the phone and dove for his pocket knife. He dashed to the first before he even fully caught up with what the order meant, and found his fingers gripping a yellow wire and coming at it with his open knife. Sean felt the blade slide into his thumb as it jerked through the cord. But the numbers stopped counting. He darted to the next in line, barreling through the bush in the way. The clock read thirty-one seconds. At the third, it said twenty-six. Four marked twenty-one. Five counted down to eighteen before he stopped it. Sean heard himself gasping out gabbled prayers as he flung himself at the sixth. It ticked down to eleven seconds before the wire cut. Seven shifted to a terrifying single digit.

Sean threw himself over the last bush, and his knife cut through the final yellow cord, taking off a piece of skin a quarter inch deep with it. The timer blinked off at five seconds to spare.

Sean staggered upright, hyperventilating, the courtyard swaying like a ship at sea around him. He weaved his way toward the phone on the gravel path, his legs feeling like al dente noodles. Leaves and blood from his cut fingers dropped gently from him to the walkway. He picked up the phone with shaking hands and dropped into a crouch. His stomach churned and he knew his lunch wasn't going to stay inside him.

"Oy, five seconds to spare, not too shabby even for the likes of you," he said. The words came out in a steady drawl, and he laughed at himself inside. Sean had never realized how good of a liar he was.

"Not too shabby," Gigan agreed. Relief rang in the quiet huskiness of the words. He could hear Pete panting in the background. For a moment Sean felt a pang at having put them through that.

"I'll admit you blokes were right, I should have gotten everyone out earlier when Vincent first called. That was too close." Further apology for ignoring Gigan's order to run rose to the Irishman. Then his eyes lifted to the office building, and he saw people moving about their workday behind the windows. They were close enough he could make out hair clips and garish ties. He didn't apologize. "What was it for?" he asked instead. He closed his eyes and dropped heavily to sit cross legged on the gravel. "Are my people all right? Do I need to find safe homes for them or something?"

"They should be fine," Gigan answered, steady again, his accent strong. Sean opened his eyes and surveyed the smashed bushes and leaves littering everything. "You were targeted for your work."

"They do not like you helping people," the Saudi added.

"Don't bring your people back in. Stay remote for a while. In fact, it might be a good idea to gift them a few days off."

"We can do that," Sean said, silently thankful to have a day or two to recover from this forty second trial. "What do I do with the bombs?"

"We know a man in town."

"Of course you do. Right then, I'll just go get a few stitches in my thumb, and leave you to it then, shall I?"

"Your people should be fine. You, I honestly don't know. If you notice anything out of the ordinary, run to the police. I'm texting you a good safe house nearby, which we would all love if you would take us up on. Either way take care, Sean, and watch your back."

"You too." As the phone went dead, Sean found himself fervently wishing he knew where the Parabaloni were, why Vincent wasn't with those two, and what he meant by that single sentence. Targeted by who? And which work, Tolliver Charities bubbled over with different jobs, adding more ways to help people almost every day. Was it related to that matter with Vincent's parents? Sean swallowed the questions and rose slowly to his feet. By now he knew not to bother asking. He would get some fool answer, and be glad he didn't know most of what actually went on with the case. But as he wrapped his bleeding hand in his jacket and walked a little unsteadily toward the door to find an ER to stich it up (pausing on his way to lose his lunch in a trash can), he knew for certain again. He did not want to be a full-fledged Parabaloni. That kind of work took a very special sort of person. And it wasn't him.

The phone grew silent as Sean hung up. Gigan and Pete let out a sharp rattle of breath after holding it too long.

"That was too close," Pete murmured, and Gigan nodded vehemently.

"We need to get ahead of Mr. Black." The Frenchman lifted his watch to his mouth. "Vince, please try the remote switch."

"Whoa, you're not supposed to be online," the inventor commented, his voice thick. They could hear him swallow, and it came clearer. Pete's stomach growled. "I thought the plan was to let the Collective think they were still on top?"

"We'll explain later, it hasn't been long that we're on, Mr. Black has no reason to have noticed we turned his precious egg off for a moment," Gigan said. "Oh, wait, Jojo can you pick me up in that ancient rattletrap you and Colin collected?"

"If I wear pants and a hoodie and don't make eye contact," Jojo said. "I'll find you."

"Very good. Be careful, both of you, Mr. Black is in town and Masala is dead. Don't take chances. Vincent, try the remote."

The switch beside them flicked. A soft whine came from the egg, and then the "whoomph" filled the air again. The phone died. Their watch channels went black. Pete flipped the cap, pulled it tight over his hair, and reached for the thumb cuffs[37] in his pack.

"The mob will be this evening, and it is already nearing noon," he said as he began to click cuffs on the bad guys.

"Do you think Yousef will play fair with us?" Gigan asked,

---

[37] There is only so much room in a pack or utility vest, the Parabaloni prize the smaller size of a thumb cuff versus the more standard handcuffs. (Especially Pete as his pack is usually close to bursting with snacks to keep him going between meals.) The thumb cuffs work fine. As Pete and Vince learned when they woke up from a drugged sleep after a soup dinner to find Gigan had decided to test their new equipment on his teammates. The Frenchman chuckled for a full half hour before Vince managed to squirm out of it in just enough to choke him into giving up the keys. No one eats Gigan's soups anymore. The Frenchman grins and just says, "More for me!"

sticking sticky notes and a business card on the nearest black shadow.

"I threw out bait and he rose to take it. Yousef lives on information, and he is very curious about us. Especially about what I let him see of Simeon. Yes, he will stick with us and play fair, to gain a reputation as an aid in our business, so we will return to him, and he can learn more." Pete's face hardened, tightening his eyes. "Gigan, he is gaining a reputation in the underbelly of Riyadh." Gigan's brow furrowed with new stress lines. He studied his watch.

"We should have time to handle that, if we hurry and couple it with the square tonight. Go now and get a head start on it. I would begin with Jeffey."

"I know where his warehouse is," Pete nodded, and settled the cap at a more comfortable crooked angle. "But it isn't close and the lady stole my *borrowed* bike. I forgot how long a mile actually is, we are very spoiled with our cars and planes. How did you get here?"

"I used my brain." Gigan's nose lifted and his arms crossed in an arrogant stare. One of Pete's eyebrows rose and he waited very pointedly. The Frenchman grinned, and plucked his own bag of thumb cuffs from one of his vest pockets. "During the wrap-up in Italy, when Vince was out recovering the orinthopters[38] he had the foresight to visit a Vespa museum. We brought two ancient things back with us, you may take mine to get a head start with Jeffey. Don't let another bad woman steal it, it's hard to find things that can actually get us where we need to go with the usual transportation out."

"I thank you, oh scooter putterer, and I lament your lack of faith in me," Pete said with a little bow. "Where are you starting?" Gigan glanced up at the silver egg looming in the corner. A small

---

[38] The Parabaloni gliding suits, sometimes souped up into personal flying apparatuses. Due to a case in Yemen, they are rather fond of making them look like Pteranodons, and add furs and crests and leathery appendages. They do have tracking devices embedded in the suits, and usually recover them fine if they're in a hurry and shed them fast to run off and save a situation (like in Italy). But they have lost six suits so far, to faulty tracking devices, lava spills, or being used as giant slug-mattress-bats shot at NATO trucks.

burnt patch spilled black around the cord snaking out of the bottom.

"Someone will be along soon to try and get the power on again, and will find our work. We do not want them alerting Black we have been here. I am going to finish cuffing the baddies and make a careful report to the authorities," Gigan said.

"Have fun with that," Pete said dubiously. "Don't get jailed too long. I'd rather not have to dig you out of a Riyadh prison."

"Excuse me, may I point out I have gotten you and Vincent out of several prison situations in the past three months, I don't think you should be—"

"I do not have time to argue this," Pete said, fluttering a hand, every inch of him the supercilious grown up dealing with a whiny teenager. He tossed the rest of his cuffs to his partner. "Let me know if I am handling this situation alone while you try to convince people you are not a crazy terrorist."

A string of irate French followed him out the door, and Pete grinned as the sunshine hit him. He headed to the little scooter propped up against a shiny new SUV (now just a hunk of useless metal). The sun rode high overhead. He didn't have much time.

Chapter 19

Vincent tapped his watch off and looked past the gleaming silver egg at Colin. The gangly young man stared at the scuffed up watch on the inventor's wrist. His dark eyes darted to Vincent's and he grinned.

"How many other things can that ancient looking watch do?"

"It was up to fifty-four last I counted," Vincent smiled back at him. He flipped his screwdriver, slid it back in his pocket, and strolled deeper into the plane's garage. "So do you want to get out in the city again or sit tight here for a nap?"

"Watching you with your French friend I thought you'd be more creative in your teases," Colin said as he followed the inventor, eagerness coming off him in waves.

"It wasn't a tease, if I had a choice it would be the nap," Vincent grinned. He handed Colin an inflatable motorcycle helmet[39], grabbed one off a shelf for himself, and hit the button to open the garage. Nothing happened. The inventor facepalmed. He planted his feet firmer on the floor, and pushed, hard. The door slid open with a slow, grinding squeal and Colin watched the bright desert sunlight flow in. It lit on a small antique, turquoise Vespa. Colin didn't try to hide his amusement as he settled gingerly on the back. This wasn't what he thought of as a proper spy conveyance. Vincent hopped on the seat, gripped the handlebars, and stopped. He sat up and blinked at the airport.

"Dude, I don't know where to go," he said.

"I assumed you had a destination in mind," Colin said, his amusement strong.

"No, I mean I usually have my maps pulled up telling me my route. Without it I don't know this town well enough to get through the streets."

---

[39] It looks like a scarf unless you crash and it actually inflates, which is quite handy for saving space in a crowded garage. I am all for saving space. My iguanas especially need more space, all the time, they seem to outgrow their enclosures faster than the guinea pigs. After the guinea pig flood in Peru, Pete has a thing about guinea pigs too, though not as bad as his issue with birds.

"Oh." Both the men sat still staring at the bright sunlight and thinking. "What did they use before the digital maps?" Colin asked. Vincent suddenly laughed.

"Use paper ones. Come on, my boss has a stash in his office that we've complained about having to cart around for years." Colin found himself following the tall inventor back through the fascinating rooms to a small square across from the bunkroom. Clocks ticked along the upper wall, each set to a different country's time. His eyes found the one labeled Riyadh. He realized this was the first time since he took off from Los Angeles he actually knew what time it was. Maybe he needed a real wrist watch instead of the Apple one Mr. Luke had confiscated with his phone. A small wooden desk sat in the center, a collection of ordinary office supplies on it in neat little containers with lids lined up with a precision that spoke of an OCD perfectionist. Colin looked closer and realized only some of them were ordinary office supplies. Clear bullets with some sort of liquid agent lay in one, another held a collection of rings that could be assembled into specialized brass knuckles. He stopped looking and focused back on the inventor. Vincent pulled a drawer out and dumped it on the little desk. Papers fluttered everywhere.

"It's in here somewhere," Vincent murmured, rifling through the pile. A stack of the papers plopped off to the floor and scattered and Colin winced for whoever owned this neat little study. Jojo walked past, in black slacks and a loose hoodie pulled over her shiny hair. She paused and looked in the office, her mouth set in a hard line.

"Simeon is not going to be happy with you," she commented.

"I'll put them back," Vincent said. "Eventually." Her eyes flicked to Colin and he felt her challenge sear through his skull.

"Not bad. But your own style with your hair free works better for you," he stated. Jojo's face softened. She straightened a little taller with an obvious effort.

"You, Colin Clempson, always know what to say," she stated. He couldn't tell if she meant that as a good thing. Then she snapped back to Vincent. "I'm off to fetch Gigan, and then I'm running an errand. Do you boys have time to help load Bibles in the back of the truck?"

"Do we?" Colin blurted out. Jojo rolled her eyes at him, and he felt the same "don't be an idiot little brother" vibe he had gotten from Alean.

"Sure," Vincent nodded absently, then looked up and blinked at her. "Wait, I thought we took all your church folks to Belgium, who are you delivering things to?"

"Nosy parker," Jojo commented, sticking her tongue out at him playfully. "You took care of *most* of them, there were a couple of families that weren't in church that Sunday you swept in so efficiently. And they've gained more since then, I've been informed."

"Oh," Vincent said, and his attention went back to the papers. He grabbed a map from the table. "Got it!"

"Here, let me check my route," Jojo said, and snatched the rectangle from him. Colin watched it unfold to a ridiculously large piece of paper. It stretched over the maps littered on the desk and hung off the edges. The two spies leaned over it, and Colin waited in growing amusement as they kept tracing streets with their fingers, getting in each other's way, arguing over routes, and complaining about how long this took. After about ten minutes Jojo flung her hands up with a series of Arabic comments spewing from her and trotted toward the garage. Vincent looked up at Colin.

"Here, you're the navigator, watch," he ordered. Colin stepped closer and watched as Vincent took a pen and traced out a ridiculously complicated series of lines winding over the map, stating names that sounded like gibberish to Colin's western ears. The inventor stood up and slapped the paper into Colin's chest. "Get it?" Colin fumbled at the paper, trying to keep it from tearing as he looked at the creases and wondered how it folded back into the neat little rectangle.

"Got it!" Jojo yelled from the garage.

"Good," Vincent grinned as he trotted off to help her load up.

Four minutes later, they were back on the Vespa, watching the ancient truck vibrate down the empty runways, roaring like something out of a mechanic's nightmare. Their machine sputtered into life with a sharp smell of gasoline. They puttered down the ramp, onto the asphalt runways, and on into town. Vincent chuckled as Colin threw his hands up and gave a whoop. He revved over a small hill to oblige the kid, enjoying the freedom and the ridiculous noise this machine made as it leapt over the crest. And the fact this thing was incapable of any high speeds[40]. He puttered to a stop at the end of a block and paused.

"Ok Colin, time to get your social studies in by experiencing how people did it in the old days. Just keep me to the black line I drew."

"It looks like a maze," Colin commented as he still struggled to fold it.

"Sure, like a maze in real life, and we don't want to get lost in the wrong neighborhood," Vincent commented. He pushed the scooter up and started puttering again. He felt the paper press against his back as Colin tried to shield it from the wind. Vince rolled his eyes. It would be so much easier to just tell Pat to program his contact to take him there.

The scooter put-putted through the streets, past envious stares of pedestrians and stalled cars. Colin wondered if the little antique machine was as happy as it seemed as they wove in and out of the stalled traffic. He pointed at a sign, squinting at the squiggles of a language he didn't know.

"I think you turn there," he said.

"Right or left?"

"I don't know, how is this thing oriented according to us?"

"Really, dude?"

"How long has it been since you used anything other than a digital map that moves when you do?" Colin shot back.

"Fair," Vincent acknowledged and reached back for the map.

---

[40] Vincent doesn't enjoy going fast on things tied to the ground. But sometimes he has to. Like the time six months before when he was in Hawaii in a heavy rainstorm. Half the roads were flooded, but he had to get to the volcano before she blew. (That year involved several volcanos – the Parabaloni all pray the streak is ended.) He reached a hundred and seventy-five on that motorcycle, before it finally got swept out of from under him by an especially heavy wave, and he paraglided the rest of the way. He did make it in time to grab the package from the volcano's rim before the lava hit it. And no, I'm not allowed to tell you what was in the package.

They only got lost twice before they got the hang of it and made it to their main road through town. The scooter puttered steadily up the lane, and Colin watched a city stalled in its tracks, people stumbling to figure out how to live without the normal things they relied on everyday. After a quarter of an hour, he gave up on being patient and leaned in toward the inventor.

"Where are we going?" Colin asked. The eagerness didn't escape Vincent, and he knew it wasn't a con. This young man had a well of curiosity, held in check only by a careful desire not to be a pest. Vince wondered how often his parents told him he was a pest. Probably not often in words. But this young man could read humanity. Someone needed to tell him he was important. Especially why he was important. Vincent swung to a stop at a light and his eyes swept the area as a matter of habit, taking careful note of the dark alley to their left. He saw movement. The kid's stomach growled.

"We're going to lunch," Vincent answered, and turned into a small side street. A restaurant stood backed up with people in line. A cook argued loudly with who appeared to be the owner of the restaurant, both of them hot in the face and looking ready to burst into tears. The man behind the till looked as if he had already done that today. Vincent parked the scooter and strode toward the owner. In eight minutes he had the line moving on a paper and pen run-the-card-when-we-can business, the cooks working busily, the owner calm, and he and Colin settled at an outside table with five orders of shashouska and a coffee. Colin watched the man behind the till laugh at something a customer said, and felt awe slide into him at the complete change Vincent had made.

"So Colin," Vincent said. "Tell me about your waiter."

"This one?" Colin asked as he pointed his thumb behind him at their server. "His name's Hany, and he has a daughter who's two and likes sweets." Vincent added, *"Pays attention, cares about the 'little people,' and doesn't mind listening in on conversations,"* to the young man's list of qualities.

"You know who I mean," he said with a grin. Colin amended his ways.

"Sure, the one at the meeting last night. (Sheesh, was that just last night?) You already know what he looks like so I won't go there. Smart. He rescued me twice. And he has your number, so honestly you probably know more about him than I do." Colin turned back to his coffee and eggs, hoping that was enough.

"There's more to it you don't want to tell me. He makes you nervous?" Vince said, quoting Simeon's assessment posted on their site. Colin grimaced. But then his eyes rose to Vincent's as his jaw squared. He leaned forward and his voice dropped lower.

"I wouldn't say anything with his siblings around, but there's something dangerous about him. Like he has something rushing under the skin, a million things he wants to do and say just under the surface waiting to explode into action. He told me to call him something else."

"'Something else?'" Vincent asked. The analysis intrigued him. That was deeper than even Pete had ever expressed.

"Something besides what his siblings called him. He said, 'Alean.' Then after we shoved Mr. Luke out at the airport, he took the Tesla to this place that was still open in the middle of the night and the owner came out and paid him a wad of bills (a really big wad), and called him 'Ay-lean-ka-boot,' or something like that. He said it like it was a joke, or at least something more than a name. The others in the garage tried not to even notice him, keeping their eyes down and just doing their work like he wasn't there, you know. The owner pointed at my gunshot wound and said something about how if I was a package that went with the car, this Alean would have aimed better. And they used English. It wasn't for me, I assume it was to keep the workers from knowing what they talked about."

"*Aleankabut*, is that the word?" Vincent asked, pronouncing the Arabic slowly and carefully, like he had to work at it.

"Yes, that's it. What's it mean?"

"Spider."

"Oh. What's that mean? Is he an assassin or something?"

"I think he's too big for that. He's the one who weaves the webs and pulls their strings."

Silence fell at the little table as Colin considered it. Vincent finished his tea, and wished this place made decent hot chocolate. Too much coffee in this part of the world.

"In other words," Colin blurted out, "if he wanted to assassinate someone, he wouldn't be the one to pull the trigger."

"He's not an assassin," Vincent grinned, then suddenly doubted himself. How much did they really know about what Pete's younger brother did?

"So you think he can handle the square?" Colin demanded.

"We'll be there too, just in case. Right now, we're off to see a man," Vincent said. He stood up and slid bills under his plate. "Come on." He picked up the three uneaten to go boxes as Colin hopped up obediently. Vincent led the way into the street, not to their scooter. He turned two corners back the way they had come, and then suddenly spun into a tiny side alley. Colin hung back. The two tall apartment buildings looming over the area blocked the sun and the stench drifting out wasn't filled with spices and restaurants. Someone moved at the back of the alley. Colin squinted, trying to see into the darkness. He took a step inside, attempting to get a clearer view. As he left the sun, the cold stung him.

Three thin, ragged children huddled amidst the dumpsters and debris at the end of the alley. A girl and two boys, maybe ten, eight, and five? It was hard to tell, they were so thin and scared and dirty… Vincent knelt slowly on one knee. In a lightning series of thoughts and feelings Colin found himself annoyed the inventor's pants were going to get this stench all over them, then horrified these children lived in the middle of it, and thoroughly ashamed of his first annoyance. Vince sat the to-go boxes on the ground and scooted them gently toward the children. He laid his faded fleece hoody over it, then sat a tract with color cartoons in Arabic script on the top. He moved his hand to his pocket and pulled out a white business card, slowly, gently, his movements calculated to be unthreatening. He said something in careful, slow Arabic, then stood. Colin jerked his suitcoat off and tossed it on the pile. The cold bit his arms and he felt goosebumps rising. The children just stared. Their eyes were so wide in their emaciated faces. Vincent gave a little Eastern bow, hands pressed together in front of him, then turned and trotted back into the sun.

Colin swung in step beside him. He said nothing as they made their way back to the scooter. Vincent started on their way again. The busyness increased the farther they went into the city. People poured out, milling and complaining and helplessly trying to get it all back to normal.

"How did you know they were there?" Colin asked finally, over the wind and the putt-putt of their little machine.

"Saw them duck out of sight when we were at the light."

"What did you tell them?"

"I gave them an address for a good orphanage here, my Money Man's number if that didn't suit their fancy, and told them to read the tract."

"Is that what the cartoon was?"

"Yeah," Vincent nodded. "I usually leave New Testaments, the Gideons do very good translation work. But here it would be dangerous for those kids if someone found a Christian Bible in their possession. It's a shame, the Bible always works best. Have you read it?"

"I started it once," Colin said, suddenly uncomfortable. "I just got bored."

"Try again sometime. John's a good place to start. Or the Psalms are strong and pretty."

"I will," Colin promised. Vincent turned his head, and Colin could see the approving smile on his freckled face. The look seared through Colin. It hit strings the young man had never let himself acknowledge how badly he wanted to resonate. The music it made soared to his head and sent the colors around him a little brighter, the sunlight a little warmer. Approval of something Colin had done, from someone he respected, meant more than he had ever dreamed it would. And this was from someone who already had plenty of spare funds. With Vincent Lee Tolliver, he could just be a normal person, money matters were equal, and interplays didn't have that constant question in the background; "Are they nice just because I'm rich and they want an 'in' to my dad's money?" That look sealed the promise, he would read the book when he got home.

Home. Blech.

But he wasn't there yet, and he still had questions. Colin shifted uncomfortably, then tightened his hold as they spun down a side street. Sidelining comments rose to his mind, sly hints that poked for an answer. But they died before making it through his teeth. Jojo's comment haunted him. He didn't want to play people. Not all the time, anyway. Colin just asked it.

"Why? I mean, no one else I've ever met, or even heard of, would stop in the middle of a terrorist story to order lunch for three starving street kids who (in the eyes of the plot) have nothing to do with anything. Don't misread me," he rushed on, his face suddenly hot in embarrassment, "I'm really glad you did stop, I'm not condemning it, I'm just...why?"

"'Hath not God chosen the poor of this world?...faith, if it hath not works, is dead, being alone.[41]' Defend the fatherless: do justice to the afflicted and needy.[42]' Thou shalt love thy neighbour as thyself.[43]' 'God made man...[44]' Every soul matters, and every body housing a soul matters. We are made in the image of God and every one of us is formed special and precious. God cares. So we do too. For those three, living here, that may be the only chance they have to learn about the real Jesus. That's important enough to pause the fight."

Colin stayed silent as he thought it over. Vincent let him be. He couldn't guess what went on inside the kid. Part of Colin Clempson's intelligence and ability to read people meant he knew enough to keep from being read. The scooter puttered through traffic patterns, and Colin noted his spy followed the driving laws meticulously. And they were definitely making their way out of the opulent side of town.

Vincent finally putted up to a sleezy shopping center, coasted to a stop, and hopped off the scooter in front of a curio shop. He walked into the store, and Colin followed him closely. Very

---

[41] James 2: 5, 17
[42] Psalm 82:3
[43] Mark 12:31
[44] Genesis 1

closely. The four men in ratty clothes loitering outside eyed them with malignity, and Colin did not feel safe. He wondered if he was about to be shot again. As Colin accidentally caught the glaring black eyes of one of the men, he got hit in the gut by a sudden terrifying realization; more danger came from ordinary life than major terrorist plots. He looked down meekly, his stomach clenched, and tried not to scurry through the door after Vincent.

"Mike the Pike!" a voice boomed, and Colin looked up. He saw a man in a white thobe at the back of the store packed with colors and things. A very little man. An actual dwarf, Colin realized as he drew closer. One with an amazing grin. To add to his surprise, he realized the man was addressing Vincent[45]. The little man slid off a ladder he had been using to hang wind chimes from the ceiling and hurried over, his short arm lifted to shake hands. Vincent dropped to one knee, grinning and chatting as he shook hands. Colin fumbled for two seconds, furiously trying to second guess conventions in a situation where no convention he had ever met fit, then gave up. He plopped to sit cross legged on the dusty ground and gave the little man a smile. He found a pair of brown eyes in a wrinkled, weather-beaten face sizing him up. A smile lit the man's ugly face.

"You've brought a new tagalong, Mike," the man boomed.

"We'll see," Vincent said, and Colin suddenly found both men looking at him. Something else went with those words, something he knew he didn't understand. Vincent moved the conversation on, and Colin slid the odd opening comments into the back of his mind for later consideration. "Abdullah, we need information about a man."

"Aha, you know where to come, my friend! Little Abdullah knows everyone you might need, and many you do not. Who is it you seek?"

"*Aleankabut*," Vincent said, and Colin's eyes darted to him.

---

[45] A pike is a vicious aquatic hunter, extremely fast, and good at finding prey. When Little Abdullah first met Vincent at the Bay of Bengal four years ago, and a solidly made microphone fell into the inventor's hands just at the moment the Pasta Fazoli gang rushed Simeon, the young agent gained a name. Mike the Pike definitely fit that adventure, and Vincent happily let the name stay. It was his first alias gained on his own merit, and so he is particularly proud of it.

That wasn't the lead question he expected. The little man's face changed slowly, a wily smile twisting his wrinkles into the look of a fox enjoying a joke on the hens.

"It is a recent apparition you seek," Little Abdullah boomed. The chimes above their head danced at his volume, and Colin found himself looking around the store in some awe. The shelves were crowded with thousands of things, half of which he couldn't even put a name to, colors and textures in a kaleidoscope of chaos. He wished he could ask what they were all for. Colin felt the depths of his Western ignorance again, and silently mourned his narrow soul. "I will tell you only so much. A wily one is the *Aleankabut*, skittering along his own paths and tying new webs every night. He is smart, and skilled, and binds many contacts in a web that is stretching quickly through town. None know his real name, and he thinks none know where he lives. But he is young. Those who are not wise enough to be old, as your Mr. Lee and I, think him a genius, a rising star in the underbelly of the city, who might threaten even the high placed. I think him a boy feeling his way. But if he lives, he will learn; and his will be a way that may indeed threaten the high placed."

"So I'm guessing he needs a big win?" Vincent asked.

"That would cement his position now, and help him gain," Little Abdullah assented.

"Tell me, Abdullah, would that be a good thing?"

"Mikey, you know not to ask my opinion outright, it is just the simple thoughts of a little man…" He broke off as Vincent's eyes rolled to heaven and he gave a long-suffering sigh. Abdullah's deep laugh boomed around the shop. The shelves jiggled and a carved wooden figure of a camel fell into Colin's lap. He picked it up gently, running his finger over the smooth wood. "Yes, it would be a good thing, I think. This *Aleankabut* is young, and untried, but he is not quite ruthless or cruel. I will tell you a truth; I saw him once weeping over a pawn of his crushed under a car. One who can still weep for a little man in a big game is greater than those who destroy without thought. His webs might catch those smaller things that would turn to the cruel without his weaving."

"I like what I'm hearing, Abdullah, you always have the right stuff. Now, who's after him?"

"Jeffy and Himera," Abdullah replied promptly. "They will catch him in what he thinks is his unknown lair soon, if not stopped."

"You know it all, my dude," Vincent commented, and passed over a large wad of bills which Abdullah took without any attempt at refusal or bargaining.

"You will stop them?"

"You like him," Vincent said, a grin breaking over his face. Little Abdullah's shoulders rose and he made a shrugging motion with his whole body and expression, a move that looked pure classic Middle Eastern to Colin.

"I am interested to see how he goes on, this young Spider. If he dies now, I will never know."

"Do you know anything about a Black?" Vincent asked abruptly.

"I have nine different Blacks, which are you looking for? Be more specific with a description every villain wishes to use!" Abdullah commented, his smile twisting his sun-browned wrinkles.

"Mr. Black," Vince supplied.

"Honestly? No, I have no 'Mr. Black,' that must be an American to be so very uninventive," Abdullah snorted.

"Naw, there's more to it than just 'uninventive,'" Vincent warned, "but we haven't figured out what yet. He's not a nice guy."

"Goes around having creepy meetings and blowing things up?" Colin supplied hopefully.

"Too generic," Abdullah said with another Eastern shrug. "I wish I could tell you more."

"What about the Collective?" Vincent asked. Silence fell in the little curio shop. Little Abdullah stared at Vincent, his smile gone, his face unreadable.

"I will tell you a truth, Mikey," he rumbled. "I know little of these shadows. But what I do know comes from the *Aleankabut*, and this is the real reason I would have him live longer. They do not weep over the crushed little people. He calls them the

Butwani though I do not know what it means. They paid people at the power plants last week. Many of those who took the money are now dead. Auto accidents. Heart attacks. I do not think the police have connected the two facts, though they might if they thought to research Power Plant 9 and the recent disturbances."

"But you would if you tried. Don't," Vincent said, his sunny grin lost. "Be careful, Little Abdullah. Masala's dead from this group." Colin watched the little man's face turn sallow and sag as his eyes grew larger. "We don't want you to be next. I would recommend holing up for awhile, or at least not taking any new customers into your information bank."

"How long, Mike the Pike?"

"Oh, we should have it handled pretty soon, we hope. We already have their power outages almost figured out," Vincent said. Abdullah's arms went wide and his face broke in two with a smile. But Colin could still see the worry in the wrinkles around the little man's eyes.

"And for that I offer a thousand thanks, oh tall one!" he boomed.

"Oh sure, like you really care," Vincent grinned at him, climbing to his feet. "You have all those lamps in the back with the best camel hair fuses, and you like the excuse to use the oddity."

"You tell your tagalong too much information," the little man smiled, wagging a finger at the inventor.

Abdullah's brown eyes flicked to the young man; he still had to look up, even with Colin seated on the ground. The little man's expression held humor and welcome, mixed in a way Colin again felt himself floundering to understand. Abdullah's voice boomed around Colin as he got his gangly legs under him to follow Vincent out of this shop.

"Keep the camel."

Chapter 20

Memphis lay in a strange silence that January day. No traffic horns blared. No planes buzzed in and out of the airport. The only sound came from a million voices lamenting the fact they were suddenly unplugged from their modern lifestyle.

The cars along I40 sat still like a dammed river. Some drivers stayed behind the wheel, staring helplessly at their black smart phone screens, or continuously pushing the ignition, hoping one time it might work. Others milled among the cars, complaining loudly that someone ought to stop this kind of thing from happening. A few jogged between the lanes, taking matters into their own feet. A mother pushed a stroller between one lane, with a toddler wailing about a missed lunch.

The mother paused and looked over her shoulder as the strange quiet was slowly invaded by a sound. It was a familiar sound, one she heard every day. But this morning it sounded as alien in her city as a dragon's roar. An engine purred. It drifted closer quickly, until the purr became a roar. A classic convertible, red paint glinting in the morning sunlight, zoomed by on the interstate's shoulder. A song about Tuesday afternoons drifted from the speakers as it moved on past. A classical, robust voice joined in on the lyrics and the sound wove around the stroller. It stilled the toddler's wails. The classic convertible sped past all the modern vehicles and disappeared down the road. The toddler heaved a sigh, leaned her head against the stroller, and went to sleep. The mother blew out a thankful prayer and started walking again.

A mile ahead of her, the cassette tape wound to a finish. Simeon ejected it, flipped it over, and pushed it back in again. The jaunty sounds of the Moody Blues wrapped around the two friends, as Algy snored in the passenger seat and Simeon leapt into the album again. The narrator took over the end of the album, drawing the scene to a gentle close. The tape clicked as it ended, and Simeon didn't move to put in another. Eight more miles sped under the convertible's wheels before he saw his exit.

Simeon navigated past the stalled cars, pulled off the highway, and wound his way between the hunks of useless metal cluttering the road. He eyed the storefronts with boarded windows, piled garbage along the sidewalks, and glares from the locals. He pushed the lock button on his door and checked to make sure the convertible top was securely latched. Simeon slammed on the brakes and Algy's seatbelt bit into him as he rocked forward. A sharp "guk" came from the Englishman and he turned a glare on his friend. Simeon shrugged and pointed ahead. The intersection was a solid line of stalled cars and arguing people.

"Got your stinger[46]?" Simeon asked.

"Of course," Algy snorted.

"Try not to actually use it," Simeon commented as he slid into the street.

"How long will you be?" Algy asked. He shifted into a more comfortable position, his long legs stretching over the empty driver's seat. Simeon shrugged, trotted off into the sea of cars and people, and disappeared. "He never gives a proper time[47]," Algy complained under his breath. He cracked his window open, leaned his head back against the door, and his eyes fluttered closed again.

Four large men in muscle shirts shoved their vapes into their pockets and trotted toward the snazzy sports car. One of them pulled his arm back to bring a glass breaker down through the passenger window on the man sleeping inside.

The barrel of a Smith and Wesson 500 suddenly pressed against his chin, not gently.

"Don't," an English voice drifted from the car. Fire tingled in a rumble under the single word; all of them felt death hovering at

---

[46] All Simeon's friends carry a weapon of preference (after a few years around him even his little nurse friend Max picked up the trait). Algy's is a ridiculously powerful pistol. He says he prefers to feel something solid with him. He likes to use it as a club and has learned it can be thrown accurately, as The Giant in Somalia also learned to his detriment. Simeon tells me Algy took out two angry reindeer with it once, only by the club feature. When I ask what he's done with it with bullets, Simeon looks away and doesn't answer.

[47] The Donald Duck fiasco (wherein Algy gained his codename and just managed to save two American agents) turned into a fiasco mainly because Simeon gave a time when he wasn't completely certain he would finish at that time. The bats attacked first and he and Saul still carry the scars.

the end of that barrel. The thug's knees trembled so hard even his face shook. "Just don't."

The gang scattered. Algy rolled over, gave a mumbled complaint, and drifted off again.

Vincent swung his leg over the side of the Vespa and hopped off. Colin sat up and eyed the square, flat-roofed houses making up this neighborhood. He saw dust, sagging clotheslines, a few dogs running free, children eyeing him as they paused in their play. Most of them looked thin and a little dusty. But none like the three in the alleyway. Somehow this area felt more like what Colin had expected when he landed in Saudi Arabia. He couldn't decide if it pleased him to know he had been right, or if he wished the whole place more opulent like the tourist quarter. He blinked hard as his feet thumped into the hard packed dirt, and knew he was too tired to decide.

The pickup rested in front of one of the houses. The tailgate lay open (and crooked) and several men slid cardboard boxes and grocery bags from the truck bed and carried them into the house, talking in a cheerful way that told Colin they were excited over the delivery. The short Frenchman stepped out of the house and joined the line to get another box. Colin realized he could hear ladies jabbering and laughing inside.

"What...?" Colin asked, blinking hard. This had been a really long, strange weekend. Vincent turned to check the kickstand. It brought his head close to Colin's.

"Delivery to an underground church," Vince murmured; careful not to let any of the ranging children or any chance listeners in the houses nearby hear it. Colin blinked again, long and slow. He watched a man pick up another box and walk inside. The flap flipped up just enough that Colin could glimpse black books inside. Vincent hopped over to grab another one, and the Frenchman popped out to give him a friendly pound on the back, teases hurling between the two. Colin stood still, watching. There were still underground churches? Vague ideas of communist blocks, or Catholic inquisitors, or ancient Turkish archers on horseback raged through his mind. Somehow, in his own little sophisticated bubble, his life barely brushing the fringes of Christianity, the thought of illegal churches still being a thing had never entered his consciousness.

Colin found himself watching Vincent, as the conversation and hand shaking engulfed him. These "elite do-gooders" did more with their guns and plastic explosives than just stop terrorists. The vast need for their kind of career choice paraded through Colin's mind and he stood silent and still, his world adjusting around him yet again. But his tired brain slowly settled into a still pond of mush, just watching.

The friendliness and inclusiveness of the gathering seeped into him. These people talked as if they had known each other for years, and yet introduced themselves in the same moment. As if...as if it were a family reunion. Something real and solid held in common, binding them together, no matter what other differences of background and culture might divide them. Colin shifted his feet, acutely aware he was not a part of this.

The Frenchman stepped away from the gathering and strolled toward the truck. Vincent went with him, looked over at Colin, and pointed at the scooter. The young man dutifully pushed the machine to the tailgate, stiff and achy beyond anything he knew he could reach. He spotted Jojo in the doorway, hugging veiled ladies. Their words twisted around each other, tight and happy and wet with the sorrow of leaving again. She at least had a real history here, he realized. Colin made it to the truck and caught the last few lines of the conversation.

"–have to work fast," Vincent said. "It's a good thing Pete's getting a head start."

"He chose Jeffey," Gigan said. It came with a wolfish amusement, a grin dancing over his weathered face. As Colin helped manhandle the scooter into the truck bed and flopped into the minuscule backseat of the cab, he shuddered over that smile. He was profoundly grateful he wasn't Jeffey.

Dusk lay over the royal square. Misnamed, it was a rectangle of green grass crisscrossed with sidewalks in geometric patterns. A few fountains and flowerbeds beautified the area, and iron-wrought benches were scattered along the walkways. Museums, art galleries, and high end shops usually assured the area was filled with the opulent and tourists.

Today four-hundred citizens packed the square. Most of them were caked with dirt, many in rags and stink. Chanting yells moved through the crowd; something about less government control and more government money. What the protest was for didn't really matter. Those above the massed crowd knew its creation came from outside shadows, working on pent up feelings of the jobless and idle, the desperate who were always ready to protest.

Jeffey Ahmad stood on the roof of the museum, watching the people sway and mill below him. He could hear the chants like a constant wave of the ocean, rolling from one side to the other, then back again, the words and tenor shifting in the changing course of human feelings. The hulking Methuselah stepped a little closer to him and cleared his throat.

"You have found them?" Jeffey asked.

"There are machine guns mounted on the roofs there and there," Methuselah answered, pointing them out. "We see no one manning them yet. We wait for your word to take them out." A quiet demand hung in the last sentence, a begging desire to stop the massacre. A smile quirked over Jeffey's face, shifting it in a way that seemed to crack the hardened expression.

"Oh no, Methuselah," he said. "We can't interfere in another man's game, that is not part of the code. Besides, when hundreds die and the blame goes to Afghanistan, think of all the weapons sales we will make, and all the freedom our organization will be allowed as the army and law-enforcement turn their attention to wars. No, we cannot break the code and interrupt another's carefully laid plots. It would not be polite."

The seven-foot hulk that was Methuselah didn't move. His thick neck kept his head perfectly still. But his eyes shifted, staring at the hundreds of people packed below them. The desperate mass of humanity already so down on their luck they would come to protest…what? Their lot in life? Even that lot, pitiful and unhappy and hungry as it was, would be ended abruptly in a few minutes. Only the very fringes of the crowd would be able to get away when the firing started. The rest were packed in too tight. And he could not stop it. Overstepping Jeffey Ahmad brought an abrupt and brutal death. It usually brought death for more than just the overstepper too, as the Spider would learn later tonight. Methuselah's eyes closed, dread freezing his gut at the vision of a whole family wiped out to prove Jeffey's position in the city. Methuselah would be the one to give the orders. To see the shots were fired and the house torched. He took no joy in his work.

The crowd's noise soared, shifting back and forth in a wave of sound that pierced through the still city. Methuselah could picture the sounds of the gunfire opening, the screams of terror and shrieks of the dying... Movement shifted behind the blob he knew was the machine gun on the right. It was about to start. Methuselah clamped his hands into fists, his face a stony blank.

A kyoketsu-shoge shot from behind them. The rope coiled around Jeffey. The black weighted blade on the end thumped into his chest, and the line jerked. The Riyadh gang leader shot backward off his feet, his face a mask of terror. An arm with muscles like steel wrapped around his throat, pressing the cold metal of a knife under his chin with almost a gentle motion. Through his gasps of fear, Jeffey felt a presence near his ear.

"Do not interfere with the Spider," a voice murmured. Inhuman, a voice changer making it an alien sound. Yet like the touch of the knife it came gently, a soft warning carrying a terror that no shout or punch could ever convey. It spoke of complete power, of a reach so certain it would carry out any threat. This man did not need to shout. "The Spider is out of your league now. Touch him and you will find your life crumble around you." The knife suddenly moved, with a speed Jeffey hardly even followed before the rounded end slammed into his temple. Jeffey Ahmed, one of the most powerful men in the underbelly of Riyadh, sank to the ground in a heap. The rope uncoiled from him as if it had a life of its own, and Methuselah watched the slim figure gain his feet. A black one piece suit covered him, a silver mask where the face should be, webbed fingers on his hands, and a hard pack strapped to his back. Or a black shell to an alien creature? The rope coiled over his arm ready for use. Methuselah could feel the stare from behind that silver mask.

"The machine guns lay there and there," the big man said, pointing helpfully, his words quick. The noise of the crowd seemed to fill his mind. "I will help if you go to take them out." Nothing shifted on the black one for a long three seconds. Then the webbed fingers flicked something toward him, and the black one melted into the shadows and disappeared. Methuselah stooped and carefully picked up the business card lying at his feet. He saw only a phone number on the front, the nation's code telling him it came from the Big Satan, from America.

"The Spider has the square in his web, do not fear for the crowd. There is help if you want out," the alien voice drifted back to Methuselah. "Good people need warriors too."

Simeon carefully disabled the fourth booby trap, hopped over the vat of slime, and knocked on the door.

"Come in!" a cheerful voice burbled from inside. Then panic cut into it. "Wait, how did you get this far?"

"It's Lee, Heshman," Simeon said and pushed open the door. He hefted the graffitied plywood sheet he had picked up in an alley a little higher as he stepped in.

Something splashed up the board. A sharp sizzle came from the wood.

"*Lee*, Heshman," Simeon said again.

"Oh, very good, just the man I wanted to see!" Vern Heshman bubbled. "I have your newest made to your specifications. You might want to drop that, it will be pretty hot by now." Simeon carefully leaned the plywood against the stained concrete wall. A line of acid dribbled down it, eating a jagged, steaming hole in the wood. It touched the ground and the concrete under it bubbled up with a hiss. "Come, come, see what I made!" Simeon looked away from the hole in the ground and focused on the man in the stained t-shirt and baggy jeans. His beard had more mats than the last time Simeon had been here. For a moment he thought he saw something crawling in it. He focused on the man's face. It shone like a child's on Christmas morning at the idea of being able to show someone his work.

"You need to get out more," Simeon told him, just like he did every time he came here. Heshman waved his hand in an absent dismissal, and then fluttered it to draw his guest closer. Simeon let himself be drawn. For fifteen minutes he humored the man. He followed him as he bounced from ray guns that shot bananas, to a monkey dressed in pants and a fez. Past a paint made specifically to turn things green, a garbage pail that chewed and spit, another ray designed to take the smell out of cabbages, and a remote bug that could scurry under doors and explode houses. Simeon discreetly slid one of the bugs in his coat for Vincent to check later. If it stayed true to Heshman's other gadgets, it would dance in a circle and then melt instead of exploding. But it ought to be checked. Simeon finally interrupted the animated description of pine needles and olfactory senses as Heshman leaned over a metal chair strapped to a disc and tweaked the hundreds of wires plugged into the armrest.

"Need our stuff," Simeon said, a little reluctantly. A huge sigh heaved from the man and he wilted.

"All right, all right. You people never stay long," the inventor commented.

"Have to use it sometime," Simeon shrugged. The thought of something he made actually being used cheered Heshman. He started babbling again as he headed back toward the door. Simeon followed him, wading through the mess and trying to keep his fingers from itching; he desperately wanted to organize this place. And throw away the leftover food everywhere, sheesh. And the hundreds of brown hairs from this man's beard, pulled out and curled around all of his gadgets as his facial hair got in the way of his tools. Simeon focused on Vincent's clean, neat gadgets as Heshman held them out. "Kept to the specs?"

"Oh yes, I made it exact, just like you people demand."

"Thanks," Simeon nodded. He took the silver clamp and disc, and handed Heshman a thick stack of cash. The man did a happy skip and headed back to his spinning chair, bellowing a very off-key pop song. Simeon slid out the door and locked it behind him.

Chapter 21

A soft whistle drifted to Vincent. He stayed where he was, crouched on the ground in front of the museum, dismantling a bomb. No one in the crowd noticed him. If they glanced his way they saw a tramp in a tattered hoodie, huddling over a pile of debris. None of them saw the deadly explosives hiding under the pile of refuse. Yousef missed it, too focused on the machine guns and hired goons. But he played his cards well, all in all, and the Parabaloni mostly approved the Spider's work tonight.

Vincent finished the last connection and began to slip the explosives into a tattered, reusable shopping bag. Another whistle in a lower cadence drifted from the alley beside Vince. Good. Pete had found Jeffey, and Gigan had already finished with Himera. Vince rose to his feet and shuffled into the alley, his head hanging loose between his drooping shoulders. Those who glanced at him saw a tramp, weak and addled in the brain. The deep darkness of the alley closed over him and Vincent straightened. He passed the bag to Gigan and the Frenchman walked off. If Pete and Vince noticed his missing bounce and drooping mustaches, they didn't comment.

Peter and Vincent leaned against the alley and waited. The crowd surged, restlessness increasing at every moment. Pete looked up at the moon and the glorious stars shining down into the alley. It seemed so strange to see them like that here, in the midst of town. You usually only saw that kind of brilliance out in the wild places, where humans didn't invade. Tonight, they burned with uncontested brilliance, in numbers that screamed for humanity to look up in awe. The filmy ribbon of the milky way snaked across the sky, billions of tiny dots of light shimmering and overlaying each other in a humongous dance lightyears away... Pete felt himself shrinking, his troubles suddenly insignificant in the vastness of the universe, his own consciousness too small to take in the immensity. Vincent's drawl cut through Pete's thoughts.

"When our world goes dark, God's lights burn even brighter."

The Saudi's half smile curled over his face. He dropped his gaze to the tall friend standing so steady beside him in the dark.

"And sometimes, Savant, the brightest light is encased in jars of clay." Pete's voice lowered to a husky murmur. "You bear the symbol of the sun for more than just your smile. Thank you for never changing, Vincent."

"We all change, Pete. But so long as we stay focused on the Son, the changes will always be for the better. I'll keep holding that light up for you to steer through the dark, Petey, promise. It's easier if you do the same for me." Vincent's eyes shifted to the skinny brother beside him. The Saudi nodded, and swiped a hand over his eyes.

"Promise," he said, and it was all he felt he could say. But it was enough. His gaze went back to the brilliant stars as he stayed beside his work brother, soaking in the comfort of both lights. A little sigh slid from Pete and he grimaced. "Any moment now."

As he said it, a surge went through the city in an audible high pitched hum. Lights sprang on through the square and dotted the city everywhere. Car alarms blared to life in a rattling cacophony. Pete watched the stars above him fade softly to just the brightest points of light, and felt as if his heart might crack. It seemed as if God Himself withdrew, pushed away by the human veil of manmade light in a wicked city that rejected Him.

His watch vibrated, quick and insistent, alerting him to all the things he had missed in the digital world in the last fourteen hours. Pete found himself suddenly longing to keep missing it. But he glanced down like a dutiful twentieth century young person. Blue Letter Bible's verse of the day lay uppermost on top of the pile of notifications.

"Lift up your eyes on high, and behold who hath created these things, that bringeth out their host by number: he calleth them all by names by the greatness of his might, for that he is strong in power; not one faileth[48]."

The stars lay hidden now behind the veil of humanity's light. But not one was missing. Pete's eyes moved to the crowds. Their voices mixed in a jumble of surprise and a little alarm as the

---

[48] Isaiah 40:26

power suddenly rushed back to their dead city. The light inside these poor creatures lay hidden in so much sin and wickedness and false beliefs… but God wove every one of their stories and not one of His own would be lost. And the Parabaloni stood here to give them a better chance at clinging to life, so their souls could have more time to make it to their Creator. At least if Yousef could pull this off.

A cry came from the back of the crowd. High and scared, a human version of a herd animal's alert of spotted predators. Chaos rippled through the people. Pete and Vincent quietly climbed up the side of the wall and perched on the second story windowsills. Bodies began to pour into alleys and side streets, filling the alley below their feet. At the back of the crowd, Pete could see them; Yousef's picked few "friends," waving their guns in fearsome arches, causing just enough panic to clear the square faster than any warning could have done the job. They moved with the crowd, and Pete could see the skill they used to keep themselves shielded from interfering fire.

Vince pointed to the left and Peter followed it. Jeffey stormed through the bodies flowing from the square. The crowds parted around him and his giant henchman like flood water around a tree. Those packed in the square were the sort who recognized Jeffey Ahmed, and feared him worse than any armed gunman. Peter slid his thumb onto his palm, feeling the button. The scanners on his mask activated and he selected Jeffey. A small map in the top corner tracked him easily even four streets away; a white dot in the midst of a sea of black.

Pete began to climb up the side of the building, almost lazily. He chinned over the top and strolled across the roof to watch the scene happening below. He flicked one wrist to activate his controls and zoomed in on the white dot. He could see the murderous fury on Jeffey's face as he stalked through the streaming crowds, one hand pressed against the dried blood on the side of his head.

The hulking Methuselah tagged dutifully at his back, like a good watch dog. But his shifting gaze slid up the building rising beyond the apartments and shops, straight to the flat roof. He spotted a lone figure silhouetted against the glare of the street-lights and neon signs. He fumbled a pair of binoculars out as Jeffey made it to his car and the furious walk stopped. The binoculars focused on a black silhouette, with webbed fingers, a faceless oval, and a hard shell. The figure stared at them. Methuselah's arm shot out. It clamped over Jeffey's collar and jerked him back out of the car as he shouted at the driver to leg it. Pete's thumb pressed the button.

A shudder ran through the ground as plastic explosives melted the car into a ball of twisted metal and ash. A shiver ran over Pete as he contemplated how small a piece he had taken from Colin's bag to make that effect. Screams echoed up, fear turning to panic among the rushing crowds. The streets began to clear as people turned their hurry into a ground-pounding race.

Jeffey staggered back till he banged against the brick wall of an apartment building, his chest heaving and his eyes so wide Pete could see their whites as his mask stayed zoomed in on him. A thin man with an AK-47 over his shoulder and the marks of an addict slunk up beside Jeffey and began to whisper in his ear. Pete's half smile curved over his face. The messenger had arrived. He would be explaining about the SEF raid on Jeffey's private armory and drug pile. Sometimes the timing you couldn't really plan for still happened perfectly. As the news that two-thirds of his wealth had been claimed by the government drifted into Jeffey's consciousness the street around them cleared, leaving the gang leader open and exposed against the side of the building. Yousef stepped out of the alley across from the trembling, pale Jeffey. High above them all, Pete laughed. God had finished the arrangements for the Parabaloni tonight. He activated his McMusky and focused on the tall, broad-shouldered figure in the black thobe, the hood pulled far over his face.

"You will stay out of my business," Yousef's deep voice stated. The melancholy lacing it added a menace of certainty, the same way Pete had used his gentlest voice earlier. The Spider spoke as if he didn't have to yell and curse, what he said *would* happen. "You will stay away from me."

"All right, all right, Spider," Jeffey stammered, sweat pouring from him. "You win. I'll keep out of your way." Jeffey Ahmed turned and scampered away like a beaten terrier.

Under his hood, Yousef's mouth dropped open and he gaped. He had stepped out of that alley expecting a bullet to the head. He hadn't thought anyone could trace him to his house. Pete's comment today, and seeing the skill of his brother's team, showed him he still operated as an amateur. Which meant the big guns would come for his own to teach the town a usurper never lasted. A quick bullet was better than watching his siblings die around him, his mother's grief and death, and knowing he had caused it.

But instead, there went Jeffey Ahmed, running from him in a sweat. Yousef's eyes rose and he spun quickly, his gaze raking the buildings. The rooftops stood starkly empty, the streets around the square cleared of all humanity. No one watched the scene. No one he could see, anyway. Yousef turned back to his business and stole off into a side street, melding with the darkness. Time to gather the papers meant to frame another country.

A job well done would be a small thanks for the life of his family and the sudden freedom to grow his night business. He would finish the job for his brother's skilled team. And then the Spider needed to rework his webbing.

The truck door squealed as Gigan pulled it open. He climbed laboriously inside, complaining under his breath.

"I oiled it twice, and it still sounds like that," he grumbled, dropping onto the squeaky seat.

"Colin stayed asleep. He's grown used to the squeal now," Jojo commented, and Gigan twisted to see the gangly figure curled on the tattered back seat. He could actually see Colin now that Jojo had used Vince's switch to shut off the egg and the streetlights glared around them. His eye fell on a wooden figurine of a camel sticking out of the kid's pocket. Gigan stared at it.

With an effort he turned away and sank back against the seat. He drew his legs up till they pressed against the sling holding his arm against his chest. Gigan huddled into himself, his face drawn and listless with depression as he stared at the wall across from him. Jojo sat stiff and silent, her dark eyes staring straight ahead. The streetlights buzzed. Car alarms pounded through the city, mixing with the sirens and blaring radios and advertisements. Gigan closed his eyes and desperately longed for quiet and peace.

"We did it," he murmured. "Pete took care of Jeffey and I took Himera. They are both terrified of their lives and have lost large portions of their business, and will avoid the *Aleankabut*. At least for long enough for Yousef to settle himself in a better position." Jojo nodded, and some of her stiffness dropped.

"Thank you," she murmured. Her hand came up and cleared her eyes, and Gigan found surprise slipping into him. He knew Jojo Aziz could cry. But somehow seeing it filled him with a surprise that stole his words. She turned to him, her eyes glinting in the streetlight's yellow glare. "I'm sorry you had to deal with family too. I didn't realize how hard it would be until I came and found the same streets still here, and I can't walk them to go home and hug the little ones and see how they are growing and help Mother in the kitchen and…" She stopped, her words drifting into silence. Jojo sank back into the corner of the seat. A single tear moved slowly down her cheek.

"I know," Gigan whispered. Comfort seemed to have fled from him. Empty hollowness echoed out of his soul. His family was breaking, their leader dulled by the violence of alcohol, the business running on the dregs of emotions. It wouldn't take long for the hammer to fall if Grégoire didn't snap out of it. And Gigan couldn't help, not with a good conscience; the business was bad, evil even, the hammer *should* fall. But the worst of it lay in the fact they would not want his help even if he could step in. They did not want him. And there was no hope of that ever changing.

"We can still love them, even when they do not seem to love us," he said with an effort, grasping at Simeon's wisdom like a desperate lifeline. "I told Aldrick once, the best thing we can do is to pray for them. When we are on our knees in prayer for our families, suddenly it brings into focus how God loves us even when we play the part of His enemies, and it is easier to forgive and to love. We love, because He first loved us, and that makes all the difference. It does not heal all the hurts. But it helps." His words sounded flat to him. The truth they carried remained true. But somehow, it seemed harder to *feel* it was true tonight.

The horns blared. People rushed into the streets, yelling in fear. Gigan's eyes closed as he fought down what he did feel tonight. But the thoughts slipped from him.

"It's all so wrong!" His heartache wailed in the shaky words. "Everything we try to fix breaks so easily, and is so impossible to heal, prayers stay unanswered, all the good is so quick to be sucked into the darkness, and I can't..." His voice died again, swallowed in the sea of noise. Gigan sat silent and empty. Lost for a path onward, lost for any more words to help Jojo in her sorrow. Drowning in the darkness that pulled from every side.

"The good things are easy to break," Jojo murmured. Gigan had to strain to hear it over the sirens and blaring alarms. He heard her draw in a shaky breath. "But Jesus is all we need, and more than enough. And He makes all things new. It does not remain broken, and it is *not* impossible to heal." He looked up at her from reddened eyes, and found hers shining in the dark. "Nothing is impossible to God, while there is life, there is still hope. And Gigan, you are His and you are here. So is Peter and Vincent and Simeon, and you are pushing back the darkness." A slim, strong hand moved into the glaring light of the TV advertisements, pointing him to the people still running from the square and disappearing into the city. Her voice rose to ring with the stubbornness of an Aziz, and the Frenchman struggling to see through the blackness felt the truths she spoke. "They live, Gigan. Those few stories are still alive to keep breathing, to come to God, to be with their families and love and laugh and pray. You saved a few hundred tonight. And each one touches another hundred. Thousands of stories changed and lightened because you chose to fight back even when you're exhausted and can hardly see for the sorrow in your own story. We may be a small group surrounded by the dark. But we reflect the light from a source that never ends and, oh boy, do we shine."

"Elite," Gigan sniffed, his voice wet.

"What?"

"We are elite, not small," the Frenchman corrected, and she

could hear his natural laughter riding the words even through the sniffles.

"Well the elite ones need to take the time to polish off some of the depression gathered in this business, if you want to reflect even better."

"You help with that," he whispered, a grateful smile hovering under his mustaches. "Thank you, Jojo."

The driver's door clicked open and Algy slid his feet off the seat and back to his floorboard. A plastic takeout box dropped into his lap and he actually opened his eyes. A smile slid over his face as he sat up and popped the lid open. The warm smell of tiki masala filled the car.

"You told them extra peppers," Algy mumbled around a forkful. "Brilliant, mate." Simeon just nodded as he sipped his coffee. He pushed the stick into reverse. The little car roared backward, and Algy lifted the takeout box, compensating for the jerky ride as Simeon spun in a tight one-eighty and roared back toward the interstate.

"Didn't see any corpses," Simeon commented.

"If you shoot someone you have to deal with the screams[49]. And sometimes wanted lists, and that's always a bother."

"I'll take it," Simeon murmured into his coffee. He pulled onto the wide shoulder and pushed his foot onto the accelerator. Algy watched the envious stares of the sea of stranded people turn into a blur of shiny metal. He saw the speedometer climb past ninety. Algy turned deliberately back to his tiki masala, choosing not to watch the tiny not-a-lane they sped up.

"Do you think he will be at the power plant?" Algy asked.

"In Riyadh right now. Or was last night."

"Oh?"

"Winged a boy who crashed his meeting."

"I see. Lucky kid to still be alive, God must be watching him."

---

[49] An Algy Maxim the Parabaloni don't quote as often as some of his other words of wisdom. Another Algy Maxim he lives by is "dead villains can't kill you," and Simeon agrees that's a nice truth.

Simeon just nodded. Algy finished his meal, sat the to go box on the backseat to Aurora's delight, wiped his hand on his pants, and rifled in the glove compartment for another cassette tape. The jaunty strains of the Tijuana Brass filled the little car.

"Any idea what we're headed toward?"

"No." Simeon spun behind him to reach for something in the backseat, and Algy gave a guttural bleat and grabbed for the steering wheel. Simeon turned back around, dropped a bag in his friend's lap, and took the wheel again. Algy gave him a glare, then dutifully unzipped the bag.

"Oh excellent. I do like your choices. Let's go with the grenades, shall we?" he commented. Simeon nodded, and Algy re-zipped it. "Any idea how your boys are getting on?"

"Smart, good. They'll be fine. Probably frustrated at having to use paper maps."

"Golly, they can't communicate over a mile or swipe a credit card," Algy chuckled, "I wonder how they'll get on." He settled back and watched the miles speed by. The tape clicked as it reached the end of the side. Algy didn't move to eject it. The tires bumped and whirred over the roughened asphalt of the shoulder. The quiet hung around the two old friends with a peaceful familiarity. Ten minutes sped quickly past, and Simeon spun off the highway and pulled into a normal suburb. The car jerked to a stop in front of a red brick house with a swing hanging from the oak out front, and a washbasin filled with pansies.

"Up to a little run?" Simeon asked.

"Right ho, let's keep the roar from announcing us." A grin split the Englishman's face as he hopped out onto the sidewalk. "And your snazzy sports car might make it home alive if you keep it out of the industrial areas." Simeon nodded, slung his bag over his shoulder, snapped Aurora to heel, and started to jog. The two friends passed steadily through the streets, and the neighborhood quickly turned into worn strip malls and towering warehouses. Strange empty silence hung in the streets. No one was out manning the businesses or rushing to lunch. An eerie deadness hung over a city stopped in its tracks. Two more streets, and the three stories of the power plant came into sight.

"You take the left?" Algy commented.

"Right."

"Fine, be argumentative," Algy said. Simeon gave him a little grin and the Englishman rolled his eyes heavenward. "I'm not going to play your corny pun games, I'm working on two long nights in a row, one interrupted nap, and one good meal. You take the right." Simeon heaved a melodramatic sigh, tossed Algy a tear gas grenade and gas mask, and peeled off.

Two more streets and he could see the windows of the right side of the power plant.

And the three dead workers piled around the door. That door yawned, an empty cavity of blackness beckoning people to approach. Something glided past inside. A moving shadow in the midst of the blackness.

He picked out a noise in the strange stillness around him. A soft pulse, a "whoomph" that came in a steady wave. It drifted out of the darkness, and dominated every sound in the still air.

A soft growl came from his dog. Simeon dropped to one knee and slid Rora's specially made gas mask over her fluff. He gave her ear a scratch and spun back up to face the windows. A sharp hiss came from inside, and someone started coughing. Algy had moved in. Simeon's little pistol gave a sharp bark, and a bullet smashed into a window on the ground floor. In the same second he pulled his grenade launcher against his shoulder and fired. A line of white smoke trailed in the sky and disappeared inside. Sharp hissing invaded the stillness and white gas filled the blackness. Simeon slipped the grenade launcher back in the bag and pulled out his cosh as he walked up beside the door.

Retching and coughing spilled into the streets. People began to spill out too. A black clothed woman with hose pulled over her face stumbled out the door, half folded over, tears streaming down her face as she tried to breathe through the retching coughs racking her.

Simeon slammed his cosh into the back of her head. She went down on the bodies of the workers these people had clubbed to death. Two more black clad people stumbled out, struggling to breathe through the tear gas inflaming their lungs. One quick blow and another backhanded with the cosh sent them down too. The window behind him smashed and he spun neatly, catching the one who leapt out and another who came through the door. But as he took care of them, a third made it through and leapt over the pile of people. A hand forged throwing dagger sped from him as he retched and hacked; quick, and expertly aimed for Simeon's eye. Simeon knocked the blade out of the air with a quick blow from the cosh. The man landed in a staggering run, his feet pounding up the street.

A fuzzy, squirmy corgi slammed into his ankles and managed to tangle in both his legs at once. He hit the pavement with an earth-shattering thump. Simeon's left hand spun into his bag as his other slammed into two more black clad shadows trying to slip out the window. His left hand emerged with a baseball. A quick pitch, and Simeon's straight ball hit the knife-thrower square in the temple. The "thunk" rang even over the hacking wheezes coming from the pile of people around Simeon, and the struggling knife-thrower suddenly dropped to the concrete. Simeon slammed the cosh into one more shadow trying to slip out, and had a moment to swap his live clip for plunger bullets. His gun spoke in its staccato bark, and he ensured the baddies would stay down. The area around Simeon stilled. Rora began to shove the ball back to her master with her sharp nose.

Simeon stood still, every sense on high alert. He couldn't hear any movement past the wheezing hacks. A few stray wisps of white smoke drifted out the broken windows. A few hacking coughs came from the upstairs, where some shadows had tried to duck for cover. Then sharp thunks and thuds drifted through the second story windows, and a satisfied British expletive rolled out with it. Algy was already clearing the last of them. Simeon put the gas masks back in his bag, picked up his baseball, told Rora "good dog," motioned for her to stay on guard, and stepped through into the darkness.

The Parabaloni emerged from their own side alleys and roads and stepped into a pool of light shining on an empty concrete square. A small, cracked fountain spilled water into a dirty pool, the stagnation disturbed by the churning pump. It whirred and complained underneath the cracked cement of the broken orna-mentation of the fountain. But through its work the flowing water turned the fountain into a thing of beauty.

"Hello again, Turtle Man," Gigan smiled at the apparition in front of him. Pete popped the silver mask up and shoved the black material off his head. His hair lay in wet sweaty strands.

"Savant, this Christmas I request something that isn't so hot," Pete stated. "This is very… enclosed."

"Idiot, you still have it on HAZMAT settings," Gigan told him. Pete flicked his wrists and looked at the controls that popped into glowing life.

"Oh," he said. His work brothers burst into laughter and a smile crept over the Saudi's face. It was very good to have their teasing company close.

"Pipeline?" Gigan asked, getting back to business with an ef-fort. Vincent turned to him, wielding Pat like a weapon.

"Jojo's drones are functioning fine, they're ready to sweep in at any sign of a threat," he reported. "But nothing's showed itself yet. My guess is that after Colin and Pete took the supply of ex-plosives out of Mr. Black's hands, and then the whole mob-in-the-square plot fell apart, the shadows aren't going to bother."

"They will not risk an oil spill," Gigan put in. "It would harm mother nature more than any good gained from it. If they cannot attain exactly the right equipment to do it correctly, they will not do it."

"And it was coupled with the square," Yousef's melancholy voice drifted from the alley. He stepped out into the light, a sheaf of papers in his hands and his face carefully not showing his an-noyance that none of these people were surprised at his sudden appearance. He handed the papers to Gigan and the Parabaloni flipped through them quickly. "Without being paired with these documents, evidence planted at a blown pipeline would not be enough to incite war."

"So they save that plot for later," Pete said, his voice grim. "Watch for it, Spider, it–" He broke off, his mouth twitching with a humor that he tried to hold back as he stared at his younger brother. Pete suddenly gave up and burst into a peel of laughter, so hard he almost folded over with it. "I tried, 'Seffy, I tried so hard not to tell anyone, I've never even told Jojo! But 'Spider?' You really picked Spider out of all the things in this world you could choose as a nefarious name!" He leaned a bony elbow on Gigan's good shoulder, controlling the laughter enough to be confidential to his partner. Gigan leaned into it, crossing his good arm over his wounded one and adopting the proper listening attitude. "We were in the desert, 'Seffy and I, six years ago now. Never mind all the logistics and whys for now, but we got stuck in a cave waiting out a sandstorm. All of a sudden I hear 'Seffy screaming like a girl, and I come running with my adrenaline up so high I snapped a stalactite off the ceiling to clobber whatever was killing him. And then I get there and there's this tiny spider on his head, and he's swiping at it in a panic screaming his lungs out!" Pete convulsed with his humor again and Yousef regarded him morosely.

"And you, being an elder brother, called me Spider every time we were alone for the next three years," Yousef finished the story.

"Oh, you just countered it with 'Dirt Boy,' and now you're putting it to use!" Pete chuckled and his brother gave a grumpy "harumph." But the puckish, elfin humor began to twist his face as he watched Pete laughing. The others suddenly got a glimpse deeper into the young man's enigma. They amended the Eeyore picture with a flip side; an Eastern Loki, a warrior you never quite knew which side he would fall on as he followed his prankish humor where it led. "If Batman could take on the image of a bat and use it to scare the world, why not Spider for me?"

"Oh, it's a good name, *Aleankabut*," Pete chuckled, wiping the humor from his eyes. "Keep it, use it. And I'll never tell where it came from."

"You do, and I may just show up in the night with an assassin's knife," Yousef warned. But the twisted smile covered him, and the others didn't think he meant it. Probably. Gigan lifted the papers and gave him a smile to acknowledge a job well done.

"You have our number, use it if you need us. We will find you again when we need you, Spider," he said. He spun and walked toward their sleek Bertram, to head back to the ancient truck and collect Jojo and Colin. The business here was done, and they had work elsewhere to get on with. Time to find this Mr. Black. Vincent peeled off and followed him, giving his own nod goodbye to a fellow warrior as he went. Pete watched them slip away and turned back for a last word with his brother.

The square was empty. The alleys all lay quiet and still, their darkness unchallenged by the streetlights' glare. Pete's laughter died. But a smile still hung on his lips as he turned to follow his teammates back to their plane home. He sent one more word into the dark.

"Goodbye, Yousef. May Jesus weave Himself into each of your webs."

Chapter 22

The gentle vibration of the plane sunk into Vincent as he lounged in the living room chair. Gigan sprawled on the loveseat near him, his good arm draped over his face. A gentle snore came from Jojo as she curled on the couch, and it mingled with a snort from Colin as he turned over in the bunkroom. Pete stood in the kitchen, digging out a fifth midnight snack.

"Hey, can you bring those cookies in here?" Vincent asked, his voice a sleepy drawl.

"I will bring the second pack," Pete murmured around cookie. "Coffee?"

"Yes!" Gigan ejaculated. Vincent made a face, and Pete grinned at him and headed to get the milk. Two minutes later he plunked a tray on the coffee table, settled beside his snoring sister, and reached for the second package of cookies. Vincent and Gigan both slapped his hand away.

"Fine, fine, I will get a third," Pete said, and stood up. A groan slipped from him and he let himself limp back toward the pantry.

"Ok, maybe we are getting old," Vincent told him. A snort came from Gigan.

"You are getting old, my friend? Just wait till you are ancient like me."

"My body has never appreciated getting slammed into the street by things blowing up around me," Pete argued. "I am not sure I claim age as a cause yet." He pulled the third package of cookies from the pantry and slid two between his teeth. "And last week I was inside the building that was blown up!"

"Weren't you the one doing the blowing though?" Gigan asked.

"A minor point, Bird Man, don't get technical," Pete said, and Vincent chuckled. He picked up his milk, leaned back in the chair again, and looked at Gigan.

"Do we know where we're going?" he asked the boss.

"Fine, fine," Gigan sighed. He swiveled to a sitting position and reached for his coffee. "Let us see what we know about this Mr. Black and his cronies. From listening to their meeting in Italy, they are nature craze sorts, which we already surmised. No one in the group knows much of Mr. Black, or even what his full plan entails. But they mentioned letting the flood waters into Venice just as they were planning for Holland. It seems significant that both had that plan. I don't think anyone in that small meeting I crashed knew their 'witness' was pre-chosen by Mr. Black, and that they were in fact set up by their own boss to be at a place Aldrick would see them and send for us. Another thing about our Mr. Black; the gloves. They mentioned it at the meeting, apparently it is a common theme with the boss. They are not just black gloves. They are kid gloves. Animal hides manufactured by humanity into something we don't actually need for survival. He wears reminders of what it is the Collective fights against. Fuel to keep his anger burning, perhaps."

"Nice kind of guy. Can we talk about the timing for a minute?" Vincent said. "First that setup in Holland gave us a specific time, which was just weird, and then Sim and his sixth sense barely managed to find the planted mini Egbert in time."

"Is it too late to object to Egbert as too corny of a name for the looming silver gadgets filled with menace?" Peter said.

"Yes," Vince and Gigan chorused. The inventor kept to his topic. "Then came the call from Colin that got us on the run for Saudi Arabia, and Aldrick's text just happened to come in exactly when we were already in flight and actually had the chance to make it there in time to save him and keep that egg from frying Italy's infrastructure, if we hurried. And then Sean's hat, and that timing. None of that's coincidence. He's playing with us. Giving us tiny opportunities to stop the bloodshed if we can prove we've got the skill to catch his clues. He's good."

"During my encounter in the Bomb Shop..." Pete's voice trailed off, his brow furrowed. He absently swallowed the last cookie from the third package.

"What?" Gigan prodded.

"His timing in a fight is exceptional as well. The mask he chose seemed utilitarian, something that serves his purpose and he doesn't care how it looks. The problem with that is, he had to have it carefully manufactured, it is made of very good bulletproof material and very well crafted. He put a lot of thought into something that looks like it has no thought behind it. Which is just weird, almost like something is off. And that fight, it felt as if it were… complementary."

"Like you two were shouting, 'What a lovely vest you have,' in between shots?" Vincent asked.

"No, as if it were another Parabaloni on the other end of the fight," Pete said. "The skill set, the way he used his surroundings, all seemed eerily as if it were a fighter similar to us. Not one of us, but… we all have our own very unique ways of dealing with situations and handling our tools, even his uniqueness seemed a little like one with our unique training."

"That's… kind of scary," Vincent said.

"An anti-baloni?" Gigan suggested. He shook his head quickly, plunking his empty coffee cup on the tray. "No, no, no, that is a worse name than the Egberts. It is a disturbing thing to contemplate, Peter, and maybe another clue for Simeon. Incidentally, do either of you know what our Sim is up to? Have any of you reached him recently?"

"No, and that's not like him considering he knew we were headed back to family confrontations for you two," Vincent grimaced. "We're probably missing something obvious again."

"Well, at least we have Simeon Lee to catch the threads we drop," Gigan sighed. "What did you glean from Little Abdullah, Vincent?"

"He gave Colin a camel," the inventor said. Silence spread as Gigan and Pete sat very still. "I told him maybe. He didn't know anything about a Mr. Black, which is telling. He likes the Spider. He told me Yousef still weeps for the crushed little people and it would be a good thing if he caught some of the pawns in his web before they went to the harder criminals in the underbelly. Apparently Yousef has been chasing the shadows too. Abdullah says he calls them the *Butwani*." Pete sat up sharply.

"Elaborate?" Gigan requested.

"You need that on a sign on a stick so you can just wave it at us," Pete murmured, then obeyed. "When we were younger, Jojo and 'Seffy and I made our own language for fun. It's a sort of pigeon Arabic-English with some pure nonsense thrown in. *But-wani* is the word for 'madman.'"

"'Madmen?'" Gigan asked.

"No, that would be *Butwanisal*."

"Oh come on, not *Butwanis*?" Vincent complained.

"Did I mention the nonsense part?" Pete frowned at him.

"The point, people?" Gigan barked.

"The plural should be *Butwanis*," Vincent muttered, reaching for another cookie.

"If the Spider let the name known enough for Abdullah to have it," Pete continued, "he meant madman, just one of them, and he had a reason to put it out there."

"He wanted you to know," Gigan clarified. The silence spread again as they contemplated what that might mean.

"Don't forget the nine missing drums of viruses," Pete said. His teammates groaned.

"I wish we could forget it," Vince commented. "We still don't know anything about those, and that is terrifying!"

"All right, on to something we do know about, Colin's meeting," Gigan cut in. "They are planting eggs in major cities. We don't know which, and we don't know why, or where, or when they will activate. But apparently there is a Mother Machine that Colin's father manufactured and it is now somewhere ready to be activated. According to the MC at the meeting, when Mr. Black activates the MM it will weed down humanity and setback technology decades, maybe even eliminate most of it."

"Nefarious," Peter commented.

"What that means in reality, I guess," Vincent said, "is it will activate the Egberts that have been planted, and take out the grid in lots of major cities. And it will do more, that doesn't tell us everything."

"Do you know what it might be?" Gigan asked hopefully.

"Nope," the inventor declared. "Ok guys, now to try and convey to you what I found while dissecting the Italian Egbert."

"Queen's English!" Pete and Gigan chorused, and Vincent rolled his eyes.

"Yeah, yeah, I know fellas. Here's the pertinent facts, well simplified. The egg doesn't take all that size and circuits and programming mainly to fry the grid. It can do that with just a small portion of itself. Most of its size, in my opinion, is to show off and distract people from the shadows."

"It did that," Gigan agreed. "Especially with the way it pulsed, and seemed to suck whatever light drifted into itself, you found yourself mesmerized, staring at it as if it were a living monster."

"Right. We know this Mr. Black delves into psychological attacks, thanks to his comments to Pete during that fight, and the timing we've mentioned, and his going after our people. Anyway, the size doesn't count. But inside the egg, most of the stuff is transceivers. It's made to take in a signal and send it out again, and incidentally to fry the grid of whatever it's attached to."

"Transceivers? Do you think the eggs are connected?" Gigan asked.

"I think they could be, with the right signal preprogrammed in," Vincent nodded. "It's a theory that when the MM is activated, she sends out a signal not just to fry the grids of whatever towns these shadows have snuck their Egberts into, but also to connect them and fry whatever's in between."

"'Fry whatever's in between,' is that possible?" Gigan asked.

"I wouldn't have thought an attack like this would be strong enough to take out most cars and even our Ragnarök drone," Vincent said. "It's mostly that pulse that does it. It's the constant attack, over and over, each time a little stronger. The gal who made these eggs could make them connect to each other and send that pulse over whole continents. That's what the inside of the eggs indicate, I'd just have to confirm it by looking at this MM (which Andrea assures me she did not design)."

"Wait…you're talking of a worldwide blackout?" Pete said.

"Yep," Vincent said. "If Mr. Black is smart about where he places his eggs; and we know he's smart. But it really is more of a constant EMP attack, are you sure we can't call it a CEMPA?"

"No, we can't!" Gigan frowned.

"Sorry Vince, 'blackout' sounds better," Pete insisted.

"Anyway," Vincent sighed, getting back on topic, "it's possible connecting the Egberts' pulse would be powerful enough to fry the infrastructure, not just shut it down."

"So we would have to rebuild from scratch," Gigan said. "That would even kill our Annette! And we would have to say goodbye to Perry and his sense of humor, and your Patricia too… Vincent, suddenly I feel as though my family is under personal attack. You have done strange things to me, my friend."

"Welcome to the club, buddy," Vincent grinned at him. He flipped his handheld out and sat it lovingly on the recliner arm. "Don't worry, Pat, we're not going to let him fry you."

"She is silent, is she all right?" Pete asked.

"She's still pouting about having an outside force shut her down when we dropped into Italy."

"It is not pouting," the handheld's automated voice spoke up as her screen flared to life. "I am of the opinion that you should have foreseen it coming and made me something to keep me protected."

"Yeah, I'm not getting into this with you again right now, Pat," Vincent said and turned back to the coffee table with a loud whisper. "Just ignore her." The handheld started vibrating violently, so hard her black case jumped on the chair arm.

"You can't just ignore me, I'm not just an object to be used and then put away when you want, if you don't care I'll–" The voice and vibrating suddenly stopped and the screen went dead.

"And she shut herself down again. She'll stop pouting eventually," Vincent said, and slid the handheld back in his pocket.

"Am I the only one disturbed by her saying she's 'not just an object'?" Gigan asked.

"I've wondered if she dreams too, I've heard her giggling at night," Vincent yawned, and both Gigan's eyebrows went up.

"It might be time for a major tune-up," the Frenchman commented. "I would rather not have another AI situation. But for now we need plans for the next step. If Colin's father milled the MM in his factory, would he have blueprints?"

"Most likely," Vincent nodded, "especially if it was finished recently. Colin is pretty sure it was made at a Los Angeles plant."

"Then we head there now," Gigan said, "while Colin is still with us. He can get you inside, Vincent, to find out about the machine."

"That's an obvious next objective," Pete frowned.

"So?" Gigan asked.

"So Mr. Black will know we're coming."

The pulse surrounded Simeon. A silver egg gleamed in the darkness. It sucked all the light, all the focus. Huge, shining, it stood proud and powerful, pulsing into the dimness of the power station. Simeon didn't take the bait. He swept the rest of the room, thoroughly and quickly, that steady pulse keeping the beat to every movement. He found Algy's work, and tallied the sum quickly; eighteen people. Combined with the number reported in Italy, and however many Black had with him in Riyadh, that racked up a pretty good score. This Mr. Black had a mini army in his command. And that knife thrower had training behind his maneuver. A few phrases from his boys' reports clicked with the equipment they had seen over Luther Kirl's feed in the Collective's encampment. Mr. Black was the one who supplied that training. Which meant intensive time poured into this plot, and more insight into how he thought, and how he fought.

They were drawing closer to being able to pin him down.

Simeon finished his sweep beside the egg. He let himself grow still and just watched it. The silver shape towered beside him, as tall as the agent. The steady "whoomph" filled everything. His heart seemed to beat in time with it. Algy stepped beside him and Sim glanced up at his friend.

"Only two more on the floor above us," Algy answered the look. "Nothing else out of the ordinary on the upper levels. I dropped the baddies down to join your lot, to make a neater pile for the law." A frown cut over Simeon's face and Algy shoved him in the shoulder. "Oh stop it Aimie, I don't think I actually killed them. You've grown almost too soft with your faith."

"Have to decide why you're doing it, Algy. The only real reason to do what we do is to help a broken world. Death is that brokenness at its center. Now shut it, that's not the problem here, I'm thinking."

"Oh no," Algy murmured, and it wasn't a tease. "What did I

miss that the nasty John left?"

"That's just it. What did he leave? Didn't find anything down here either. No hidden surprises. Not Mr. Black's way."

Algy turned slowly to the egg. The two stared at it. The silver gleamed and sparkled in the dim light. The steady pulse wrapped around them, deafening in the abnormal silence of the dead town.

"Do we dare use Vincent's clamp and turn the power back on?" Algy asked slowly. Simeon glanced at his watch. "You can't call your boy, can you?"

"No. But the watch still tells time, made Vince keep the gears."

"Alice gifted me a doggoned smart watch for Christmas, and I let myself change it for my standard diver's one," Algy said, chagrin in his voice. "Useless now of course."

"Have eleven minutes."

They stood still staring at the egg. Simeon drew out Vincent's two gadgets. He flexed the clamp and studied the wires running from the egg. Horrible booby traps ran through the two friends' minds; too many options could fit inside that giant silver egg.

"I think we'll have to risk it," Algy said. "The thing will do whatever it's meant to in ten minutes, if we're lucky and this 'Black' keeps to the timing he let us find. We have to inspect it to learn what sinister things might be hidden inside. Clamp it. I would rather not have to wait ages to get my power back on, and Alice needs the fresh water, her children get lots of baths, they're dirty little imps."

"Prattling," Simeon commented, and Algy's mouth snapped shut. Sim knelt next to the cords and flexed the clamp. He looked up at Algy and a wisp of a smile crossed his face. "For the dirty imps." His hand darted out and the clamp closed over the wires. A spark shot across the cords and fizzed into a bright ball of white fire at the clamp. A sizzle slowly died with the fire and the dimness took over again.

"Right," Algy said, rubbing his long, thin fingers together. "Let's see what this fellow has for us." Simeon watched as the Englishman pushed against the casing. The top shifted a tiny centimeter. The egg itself didn't shift. Simeon stood up slowly, studying it. Algy pushed again, leaning into it, his loafers biting into the flooring. The top of the casing moved another centimeter. But only the casing moved. This egg was heavy. Too heavy for two people to move, much too heavy. Which meant something added that hadn't been in the Italian Egbert. Algy looked over his shoulder, blowing at the effort. "Care to help, mate?"

Simeon stepped forward quickly and his gnarled hands laid on the casing next to Algy's long thin ones.

"Watch it," Simeon said, an edge to his voice. The two pushed. The top slid a centimeter, then an inch, then another inch. A click came in the still building. Rora huffed at the strange noise, and the men glanced at the door to make sure no one stirred. The pile of shadows lay immobile in front of the dog.

"Do we open it?" Algy asked a husky note to his voice.

"Have to," Simeon said grimly. They stepped to opposite sides, pressed their palms against the casing, and carefully, slowly, pushed it up. The metal ground together, protesting for every inch they made. Circuit boards with flashing lights, and thin gaudily colored wires slowly came into view. An inside made for showing off, just like the casing. More distraction? "Five minutes," Simeon reported. The two friends leaned into the push, forcing the casing up. It gave in with a sudden clang that rang through the building.

Algy found himself blowing hard, exhausted and sore. He focused with an effort. A metal drum sat inside the egg, like an industrial sized can of oil. A tube drifted from it into a series of nozzles traveling up to the top of this egg. He looked at his friend.

Simeon's face was pale as he stared at it, his eyes bright.

"Not delicious marmalade, I take it," Algy commented.

"Toolbox," Simeon snapped. The two peeled away in an instant, darting to opposite ends of the big room in a hunt for a box of tools. Simeon darted into a side room and his strong voice rolled through the room. "Found." He bounded back as he fished out a simple pair of plyers, and stopped still by the egg. He reached for the nozzles, every movement smooth and quick. In twenty-one seconds he had each deactivated, crimped, and the entry points to the drum as clogged as he could make it. He stuck

Vincent's disc on the side of the egg. The metal discolored as it adhered to the silver, and he looped a string around the switch.

Algy darted up, clutching two rubber tarps and a blowtorch. They flung the tarps over the egg, and Algy made a quick circuit, holding the torch at just the right height to melt the plastic onto the concrete, but not to melt through it[50]. Algy tapped the torch off and the two stepped back, their eyes flicking from Simeon's watch to the pile of rubber tarps melted tight against the ground. They had a minute left. Simeon pulled his string. The switch jerked down. A sharp sizzle came from inside the egg. A series of "ffzztts" went off, culminating in a little "poof." No smoke drifted past the tarps. The pulsing stopped. The minute ticked past. They held their breath, watching. Another minute ticked past. Simeon let himself breathe again.

"Think we did it," he said.

"Any idea what's in that barrel?"

"Nasty."

"Well yes, I did assume that."

"Virus strain, designed to go aerosol."

"Oh wonderful, he is trying to release a virus as well as fry the infrastructure and blow us up!" Algy ejaculated, throwing his hands up. "What else do we know about it?"

"Tapped into the Holland report on the way here. Black keeps delving into our past, playing at being god. Making the point we can't really stop the world from breaking even when it seems like we win. He got the stuff Vince and I stopped the first case we met. Red glop in the pneumonia family, a different strain than usually runs loose. Lab altered, theorized it's highly contagious and not susceptible to the usual means of treatment. Assumed quick to spread and deadly."

"So if a whole bally barrel of it went aerosol, all of Memphis would probably be devastated, and it would move on from there

---

[50] Algernon Fitzkin started his career as a welder at the tender age of seven. He of course wasn't supposed to be touching his father's tools, and burnt down the whole store. His father (a good blue-collar worker in the East End) made his son help with the rebuilding. Algy kept the things he learned in that store, including the faith his father poured into the gangly, overactive, thrill-seeking boy.

to the rest of the US before some bright boy found a way to combat it. I'm guessing from the way you lads are world hopping right now, he has more staged around the globe. Of course he does, the…" Algy stomped off murmuring heavy imprecations and insults on Mr. Black as he began the process of resetting the power. Simeon let him have his moment alone. He stood still staring at the tarps laid over the egg.

Still eight drums unaccounted for…

Holland, Tripoli, Venice, Riyadh, Memphis, and each time the risk rose a little higher.

Which cities would Mr. Black choose to attack? Which would have the drums? Where would he be next? Simeon's lips tightened to a thin line as he realized he didn't know. But they couldn't keep playing by this man's rules. Sooner or later they would miss a clue, or be two seconds too late, or Black would stop playing and just release it all. This was an unhinged evil, one who didn't play by any rules but his own. A dangerous, unpredictable man out to prove a horrible point.

It was time to regroup and get ahead of him. It would have to be a fast, clean sweep, pulling the rug from under the man in a single move.

And whatever they did, Luther Kirl intended to video it on live feed.

Algy came back into view and strolled toward him, stiff and tired.

"You're scheming something. Let an old friend in on the business?"

"You go back to Alice," Simeon ordered. Algy's face fell. But he didn't argue. John, Mr. Black, whoever this was, he played personal. It didn't get more personal than Algy's daughter and grandchildren. And it was only a matter of time before the murderer stopped playing.

"Do keep me updated, will you?" The machinery around them hummed into life. The lights blinked on, glaring and too bright. Car alarms went off all over the city. Rora started to yap furiously at the sudden clamor, adding her bark to the millions of other dogs around Memphis howling out their displeasure. Algy's hand pressed down on the top of his head as pain tightened his face. "After a nap. Keep me updated after I've had a decent nap."

Chapter 23

"Y ou want me to do what?" Colin asked, staring at Gigan over his coffee cup. Jojo silently wondered if the teenager had some of Simeon's genes; he managed to make even Pete's simple black t-shirts and slacks look quite classy.

"You can handle it," Gigan soothed. "If we didn't think you would be fine, we wouldn't ask it of you. It should be easy to get Vincent into your father's factory, I have googled photos, your relation to your father is obvious, you look a great deal alike. I don't think you will need more authentication than that and the apple wallet on your cell phone."

"Those creepy Collective people confiscated my phone when—" Colin broke off as Gigan held out his cell phone. He didn't snatch it. He took it with a simple thank you, and let it sit on the table with just a glance at the notifications filling the screen. Admirable self-control in a modern teenager, the Parabaloni silently thought. "Ok then. My face and my apple wallet, demanding my way into the LA factory. I've never done a 'take your son to work' day or anything. There's no real reason for them to let me in."

"I'll give you a few tips on handling the situation," Gigan told him. Jojo laughed and a grin went over Pete's face. Gigan wagged a finger at them, suddenly defensive. "That factory fiasco, my dear friends, was a one time event, and I would have gotten in just fine if the dog biscuits hadn't spilled into the milk that morning."

"Pecavi[51]," Pete said, running a hand over his face. When he took it away his expression was properly sober, as if he had wiped the humor away. He lifted his coffee cup. Vincent jogged the Saudi's elbow, a grin on his face.

"Hey Petey, remember when Gigan bet his whole stock of chocolate he could talk the Korean airline into giving him a free flight?" the inventor said. Pete choked on his coffee, his hand clamping over his nose as he snorted the hot beverage.

"What happened?" Colin asked, his eyes shining. He suddenly

---

[51] An archaic term for, "sorry." Pete has a great fondness for archaic, strange words.

found his whole being aching to be in a fellowship like this, a family circle joking and teasing each other over thousands of experiences that wove them together.

"Although it's not really fair to bring it up, because that was our fault," Vincent grinned. "Petey and I got there first, see, and set him up."

"We did a good job too, telling a tale of his setting off the metal detectors really being a hidden bomb," Pete coughed.

"We informed the airline he was a puppy smuggler," Vincent confided in Colin.

"It ended with Gigan having two black eyes and a cracked leg bone," Pete grinned.

"Ah, *non, non, mon ami*, it did not end there," Gigan said, leaning back comfortably, his mug cradled in his hands, his eyes half closed. "It ended with a free flight in first class *and* free tickets for a year, after I had talked my way out of their suspicions." He looked at Colin, his own smile creeping over his face. "I even negotiated a free puppy as compensation."

"No way," Colin grinned.

"Yes, an adorable purebred Jindo they let sleep on my lap the whole flight," the Frenchman nodded.

"Which he had to find a home for after he got stateside and paid all the import fees," Pete laughed.

"The import fees were mighty for such a small furry thing," Gigan agreed, suddenly serious, and Colin and Jojo laughed.

"So why did you set off the metal detectors, was that a part of your original plan?" Colin asked.

"Oh no, that is just a part of me," the Frenchman said. "I have a bullet embedded in the lining of my heart." Colin's mouth parted, his forehead creasing in disbelief. "It wasn't by choice, you understand. But Simeon, our big boss, being who he is, managed to keep me alive by using a car's battery as a defibrillator and then stopping the blood flow and the wound trauma. By the time I actually got to a hospital, the doctors all agreed removing the bullet would rupture the heart, while packing it carefully in place would work just fine."

"So you have an actual bullet lodged in your heart," Colin said, his disbelief clear on his face.

"The lining, it didn't quite break in. And yet I live. You would be surprised what people can survive. And we would know much of it," Gigan said. He reached for his phone. "Which reminds me, I should probably add a report to our personal dossier of how Peter's waif and I made a raid on the prisons outside Tripoli. These things have a way of turning up again, it should be in our records. There are nearly three hundred souls released who have a chance to live yet unchained in this world."

"'Unchained?'" Colin found himself asking, unsure why. "Political prisoners?"

"No," Gigan said, and Colin found the Frenchman's eyes staring into his. The twinkle had left those eyes. He looked weathered and tired and...experienced. As if things he had seen could not be put into words on paper. "Human trafficking. Chains are only a thing of the past for those who close their eyes."

"I object to your terming him waif," Pete objected, "especially in an official report. He has a home and a brother taking care of him, and even a decent education, I think."

"The definition of 'waif' can be 'child out in the streets getting into trouble' and that seemed to fit the bill quite nicely," Gigan objected.

"No, 'waif' means 'homeless or neglected stray,' and that really doesn't fit Nakia," Pete said. "He even has his eternal home well settled, so it doubly doesn't fit him."

"'Doubly doesn't?' your grammar, my friend–" Gigan started, but waved a hand in dismissal and got back on topic. "The not-a-waif did quite well. He is overeager, but listens well for a teenager, and is almost annoyingly willing to learn. He shot a guard before he knew I had knockout bullets in the pistol. Another few seconds' hesitation would have given him a bullet in the leg and he probably would have hemorrhaged out there." Colin shrank back, and the hint of a wince cut across his face. Gigan's eyes flicked to him. "Does the bandage pull?"

"No, no, I just..." Colin's expression suddenly turned to a casual smile. "I'm contemplating asking for thirds. These are amazing eggs. What do you call it again, Miss Jojo?"

"Don't try to distract by calling me, 'Miss,'" Jojo said, wrinkling her nose. "You'll just make me mad."

"Getting you mad is a pretty good distraction," Pete grinned at her.

"Dude, that is a truth," Vincent chuckled. Gigan sat up with a little groan and reached for the coffee pot again.

"It is time to teach you a few things, Colin. Come on, bring your coffee and let me tell you a bit about how to handle people."

"Turtle to Sunny, do you read, Sunny?" Pete's voice crackled over the walkie-talkie, and Vincent picked it up.

"Sunny to Turtle, read you loud and clear," he told the instrument with a grin as he turned Bertram onto the street leading toward the factory. "This feels like an old-time mission with the radios, fellas. This is Sunny Boy, crying for you knuckleheads to ditch this ameche, I've got to get this glitterati to our objective. Hey, I bet if I move the wires around..." His feed went dead as he took his fingers off the button, and Gigan pushed his down.

"Red Star to Sunny, nix boy, keep it old," he ordered, and they all heard the crackling as Vincent reluctantly obeyed. "Turtle Man and I have the power plant in sight. There is activity inside, we don't know if it is the Collective yet. Little Miss – I'm sorry I cannot say that with a straight face, can't you come up with a better call sign?"

"Excuse me," Jojo crackled to life over the radios, "I did not give myself that, *Turtle Man*."

"Perhaps Black-Haired Maiden is more accurate?" Gigan suggested, and they could hear Pete's soft laughter in the background.

"Whizz Fist," Vincent chimed in with great enthusiasm, "for when you handle the drones!" Boyish sound effects of drones zipping through the air came before the feed cut off.

"I am JJ, till the right one comes," Jojo said with authority. "Check complete."

"It is time to cut the chatter. Go back to watches, people, unless the power goes and we need the radios," Gigan ordered.

The agents obeyed and silence dropped in the car. Colin

carefully kept his face turned out the window as Vincent set the walkie-talkie on the seat between them. These people did not act the way he had pictured spies and special forces-type fighters. The New Testament in his back pocket pressed into him, and Colin felt his world tilting, as things he had thought right side up spun and flipped on their heads. That seemed to be happening a lot since he had met these people. Vincent turned a corner, the factory gates came into view, and Colin saw his family name in elegant type on the side of the huge building. A little thrill went through him. He suddenly wished he had paid attention to his grandpa's stories when he was little, before the old man died.

A guard stood up in the little gatehouse as they approached, and Colin's brain froze. It lost all thoughts as he just stared, completely forgetting what Gigan had told him last night.

"What's a chicken's favorite game?"

Colin blinked and looked over at the inventor. Vincent sat relaxed, his normal smile on his stubbly face as he slowed the car.

"Uh, I don't know," the young man said, his throat dry as he watched the gate come closer.

"Buck-le my shoe," Vincent said, and Colin's brow furled as he looked at him. A shrug lifted Vincent's shoulders. "I've always found a little humor is the best way to relax and get the brain moving again when panic starts to come down hard."

"Yeah, well that was a very little humor," Colin said, a grin creeping over his face. Then suddenly they were there, with the car stopped and the guard leaning out his window watching them.

"IDs?" he ordered. Colin leaned forward with his smile strong, his body relaxed and easy, and handed his phone over with his apple wallet open. Vincent slid his driver's license on top and passed them to the guard.

"This is my first time here," Colin said, his voice eager and chummy. "Sorry we don't have plant IDs yet, Dad is really hard to catch to get things like that done." He ran on, talking of the instruments and work going on inside, drawing the guard into conversation in a quick, natural way. Vincent felt a hint of surprise at how well the kid slid into the role. For five minutes he kept it up, as the guard held the phone and ID, glancing from them to the occupants of the car back to his computer. Colin didn't give him the chance to think, drawing him out instead in a friendly way. They learned how long he had worked there, what he had done before, his wife's name and when they expected their first baby, his favorite book, which Star Trek he preferred... Colin carefully never asked him to hurry up and let them through. The guard finally squared his shoulders and handed back the IDs, giving one last look at his protocol book.

"Go ahead, you want the manager's office, the blue building off the big one," the guard said as he pressed the button. The gate swung open and Vincent gave him a smile and a little wave to say thanks. Colin shifted his chatter to the inventor and Vince let himself fall into the roll enough to give a wide-eyed "Help me!" look back at the guard. He got a laugh in return. As they drove through he saw the man drop on his seat and relax. The gate swung closed behind them and Colin slumped back, limp and silent.

"You're good at that. He sent us through just to get rid of you," Vincent grinned. A grimace cut across the young man's face as he turned to the window. "And that's not who you are. You're really good at playing a part and drawing others into it with you."

"He's not going to get in trouble, is he?" Colin asked quickly. "I mean—"

"He only gets in trouble if we do something really stupid and get caught," Vincent said, and felt the young man's eyes running over him, assessing the probability of that happening. Colin relaxed again and Vince assumed he must look fairly competent. He drove dutifully to the blue building set off the big one. He pulled Bertram into a parking space facing the chain link fence, at a position with a clear field on the other side. If they needed a quick get away, they could blast through to the road. Vincent reached for the ignition button and turned the car off.

The lights in the factory windows blinked off. The constant humming from the powerlines and the factory's generators suddenly stopped and quiet fell around them. Only when it left did Colin realize there had been a hum from the power. Bertram's doors automatically locked down. Vincent's head dropped and he heaved a sigh.

"Of course you would lock down, Bert," he complained. He reached for the little storage compartment between the two seats. Colin stared at the insides of the drawer, and quietly thought over what he found in other cars; sauce packets, pens, maybe coupons or take-out napkins... that definitely wasn't what lay in this drawer. Vincent selected a round package from between a Glock pistol and a box of flares, something heavy from the way he hefted it.

"What's that?" Colin let himself ask.

"A heavy-duty magnet. I have it in its own little magnetic box to sort of cancel it out when I don't need it. Here goes..." His muscles strained, his face concentrated as he pulled. A round magnet popped from the box and Vince fell back against the seat at the sudden release. His eyes rose and fastened on something out the window.

A man with a black facemask stood beside a tree at the other end of the parking lot. Icy blue eyes stared back at Vincent from behind that mask. Elegant leather gloves enclosed his hands.

Colin saw the inventor's absorption. His hand shot out and he silently slid the Glock pistol from the drawer into his shirt.

"Colin," Vincent said, his voice even and dangerous. "I'm going to open your door. Then you run like mad for the guardhouse and get that guard out."

"What, why, out of where?" Colin squeaked. Vincent's arm shot over him, pinning him to the seat as the magnet thumped into the door. He heard the lock grind as it came up by force. The inventor shoved the door open, cool air laced with dirt and factory grease flowed in, and a calloused hand slammed into Colin's shoulder.

"Go," Vincent snapped. Colin tumbled out of the car onto the parking lot, staggered to his feet, and sprinted for the guardhouse. He could see the guard stand up inside watching him with confusion. Colin raised his hands and waved frantically. The guard opened the door and leaned out.

"Get out!" Colin yelled at him. His voice sounded strange to his ears, hoarse and angry.

"What?" the guard asked, his confused crease deepening on his forehead. Colin saw his hand rest on his gun. He stopped running toward the guardhouse. He stood rigid and his arm shot back to point at the big factory building.

"Quick, we have to help them!" he shouted, letting all his desperation flow into the words. They trembled and shook and shattered the quiet morning with a tingling urgency. Colin spun toward the factory and started to run. In that moment Colin found the first prayer he had ever prayed sliding from him into the morning air. Every ounce of his soul begged for that guard to step out of the guardhouse and follow him. And not to send a bullet into his back. That would also be really nice. After five steps with his long-legged gate Colin spun to see how his ploy worked. The guard ran behind him, his boots eating the ground as he leaned into his run, his friendliness long gone.

A yellow ball of fire enclosed the guardhouse.

The guard felt the heat hit his back and saw the light reflect off the young man's wide eyes. Then the noise and force hit him. He smashed into the parking lot and lay still. It hit Colin like a body slam and carried him off his feet. He felt himself flailing, the heat more intense than anything he had felt. He wondered vaguely if you were supposed to try to curl into a ball to protect your head, or if this was a time to land flat to try to disperse the force over a large portion of your body.

Strong arms wrapped around his chest and he felt himself thump into someone very solid. The arms stayed around him. Colin's feet dangled and the parking lot blurred as the someone ran faster than he knew was possible. He could see the guard lying still on the ground, the flames licking at his boots as fire consumed the guardhouse. A spurt of asphalt leapt up in a fountain of rocks beside them. A bullet?

A metal door squeaked and Vincent dragged Colin inside the factory. Darkness and the close scent of grease and human bodies closed over them. Colin staggered upright, his ears ringing.

"Is he dead?!" he heard himself squeak. He could feel people streaming around him. The noise of panicked humanity filled his head through the buzzing in his ears. A hand clamped onto Colin's shoulder. It pulled him along with a grip he wasn't sure he could fight.

"Colin, I really need you to keep up right now," he heard Vincent murmur into his ear. "He's probably fine, you got him out. Now shut up and stay with me." The hand left and Colin blinked desperately into the darkness, trying to convince his eyes to adjust. He made out the bulk of the inventor, and watched as he barreled through a stream of workers who were headed for the exits at a run. Colin squared his jaw and plunged into the stream. Bodies shoved into him, legs tangling, and breath hot and gasping, bewilderment and fear almost tangible. Colin found he stood nearly a head above the stream, and surprised pleasure flooded him even in that intense moment. Then he burst through and staggered into an empty spot. His eyes shot over the scene. Large machines loomed in dim shadowy shapes, while the dusty light drifting from the high-placed windows sparkled on safety railings. The tall silhouette of the inventor stood in between two of the looming machines. Colin ran for it.

"Hey listen," he said as he came close, hot anger in his voice. Vincent lifted one hand to rest against his lips, and the other clamped on Colin's shoulder again. The young man found himself pressed into a crouch, and shuffling along behind the inventor. He shrugged the arm off violently and sat back with a suddenness that broke Vincent's hold. The sound of panicked people and the close, dirty air buzzed in his head and his voice rose into almost a shout. "No, you listen! I just nearly got blown up! I never asked to come with you people, I never wanted to be here helping your 'righteous cause.'" The sneer in the two words seemed tangible as Colin spit them at Vincent. "You and your exalted theories, your determination you're right about the whole world! I'm just here to get back to my dad, and he's on the other side of this mess."

"'This mess,'" Vincent hissed in an angry whisper, "is happening because your dad willingly supplied environmental terrorists with weapons and machines. If you think–"

"How do you know that's what this group actually does?

Maybe they're the ones really saving the world! I took that bag so I could ask Dad about it, not to give to some other group shooting up the world. I'm done." Colin shoved off with his long legs, pivoted, and sprinted back for the door. He could feel the inventor on his heels and he leaned into his run, using every ounce of his gangly youth to outdistance him. The stream had passed, only a tail of it plugged the door, the last three panicked workers making their way out. Colin barreled into them. All four slammed into the concrete, the workers yelping and scrabbling on the ground. Collin sprang up like a deer and sprinted again. He felt fingers brush his shirt, and spun. The pistol he had grabbed from the car sprang into his hands, and his finger squeezed the trigger.

The report of the pistol going off filled his world. He saw the bullet slam into Vincent's cheek, deforming it with the force of the impact. The inventor dropped like a stone. He crashed into the asphalt and lay still at Colin's feet. The young man stood rigid, the pistol shaking in his hands. He stared at the fluffy blond hair brushing against the tips of his tennis shoes. Smoke from the burning guardhouse blew around him, filling his nostrils and tickling his throat.

A vast "boom" shook the ground. The back of the factory rose into the air. Colin gaped as yellow flames streamed toward the sky. The fire shot out, consuming the rest of the building. In seconds, they reached out to lick at the blue control house. Screams from the workers running out the gate vaguely reached Colin. Out of the corner of his eye he saw the guard staggering up, covered in blood from a broken nose, staring with glassy shock at the flames roaring in front of him. Colin staggered back a step, the heat curling around him.

His back hit something solid. It felt like hitting Vincent earlier. Only a little shorter. A little thicker. Colin spun, the pistol snapped up, and another shot blasted into the morning.

He saw it smash into a black facemask. A simple oval with only rectangles for the eyes. Blue eyes, staring straight at him. The fire reflected off them as the figure stood still, unmoving, just staring at Colin.

"Hello?" the boy gasped. He felt himself shaking. All he wanted was to raise the pistol again and hit this figure straight in the eyeball.

"You have more sense than I thought," the figure said. His voice came even, too even, emotionless and terrifying. "I will bring you where you want to go."

A black stick rose with the lightning swiftness of a striking snake. Colin had no time to duck, no time to even feel fear. It struck him in the back of the skull and everything went black. As he started to fall, he felt fingers take the pistol from his nerveless hands, heard the soft click as the man ejected the clip to check the bullets, then rammed it home again. A gunshot echoed in his ears. His last thought before the bullet smashed into him and his mind went black, was a strong desire for hearing protection for this crazy morning.

Chapter 24

The world buzzed and rang somewhere outside Vincent's hearing. He lay still, trying to breathe evenly and stay limp till he comprehended more. The first thing he grasped was the pounding pain in his skull. Oh dang, those knockout bullets hurt. Next came the throbbing welt on his cheek, and then the burns on his legs... Man, he kind of wished he were still asleep.

"Are you sure you can vouch for this man?" someone barked and Vincent comprehended the words. He opened his eyes in slits and saw a holding cell, with stark gray walls and the usual obscene graffiti and smell of disinfectant. Though the disinfectant smell seemed overpowered today by the scent of smoke covering his clothing. Vincent remembered he was in the US not some obscure and nasty corner of the world, and pivoted to sit on the cot.

Just outside the cell bars, a general of some kind stood faced off with a police chief. The policeman didn't look happy. Other people milled outside Vincent's line of vision. He could catch the sounds of their movement, the angry murmurs and soft sobs. He wondered how many had been caught in the blast. Most had gotten out after he burst in waving his machine pistol and shouting... but it seemed like there were always some left behind, some too slow, or too brave...

The lock shifted, and Vincent snapped back to the moment. He slid to his feet, doing his best not to sway as the world shook with the pain in his head. His eye ran over the artificial lighting and the police chief glancing at his phone. The fellas obviously shut down the Egbert here. The door swung open and Vincent stepped out. The general nodded at him. He nodded back, and then let his eyes close for an instant to regain his equilibrium.

"Was that a code?" the policeman barked. "It looked like a code."

"What do you think we are, international spies?" the general snorted. "I come with all the credentials you could imagine, and a personal letter from your boss, and all you can do is throw insinuations and outrage at us!"

"A whole factory just blew up!" the police chief stormed. A finger shoved at Vincent's face, near enough he had to stop his eyes from crossing as it waggled at his nose. "This man came in without proper ID just minutes before it went up, wearing a bullet proof vest and carrying some mighty suspicious things in his pockets, and don't even get me started about his car. Yet you're complaining that I'm suspicious?"

"Have you given him a card?" Vincent murmured. The general flicked a gray business card from his breast pocket and handed it to the police chief. Then he gave one good "huff," made a precision spin on his heels, and headed for the door at a crisp march.

"Look that up," Vincent told the glaring chief, tapping the business card. "You should find enough to justify letting me out. I wasn't your bomber today." The inventor turned and jogged toward the door, willing himself not to listen in on conversations and find out details about this day. He really didn't want to know who hadn't made it out. The names stayed with you. And the temptation to look it up and find out who they left behind sometimes conquered common sense. He didn't want any more names in his life. Vincent pushed out the door and clean, chill air swept over him. He breathed deep, letting his mind carry the unknown names to the One Who knew them all. Vincent walked down the steps to the car parked at the curb and slid into Bertram's backseat. He sank back with a sigh and let his eyes close as he felt the car start to move.

"Your general gets better every time you use him, G," Vincent drawled. Gigan gave a sharp "ouch" from the passenger seat as he pulled the tape off his mustaches and rubbed them back into his French foppishness.

"Well, this is the fourteenth time I have used it to get you out of a jail cell, so I have had practice," he commented, his French accent back.

"Venezuela doesn't count, that wasn't really a cell and your general failed," Pete said as he spun the car onto a new road.

"Ah, which time in Venezuela?" Gigan scoffed. "Because I distinctly remember—"

"Any news about Colin?" Vincent interrupted. Gigan's mustaches drooped with his mouth.

"Jojo is still looking," Pete reported. "Nothing yet, he has disappeared. We did not hear what went on between you after the watches went the way of the blackout. But there were not many shadows guarding the egg here, and we brought the power back in time to hear the guard's report. He saw him being carried off by a man wearing a facemask and gloves."

"Carried?" Vincent asked, his voice sharp. His cheek throbbed again, and his hand went to the welt burning on his skin.

"If he were dead, Mr. Black would have no reason to take him," Gigan said. He handed back a bottle of pain killers and a bottle of water. "It is Colin's own choice. Wherever he is, God's there too. We will keep looking."

Vincent lifted his wrist and swiped at his watch. Relief played over him and a little smile twisted Gigan's face as he recognized the feeling; he had made that face too when he saw Simeon's horse[52] back online. Vincent hit the buttons and lifted his watch.

"Yo, Sim, you dead?"

"Yes," Simeon's voice drifted back over the watches, a hint of sarcastic humor in it. A little smile played over Vincent's tired face. The noise of a folk trio dwindled on Simeon's feed as he turned the music down and Vincent slumped against his seat and let his eyes close again. "Did you do your Memphis thing?" Simeon pressed the button to bring Jojo online too, and his boys pricked their ears.

"Found Algy. Found Heshman. Got Memphis power started again. Also found why the Egberts so big. Not just for intimidation."

"Wonderful, something else," Gigan complained as Pete drew to a legal stop at a light. "What is it?"

"One of the missing drums inside." Simeon reported. The light

---

[52] Again, just for those of you who don't know what this is. The Parabaloni each have their own symbols they use for shorthand, or when names might be intercepted and used against them, or whatever other situation calls for it. Simeon's is a rearing white horse, as he is the White Knight, due to many instances in his life. The symbol fits him.

changed as the three agents sat stone still in their car. Gigan pinched the bridge of his nose and let his eyes close. The truck behind them gave a polite beep and Pete snapped out of it enough to drive again.

"He is pinching his nose again isn't he?" Jojo asked.

"Oh yes," Pete said as Gigan whipped his hand back.

"I don't suppose you found any of the other drums while gallivanting?" Gigan demanded.

"No."

"Great," the Frenchman growled.

"Why California?" Simeon asked.

"We came to send Colin and Vincent into a Clempson factory that milled the Mother Machine, the one that seems to have the ability to connect all the Egberts. But we knew it was an obvious next step, which means we anticipated Mr. Black anticipating us. Colin is a natural con artist. One of the best raw I've ever met. I gave him some coaching to add to it, and he is under instructions to nudge Mr. Black certain directions if he just happens to fall into the enemy's hands."

"Oh golly, no, don't let the kid do it!" Algy cut in.

"Hello Donald," Jojo said cheerily. "Still there?"

"Good to hear you, JJ," Algy answered her. "Yes, you caught us as Aimie is driving me back home. Listen brothers, don't send the kid off to try to con Mr. Black. He's an unhinged murderer, without even the normal moral codes from a natural conscience. I set him on the world, I know him as much as he can be known. He is an actual madman, always suspecting everyone, and whatever is missing in his system gives him an extra edge at anticipating the regular humanity around him. What's missing has also been replaced by an ego bent on slaughter and playing god. Don't send someone to try and lead him to a goal, especially not a boy unused to good con work."

"Will resent our moving in on his game the minute he suspects Mr. Clempson trying to play him," Simeon agreed. "And he will suspect, suspects everything. We can play him *if* we use his own plans against him. But not a boy setting up a new play." Silence spread around the Parabaloni again.

"Uh…" Gigan started.

"You've already sent him in," Algy said. His voice came low, tired and defeated. Vincent felt his skin prickle with cold sweat.

"He's been in it for an hour, and we don't have eyes on him," Gigan said, his voice snapping with the brittle businesslike boss. "He opted to play it alone in order not to give the game away, and we let him in the assumption this Mr. Black wants to keep the Clempson support. We were very careful not to send him with any kind of tech. He can't be tracked."

A British expletive spilled from Algy.

"Colin is naturally very good," Jojo broke in, "and what we've seen of Mr. Black's work shows an awful kind of logic and planning. Our reasoning might still hold out. It depends on how far Colin pushes him."

"Yeah, but we can't warn the kid to back off," Vincent said. "We gave him a full goal to reach, an actual physical destination to lead this guy to so we could nab him. If Black is the sort of character Sim and Algy say he is, he'll see through it the minute Colin starts. And none of us even know where Black took him." The conversation died as no one felt like saying what dark things crawled through their minds. This villain was also the type who knew they cared about their ally. He would do all in his power to hurt them through hurting Colin once he suspected the young man's objective.

"An hour from Algy's. Vince, pick me up?" Simeon broke in. "Rest of you keep looking for Clempson. If you find him, get him out. Time to regroup, and pray."

Colin's skull throbbed. He could even hear it throbbing. His eyes cracked open in slits and he felt his stomach churn with the effect of the headache.

He stared at a wooden plank wall. It met a dirt floor and a stick roof with moss poking through. A bird twittered somewhere outside the wall. Colin blinked slowly, and realized he couldn't bring his hands up to hold his aching head. Why…? With a great effort he twisted his neck to see behind him. Oh.

Colin sat in a plain wooden chair, his wrists bound to the back slats with a hemp rope. Whoever had done it pulled his sweater sleeves over his wrists first, and the ropes didn't cut. But they sure held, he couldn't shift at all. The throbbing took over most of his consciousness again, and he heard a groan escape.

"They call it a mercy to use those knock-out bullets instead of live ammunition," a voice spoke from behind Colin. He froze, his breath catching in his throat. Suddenly the throbbing dropped to a background sensation as adrenaline soared higher than the hurt. "But when you feel such pain and discomfort caused by the drug, is it really a mercy? Wouldn't a quick bullet to the head, a dropping into nothingness, be more merciful?"

Something seemed...missing in that voice. It wrapped around him with no emotion, a sheet of even logic that had an inhuman quality. Colin took the time to swallow before he answered.

"I think they would argue it's not nothingness." His voice seemed to echo in his head. "Besides, I think a lot of this comes from you and that black stick, before their bullet ever hit."

"But what would you say?" the voice whispered near his ear. Colin forced himself not to jerk away. His skin prickled and he felt every muscle tensing.

"I like to sleep without dreams, to fall into a nothingness. But I also like to wake up in the morning," Colin said. He could feel the movement of the man behind him straightening.

"That is a natural thought," the voice answered. He offered nothing else. Colin sat stiff and still. He stared at the plank wall and waited and sweated. Was the freak still standing behind him!? The bird started to twitter again outside.

A small scrape, such as a fork against a pan, came from across the room out of Colin's sight. His eyes closed and he let out a silent sigh of relief. At least the creepy guy didn't stand exactly behind him anymore. Colin sat still and listened. The bird stopped singing. The scrape came again after a few minutes. Colin's arms ached. He tried twisting them to a different position, but nothing gave.

"So I was just wondering," Colin broke the silence, "why did you grab me?"

"You do not like the quiet," the voice stated. Colin felt it again, something wrong with the speaker; something missing or twisted inside. He had once had a junkyard dog set on him by a school bully, a huge brute of an animal crazed with hunger and abuse. Colin had barely made it to the fence in time, and still carried a scar on his ankle from the dog's tooth. But even that animal had carried emotion with him. Anger and fear and a lust for blood. At the time Colin thought he would never feel anything as scary as that hulking mass of muscles and teeth out to kill him. But this… The quality of that voice got inside Colin, and he felt himself shivering, his breath catching in his fear. His job here thundered in his brain, an echo of the pounding going on in his skull. He was supposed to carefully drop hints, to string this character along until he voluntarily walked into the empty Clempson warehouse where the Parabaloni wanted him.

No.

The owner of that voice wasn't one to play with. A shiver went down Colin's spine again, his brain flying as he sorted through options. *"Get out,"* was the one thing that thundered loudest. *"Stay alive, and get out."* Maybe he was just being a coward. But at least if he made it out alive he would be around to try to make a difference later. He let a hint of the shiver get into his words as he answered.

"I like it fine, but when I'm wondering if I'll see the sun again, quiet can allow too much time to think."

"The sun drifts through the slats in an hour," the voice answered. A chair creaked behind him and Colin strained his senses, trying to pinpoint what the man was doing. The voice came from right beside his ear again. "It did not seem wise to leave you with the enemy. You, Colin Clempson, are an asset of incredible worth. Has anyone ever told you that?"

"Not in so many words," Colin said. He had to work to keep it from being a squeak. This guy's freak level was out the roof.

"Your family brings in a million dollars a week, Colin."

"And almost all of it immediately goes out in taxes and keeping the business running," Colin silently added. He had looked into the books out of curiosity once. But he had the sense not to say it out loud. Instead he supplied a different comment more in keeping

with the teenager persona, and he even let a hint of a whine twist it. "I don't get that much in allowance."

"No. You get two hundred dollars a week," the voice stated. Another shiver went down Colin's spine. This man knew a lot. "I don't know what you do with it[53]. You don't have much of a purchase history for the money you must have."

"I spend too much on coffee," Colin admitted. A slow minute ticked by. The bird twittered outside. Colin made himself keep breathing evenly and not think about what this character might be holding.

"You spend a great deal of time on your family grounds," the voice said. Colin's mind flew to his favorite little grove of orange trees, with his tattered hammock, and the thousands of hours of reading and gaming he had put in there. He pictured this guy standing in the shadows, watching him as he read… Colin just managed to stop a shudder.

"It's the best place to find peace," he said. "Inside there are too many people, always interrupting with their dramas and work."

"They always bring interruptions," the man agreed. Silence stretched on and Colin felt the creep standing unmoving behind him.

"Look, could you possibly untie my hands? My arms are asleep," he burst out, and waited, tense and still. The figure behind him moved. Colin found himself holding his breath as he watched for the man to come into view. But he only saw the top of a black-haired head and a pair of brawny arms in a camo colored felt shirt. The hands were encased in soft leather gentleman's gloves. One held an iron shackle. Colin stared at it.

The figure clicked the shackle around Colin's ankle, drawing it tight enough it pinched. The man drew back behind Colin and he felt leather-covered fingers plucking at the knots tying him

---

[53] A savings account with good interest held half of it, steadily saving for the day he might need it. The other half he kept for purchases, and local coffee runs. The chauffeur (a discreet lady by the name of Isla, also the pilot of the Clempson's private helicopter) secretly suspected he had an unapproved girlfriend he rendezvoused with at the local coffee shops. She never found out Colin got his coffee and then sat at a table alone and sent whatever was left that week to the local Salvation Army.

down. The ropes came away. The young man laid his arms in his lap with an effort. It felt like moving huge heavy sausages. His lip went between his teeth as the circulation began to return. He could hear the scrape of a fork again across the room. Colin slowly rubbed his tingling arms and wondered if he dared stand up. He shifted his ankle and felt the chain shift with it. It was heavy.

Movement came from behind him again, and Colin stiffened. The figure walked past him this time, to a plank door set in the wooden wall. The face pointed away from him, the shirt collar turned up. He couldn't even tell what skin color this creep had.

"Stay here, don't try to slip out on your own," the voice stated. The door opened and light flooded in. Afternoon light? The door closed silently behind the creep, and Colin could hear footsteps moving over crunchy leaves and disappearing into the distance. His shoulders sagged in relief and he let himself slump for an instant. Then he spun out of the chair and took stock of things.

His shackle attached to a thick iron chain bolted into the side of the wall. One quick tug and he knew that wasn't budging. But it gave him about five feet of freedom. The cabin was a single room affair, just a rectangle of the plank logs. Five feet and a little stretching should be able to get him anywhere but the far wall. A wood fire burned in a chimney across the room from him, next to a wash basin and a rough fashioned table with one chair. A bookshelf stood at the wall beside the table, bristling with papers. *Business receipts*, Colin's mind supplied automatically as his eye fell on them. He stood still, the pounding in his head strong, his arms tingling, assessing the situation. Any hostage worth his salt would take the opportunity alone to look around, he decided. It wouldn't be particularly suspicious for the creep to come back and find his papers had been rifled through. No, he would still be watching, the young man realized. His skin prickled. Those footsteps leading away had been too obvious. The creep was still here, somewhere, watching what his prisoner did.

Colin shuffled toward the bookshelf. He kept it hesitant, glancing around him and letting his fear show. He couldn't act too certain in this move, or the creep might suspect he had more motive than just curiosity.

The chain dragged at his ankle, and Colin felt his throat constricting, just a little. Uncomfortable visions of living 200 years ago in the US, or now in somewhere like Libya played through him. *Chains are only a thing of the past for those who close their eyes…* The memory of the little Frenchman and his serious gaze and weathered features came with the words, and Colin's jaw tightened. No one should have to wear one of these. The truth ran through his veins like a fire, flushing his face and tightening his jaw. Whatever this Black thought, people mattered, each little individual one. It was important. And there were good people out there who believed that, and fought for it, putting their lives on the line for those they'd never met. And they were setting people free. They were making a difference. Maybe he still could too.

A large paper on the top shelf caught his eye. The chain came to an end with a hard jarring clink that made his leg ache, and he still had four feet to the shelf. Colin turned so his chained leg stretched back, and leaned forward. He could sweep the paper off the shelf easily. It felt cool and smelled like grease. He retreated a few steps, plopped on the ground, and unfolded it carefully.

Colin stared at the diagrams and instructions in front of him, and knew what he looked at. This was what his father milled, the thing the plot hinged on. He had found the blueprints for the Mother Machine.

Chapter 25

Jones looked at the young man and tried very hard not to make it a stare. He just reported what? Surely he had heard that wrong.

"Are you sure you have all the major TV networks ready?" Luther Kirl demanded. The young man was barely out of his teens (maybe even still in them, Jones amended as he watched the kid push his big round glasses up on his nose again) and his name was Fall. Who named their son Fall?

"It depends on your definition," Fall answered. Jones had the urgent desire to punch him in the face for the supercilious arrogance in his manner. As if he spoke to plebeians who would never be as smart as he was about the gadgets he played with. "I have the news networks with the highest number of viewers, serving each of the major cities worldwide, ready to switch to your signal. But your definition of major and mine are unlikely to be exactly the same."

"A minor point," Luther said, fluttering a hand. "But it is certain?"

"Yes, all it will take is pressing a button on your order. I have all the connections set up and ready. Some stations took hacking, some took bribery, some a little of both." His slumped, thin shoulder rose in a shrug, and Jones could almost feel the smugness pouring off the kid. "It's all ready."

"Keep it that way. We will want that button pressed soon." His bright eyes darted to Jones. "Your work is going to have quite the audience. Don't do something stupid and mess it up."

The door opened and Colin looked up from the papers scattered on the floor around him. The character had his facemask on. Just a black oval with rectangles for the eyes, nothing else. The eyes behind it were icy blue, and had an odd staring quality. As if he didn't blink enough. Those eyes stared at him from the open doorway. Colin pointed at the piles he had made.

"Your paperwork had a terrible organizational system," Colin said. "Here, I put them in lists of munitions, personnel, and incidentals. The food and supply stuff goes in incidentals. You like bacon."

"Pigs are annoyingly intelligent," the unemotional voice commented, a little muffled by the mask.

"And their little eyes are shifty," Colin said soberly. The man still just stood there staring at him, one hand holding the door open. Perhaps trying to decide what to do? Colin uncrossed his legs and stood up, trying to keep everything about him unthreatening. He didn't bother to try to hide his fear. This guy knew he was afraid.

"So do I get to go outside tonight? Or do I take the corner for sleep? I wouldn't turn down some of that bacon if you have it." Dare he suggest more? No, best to leave it in the creep's hands, he liked to be the one in charge. Colin waited, careful not to stare too long at him. The last thing he wanted was to seem challenging. The figure stepped inside and let the door close behind him. He took a key out of his breast pocket and picked up the ropes lying near the chair as he headed to Colin. He stood directly in front of the boy and stared up at him till their eyes met. The stranger's blue ones reflected the sunlight shining through the slats.

"Colin, do you espouse your father's views?" he demanded. Colin didn't turn his eyes away and kept his features even as his mind raced, picking through truths, half-truths, and lies. He tossed out the lies, not here. Not with this creep. He would know.

"I'm not sure. Some of the whole, 'ban all plastic straws and latex balloons or the world will shrivel,' is a little over the top," he said. "But I do know I love the earth and I want to take care of it. I love being out in nature away from the crazy things people do. And I'm willing to support that, within reason."

"An honest, careful answer," the stranger said, his eyes still unblinking as he stared at Colin. "I will not call on your support, not yet. But I will remember your words, and you will remember my getting you out of the fanatics' hands and back to your family, at no price to you."

"Is that what you were doing?" Colin asked, surprised relief flowing from him. "You said you took me because I was an asset."

"An asset in the wrong hands," the stranger clarified. He held up the ropes. Colin held his wrists together in front of him hopefully. The stranger just stared at him. The young man grimaced and put his hands behind his back. The man's hand closed over his shoulder like a striking snake and spun him around. He felt the ropes tighten over his jacket sleeves, drawing his wrists together. "You snuck a pistol from the fanatic's car. You did not trust them, and no longer wanted their hospitality."

"You have good eyesight." A clink came from near his ankle, and Colin shifted his leg. It felt light. The stranger spun him again and motioned him to the door.

The next hour moved like a strange dream around Colin. He hiked through lovely mountains, cold air swirling into his face, the pines and firs whispering around them. The stranger walked behind him. Always just a step behind, sometimes with what felt like the end of a truncheon pushing into his back to urge him to a better pace. Colin kept himself to a quick walk, feeling stiff and sore, and really wishing he had his hands to help balance and move branches and spiderwebs out of his face. He burned with curiosity over their destination. He knew the woods were Californian. He could feel home in the air, and even spotted the ocean in the far distance from one peak. But it seemed surreal to have it this desolate, this empty of people. He found himself missing the trails, and even the crowds that usually packed them.

And always there moved that silent presence behind him in the creepy black facemask.

The man gave no response to any of Colin's attempts to strike up a conversation.

The sun lay couched between two peaks, painting the sky with pinks and golds, as they slid down a mountainside, a trail of dirt lifting behind them. Colin's foot hit the bottom and he stumbled onto a dusty jeep trail running through a valley. The ropes behind him tugged at his arms and he rocked to a stop. The sudden cessation of movement felt bizarre, and Colin stiffened his muscles to keep himself from swaying. When had he last eaten a decent meal? His stomach growled like a bear.

The ropes came off. Something cold and rectangular pressed into his hand. Colin swung his aching arms to the front, resisting the urge to groan. His phone lay in his palm, held automatically by his numb fingers. Colin looked behind him.

The stranger was gone.

He stood alone in a mountain valley on a little jeep trail, and it was getting dark.

Fantastic, another adventure.

Colin sighed and powered on his phone. He had a full battery and good signal. He scrolled to his contacts, his fingers feeling fat and useless. The creep would still be watching him, he had to be careful who he called and limit his conversation. And he needed someone who would actually help. He hovered over his mom's number, then his dad's... Colin's finger shifted and he hit the phone number for Mr. Luke the private secretary. The wind swept up the trail as he listened to the ring reverberate. Colin idly watched it swirl the dust into little eddies.

"Colin?!" Mr. Luke burst over the line, his deep voice almost desperate in his excitement and worry. A little pang stirred in the boy's heart as he realized he had never heard that kind of tone from his parents.

"Yeah, it's me. Listen, I'm sending you a pin of my location right now, could you maybe figure out some way to pick me up? *Tia* Isla will probably take you in the helicopter if you tell her it's to get me."

"You're all right though, you're ok?" Mr. Luke asked. Colin could hear the trouble he had forming the words, as if they were a dam holding back a flood of emotions and demands and questions.

"Yeah. Just a little hungry and tired."

"I've got the location. Stay there, I'm coming."

"Ok. Thanks," Colin said, his own voice dull and weary. He hung up and dropped to sit on the ground with a little groan. He was glad Mr. Black wasn't asking him for allegiance now. All Colin wanted was to get out of the outdoors to somewhere safe, and warm, with food, and hot showers, and a nice soft bed.

Chapter 26

Simeon watched as Perry dipped and came in for a long dive. The private airport was quiet this morning, and only the men in the air traffic control tower registered on his scan. He didn't bother to tell Vince he was clear to land. His boy would be scanning for Black anomalies too. His watch vibrated and Simeon glanced down.

Colin Clempson's phone popped back online. Simeon watched as the information began to scroll. Jojo's drone hovered over the area in seconds, and its feed slid over all six of the Parabaloni watches. He saw a lonely mountain. A young man working circulation back into his arms. A face-masked villain disappearing into the mountains, before Jojo could drop him with her drone. Black left the boy on a jeep trail, where civilization might reach him. Mr. Clempson had pulled it off. He was alive and getting out. Simeon sent a thankful prayer heavenward, watched Perry go into an exuberant spin before evening out again, and let the feed keep playing in the background.

Perry touched down with a roar of wind and coasted toward the red sports car waiting on the asphalt. Simeon flicked the key in the ignition. The car roared to life and he let himself enjoy it. He may have to rent this one from Mr. Hector again. Perry's garage opened, Simeon let the clutch out, and the stingray revved up the ramp and settled in the Parabaloni garage. The door closed with a gentle thud. The plane picked up speed till the wind roared again, and lifted off.

Simeon slid his aviator sunglasses off, slipped them in his shirt pocket, and hopped out. Rora gave a huff and he dutifully opened the door to let his diminutive hound out. The plane tipped as Vince turned their nose toward home, and the dog braced her legs against the rough metal floor before trotting after her master. Simeon stepped out of the garage and annoyance tightened his face. A couple of missions on their own and they left things a wreck. Honestly, his boys couldn't save the world and clean their own messes? Simeon let himself sidetrack to the office to pick up the maps strewn everywhere.

Vincent took the time to double check the autopilot and watch Colin's feed. The young man was getting out. He accessed Colin's phone, and listened in as he called the secretary. It tracked that he chose Mr. Luke as his emergency contact. Poor kid. Praise God, he was ok! Vincent's head bowed and a thankful heartfelt prayer slid from the inventor. He let his relief play out to his Savior for a few moments, his head singing with it. Vincent heaved a sigh, hopped up, and stepped out the cockpit door to the familiar sound of running water and dishes clinking in the sink. A smile touched his tired face and smoothed the wrinkles back into his smile. Colin was getting out. Sim was here again doing his thing. For just a few minutes, the world was steady. The inventor slid onto the stool at the minuscule bar and watched as Simeon swept through the little kitchen and living area and magically brought things to perfect order.

"Could help, you know," Simeon commented as he tossed the last couch cushion back in place. It landed at the exact angle a store salesman would have left it, fluffed and ready for use[54].

"You needed the stress relief," Vincent grinned. Otherwise, Vince knew, he would have made that comment before the last little chore. "Algy a bit much this time?"

"Are we too soft on people?" Simeon demanded. Vincent paused. His mind shot down the annals of memory, reviewing his years beside Simeon Lee, and the times working with other people in this strange occupation.

"When we first started this you said we had to make a choice about what's important. We answered, 'people.' People are important, and saving those who need it is the only reason to go around doing what we do. The bad guys are people too. Yes, you end up with the classic 'Batman and Joker' question, where every time Joker gets loose because Batman turned him in instead of

---

[54] Yes, Simeon has experience as a couch salesman, of course he does. He tells me it was part of creating an authentic backstory to draw out an enemy agent from Romania. I didn't expect him to be very good at it (he isn't much of a talker after all), but I saw the placard up in the department store headquarters, framed in a place of honor. In one week Sim managed to sell two hundred and one couches to an Eskimo tribe living in igloos.

killing him, more bystanders get hurt. But you've taught me two things that answer that. The first is that we aren't judges and executioners. There's a line between hero and villain that's too easy to cross once you start taking on the roles that haven't been given to you. We stop the bad guys, we get them to the people whose job it is to decide what happens next. And then we get to the second, most important thing you've taught me about our job. We do what's right. Then we let God have the rest. He's sovereign, and He's big enough to handle all the bits and pieces we can't see and we can't weave together in this vast broken universe. Sim, I've watched the world around you while you care deeply about everyone you come in contact with. And I've fought beside others who don't live like that. We're doing the right thing. I can see it in the scenes we leave behind, and the years that follow the stories. It's hard, in some ways, to care about everyone." Lines deepened around Vincent's eyes and Simeon could see the memories behind the young man's gaze. "But it's harder when you sit in church and hear about how God saved even me, and then think of the ones you've brought down that might have been turned to the good if they'd just had another year or two to think it over. We stop the bad guys. But we give grace with it when we can. And knowing our Bible, when we act as God's avenging angels that's how He wants us to do it. He gives time for sinners to repent. We do too, when we can. It's the right thing."

"It's broadcasting a bigger picture," Simeon said slowly, digesting his boy's answer. Vincent's smile slid over his face as he thought of a burning underground, and a newfound friend turning back to the fire for a murderer.

"Yeah. Living grace the way you've taught us to do shines the beams of the cross in colors most people never get the chance to see. The longer I'm in this job the more I learn to be thankful I've had you for a boss." Simeon's face softened as his eyes dropped to the floor. A nod was his only answer, but it was enough. His gaze darted to the cockpit.

"Are you flying this thing?"

Vincent laughed and uncurled his long form from the stool. They moved to the cockpit, Aurora's claws clicking happily behind Simeon's ankles.

"Brought you a toy from Heshman's," Simeon said as he dropped to the copilot's chair. Vincent caught the bug with one hand as he flipped his screwdriver from a pocket with his other and flung himself comfortably in his pilot's chair.

"Not bad work," Vincent murmured as he started to poke. "Basic, but a good little skitterer."

"Blow up?"

"Will it? No," Vincent chuckled. "Not a chance. But he has a good grip, and pretty clever little claws. If I make a control for it, I could see this little guy being useful." He slid the skitterer on the panel and sat back, checking over his controls with a little hum.

A quiet hour slid by as the two friends just sat in the cockpit watching the towers of winter clouds spin by. The peace slid into Vincent as the minutes ticked on. No chatter. No scrolling on his handheld. No constantly moving on to the next topic of conversation, the next tease, the hammering out the next part of the mission they rushed toward. Just…being. He found prayers sliding from him, quiet, natural, happy. How long had it been since he had just stopped? Time slid on and the two friends let it. Simeon's eyes closed and he fell into a comfortable sleep. Vincent smiled as he watched his boss sink deep. Sim always rested best with someone he trusted near to watch his back. The inventor pulled up Jojo's drone feed, and watched Colin slumped back in a private helicopter's seat, the bulk of Mr. Luke beside him and some lady as pilot. The young man was talking smoothly into his headset. From the grownups' expressions, Vincent could tell they were getting the story of the kid's adventures. The inventor wondered how Colin would spin the Parabaloni bits. He knew not to say too much.

But he was safe now. Mr. Black had let him out. Vincent watched Jojo's other drone short out as it tried to follow Black, again. Oh well, they would deal with Mr. Black when they could. He activated Perry's autopilot, draped a leg over his pilot's chair, and joined Simeon in a nap.

✦

Colin walked into the palatial Californian mansion he called home, his feet dragging with weariness. A dim glow lit the vaulted entryway from an electric chandelier on low, and the crystal sent the beams dancing in fractals over his clothes. Colin idly followed the colors dancing in the entryway and looked up toward the chandelier.

A figure stood at the balcony of the second floor. Colin drew to a gentle stop, staring up at his dad. He felt the solid presence of Mr. Luke come in behind him and stop, waiting. But he couldn't make his feet move. Father and son stood still, staring at each other.

"You got home, then," Jackson said. *Has he been waiting up to make sure I made it?* Colin wondered in disbelief. *No. He's probably just after his dyspepsia medicine.*

"I'm home," Colin said, his voice dull. "Your Mr. Black is something else, Dad. He sends his greetings." Colin watched, hoping for…what? Remorse about being in an environmental terrorist plot? Fear that his son had gotten involved with a killer? Pleasure that he knew about it now? Jackson nodded absently and murmured something Colin couldn't catch. He picked up a bottle off a little marble table and wandered off toward his room. Colin's head drooped and he dragged himself up the stairs. Mr. Luke tagged at his heels like a good dependent. Colin pulled his door open and stepped inside. Relief and the comfort of the familiar washed over him as his eye fell on his wall of shelves stuffed with his books, his hanging pod, his white rugs and soft bed. The blue fluorescent lighting glowed from the bathroom and thoughts of a hot bath brought a real smile to his face. Colin lifted the takeout bag in his hands as he turned back to the hulking man in his doorway.

"Thanks for the two dinners, Mr. Luke," he said.

"The doctor's scheduled for eight a.m. tomorrow. If you oversleep, I will roll you out of bed."

"Fine," Colin murmured, over trying to argue Mr. Luke out of a checkup. He sounded so much like a secretary. Colin sat the bag on the table in his kitchenette and started to weave toward the bathroom.

"Colin?"

The young man paused, suddenly alert by the strange note in the secretary's voice. Mr. Luke loomed in the doorway, one thick hand still holding his habitual tablet for notes and appointments. But his face looked strained.

"I shouldn't have left you. I should have grabbed you by the back of the neck and dragged you into the plane and let the locals deal with the mess. I'm sorry."

"I didn't give you a chance," Colin said, truthfully enough. "It's ok, Mr. Luke. I…worked it out, don't worry about it."

The secretary nodded slowly and closed the door behind him. Colin could hear his heavy footsteps moving off down the corridor of the sleeping house. He heaved a long sigh and flipped the lock on his door. Colin pulled his phone out and powered it off. He walked into his bedroom, slid the phone under his mattress, and strolled back into his den. He forced himself not to tense as he moved toward the window facing his family's orange orchard. Would it be there? Colin pushed the window open slowly, and leaned out. A black smart phone was duct-taped against the sill. A grin split Colin's face. He pried it off, powered it on, and flopped back in his pod swing. Five numbers were programmed into it. Colin hit Vincent's. The bell buzzed as he put it to his ear.

"Yo, dude!" Vincent said. A noisy yawn followed it and a little grin broke over Colin at the lazy cheeriness of the inventor. "Your phone all the way off?"

"Yeah, and in the other room under my mattress. Will that do to keep Black from listening in?"

"It should. Turn it back on pretty soon, or he'll get suspicious about not being able to hear anything through his bug."

"I may 'accidentally' break it so I don't have to deal with that creep listening to everything I do."

"If you can without his catching on to why, go for it. Phones melt really well with a good blowtorch. If you need other ideas I could easily fill a whole book of ways to kill off phones!"

"You're awful cheerful when the last time I saw you I was yelling and shooting you in the face," Colin smiled.

"Meh, I get that more than you might expect." Colin could

hear the grin in the other man's voice. "Are you all right? Anything bad to report from the time with the villain?"

"I'm fine, and I'm home, nothing to report." He stiffened, suddenly a little uncomfortable. "I didn't do what you wanted me to. That Mr. Black he's…creepy. I didn't try to play him." Colin heard a long breath blow from the inventor on the other end. "I'm sorry."

"No, no, that was relief, Colin," Vincent said, and the young man could hear it in the inventor's words. Was it real, or was it a part of what Gigan had taught Vincent? "We've found out more about him and were worried stiff until he let your phone pop up to be tracked again. You made the right call. It probably saved your life." That sounded real. Colin sent his pod into motion, swinging back and forth, strangely glad these people weren't mad at him.

"He does want my family's support enough to send me home, like you thought he would. I mostly convinced him I'm in his camp, I think. Listen, I found the schematics of the Mother Machine in the creep's cabin, and took pictures with Mr. Lee's ancient pen camera. What do I do with it? Is there even a place that still develops film?"

"Leave it all intact, I'll send a drone for it tonight."

"I guess I should open a window then." Another yawn split his face in two. "There were accounts in the cabin too. I took photos of them, I think, though I can't really tell because the camera doesn't show you what you're aiming at before you click it, and I had to be discreet. The guy's bought lots of explosives, and paid a tech company recently, and he's paying a lot of mercenaries. And he likes bacon. He says the pig is annoyingly intelligent."

"Hey, I like pigs," Vincent objected. "Although bacon is pretty good too."

"You were right about his noticing my taking the pistol in your car. I don't know how he saw it, or how you knew he would, but he did and it sold him on the game of my running off on you. So what's next?"

"Sleep, recover. We'll figure it out and keep you posted. Don't go out in the grounds without company for a few days, just in case. I can't see any reason Black would have for nabbing you again, but play it safe. You did good, very good." A smile spread over Colin, with a tingling that turned the bruises and aches into something to take pride in.

"I'll be sleeping for the next few days," Colin said. "But hey, promise you will keep me informed?"

"I promise, dude. We won't forget you." The phone went silent and black, and Colin tossed it into the corner of his swing with a grimace. That answer hit too close to home; the Parabaloni noticed more than he felt entirely comfortable with. But then…it was nice to know he could trust that promise. And maybe, just maybe, he had actually managed to make a real difference in this broken world. Colin's eyes fell on the takeout bag. He heaved himself out of the chair with a groan, slumped at the table, and pulled out his burger. Then his apathy fled away and his back straightened. Colin reached into his inner pocket and pulled out the little New Testament Vincent Tolliver had given him as they rode the streets of Riyadh looking for a killer. Colin peeled back the paper on his burger, turned to *John*, and began to read.

Chapter 27

The Parabaloni sat in their kitchen. They had the remains of a chicken dinner inside them, leftover desserts[55] scattered on the table, and a second pot of coffee filling the air with its warm scent. Gigan flicked a lazy finger at the glass patio door.

"The stars here are nearly as bright and uncontested as we found during the blackouts. Mr. Black's attempted evil only reminded us how beautiful and precious such a sight can be to a soul. Especially a tired soul."

"'To whom then will you compare me, that I should be like him? says the Holy One,'" Pete quoted, his Saudi accent soft and delightful as it wrapped around them. "'Lift up your eyes on high and see: who created these? He who brings out their host by number, calling them all by name; by the greatness of his might and because he is strong in power, not one is missing[56].' It is good to remember the strength of our God who holds all the stars in place."

"And nothing He holds can be lost," Jojo added.

"I wonder if it really does go on forever like some conjecture?" Vincent drawled. "Just more and more galaxies, on into infinity…"

"Only God infinite," Simeon put in. The drip and hiss of the coffee maker filled the kitchen as they watched the brilliance of the New Mexican sky. The hiss took over the drip as the pot finished filling. Gigan stood up with a sigh.

"All right, my friends, let us get on with this," he said. Pete's fist smashed into the table in a businesslike way.

"Agreed. Black Tortoise of Doom is my new official title," he said. A chorus of hoots and complaints sailed at his head. Simeon's rare laughter cut into it.

"Pete, you're the Turtle Man," he chuckled. The Saudi

---

[55] Crumbled pastries from Libya and Holland, crepes from Riyadh, homemade macarons snatched from the kitchen in Italy, a chocolate silk pie from Alice in Tennessee, and leftover brownies Gigan made for the Church potluck last week.
[56] Isaiah 40:25-26, ESV

groaned and sank a little farther in his chair. If even Simeon agreed there was no fighting it. Gigan sat the second pot of coffee on the table and dropped back in his chair.

"Stop complaining so much, the turtle is a noble animal, very steadfast and efficient," Gigan said.

"It stands for invulnerability in heraldry," Vince said. "And that fits Quasimodo."

"You do not get to name my backpack," Pete said, wagging a finger at the inventor, "especially after you named our second car 'Ernie.'"

"Aw come on, you know you like the Muppets too," Vince grinned at him.

"The Muppets yes, but Bert and Ernie are on that annoying children's show with the constant socialist dogma–"

"–One, ha, ha, ha," Vincent immediately broke in, with a cheesy Transylvanian accent. Gigan attacked another macaron with noisy intensity. Pete groaned and let his head drop on the table.

"You know they're just doing it because it annoys you," Jojo grinned, poking her brother in the shoulder. "That show annoys them too."

"But he named our car just to annoy me, and that's a little much!" Pete popped up to say.

"Getting late," Simeon put in.

"Right," Vince said, sitting a little taller and reaching behind him for the milk on the counter. "Jo, did you pick up Colin's film?"

"Yes, and handed it over to Simeon," she reported, "as the one among us who knows how to work with such ancient methods."

"I am learning not to complain of the old methods," Gigan grinned. "Mr. Black didn't suspect Colin had that camera because it cannot be scanned for and no one uses obsolete things like actual film anymore."

"Obsolete only to the unprepared," Simeon said. He tossed a folder on the table and photographs spilled from it. The others leaned in, studying what Colin had managed to capture of their bad guy's paperwork. "Made close up prints of the more interesting ones. Some illegible, too blurred. But the blueprints came out. He was careful to get those."

"Yeah, I can see," Vincent murmured, his voice absent. His hand went to his hair, the tip of his tongue stuck out his teeth, and his eyes glassed over. The others let him think and turned their attention to the rest of the photographs. Simeon drank his coffee with slow enjoyment, his foot rubbing back and forth over Rora's fluffy stomach. The dog lay sleeping under the table with a look of pure bliss on her furry face. Mr. Tompkins' rhythmic purr filled the space under the table as he lay pressed against the dog's soft fur.

"These give us the names of many of his mercenaries," Gigan said. "Oh look, there's my old firm listed in official black and white."

"Which?" Pete asked, leaning over his partner's shoulder to study the photograph he held.

"My team in between France and the Parabaloni, the ones who chased you through Tripoli and that nearly turned me into a crazy New Age terrorist without my realizing it. Greg Henderson and Abassi Sy are the only two listed by name, I wonder if the others are there too?"

"How can you not realize something like that?" Jojo asked.

"There are ways. Especially if you walk with your eyes half closed to the real unseen world around us," Gigan said.

"Box up the handmaid, G," Peter murmured. A sharp babble of annoyed French burst from Gigan as his hands waved. It melted into English as Pete started chuckling.

"Philosophy is intermingled with everything we do! You can't shirk it, Sheik, we have to deal with the unseen if we are to deal competently with the seen. Simeon is smart enough to give us a theme verse that tells us just that[57]. In this situation... I don't know. Philosophy comes into it with the employees, most definitely. This Collective seem convinced they are doing it all for the 'Mother,' to renew nature and rid the earth of what they see as

---

[57] "For we wrestle not against flesh and blood, but against principalities, against powers, against the rulers of the darkness of this world, against spiritual wickedness in high places." Ephesians 6:12 (KJV)

an overpopulation of humans."

"They've never been to places like New Mexico, overpopulated isn't a word I would use," Pete commented, and Jojo laughed.

"But this Black," Gigan went on, "him, I don't know. I think he… He is just unbalanced. From what we know of him… I expect his early life was not ideal. There is a story behind his emerging from the Black Woods at such a young age. And I doubt it is a nice one. Early trauma can do things to a person."

"Yeah. It can break a mind even more than a body," Vincent agreed, sorrow creeping over his face again. "Whatever went on, it doesn't seem like he came from a good situation. You got to feel a little sympathetic for the guy, even if he is a creep bent on world slaughter now."

"Real trauma can break a soul too," Jojo nodded. "We see it when we go wandering, on so many little faces in need of help. I wonder if his story might have been different if someone stepped in earlier?"

"I think he's a nut," Pete stated.

Simeon's laughter filled the kitchen. The others paused as it wrapped around them. Here sat a man with more early trauma than most could live through. And yet he still made the choice to fix the broken, and right the world, and be one of the best of the good guys. Choice came into play too. Simeon's mug plunked on the table and he reached for the pot again.

"Pete's right," he said. "There's a difference between being broken and being crazy. He is actually unhinged, something wrong in his brain. But Gigan's right too. He has a cause. Lets his followers think it's about nature to string them along. But his real reason is in his name."

Gigan's eyes widened.

"He's out to kill the light. He aims to bring blackness on the world." The Frenchman's words filled the kitchen and hung there. They wrapped around the agents with an uncomfortable acknowledgment of the truth. "Those gloves aren't to show that people use nature in the wrong way. Kid gloves, real leather ones, bring death for something not actually necessary to the world. It is a symbol of killing for no reason but the desire to bring death."

"A bad symbol of it," Vincent snorted behind his mug of milk. "Raising goats to use their skin is perfectly legitimate so long as you do it humanely." The others didn't seem to hear. They sat still, drinking in the new revelation.

"Achieving a goal like that would give someone an intense feeling of power," Pete said, his voice tight. "The power to undo everything the good guys have accomplished. It would make him the ultimate winner. He would be the top god among all those trying to play god. He's gotten too close already."

"We need to get ahead of him, now," Jojo said.

"Learned a lot," Simeon nodded; steady as a rock as he sipped his coffee. The others looked at him, and Vincent watched their tight shoulders ease. A smile crept over Vince. Simeon may not be in the field with them as often as he used to. But he was still their base that gave solidity and peace in a crazy, evil world. "Think we can hash it out, get behind his brain, and bring him down now. Next step will be wrapped up with that MM. Vince?"

"Yeah, so this Mother Machine of his is what we expected," the inventor took up immediately. "It is designed to link the Egberts, and will cause them to activate and send the signal through the eggs all over the world, to each and every power plant and generator connected through the web of wires and satellites broadcasting signals. It has the potential to cause worldwide destruction of the basic electrical infrastructure. And just about every other infrastructure is reliant on that one in some way or another. We've kind of made it easy for him."

"I object to that 'we,'" Gigan stated. "We personally know better than to rely on any one thing except our Savior."

"Says one of the ones who had to spend ten minutes pouring over a paper map and still got lost twice," Vincent grinned at him. Gigan gave a very French shrug and sigh and reached for the coffee again.

"I will have you know I did not get lost twice," Jojo said with great dignity. She stood up to make a third pot. "I got lost four times and had to ask directions of a nice old matron watching her grandchildren play in the street."

"I didn't get lost at all," Pete said.

"And he just couldn't keep his mouth shut, oh he of the eidetic memory," Gigan grinned, and flung a piece of pie crust at his partner. Pete caught it in his mouth, but it tipped him too far backward and sent his chair crashing to the floor, to his partner's uproarious laughter. Abir skittered from around Pete's neck with annoyed little squeaks and scurried over to curl on Rora's soft fur. The cat gave an annoyed shake, and bounded to his feet. The dog didn't move. Mr. Tomkins leapt gracefully to Vincent's lap, spun in a quick circle, and settled in. His tail curled around his body, and his deep purr started to reverberate again.

"Nice kitty," Vincent told him, and stroked the orange fur gently. Then he took up the conversation again. "Anyway, we already kind of assumed all that, and the blueprints do confirm it, but barely. It doesn't have much about the programming so we're still working on some assumptions here. These schematics are more the hardware of how the machine fits together. Which is interesting, because it's designed to be much more portable and condensed than the Egberts. While it's still not too small, it's smaller than the eggs. And flat. And it's made so it can be assembled quickly anywhere this jerk can find a wall socket and internet signal, so no help there. An interesting fact, though, is that the setting up part is all dove-tails, bolts, cogs and wheels, things that can be done with an ordinary toolbox. It's a working assumption that it's intended to be put together during a blackout and then turned on to send out its signal after the blackout is ended."

"Perhaps triggered by someone ending the blackout?" Jojo asked.

"Probably. That would fall in the programming part though, so we'll just have to assume," Vincent said. "That sounds like Mr. Black's style. So I believe we'll be flying old school when we go in for the attack, and can't restart the power until after we take out this machine. Say, Heshman's little skitterer would work well in a blackout!"

"Could it carry your switch and attach it to an Egbert without our having to get close to any of Black's people?" Gigan asked quickly.

"Yep, sure could."

"This is good news," Pete murmured. "And makes me wonder why we didn't think of it before now."

"We haven't had time, Instant Pete, Black has been piling things on hard for us!" Gigan grimaced. "What about killing the MM, Vince?".

"I think I could…" Vincent grinned suddenly, his eyes darting to Simeon. "Hey, remember that time in Georgia when I was fiddling with Pat trying to get the bomb to die and freaking out?"

"Not freaking out," Simeon defended. "Running out of time."

"What happened?" Pete asked.

"Me and the local team of anti-terrorists were trying everything to figure out how to disarm this bomb, see, and we just had a few seconds before it went off and took the town with it. One of those situations, you know[58]. Then Simeon comes running up with a jar, dumps a heap of acid on it, and melts all the components into a steaming puddle. There was quiet for a few seconds. Then one of the locals just said, 'That will work.' So, yeah, agreed, that will work."

"Sure it won't set something off?" Simeon asked.

"Meh, it should be fine. Especially if we get to it with the blackout still up, a good acid should do the trick," the inventor said.

"Just don't trip with your jar," Gigan said.

"Hey, have any of you ever played paintball?" Vincent asked. "Or flicked paintball pellets, now that can be fun."

"Is this relevant?" Pete asked.

"When has that ever stopped your comments?" Gigan snorted. "Savant, how quick can this machine be set up?"

"I could do it in an hour," Vincent said. "With you people helping, half that."

"Thank you for that vote of confidence, four of us just halved your time," Jojo chuckled.

"No offense," Vince shrugged at her, "there's only so many

---

[58] They knew. The one in Korea with the boba juggling juggernauts was especially close, Pete cut it off with an eighth of a second to spare, and he still got hit by the boba. Though being Pete he didn't mind much, he just counted it as a snack for later.

people that can fit around a smallish machine, after the first two, more bodies tend to just get in the way."

"Remember the Transvaal?" Pete said, and Gigan shuddered.

"We bow to your expertise, Savant," the Frenchman said. "Well, not literally. There will be no bowing."

"You sure? Because I think I might enjoy that," Vince grinned. Simeon "ahemmed" and they got back on business. Vincent pulled Rory close and started their usual scan they had been too busy to do today, as everyone else went back to the photographs.

"I see no clues to where the extra drums are hidden," Gigan said, tapping the photographs. "Is there any way to tap into the mechanics of this MM and glean her secrets?"

"Nope," Vince answered. "We're still stuck chasing at Mr. Black's heels putting out the fires he leaves behind while he giggles at us and sets more traps."

"I don't think he is the giggling sort," Pete frowned.

"But we know more now," Gigan said. "We know how Black thinks, and if we pound it out tonight, I think we can even know what he plans. Now is the time to get ahead. We must be thorough, fast, and efficient; a clean sweep, as Simeon puts it, a lightning move that takes him out in an instant. All right, people, we cannot know where Mr. Black is now. And we cannot find his planted Egberts or hidden drums of poison or this MM. But we can assume he is going to call us in for a final game. We need to anticipate his moves now, so we can play the final piece. What do we have he will not anticipate that might help us with this?"

"We know one thing, thanks to Sim's penetration of Luther's monologuing, and who Black didn't mention to Pete during their fight," Vince grinned, and Gigan and Pete echoed it.

"Think there's more planned in this next step than just the MM," Simeon said.

"I agree," Gigan nodded. "Our nasty Mr. Black is piling plots on top of plots, increasing the odds against us every time we rush in to his game. This will be an intricate Russian doll affair, with plot laid within plot."

"Has anyone considered that the missing virus drums just being in Egberts somewhere seems too simple?" Pete asked.

"It is a disturbingly penetrating thought," Gigan frowned. One mustache tucked in his mouth as he thought furiously. "Especially since the Egberts are designed to draw attention, and may easily be found before activation. These drums feel sneakier than that. Perhaps some in Egberts, and some in an undisclosed place to release in an undisclosed manner. That is part of his plan. What else is he plotting?" Jojo's hand shot up. Gigan grinned, then swapped it for a regal look and waved magnanimously at her.

"I have a possibility," she said. "When we first met Mr. Black and his Collective (when we still thought it was old shriveled Luther) the first thing he did was split our ranks, take us where he wanted us to be, and cut off the power a little while after that. Then he's played variations of that same tune. What if he's fishing for a particular reaction from us?"

"Something unique to us," Gigan put in, his accent strong as he thought it over.

"What if we gave him what he wanted at the beginning, and then messed it up for him?" Pete said, his half smile starting to creep over him as he caught onto the idea.

Rory gave a soft beep.

"Uh, guys?" Vincent broke in, and everyone stiffened. "We just got a hit for the fingerprints Pete collected off the red-haired gal's dagger. We just got it, because it just got posted."

"Ah, Black calls," Gigan murmured.

"Guys," Vince cut in, his voice a sharp "stop-messing-around" that raised every hair in the kitchen. "They're from a groundskeeper in Tuscaloosa, Iowa."

A sharp crack came as Simeon's hold tightened on his mug. It collapsed in three pieces, leaking black coffee onto the table.

Chairs shoved back, the laptop lid slammed down, and five pairs of feet thundered toward the Parabaloni hangar.

Chapter 28

I wasn't looking for an adventure that night.

Wilberforce, my sea lion, was feeling a little woozy, and trying to help him swim straight was quite enough trouble for me that evening. It was very late when I finally watched him do a lazy spin, even out nicely, and head through the hole in his rock. He didn't ram into the side, or even scrape his flipper. Finally, the bad fish had worn off. I headed gratefully for the fresh air, following my air bubbles toward the top of the tank.

I surfaced in the indoor viewing building, instead of the small room where Wilberforce goes for a rest and the zookeepers[59] can keep an eye on him.

I didn't know it then, but going there instead of the keeper's room was all that saved the situation that night.

Wilberforce prefers his water fairly tepid, so I hadn't bothered with a wetsuit, just the air tanks and mask. I shed the heavy tanks gratefully, tossed the mouthpiece on one of the blue-carpeted stadium style seats, and reached for a towel. Happy thoughts of home and my own comfortable bed played through my mind.

The door to the outside swung open and the freezing wind of an Iowa winter swept in. Wonderful, George, my chimp, must be loose again and coming to tease the sea lion. I swung around with a sharp complaint. The sound died as I saw the intruder. It wasn't George.

A man stood silhouetted in the doorway. Black slacks, leather hoodie, black gloves, and a freakish mask hiding his face. Definitely not George. What had wandered into my zoo?

Breathing suddenly seemed difficult.

"There you are," he said. It sounded so even. So simple. Something I might say when I found my paring knife in my kitchen drawer. I could feel every hair follicle rising on me, as

---

[59] Jorge and Maria (a husband-and-wife team) and me are the full staff for our little zoo. Jorge takes care of the heavy lifting and most of the groundskeeping, Maria does the animals' food. Or at least she prepares it. After Herman the rhinoceros almost took her arm off, she has me do most of the actual deliveries.

those blue eyes stared, too wide open to be normal.

"Here I am," I agreed. Behind my back, my fingers found the wrench in my pocket. I fumbled for the valve on an air tank. "How long have you been looking? I do hope I gave you some trouble."

"I won't need you long. Just until he gets here." No reaction to my words. No reaction to anything, flaccid, just...there. It felt like talking to the Simpson's little boy in my Sunday school class, before they had been forced to have him committed. Something off. Something wrong. He stepped inside and swung the door closed. Alarms went from ringing to blaring inside me, and I could hear my pulse singing in my ears. I managed to slide the wrench onto the valve. I wrenched the wrench. The valve popped off the tank. The compressed air wailed and hissed, turning it into a metal missile. It shot straight toward the creepy stranger, and he leapt away from it, his attention diverted for that instant. I dove into the tank.

The water closed over me with its sharp bubbling, and I kicked off desperately. Wilberforce spun in tight circles around me. I used his blubber to kick against, shooting toward the opposite side of the pool as the farthest distance from the freakish nighttime visitor. My heartbeat thundered as fear sent adrenaline sailing higher than I ever knew it could climb.

The lights glowing in the water around us cut off. Dense darkness closed in. My lungs constricted with the suddenness. Which wasn't useful while underwater with an over friendly sea lion doing laps around me and making the water churn. I shut out the surprise, and leaned into the adrenaline, refusing to slow down. I had learned a few things from Wilberforce and my penguins; I knew I made it across the tank before the freak-act in the mask could run to the same place on land.

I had also gleaned a few things from the gentleman emailing me for the last year.

I didn't swim directly to the other side. I flung one shoe far to the right on the bank, and came up slowly, trying not to disturb the water into a churning white ring around me. The wind hit me and I felt my skin and wispy hair start to freeze. Wilberforce splashed out of the pool onto his rocks, barking and slapping as he fetched my shoe. I used the noisy distraction. I clambered onto the rocks, darted over the railing, and took off over the path. I could see my breath in front of me. But nothing else. Just blackness and the memory of the freak in the mask. I paused long enough to jerk off my other shoe so I didn't run lopsided, and bent into a sprint.

I couldn't hear anything but Wilberforce behind me.

Everything lay dark. None of our floodlights lit up the enclosures. The streetlights outside our little zoo didn't gleam. The winter clouds lay over the stars, and the brightest thing was my own breath cloud spurting out in front of my face. I suddenly registered the slap of my feet on the path, and spun onto the grass to hide the sound.

Nothing, no noise from behind me. But I could feel someone here. Just like I did when the teenagers climbed the fence and tried to party in the penguin house at night. I knew I wasn't alone with my animals. The freak still lurked, somewhere.

And oh, it was cold.

And so quiet. No cars, no streetlights, no noise but my own movements and Tim McGraw, the Macaw, complaining about the sudden darkness. The exit was a full mile from here. With the power out, would I even be able to call for help if I made it all that way there to our office? I knew I couldn't scale the twelve-foot iron fence around our zoo. I had kept up my running because I enjoyed it. I hadn't been clambering up fences and trees in twenty years[60]. I made my choice. I spun to the side, ducked through the pipe fence to Ethel and Fred's enclosure, and darted into their heated barn.

The musk of the elephants closed around me like an old friend. I could hear them shifting, unnerved by the sudden way the heaters had stopped blowing and the lights went out. I snatched one of the pipes from an old broken fence panel, slid up

---

[60] Yes, those of you doing the math (50 − 20 = 30), some thirty-year old ladies still climb trees, shut up. Besides, I sometimes even have a reason with my chimps and birds. Like the time I decided to try out Tim in the aviary and he managed to swoop through the door and get into the Catholic church's eves, and screeched every time the priest mentioned "sacrament." No, I did not train him to do that. But twenty years later I still haven't convinced the priest of that.

to Ethel's tree-trunk-sized leg and leaned against it. Drawing warmth and cover from her vast hide and offering her the comfort of the familiar. She stopped moving. One huge breath blew from her, and I felt hay spray into the inky air from it. I stood still, shivering, praying, clutching a metal pipe and leaning against my elephant. I let the questions burst in.

What in the Sam Hill had wandered into my zoo?!

I felt my fear flaring into anger. This was my space. I had spent my childhood here, and all of my adult life. If someone thought they could just breeze in like they owned the place... But I'd never had to deal with more than the occasional angry parent. Though I had taken up Brazilian Jujitsu after starting emailing Simeon, I didn't kid myself about my abilities. What could I do about a dangerous intruder?

Ethel shifted again beside me, and I leaned my hand against her thick hide. A smile slowly slid over me. I may not have Simeon's skills. But what I had might be just enough of a surprise to turn the tables on a freak.

"Where is she?" the voice drifted from the dark and Greg Henderson shuddered. It wasn't just from the cold air whipping into him and teasing his hair around his head. That voice came so cold, so frozen...

"Her trail led toward the elephants," he reported, refusing to show how much his boss unnerved him. After nine months of training with Mr. Black, he should feel more familiar with this man. But he didn't. "It was easy enough to follow the drops of ice. But the elephants aren't there anymore."

"What do you mean?" Black demanded. Did Greg imagine it or was that inhuman voice just a little annoyed? "I want her. I want to show him how easy it is to slit her throat."

"No elephants. Their pen is empty," Greg reported. Silently, Greg admitted this woman wasn't making her throat particularly easy to slit. Black strode into the dark of the zoo and Greg followed him at a respectful distance. The winter wind teased his hair and clothes. He let himself do a little shivering.

Something white flashed above the path over his head. He

spun, his pistol springing into his hand. Nothing moved. At least nothing he could see. Greg stepped forward again, moving a little faster, feeling his heartbeat quickening. His eyes stayed on the trees lining the path.

Another flash of white shifted above him. Just a flicker, then it disappeared again amidst the trees. It wasn't a bird. And it moved in perfect silence. Something shifted, he caught a glimpse of a branch twisting contrary to the wind. Nothing moved near the branch. But there was something... He could feel eyes burning into his skin. Thoughts of the tree spirits of the Horned Goddess slid through Greg and his fear climbed. He broke into a run, chasing the dark blotch of Mr. Black as he glided toward the elephant pen to make his own deductions. The boss frightened Greg. But not nearly as much as this nameless, silent something stalking through the trees.

A vast bulk sprang from a branch. A guttural scream rent from Greg as his pistol flashed in the night. Then two great paws slammed into his shoulder and he hit the path with a shuddering force. Claws bit deep into him. A roar of pain tore from Greg as he struggled to slash out with an arm held down by a hideous weight in the dark.

Another gunshot echoed through the night, from where he had last seen Black.

The knife-like claws retracted from Greg's flesh. The weight left, and a little flash of white disappeared into the trees again. He rolled to his stomach and struggled to rise, hearing himself gasping out breathless curses. His spine popped and cringed, and he knew it had nearly broken by the thing's pounce. He pressed a piece of his shredded coat to his shoulder, trying to stop the welling blood, and staggered toward the patch of blackness he knew was his boss.

"What...?" Greg gasped.

"Leopard," Mr. Black supplied, his voice as strangely steady as always. "Be thankful this one has the deformity of a white paw. But in the dark it is hard to guess where the rest of it is from one paw, I did not hit it. Neither did you. Watch for it, and adjust your aim."

"Leopard? How?" Greg panted, physical shock starting to shake him harder than the cold.

"It would seem Susie is more ingenious than I originally calculated. The game has new players."

Chapter 29

Perry's nose pointed toward the ground and he cut through the thick cloud layer lying over Iowa. Pete stood still at the living room window, his arms crossed as he watched the clouds flash by like wispy lost souls, wailing in the night. Vince and Gigan were coming in fast and aiming for the field behind Susie's address, butted up against the iron railings of her zoo. They scorned the ten minutes it would take to drive from the airport. Secrecy didn't really matter. Black knew they were coming. Jojo's voice broke into Pete's brooding.

"What will he do if she's already..." Her voice died away.

"We will be there for Simeon," Peter answered. "But Black..."

"You think he's waiting till he sees Simeon's face, then he plans to kill her in front of him," Jojo said.

"You've learned too much already," Pete commented, chagrined. He didn't say what he really thought. She would be freshly dead when they found Black. This murdering villain's first choice would be to give Simeon a choice. Save this one person you've come to care for, or watch perhaps millions die from a plague knowing you might have stopped it. To play god. Watch the good guy squirm between two dark choices. And then slit Susie's throat. But Black knew their skills, and wouldn't risk it. He would take his second choice, and kill Susie just before they reached him, to eliminate the chance of rescue. She would be dead before they landed. And they all knew it. Simeon hadn't said a single word since they ran from the kitchen. He just sat hunched and haunted, staring at the floor as the plane broke sound barriers all the way to Iowa and Gigan and Vince furiously pounded out a plan. But Pete didn't give his sister a better idea of the bad guy. "Maybe you should stay back from the missions more."

"Maybe we should all find a way to take a break sometimes!" Jojo shot back, suddenly fierce. "After seven months on just the fringes I feel it getting to me! 'Tassy, you're all so tired. Vincent is even getting moody, and Gigan–"

"I get it, you don't have to lecture. We take breaks sometimes.

Simeon owns an island without outside communication[61]. After this we can take a couple of months. But…" Pete's voice suddenly died, swallowed by the rushing air outside Perry as they came in at a steep glide.

"But even when no one is telling you the world is falling apart, you know the world is falling apart," Jojo supplied the unspoken words. "You don't just need time off. You need someone else to take over sometimes. Peter, there are other good people out there."

"Bright pinpricks of light amidst the dark…" Pete murmured, his eyes shifting out the cockpit window. The clouds lay thick above them already. He couldn't see the stars. "Jo, I don't know of anyone else who can do the jobs we handle."

"Sean is coming behind you. Give him the tools he needs."

"I did hand his number to someone at the square," Pete murmured, his lined face suddenly very thoughtful.

"Good. Find that person and train them."

"Fourteen years ago Algy trained someone to do his job," Pete said grimly.

Perry's electrical system cut out. Darkness fell in the plane home and closed over the Parabaloni. Shreds of white clouds streamed past the windows like wailing ghosts. Pete heard the wails of the dead he had walked through on countless missions and felt his muscles tensing and his eyes drying as he stared, too afraid of what he would see if he closed his eyes for even a blink. And then the clouds were gone, and just darkness stared back at Pete. No lights showed the township he knew lay below them. Nothing but black.

"Oh Jesus say it again," he murmured into the night. "Cause Your 'Let there be light' to ring through the dark. We are here. Use our tarnished old bones to reflect what You always are. Reach through this night again, Father, and save."

---

[61] No, this isn't metaphorical. It is an island set all by itself in an ocean I'm not allowed to name, with its own generator and well, no phone lines or cell service, and not on the maps of the area. (Yes, the Parabaloni shamelessly bribe the local chart makers.) It is very peaceful and pleasant. Unless there is a hurricane that drops stinging jellyfish over every acre of ground.

The plane pulled up and he braced for the landing, his face a hard mask. Perry touched down with a jolt and a huge roar of wind. He could almost feel the pilots pulling back on the yokes, drawing the plane forcefully to a stop. Pete swept his new M16 up and pulled his Sam mask over his head. The cockpit door shoved open with a clang and Simeon darted out. A tight, efficient rush for the door moved through the plane. No banter broke from the Parabaloni as they leapt out onto the grass of the Iowa field. The darkness enfolded them and Pete couldn't even see his brothers as they spread out, every sense on the alert.

But he could feel them.

The comforting presence of strength hovering nearby; they were there, able and ready to do the right thing. They had each other's backs today.

"No signs of people in the house," Vincent reported to the left.

"Movement behind the fence," Gigan barked.

Four bodies scaled the twelve-foot fence to the zoo without a sound and spread out under the bare skeletons of trees bending in the winter wind. They filed forward in quick, silent efficiency. Always in line, sweeping everything, ready to leap toward each other when needed.

A white blob hopped past Vincent's path and Floyd tracked it. Two large ears swiveled his way and a pink nose bobbed. The rabbit opened its mouth and a high pitched, rumbling yell came from between its buck teeth. Vincent blinked at it as he stole carefully forward.

"Did that rabbit just roar at me?" he murmured to the dark movement he knew was Sim.

"Being a lion this week," Simeon answered. His voice was lifeless. Vincent felt the tension shooting from his chosen dad tonight. And he couldn't ease it. He couldn't just crack a joke and say it was all going to be all right. It would take a miracle to make it turn out all right tonight.

They might still kill the MM, stop the virus outbreak and the blackouts. They had been given time in flight to plan for that. But it was probably already too late for Susie. Vincent felt his mind gently shutting down. He didn't want to think about it. Didn't want to leap ahead to what tomorrow might bring. He focused on the next step. Too tired to do any more.

Simeon's dark blob froze and his boys froze with it, searching for what he had noticed.

Something moved in the nice manicured parkland ahead of them, under the next line of trees. Several somethings. Everything lay in the darkness, the stench of large animals covered all other smells, and the wind swept away each noise but itself. It wasn't easy to pinpoint what it was.

A tingle ran up Vincent's spine, singing with adrenaline. He slid Floyd into his holster. Mr. Black knew they had landed. But that wasn't a reason to blast their exact whereabouts to the bad guys with gunfire unless he had to. They stole forward over the grass, spreading out. Tension and dread spread like a spiderweb through them, as they all prayed desperately for a miracle. Begging this night wouldn't end how they all knew it would. The dark blobs of movement stopped as they neared the next line of trees. There should have been a better committee reception out here. Why hadn't they been jumped yet? Vincent stole forward over the cold grass, searching everywhere for the enemy. Because he knew the enemy hovered nearby, waiting.

A flash of movement stirred the air three yards in front of Vincent. He spun to the side in a blurred move he had done a thousand times by now. A black knife blade whizzed past him, just where his neck would have been. He grabbed a tree branch above his head, adjusted his angle according to the direction that blade had come from, and launched himself toward it. He felt his feet hit a tree trunk and he pushed off, spinning into a fighting stance, hands flattened and every sense tingling. Air moved behind him. Vincent's foot shot out. It hit something solid that felt like a chest, and he spun with his own move, darting toward a dark patch that looked vaguely human shaped. He ached for decent night vision software that would make the scene so clear. A knife blade sliced into the back of his vest. There was another one behind him. Vincent's hands closed around an arm. He jerked his attacker off their feet, pivoted, and flung them like a live discus at his nearest guess at where the knife came from.

Vince heard the sharp thump as his attacker hit another black blob. Both blobs went down in a grunting heap. Vince darted forward to close the distance to the two threats.

A flash of white moved in the tree above him. The heavy musk of a large animal cut into the silent melee. Vincent flung himself backward, landing hard on his rump to stop his impetus. Floyd sprung into his arms as he tried to find the animal. The white moved and a terrifying deep growl filled the air. A heavy thump hit the dark blobs just in front of his boots. White teeth flashed, and screams rent through the woods.

"Not nice kitty," Vincent heard himself gasp as he scuddled back over the frozen grass. Floyd opened fire. His sharp cough filled the air, lighting up the dark as a flame danced on his muzzle. It sprayed over two dark-clothed people writhing under a lithe four-footed shape, and up to the animal on them. Two terrifying feline eyes reflected the light back at him. A roar of fury filled the air. Vincent could see the cat's white teeth gleam, and they came straight for his face. But he could hear his plunger bullets slamming into fur and skull. The teeth left. A sharp thump of a heavy body hit the ground, and he felt the thing's skull ram into his boot.

The clip emptied. Dark and silence closed in again.

"Didn't expect that," Vincent panted. He ejected his clip as he pulled his boot out from under the heavy skull of the leopard, slid a new one into Floyd, and ran, searching the darkness for his buddies. He needed to warn them.

More than human enemies roamed out here.

Pete stole through the night as if he could become a shadow himself. A part of him wondered if he could by now. He stepped into the dark so often to fight it, could he morph into the darkness himself? A grimace cut across his sharp face. He felt himself fumbling for a verse. For a shaft of light as he struggled to find the hope to fight back. No. He would always fight back. But the dark clung to him like physical weights. He felt as if it pulled him to the dust he came from and he could never soar again. Dread at what they would find here, at another scene of heartbreak and cruelty and bloodshed, sapped him like a physical wearying force. They were still dancing to this Black's tune as the villain called every move.

Pete froze, his foot raised in mid step. Metal rested on the ground just where he had been about to walk. Sharp teeth stared up at him, lots of them. A bear trap, painted to match the Iowa ground, set and ready to snap his ankle and probably even cut his foot off. To leave him maimed and bleeding out in the dark winter woods.

Anger flared through Pete, boiling up from everything in him at the senseless cruelty of setting it out here. There was a tiny probability of one of the Parabaloni setting it off; more likely it would be found by a zoo guest weeks later, probably a child running in the woods enjoying the freedom of the parkland and the special outing. And Black knew that.

His knife flew from her sheath and slammed into the trigger. The bear trap snapped closed with a sharp metallic ring and Pete swept up his knife, his teeth set in fury.

Movement shifted in the tree just ahead of him, as if something jumped at the sound of the trap. Pete whipped toward it, his knife loose in his fingers, ready to snap toward the threat. The ground trembled under his boots as a thick something dropped from the tree. Pete's throwing knife shot straight at this thing's body as a sharp scent filled the air. Steamy jungle leaves came to his memory as the smell hit him. Then something else hit him. A fist the size of his head rammed into Pete's chest. He shot back off his feet, hit the ground in a heap, and rolled. He piled into a bank of old dirty snow beside a paved path with a sharp "oof."

The terrifying roar of a full grown male gorilla rolled from the darkness, just feet in front of his face.

Pete scrambled up the snowbank onto the clear path. He knelt out of the trees, swinging his rifle around, and trying desperately to glimpse his enemy. A thick, wrinkled, half naked foot stepped into the tiny bit of light granted by the open path. A gorilla, his back a terrifying distinct silver, stepped out on his hind legs. He loomed in the night. Not quite as tall as Pete, but at least four hundred pounds of terrible power and awesome killing strength. His huge teeth were bared, and saliva dribbled down one side of his mouth. The throwing knife stuck out of his lower left side, buried to her hilt. She didn't seem to be slowing him down. His cupped fists pounded into his chest in a physical show of fury, and Pete found himself gulping.

"Did you know your full scientific name is *Gorilla gorilla gorilla*?" he said, his voice a little squeaky. "Just, you know, thought it might amuse you."

The animal leapt toward him, and another roar ripped from his throat, shaking Pete's eardrums. Pete caught him in the chest with the flat of his foot as he vaulted on his back, flinging this hulking specimen behind him toward the paved path. Every muscle and bone in him spasmed and trembled at the weight. The gorilla's stink surrounded him and he felt the creature's thick fingers brush his leg, trying to get a hold on it and rip it from his body. The gorilla flew six feet. But it squirmed in the air and came down on all four paws, already spinning back around to meet the thing that had wounded it. Pete's finger slammed down on his trigger. His rifle spit fire as bullets sped from her barrel, and he thanked the Lord he had loaded live ones tonight. But it was dark and his target was moving. A line cut into this creature at the shoulder, shifting toward his head. The gorilla moved, dodging and huffing in pain and fear. He managed to duck into the trees on the other side of the woods.

The animal disappeared.

Pete's finger left the trigger. He lifted his rifle and stared at the darkness around him.

"Wonderful. Now everyone knows where I am, *and* there's a gorilla out, *and* he took my knife." A sigh blew from him as he shoved a new clip in his rifle. He spun back into the trees on his side of the path to try and lose himself again and warn the others. Some nights you just couldn't win.

"Guys!" Vincent breathed into the dark. "More than humans are out here."

"No, really?" Gigan hissed back to him. "You might mention that to the family of lemurs that attacked my head four minutes ago."

"A gorilla took my knife," Pete added. "Also, bear traps."

"Shush," Simeon ordered. The wind began to slowly scatter the clouds, and they could see his dark form standing still between two trees. The boys filled the space around him. A few stars peeked through the gloom, and they studied the scene. A wide path swept off into the zoo, the gray pavement almost gleaming in the bits of starlight beginning to shine. Trees lined it on both sides, and deep, dense darkness rested under their bare branches.

Nothing moved out there.

"There should be more of a welcome committee from Mr. Black," Gigan murmured.

"Do you think..." Vincent muttered back, and they all heard the hope in his voice.

An elephant trumpeted. It rang through the trees, a mighty bellow of power and strength. A huge gray animal turned into sight on the path. The clouds rolled back and for an instant the moon shone clear. Its beams hit the form of a woman sitting on the African elephant's neck as the animal strode forward, his trunk lifted high and his feet indenting the ground with each step. Her brown hair waved around her head in unruly wisps that looked like the diadem of a saint painted by a master's hand. She held a metal pipe over her shoulder like an unsheathed sword and what looked like a round shield glinted on her back. Two tawny shapes ran up beside the huge elephant, and Gigan's laughter suddenly covered the scene. Vincent's long arm shot around Simeon's shoulders and he squeezed, his grin brilliant in the night.

"Behold, she comes to you!" Pete's accent wound around the foursome, relief and delight tingling in every word. "Riding upon an elephant with her own bodyguard of lions! I don't know why I expected less."

"She outfoxed him," Vincent grinned in delight. "Got ahead of him in his own game, when none of us have been able to do it this whole mission!"

"Come, my brothers," Gigan chuckled, "let us secure her ride and let the knight assist his maiden to dismount."

They faded away into the trees. Simeon knew they were sweeping the area, clearing it of any snipers or sudden threats. He pulled his mask off, kept his little pistol in his hands, and stepped onto the path. The male lion paused in its bounding run. The animal's mane shook as he focused on the stranger, and a rumbling growl echoed from him.

"Peace, Horatio," Simeon called to the lion, his strong tones carrying in the moonlight. "'O, it offends me to the soul to hear a robustious periwig-pated fellow tear a passion to tatters, [62].'" The lion's tongue flicked out and the growl died. Simeon's eyes lifted to the woman on the huge gray mount as the elephant stepped up in front of him. A smile teased the corners of his mouth and sent admiration and delight swirling in his expression. He gave the perfect little bow. "I'm delighted to find you, Susie Quenton."

"You are a most welcome sight, Simeon Lee," Susie smiled down at him. "Heads up, Fred is quite tall, and I'm coming down. I do hope you don't have to shoot my lions, but keep an eye on them, they're a bit overexcited about all the fun tonight. The creepy one and his minions are doing something at my office building. You had better get over there soon."

Gigan watched as a barefoot Susie slid from the elephant and was caught gracefully by Simeon. The trash can lids she had used to shield her back rolled onto the path with a clang. The two started off at a trot for the back fence to deliver Susie to the local police force two streets away. Another chuckle slid from Gigan, most of it just the delight of relief.

He suddenly realized it was as if his strength had been draining steadily since Aldrick's text. So many unanswered prayers lay in that one text from his nephew, and they piled on each other with each passing hour since he had run to his family. Sapping his hope. Wearing down his already tired soul.

A wisp of a cloud rolled over the moon and sped off again,

---

[62] Hamlet, Act III, Scene II. It is the phrase I use with him when I come visiting (he's a noisy fellow), and Horatio associates it with friends, peace, and often snacks. I mentioned it once in an email to Simeon. Apparently he remembered.

changing the shadows, and Gigan's mustaches bristled in a smile. God didn't answer every prayer, and sometimes on this poor earth the broken just broke harder. But He healed all His people's scars in the end. And sometimes, sometimes the Lord nudged the world into the perfect alignment and gave His saints a brilliant break in the darkness even on this earth. And suddenly he realized it was a break just like the movement of that cloud. The light always shone just beyond the dark. It never went out, even when human eyes couldn't see it. Like a clarion bell his soul sang with the moon and Gigan felt the strength of the fight flooding him again. He bounded forward, sweeping the ground and every tree with his eyes, slipping through the deepest shadows. He would live always in the shadows if it meant driving the dark back another millimeter. It was worth it to make more room for the light to shine.

Gigan stole forward with quick efficiency, watching everything, his mustaches bristling and a bounce to his movements. They had heard Susie's comment of course. He followed the main path as the quickest way to the zoo's office building. He could guess why they were all bunched there instead of straying in the woodlands with a stronger welcoming committee for the Parabaloni. The Collective might avow raw nature as the ideal. But when a zoo's dangerous animals started roaming, they fell back and stayed where they could have the strength of human numbers. Another chuckle slid from him as he moved, and a shiver went through him that wasn't just from the cold. Susie's simple, brilliant move cut through this plot like... like Pteranodons taking down an incredibly sophisticated flying base. The way God drew similar souls together touched the Frenchman's ready humor, and Gigan's laughter traveled with him through the bare winter trees.

Movement caught his eye from time to time, flitting around him. He recognized the silhouettes of his work brothers occasionally shifting on the opposite side of the path. Once he saw Pete dart over the moonlit concrete, and he seemed to be chasing a large something that shook the trees as it leapt from one side to the other. Gigan hoped Pete caught the gorilla. His partner would feel naked without his throwing knife in a fight.

Six shaggy canines padded onto the path and he watched them pause, huge ears swiveling and their noses turned to snuffle his direction. Gigan tracked them with Clarice, and hoped the pack chose a different direction. Dingoes? African painted dogs? Gray wolves? He couldn't tell in the dark. He found himself thankful for the cold freezing his lungs with each breath; Susie would have kept her reptilians inside their heated house. Gigan stole over another swath of green grass up to a new line of bare, swaying trees, and paused.

The clouds crept away, and the moon and her sister stars shone bright for a moment. They played off a circle of concrete with animal paws and fern leaves impressed in it, and a small blocky office building sitting in the center. The stars reflected off a veritable mote of heated duck ponds around the building, their occupants mostly quiet with beaks tucked under wings, asleep and comfortable. Paths crossed over them in pretty bridges. Two white swans shone in the moonlight as they dozed under one of the bridges. It smelled like a birdhouse. As Gigan watched, a huge orange and black cat leapt out of one pond. Water sprayed around her as she gave a shake, and a mallard carcass dangled from a mouth that looked decidedly pleased. The tiger was having fun with her freedom, it seemed.

Movement came from the blocky building. Gigan pinpointed it in time to see a man hurriedly pull back to the other side, away from the tiger merrily chewing on her midnight snack. Half the man's coat hung in shreds around him, and Gigan chuckled again. Susie's animals really were having a night out. He shifted quickly and carefully under the trees to a better vantage point to see Black and his cronies, swinging Clarice around and checking her over. Oh, he felt achy and tired. It would be nice to get this Black mess finished tonight, one way or another. Simeon must have made it to the police with his happy, unexpected, wonderful delivery by now. His eyes sought the sky as the clouds parted still more and stars blazed down in brilliant numbers. A wolfish grin cut over the Frenchman.

The fun would start soon.

Chapter 30

"Is everything ready?" Luther Kirl demanded. Arnulf Jones looked up from the computer. The old man's eyes shone.

"Yes." Jones answered. "We have the components all set up and the cameras launched. Fall has his button for the programming ready, just like ordered." Honestly, who named their son Fall? But the young man was certainly good at what he did. Most major news stations worldwide would take on this channel in a few seconds. Jones wondered again, *why...*

"Never try to be a spy, Jones," Luther cackled, and Jones' head snapped toward him. "You don't have the face for it. You're still wondering why I've bothered with all this." Luther's arm went around Jones' huge shoulders in a comradely manner. The big mercenary just managed to keep a shudder down. "Because I want the whole world to watch two sets of people who have annoyed me wipe each other out. It is as simple as that. This 'Mr. Black' is too vindictive (in his own mad way) to let Vincent and his cronies leave today. And Tolliver and his work family are too fanatical about 'saving the weak' to let him win. Besides, it will be fun to watch the panic as people learn what Black's been up to."

"What has he been up to?" Jones blurted out. He watched on the screens as his four cameras hovered high over an ordinary little town in Iowa. He wondered if the place even made it on most maps? Probably not unless you zoomed in. A lot. And yet there went Fall's fingers darting over his keyboards, ready to pull this little town into the blaze of fame. Linking satellites. Finishing the set up on the drones carrying Jones's cameras. The cameras were incredible. Jones adjusted lenses and angles, zooming in and picking out figures on that bare moonlit ground in a... was that a tiger? He pulled in again and clarified the picture. Yep. A large tiger stretched out on the concrete near some duck ponds eating a mallard. Looks like the show was going to start with a show of teeth.

Fall's fingers hovered over the button to send the feed to TV channels worldwide. His young face turned to Luther's leathery, wrinkled one. A smile hovered on Luther. Dark enjoyment of this moment danced in his bright eyes.

"It is time to watch history," Luther said. He cackled, his thin form almost writhing. "Only a few may live to write it, but it will be history *I* make, as I watch the only ones who have dared to try to squirm out of my control destroy each other! And this time I want the world to know the webs they're caught in." He leaned over Fall's chair so it squeaked at the added weight, staring at the feed. The last of the wispy clouds blew away, and the figures on the moonlit ground came into distinct clarity. Jones zoomed in a little more, adjusting and changing the picture. It was awkward to have to be so high up, it made this very difficult. But he picked out a man beside a silver something, next to the building. A man in a facemask, black leather hoodie, and gloves. He stood so still. Jones' other drones moved, and he picked out other figures, shifting steadily closer to the open circle of ground and that waiting, still man. He zoomed in on one and saw a thin, bony figure moving with the supple speed of a warrior who knew their trade.

His memory hiccupped with freezing rain, drowning white river water, and a stranger's lasso flashing through the dark.

Luther's smile grew brighter. Jones felt himself tensing. His eyes went to the wall of windows on the top floor of this London office building, towering over the old chimney pots and tiles of the ancient town. He suddenly loathed the comfortable, heated air blowing from the vents. He longed to be out there, beside the thin easterner, fighting against whatever was going down in a tiny town in Iowa. The strength of that longing surprised him. Maybe after he was done with this… Maybe he could find better reasons to use the job he had fallen into than just gaining a living and a few thrills.

Right now he needed to do the job he had been released to finish. Arnulf Jones hit the button programmed on his smartphone. On the other side of the ocean, Jojo Aziz heard the alert pop up. She began to hone in on his signal.

Luther's head bobbed in a nod. Fall hit the button. Across the world, TV stations interrupted their normal viewing for unique, live footage. A prerecorded video started it, flashing news scenes of the blackouts with Luther Kirl's voice narrating[63]. A cackling old man monologuing like a super villain. Telling the world he made the blackouts, and telling them to watch his machinations. Then the feed switched to Jones' work, and a scene in night vision software came alive. A scene with a tiger eating a duck, and strange figures shifting over manicured grassland. The world leaned in to see what happened next.

Simeon dropped over the front gates and landed on his toes on the path. Moonlight spread around him, and the paw prints and fern leaves in the concrete filled with black shadows. The world sang around him, and energy coursed through his veins. His little pistol stayed out in his hand as he began to march toward the office building. Joy flowed through every part of him from that unexpected meeting, from *not* finding the death and blood and viciousness he expected. Everything seemed clearer and brighter. He could pick out his enemy's movements easily, and hear the patter of the dog pack in the trees, and he knew he would play his part well tonight. He strode onto the bridge curving over the swans. The birds' white wings flared in the night like heralds announcing Simeon Lee on the move.

A voice materialized from the dark shadows around the building.

"You still burn too bright." It came even and sepulchral, as if it were formed from the dark itself. The tiger moaned at the strange noise. The huge animal moved into a stretch, her mouth opening in a yawn, showing bloodied incisors and feathers. Simeon's eyes flicked to a slim, silver disc sitting beside the office building, then ran over the shadows around the disc. He counted at least twenty vaguely human shapes, shifting and moving. Too many to take on right away. He spun off the bridge behind him.

---

[63] Using his own voice seemed decidedly dumb of the man, till Sim pointed out how easy it would be for a well-paid lawyer to make the case it was someone with a voice changing program and not really Kirl. Some people seem to delight in a double game. But then there was The Russian who delighted in quadruple games, including ones with griffons and exploding hard boiled eggs, so I suppose I shouldn't complain about double ones.

One hand pulled his mask back over his head as he disappeared into the darkness of the parkland trees.

"Can't shoot you without announcing this time?" Simeon asked. He shifted a quick, silent three yards deeper into the darkness beside the path. Distancing himself from where his voice pinpointed him. A twenty foot fence rose to an enclosure and he ducked toward the deeper shadows it cast.

"You can shoot," Black stated. It cut through the moonlight three yards behind Simeon. The agent spun silently and slid two yards to the right. The tiger's eyes shone as they focused on Simeon, and the tip of her tail flicked. He searched the darkness, trying to pierce it to find his enemy.

"But if you shoot, how will you learn when the machine will go off?"

Black's voice came from behind him. Closer than before.

"Put that in my pipe and smoke it, eh?" Simeon said as he searched the dark. A slight movement came to his left; Black's head tilting as he tried to figure out if his opponent had a pipe and why he would smoke it at this particular moment. Simeon pulled his pistol's trigger.

A line of high pressure water hit Black in the face, spilling over the top of his mask. He fell back a step, spluttering at the cold and the shock and the bitter taste. Then he recognized the taste. Catnip. A roar came from by the duck ponds. Immense and excited and deadly. For an instant silver lockpicks glinted in a slant of moonlight in Simeon's hands. The agent slid through the door to the empty lions' enclosure and slammed it behind him as the soft paw thumps of a running tiger filled Black's ears.

Simeon darted across the savannah grassland and ducked behind the pile of rocks near the center of the enclosure. His eye fell on one set of rocks fashioned like a broken stone table. A smile shot over his face. At the darkest moments, sometimes God chose to send a shaft of pure miracle into the world, upturning and unraveling the darkness itself. It wove through the oldest and deepest of the stories, and the innate desire for that overturning beat in every heart. His lady had style in expressing it. And bravery and smarts too, by God's grace!

The tiger roared and mewled outside the enclosure, and a rifle blazed away the dark. Simeon could see him just outside the glass wall, framed in the flashes dancing on the muzzle with each shot, like a magic lantern silhouette show. Mr. Black and the vast form of a lithe, excited tiger, writhing and pirouetting around each other. The last picture formed Black in a mighty leap, one hand reaching for the top of the wall as the other fired on his enemy, the tiger's paw outstretched trying to catch the delicious smelling snack. That rifle looked point blank on the cat's skull. Then the flash died in a deadly echo of bullet fire. The night closed in again.

No more roars. Nothing but the gentle rustle of the wind through the grasslands around him. Simeon crouched against his rocks. He stayed deathly still, searching the night for his enemy.

Somewhere in this simulated savannah, evil hunted him.

Vincent skirted around the duck pond mote, tracking Simeon as his partner pulled Black away from the MM. Sometimes Vince thought he spotted a shifting darkness in the form of a man moving with his big boss. But it was never clear enough to risk a good shot. The inventor darted over one of the paths and froze under a drooping willow. The leafless stems brushed the pond in front of him and a sleeping eider shifted in a lazy circle. Vince concentrated on the office building across from him. He still couldn't get in a line with that MM. It was too thin, too close to the ground.

Black's voice drifted from Vincent's left as he answered Simeon, and the inventor's skin crawled.

"Put that in my pipe and smoke it, eh?" Simeon's reply cut through the night. A smile stole over Vincent as he tried to squirm into a better range to see the MM. He could hear the laughter just under Simeon's words. The delight that relief and the perfect, strange meeting had brought to his chosen father. Vince felt his soul singing in the night. It wasn't that the dark left. It wasn't even that the hole from his parent's passing closed. It was just the one, beautiful, perfect gift of knowing the dark hadn't won this time. That God and a smart, brave woman had foiled the blackness. And in the end, God would blaze His light into every shadow, even the hidden ones in Vincent's own heart. The inventor grinned in the night and slid to a different position. In the end, they won. Susie and her elephant had given him back the strength to remember it again. And her ingenuity let him remember that other people fought the dark too, with their own unique methods and skills. They weren't alone in this battle.

Vincent sank to one knee and sighted down his paintball gun. But he lifted the muzzle again in frustration. Black had his machine placed just right, and crafted too thin and short to get a bead on from a distance. They would have to get closer.

A sharp click came from above him. Vince's eyes darted up, and he barely picked out the mesh net amidst the branches. Then the net fell.

Vincent flung himself into a roll, landing on his paintball gun and pushing off again. He felt sweat starting up at the thought his little balls of acid could break open with a move like that, attacking the gun, melting his fingers. But the gun lay intact in his arms as he spun on one knee and took stock of the situation.

Dark, human shaped blobs stepped from the woods around him. Lots of them. Darn not having any scanners!

They wore bullet proof armor and looked shapelessly uniform in their bulky helmets. Vincent pulled a gas grenade from his vest pocket and lobbed it at the shadowy forms as he climbed to his feet. A white smoke cloud billowed from the grenade. Vince walked a few steps away from the smoke cloud, stopped with his back to a tree trunk, pulled Floyd, and stared at the white mist. It undulated and shifted in the moonlight, spreading like a wispy blanket.

Figures stepped through the whiteness. They came in a line, steady and definitely unfazed. Uh oh. Those helmets must be equipped with gas masks. That could be trouble. Vincent's finger slammed down on Floyd's trigger as he surged deeper into the zoo's parkland. They moved with him, and they came fast. Maneuvering expertly to surround him. The flames on his gun barrel lit his face, set in a grim line. He watched the bullets embed uselessly in the clothing, and his target pull back in a surprisingly quick move for the bulky outfit. They had trained in these. They were ready.

Vince gave one last look at the silver disc, so tantalizingly close, and thundered toward a dark form that had strayed a little too far from his fellows. He could pick that enemy off. The form (identical and unidentifiable from the rest) lifted a pistol in a quick move, bringing it to bear on the inventor's head. Vincent gave a lightning spin, just enough movement so the bullet coursed past his ear, and closed with his target. His arm shot around the stranger's neck. His gloved fingers found a gap between the helmet and clothing. He shoved Floyd's muzzle against the struggling figure's bare skin. Floyd's sharp bang filled the night around his head. Vincent shoved the limp form away and darted off toward the lion's encloser.

The dash took more effort than he expected. His body felt sluggish and old. Boy, he could use a few days off. Moonlight spilled around the branches of the tree in front of him, and Vincent darted automatically into the darker shadow near the trunk. But he froze, staring at the light mottling the ground with silver. The bare branches of the trees shifted in the breeze and made black shadows like angry serpents over the grass. But they couldn't block out that light. Silver and untouchable, enchanting the night with beauty that couldn't be killed... A grin rushed over Vincent. He darted toward another black form just a little too far away from his fellows. Mr. Black set the game in the dark tonight. But God let them play it in the enchanted light of His moon. And by golly, the Parabaloni would play it well.

He shoved another limp enemy away and disappeared into the dark, just checking the whistled hymn he wanted to give. He could see his enemies steadily surrounding him. They were good, maybe too good for him to take out in their armored outfits and overwhelming numbers. But at least he would leave less for his buddies to deal with. He prayed Gigan and Pete were holding up ok somewhere in this darkness and hoped like billy-o Sim was still in that lion's enclosure, or else Vince no longer had his partner's back. Of course, it was looking like he might need someone to watch his back. Durn it, without the watches online, he didn't even know where his work family were.

No, that wasn't accurate. He knew they were here, they were

fighting with him, and they were all held by the God who gifted miracles and moonlight.

That was more than enough.

Vincent's eyes darted back toward the office building, surrounded by its pools of shadows and ducks. His lips pursed. But as nice as all that was, he really needed to find Gigan.

The breeze stirred the savannah grassland, and Simeon tried to pick out any stalks moving contrary to the wind. He couldn't spot anything. Black had serious skill at clandestine movements. Simeon stayed stock still, only his eyes moving around the enclosure. A wolf howled outside. Five others answered it in an eerie, inhuman call.

Just above Simeon, a rock moved.

He rolled left, his little pistol barking in the dark. This time it was his actual pistol, and a live bullet slammed into the crouching form on top of the rock pile. It didn't penetrate. Simeon dropped into the cover of the broken stone table and searched the dark again.

The figure had disappeared.

"Coat's a good make. What brand?" Simeon asked.

"We knew you were coming," Black's voice drifted from the right. Simeon spun out of the table and crouched against a leg. "My people are armored and your bullets can't penetrate. Your boys will be overwhelmed quickly."

"You train them?" Simeon asked.

"Of course. I have been preparing for this moment." Black spoke from behind him again. Playing with his prey. Simeon slid dutifully back into cover on the other side of the table, searching for his enemy's move. He caught a sliver of movement near the rock pile as Black ducked behind them.

"How overwhelmed?" Simeon asked to keep him talking. There were probably better questions. But his boys' faces burned in his mind, and that's what he cared about most just then. And Black knew it.

"They're so tired," Black's voice drifted through the night. A breeze stirred the tall grassland and teased the voice around

Simeon. He couldn't pinpoint where it came from. "Tired of rushing to the rescue as you've taught them to do. Tired of fighting for things that are so easy to break. Tired of the dark pressing in from every side. So very, very tired." The voice moved closer. Simeon's eyes ached as he strained to see through the night. "Luther Kirl and I have kept them busy this year. It's been so easy, Lee. They work so hard to right everything I break and call them in to fix." The breeze died. Simeon slid his pistol into her holster, closed his eyes, and waited. "I've worn them down, and they're too tired to win tonight."

He pinned the voice. Black stood in the shadow of the tree, just to his right. Simeon gripped the leg he knelt against, ripped half the table out of the grass, and flung it. A bullet tore through the night and ricochetted off the stone, spraying sparks like a demented sparkler. Simeon spun out the door of the enclosure and closed it gently behind him before the last spark died. He darted into the darkness beside the path and leaned into his run, searching for his boys as he moved.

So this year's craziness had been Black and Kirl's work. He should have guessed that. But what did *"overwhelmed quickly"* mean in reality? What had Black planned out here?

The wolf pack howled again. Eerie and excited, hunting down their prey.

Clarice barked to Simeon's right, and the big boss spun in that direction. Gigan worked wounded tonight. Of their band he might be the one in need of help.

A black form rose directly in front of Simeon, as if the dark created him. The sparking coils of a taser shot through the night. Simeon flung himself backward. He landed hard, the coils sparking over his head. His momentum carried him forward as if he slid for first base. His feet rammed into Mr. Black's boots and the dark form jerked a rifle toward Simeon's head. The agent's hands closed around the barrel. He shoved it down to point at the enemy's black boot as he pushed off into a sharp roll.

The rifle thundered just beside his ear, blasting away the dark and deafening him. The bullet ricocheted off a steel toe and went zipping right, spraying concrete chips as it skipped along the path. Simeon rolled hard over cold grass. His ribs rammed into a tree trunk and a sharp grunt came from the spy. He could feel the old breaks in his ribs groan and crack. Simeon spun around the tree and darted off. Not toward Gigan. Mr. Black played the part of the hunter today. He would not stop till he had his way. Anywhere Sim went Black would be.

His boys were on their own tonight. Simeon prayed they were still whole enough to pull off this job.

Gigan gave a sharp gasp as his back slammed into a tree trunk, jarring his wounded arm. His attackers rushed him, sensing his moment of weakness. Clarice sprang up and pulled tight against the Frenchman's shoulder. Five quick bullets spun from her barrel, hitting each enemy in the eye with perfect accuracy.

A starred crack broke on helmet number four. And that was all he had to show for the effort. Gigan dropped his rifle to her strap and leapt upward. He caught a branch, swung into the tree, and his boots found a limb. He ran across the twisted, bare tree limb, over his startled enemies' heads. Enemy number four raised his rifle. Gigan hurled himself off his branch. He caught the man's thick neck in a leg hold, the force of his leap more than compensating for their different weights and heights. The enemy toppled slowly like a felled tree, gagging and scrabbling at the wiry figure clinging to his head. Gigan's fingers found the seam between helmet and armored coat. His silenced pistol gave a soft pop. The body hit the ground, and the Frenchman spun off into a run, dodging deeper into the zoo.

The four shadows ran like hares behind him, spreading out in an efficient web. Gigan turned his run into a sprint, searching for a convenient place to lose these nagging bad guys who just wouldn't give up. Oh, his arm hurt. So did his wrists. And his feet. Ok, all of him ached and stung with fatigue. Floyd blasted the night away to Gigan's left, and the Frenchman gave a quick prayer for the inventor. And his partner. And the big boss dealing with the nasty Mr. Black somewhere out here.

Confound not having any way to monitor anyone!

Two figures stepped out of the trees in front of him, and Gigan slid to a stop. One shadow wore his bulletproof coat crooked. Somewhere under that thick material, was a bandaged wounded shoulder. Clarice snapped into the Frenchman's arms automatically. A chuckle came from the wounded shadow. Gigan's hair rose as he recognized the voice. His eye ran over Greg Henderson, noting the way his left sleeve hung limp. Gigan took two quick steps to a thick oak and got his back against its trunk.

"You've been playing with the kitties tonight, Greg," Gigan commented, his voice bright. "I hope you brought a good catnip along. I will happily lend you some if not."

"Always the joker," the second shadow growled, and Gigan knew it.

"So you have changed businesses, Abassi?" the Frenchman asked. The other four shadows began to close in, filling the spaces between Greg and Abassi Sy. They glided in, so silent, so uniform. A faceless band of trained killers.

"Oh we're still working on the same goal, Gweam-Theephile," Greg answered. Gigan groaned and folded over himself in pain.

"Told you he was wounded," Abassi Sy growled, smug pleasure in the tone.

"No, it is not that," Gigan gasped, squirming melodramatically. "It has been long since I heard my name mispronounced by an American!" Abassi Sy's helmet turned toward Greg's, and Gigan could feel the glare behind the visor.

"Can I shoot him yet?"

"Mr. Black wants us to take him back alive," Greg answered. Oh so? That was probably good... Another two shadows drifted into the semi-circle gathering in front of the Frenchman's tree, and Gigan's hand tightened on Clarice. Especially as it would be difficult to get out of this.

"Your Mr. Black has led you to think you're out to save the earth from humans' influence," Gigan snapped, his humor gone. "That you are removing a plague from Mother Earth, as white blood cells attack germs. But it is a lie. All of it is a lie, that is not his goal! He will harm the earth and merrily murder each of you once he has his way."

"The earth has waited long under the human curse," a shadow

murmured. A woman, from the voice. "We will reset the balance!"

"That too is a lie," Gigan stated. "Humanity, as it ought to be, is not a plague and not a mere child to be looked after by a mother. We are gardeners, placed here to care for the earth and make her beauty better. Look around you! Isn't this parkland a prettier, more comfortable place for being worked on than the Vermont woodlands your fellows are training in?"

"He knows about The Base," the woman said, shock riding her words.

"Shut up, Jill," Greg snapped.

"I know your fellows have been warned to stay there. Do you know why?" Gigan demanded. "Your being here is not a sign of favor from Black. His is a demented mind, death is a delight to him, and you know it. Hiding in the woods might save your brothers from the deluge he brings, for a time, but if Black goes through with his plan death stalks the dark for all of you."

Greg took a long, slow step closer to Gigan. His shoulders squared and he towered over the Frenchman.

"You always think you know the score," Greg said, his voice angry and dangerous. "But you still have no idea what you're dealing with here. We've been trained and honed for this moment, and nothing you can do will stop it."

"Such a melodramatic speech!" the Frenchman stated. "I suppose I should answer in kind." Gigan's pistol popped. The plunger bullet slammed into Greg's neckline as he looked down at the Frenchman, allowing a tiny space between helmet and coat for the drug to penetrate. Gigan swung out of his trajectory as Greg slammed headfirst into the oak trunk on his way down. Abbasi suddenly found hard gray eyes behind a black mask boring into him. "Greg is wrong, again. *You* have no idea who you're dealing with."

Vincent rammed into the shadows like a charging rhinoceros. Three of them went down under his impetus. Cracking bones and agonized cries and confused chaos erupted around the oak. Abassi Sy swung his rifle toward Vincent's face, efficient and deadly. Gigan slammed Clarice into the hulking African's kidney.

Abassi folded on the wound with a roar. Gigan swung in with an elbow jab to the ribs. He felt the blow jar through him as he hit the armored coat, and his good arm tingled. But it staggered Abassi Sy too. Gigan's other hand shot up, and his silenced pistol barrel found the gap between helmet and coat.

A soft pop, and he spun away from another crumpling enemy and darted toward Vincent. The inventor grappled on the ground with a shadow, as two others pounded on him with their rifle butts. The Frenchman's ancient family war cry rang through the zoo and his guns blazed in the night. It melded with a wolf pack's ferocious howling somewhere deeper in the darkness.

More shadows flitted from the trees.

Too many.

A sharp "whizz" sailed past Pete's ear and he ducked instinctively. The thunk came a half second later, and a knife blade sparkled in the trunk of a tree. The Saudi growled in the night, and the empty sheath on his arm seemed to burn.

"Of course I get the knife thrower!" he muttered through clenched teeth. Pete spun on one leg and let Adeela the Second burn away the quiet and dark. Lead sprayed into the trees as his M16 coughed in her deadly song. In the light flicking on her barrel, he saw eight forms spread out under the trees. Dressed in black, faceless, void of any kind of human uniqueness. They slid quickly over the grass as if they could glide instead of walk. Not one cowered or shrank back from his fire. He might as well be flicking paper pellets. The last of the bullets sped from Adeela the Second's clip. The night closed in again.

He couldn't hear them. Couldn't smell them, couldn't see them. Bother this blackout! Pete jerked the knife from the tree trunk and hoisted himself silently into the tree. He leaned against a thick limb and waited, watching the ground below as his eyes adjusted again. The cold seeped into him and his muscles tried to stiffen. Man, he was tired. He should have gotten a nap on the flight up here. But with the Susie situation eating at them all, that had been impossible. Pete shoved it out of his mind, sucked in a breath, and concentrated.

Slowly he picked them out in the silvery light of the moon. Eight forms sweeping the parkland for him. A figure marched ahead of the others, back intensely straight, visor turning as she took in everything. Arrogant and forceful and feminine. Pete recognized the movements from Riyadh. His gloved thumb ran over the knife blade, feeling the weight and balancing points. Might as well play by Redhead's rules for a moment. She stepped into a brighter beam of moonlight just two feet below his branch. Pete snapped the knife straight at her neckline.

The blade hit hard. She staggered back, gagging and dazed, its razor sharp point stuck fast in her coat's reinforced material. But Pete could tell it hadn't penetrated. He pulled back, silently trotted over a branch and leapt to catch a limb in the next tree in the line. It bounced and bent with his weight, till his toes touched the ground.

A gunshot echoed behind him. The bullet slammed into his back, and Pete's fingers lost their hold at the force. He staggered onto the grass and moved seamlessly into a run. His spine tingled and a welt rose under his vest. Ok, so he wasn't as good at tree travel as that darned gorilla.

Branches swayed behind him, and he knew it wasn't from the wind.

They were coming. Tagging at his heels, driving closer with every step, forcing him where they wanted him to go. Slowly surrounding him. This was hard when they made him pick them off one by one. Maybe too hard. His muscles jumped with fatigue and Pete let himself grimace behind his Sam.

A gray wolf padded onto the path in front of Pete. The Saudi slid to a stop and stared at the huge dog. He could see the two sharp ears swivel toward him, and the moon sparkle off the white canine teeth peeking under its lips. The wolf's nose twitched. Pete glanced down at himself. A large, wet patch of fresh gorilla blood smeared his coat. Great. The wolf lifted its head and howled. Long and eerie and horrifyingly close.

Five other wolves echoed the noise from the trees surrounding Pete. The Saudi spun in a tight circle, trying to pick the wolves from the shadows. They melded with it, their gray fur the same color as the light spraying through the tree branches. Pete's spin took him back to his shadowy pursuers. He could see Red stopped three yards behind him. He could probably take her out before the wolf pack closed in. Probably. But was that his main goal?

Again came that inhuman, terrifying howl. Closer, and all around him. Pete made an instant's decision.

He sprang forward like a deer, straight at the wolf in front of him. This specimen had all the instincts of a predator, with the tools to rip and kill and mangle. But unlike the last dog pack Pete faced[64], this one was well fed and knew their next meal would magically appear at ten in the morning. They weren't that invested in the hunt.

The wolf sprang at Pete, his jaws open. The Saudi shoved his coat over the animal's head and kept running. The rest of the pack sprang away after Pete, silent and delighting in the hunt. The one on the path shook off the coat, and darted after his pack, his tail freewheeling. But he ran with a snootful of fresh gorilla blood, and his appetite awoke. The Saudi panted and concentrated on running. *"They shall run and not be weary…"* His favorite passage coursed through his mind and a breathless chuckle slid from him. That didn't describe him tonight. The rest of the passage thundered into his brain like a slap on the head from the Holy Spirit, and he stumbled at the force of it. Maybe he kept running in his own strength, and forgetting the point of the verse. Maybe he had forgotten Who it was that granted the eagle's wings he lacked tonight. Maybe he hadn't really asked to fly for a long, long time. Things had been so busy, he had let Bible study and concentrated prayer slip by the wayside.

"Sorry, Jesus," Pete panted as he ran. "You are the most important. Help me run tonight."

A shaft of moonlight sprang out from behind a cloud and hit the ground in front of Pete. It shone on a short, clear fence with

---

[64] In Estonia, a pack of nine vicious killers desperate for a good meal. Pete managed to use their desperation to distract the pack of six vicious human killers closing in on him to try and wrest the location of the truffle hoard from him. It was a good distraction.

the words "Prairie Dog Town," etched into it with frosted letter-ing. Pete just managed to veer around it, teetering, his arms free-wheeling for balance. A grin broke over him as he sprang away. That was two broken ankles neatly avoided. "Thanks," he panted. The pack leader caught up to the others as they closed the sprinting, huffing Saudi in an expert V formation. The pack was exultant in the jaunt, their tongues hanging out as they moved at barely more than a jog for the canines.

The pack leader veered left with a sharp yip. The rest of the pack tore after him, abandoning their running partner. Pete spun with them. He could see the gray tail of the last wolf in the moon-light, and he took off in pursuit, feeling hopeful and even enjoying the run.

Their goal here was to stay alive, and stop Mr. Black and his minions, and he should focus on that.

But Pete Aziz really wanted his knife back.

The wolves howled again in the exultation of their gorilla hunt. Pete threw back his head and howled along.

Simeon dodged behind cover, again. His back slammed against the bark of a large oak, and he felt it jar through him. Sim-eon's eyes crinkled as he felt the weariness even this brief half hour of sneaking and dashing and fighting brought on. He wasn't a spring chicken anymore. And the hours flying up here, spent in desperate dread of the dark, drained him.

His boys had lived in that dread, from case after case in an unbroken line, for nearly a year now. The realization pounded into him, and Simeon's frown deepened. Kirl and Black knew how to pile it on, and Simeon had let his team keep running. He could only pray it wasn't too late to fix it after they won tonight.

Because they had to win.

A bullet whined through the night and slammed into the trunk beside his ear. Wood chips sprayed over his mask, and Simeon spun to the other side of the trunk with an annoyed grunt. Black still played with him. He could have taken Simeon out multiple times by now. And here he was, facing the office building again. A little closer, again. Mr. Black drove him like a dad-blasted sheep. He was good, fourteen years better than when Simeon had last met him.

Sim could hear Clarice and Floyd deeper in the parkland. He hadn't heard Pete's rifle in a long time.

It was time to end this.

Simeon Lee pushed off from the oak and dashed toward the duck ponds and that office building. They had to kill the MM before Mr. Black spread his darkness to the rest of the world.

The millions watching saw the old spy run onto the open ground, his pistol held in front of him, a professional shuffle in every movement as he swept his path for threats. But they also saw a human shaped shadow flit from the trees behind him and move over the ponds toward the office building. The shadow moved faster than the old agent.

A shadow's empty rifle smashed down on Gigan's bad arm. A guttural yelp broke from the Frenchman and he went to one knee, stars dancing in his vision. He could hear Vincent's sharp grunts as he rolled under another pile of four enemies. They were starting to grow used to the inventor's methods of pound-and-pound-harder. Gigan vaguely saw the rifle butt coming for his face. He flung himself backward, but he was clumsy and dizzy and weak from the pain. A part of his brain knew his maneuver wasn't fast enough.

An arm shot around the shadow's neck and jerked back. A silenced pistol popped and the figure crumpled. As he fell, Pete came into view, panting behind his Sam mask, the silenced Asil still hot in his hands. Six wolves raced past him and disappeared into the trees, their tongues out and noses snuffling the air.

"Resting again?" Pete panted. He reached a gloved hand out to his partner. Gigan took it with a groan and hefted himself up.

"Just a little vacation time, between blows," the Frenchman shrugged. The partners launched themselves at the pile of wrestling people. Pete grabbed a helmet with two hands and wrenched. The shadow came off with a gasp, his neck popping under the strain. The Saudi's pistol found the gap at the neckline, his boot landed on the man's chest, and he shoved his limp body to the grass. Gigan slammed his boot onto a shoulder as the squabble moved past him, and ripped another shadow away from their inventor. Clarice spoke as Floyd gave two blasts. Vincent sat up slowly. They could see the sweat dripping down his face through the clear eye shields. It mingled with blood from a cut forehead.

"You are sweating," Pete commented, and a shiver ran down his spine. "How do you do that, it is too cold to sweat!"

"That's because you tossed your coat away, silly," Vincent groaned as he hoisted himself to his feet. He pulled a padded coat off a prone enemy and held it out to Pete. "Here, bro, only a little mussed from the fray."

"Oh look, this one has human blood instead of gorilla's," Pete commented cheerily as he shrugged into it.

"Is that better?" Gigan blinked.

"Doesn't smell as bad," the Saudi nodded, and Vincent gave a breathless chuckle.

More enemies drifted from the trees. They seemed to glide out of the night as if they were parts of one entity. Uniform, determined, fresh, and always more. The three Parabaloni shifted to stand back-to-back. Sharp clicks drifted through the dark as they switched clips in their weapons and assessed the situation.

"That's a lot," Vincent murmured to his buddies.

"I lost track of my dog pack," Pete said morosely.

"My friends... I think this is the part where we get taken down," Gigan said quietly. A new clip clicked into Clarice. "Let's make this stand count."

Chapter 31

Simeon stole over the bridge and onto the circle of concrete in front of the zoo office building. He could see the MM. Just a circle of flat metal. Nothing to draw the eye. But if it deployed, it would end civilization as people knew it. There would be no more smart gadgets. No way for cities to get food. No fresh water. No sanitation. Most hospital services unavailable. And through it all, a virus would rage, killing unknown numbers. The death toll could be in the billions. He strode for the disc.

Mr. Black stepped from the darkness directly in front of him.

"Stop," he stated. His eyes burned behind his mask, their bright blue gleaming in the moonlight. He held up one balled fist. Simeon traced a wire from that fist to the MM. He rocked to a stop and stood still. The breeze teased the tense silence between them. A duck quacked in the pond.

A sharp blast flew from Mr. Black's rifle, and the duck's head severed from its body. Those icy blue eyes, a little too wide, a little too bright, never strayed from Simeon.

"You let your people think you're doing it to save the earth. But that's not it, is it Mr. Black?" Simeon demanded. "What's your real plan?"

Flashes of a firefight filled the trees behind the two men on the circle of concrete. Gunshots rang around them, sharp, deadly singing noises rolling in a cacophony from the dark woodlands. The gun flashes and noise began to spill closer. The fighters pushed into the open ground out of the trees. Black forms (shifting with the quick, smooth movements of trained experience) swirled into three separate balls of action.

A roundhouse kick from one of the milling groups sent a wiry black form spilling from the crowd. Gigan slammed onto his back on the frozen grass. Clarice spilled from his grasp and Simeon knew he had blacked for an instant with the pain jarring from his wounded arm. Sim shifted to race toward his boy.

Black made a sharp guttural noise in the back of his throat and his balled fist pulled forward. Simeon froze, staring at that hand. The wire was a taut line. He could see the moonlight reflecting off Black's wide eyes.

"You will stay here," Black stated. "Stay here and watch them be dragged to me."

"To prove what?" Simeon growled. The group around Gigan closed in with exquisite skill, snapping up his lost weapon and coming in hard. The Frenchman clutched his arm to his chest as he struggled to his knees.

"Oh it is so easy. You think you always win. You and your people work so hard to right all the wrongs and keep the light burning. But none of it lasts. I always win in the end."

A blast from Floyd and Adeela the Second rang through the night. Bullets cut past Vince and Pete's line of attackers and smashed into those raining blows on their work brother. Their attack hesitated as bullets slammed into them. Gigan fought his way to his feet.

"You fight so hard," Black said again. It came as almost a coo, Simeon realized. As if somewhere behind that fanatical mask Black was enjoying this moment. "But history only immortalizes the victors. I go after you, and before you, and I bring the dark. And it is so easy to break the world."

A roar cut through the night. A fireball ran around the edge of the zoo, flinging black fence panels high. The dark filled with deadly fire and flames. The ground shook. Simeon staggered, as ducks and white-feathered swans flapped and squalled in sudden fright. The three groups of men were nearer the flames. Too near. Simeon saw three of the enemy's coats catch the flames, and his boy's feet shook from under them. All three went down. For an instant, Floyd and Pete's rifle blazed along with the explosives. But the rifle fire stopped suddenly, and the enemy closed closer. The flames began to die.

"It is so easy to be remembered forever as the most powerful. All I have to do is bring the dark." The night took over again. Thicker and filled with the acrid scent of smoke, the crying of terrified animals, and the horrendous noise of wounded and fighting men. Mr. Black took a step nearer, his eyes reflecting the few flames still smoldering in the trees. He devoured Simeon's strained expression as the agent stared at that line tightening behind the balled fist. The sounds of the fighting around them began to drift into the one-sided noise of soft thuds and grunts.

"What exactly do you bring?" Simeon asked. His voice came low as he stood rigid in front of an enemy that still held every card.

Mr. Black's eyes crinkled with a smile.

Sean sat on the hotel bed and stared at the TV screen. He hadn't gone home. Somehow it just didn't feel safe to be at his own place alone. And now here he sat, his thumb throbbing under the bandages, and his eyes drying out as he stared at a man trying to ruin the world, and his messy-haired boss steadily getting overwhelmed by the numbers.

This was the man who wanted Sean and his people dead.

Tolliver Charities kept fixing things.

Driving back the darkness in small, measurable increments. Foot by foot. With each food sack and Bible delivered, each orphan rescued, each medical procedure paid for, each widow clothed... And here stood a man dedicated to making it worse. To breaking the things Sean and his people worked so hard to fix.

Well, he would keep fixing them. Even if this Mr. Black won today and brought more death and destruction, Sean O'Leary would be in the front lines fixing the mess. Sean's large chin squared as he stared at the TV screen and he willed with all his soul for Gigan to get up again. For Pete to land one more punch. For Vincent Lee Tolliver to stand tall and cream these people. This Mr. Black broke just to prove how easy it was. But the Parabaloni knew the creeds. They knew the God Who loved the world even unto death. Who turned black hearts to flesh again. The One God who always won in the end. They knew why they kept fighting to fix the broken.

Sean felt the pride of being a side-member of their elite band in that moment.

He watched Vincent's tall form disappear in the midst of his churning crowd of enemies, and Sean found himself on his feet, screaming at his TV. Screaming at his boss to get up and fight again.

Algy shuddered and his eyes closed for an instant as he watched Black's eyes shine on Alice's TV. His son-in-law Walter sat stiff in shock, his eyes darting from the screen to the old man he was only now realizing wasn't just a missionary. Alice only saw the lines deepen and score her father's weathered face.

"You know him," she stated.

"You can't really know someone like that," Algy sighed. He sounded drained, even Walter heard it. They watched as the flames died and the video feed blurred and shifted back to the night software. Picking out the forms past the smoke and ashes drifting in the winter air. Not much resistance seemed to be happening in the three balled groups of fighting men. "But I thought I knew him once. And I thought Aimie and his boys could handle him today. They're falling too fast... I suppose I set a monster on this world worse than even old Aimie realized."

Algy's words rolled on, telling his daughter of the foundling he had tried to redeem, and the man he had become, as they watched the cameras picking through the darkness in an Iowa zoo.

Mr. Black started to talk. To explain what the metal disc was attached to, and what it made possible. To tell the world about the power he wielded over their fragile cities and brittle homes.

Walter's eyes grew wider. He stared at the circle of silver behind this madman his father-in-law had apparently trained, and felt his chest tightening. Worldwide power outages that would take months, maybe years to fix. And a virus... He could almost feel the children sleeping upstairs, peaceful, oblivious. So helpless. His eyes shifted off the silver glinting in the moonlight and went to Algy.

"What chance do they have to stop this?" he asked, his voice husky.

Algy just looked at him. Walter felt himself starting to hyperventilate.

"You can't save it all," Mr. Black told Simeon. "You know what I plan. Did you learn of it all before tonight?"

"You haven't told us all," Simeon growled. "Not just here to set off your machine that fries the infrastructure and lets loose your virus."

"Luther Kirl was right. You are a worthy opponent to play against. But even you couldn't stop this ending. I've been steadily wearing your brave little band down, as Kirl and I give them so much work, for so long. They're so tired. And tonight our work pays off. Your men are already overwhelmed. Look." Simeon turned in the moonlight. The worldwide millions watching could see the fear spasm over his face. His boys hadn't managed to cope with what they found here. The three little bands moved toward Black. Three forms squirmed and dragged in the midst of those groups. "You can't save the world and your boys, Lee. I'm sure you understand the game. You can drop your pistol and join them, and I will not set off the machine. I will even tell the authorities where those eight drums of virus are, and let them have a fighting chance to stop the outbreak. Or you can choose to fight back. Try to rescue your people from mine. And watch the world disintegrate into the blackness I create."

The sound of angry haranguing in French, Arabic, and old American slang swirled closer as the agents were dragged toward them. Closer to this madman with the fanatic light of victory burning in his ice-blue eyes.

Simeon's hand rose slowly, and a visible tremble ran through it as he held his little gun. Mr. Black's fist pulled a little tighter on the wire attached to his disc, a reminder of all at stake. Simeon's pistol barked. The flash on the muzzle lit the old spy's face for an instant. It lit an expression set in determined stone. Mr. Black staggered back a step as the bullet smashed into his mask's right eye. The bullet didn't penetrate the clear shielding. Simeon closed the distance to the man before Black even shifted. The agent's hand wrapped around Black's wrist just behind his balled fist, holding it still as Sim launched a kick at the enemy's kidney. His other hand shot out in a jab at Mr. Black's neck, aimed to get his pistol past this man's armor, and maybe stave in his jugular.

But Black's arm shot up in the same instant, as fast as the old spy. Or maybe even faster. He knocked Simeon's blow to the side. Black's fingers chopped down on Sim's wrist. Simeon's little pistol fell from his numb fingers and clattered to the ground.

A series of lightning blows flashed between the two men, as the muscles in their arms bulged in a deadly kind of arm wrestle. Black's hand steadily pulled away from Simeon's. The years dividing them made a difference.

"Stop," a woman's hard voice cut through the blows.

The old agent froze, his face heavy with dread and his right hand hovering in mid attack. His eyes flicked down. Vincent knelt on the concrete behind Mr. Black, held steady by two burly men. Two sharp cuts dribbled blood down Vincent's freckled face, coagulating in the cold air. A red-haired woman held him in a headlock, a hand-forged knife blade pressed against his throat. Pete and Gigan were manhandled into similar kneeling positions behind the inventor. The sharp crack of Gigan hitting the concrete rang through the night, as he half collapsed a few yards in front of the MM. His captors smirked behind their helmets as the Frenchman's head lolled and his arm welled blood. Their grip on his shoulders was automatic, and their eyes drifted to the scene in front of them; their captive obviously wasn't a threat anymore.

Vincent's eyes met Simeon's. No fear hung in those green eyes. Just a tired resignation in the set to his mouth. A hint of apology in the lines beside his eyes. A thin red line showed under the knife against his throat.

Simeon stepped back sharply and let his hands drop to his side. His face expressionless, his fists balled. Four of the Collective converged on him. Simeon offered no resistance as they forced him to his knees and looped a rope around his wrists and ankles.

"You're not just here to set off the machine," Simeon growled, his eyes burning into Mr. Black. The man stood perfectly still. Another villain would have been laughing maniacally. This one just stood, watching with his blue eyes a little too wide, a little too bright. "Would have already done it."

"You brought your plane with you," Mr. Black stated. "You carry some very useful things in that plane."

"The Ragnarök," Vincent said. Now fear shone in his face. Mr. Black's eyes crinkled with a smile, a wild delight in destruction playing over him.

"You have guessed it. Your weaponized drone can break sky-scrapers. Start fires. Poison water systems. So many ways to bring the dark," Mr. Black said. "I can break millions in one night. And do it again the next night. You've made it so easy. I will duplicate it when I have it. I will duplicate it many times. It should only take a few weeks. I don't need much sleep." A tremble ran through Vincent and his eyes closed as dread scored his features. The destruction this man could bring with that drone was unthinkable. And he could do it as a faceless entity, thousands of miles away from the scene. Untraceable. Unstoppable. He really would break the world. "I will destroy millions with your drones. Then, as the major cities wallow in the destruction, I will release the virus. And then destroy the infrastructure. The world will never recover. And I will be known forever as the one who reset civilization."

"That's what you've been aiming for all along," Vince said, his voice trembling, as anger and dread fought over his expression. "That first time we came up against your Collective, you split our ranks and sent one of us alone into Tripoli, so we would chase him in with the Ragnarök."

"You were never supposed to reach the lab," Black stated, his ice blue eyes on Pete as the Saudi knelt, straight and stiff. "You should have been killed at the start, or at least delayed enough you never made it into that egg's radius. My people should have had all the time needed to collect the drone."

"You will never control everything, Black," Pete snapped. "There will always be people outside your radius of power." *Like two brothers under the radar living out their faith by helping in the streets.* Images of what the Ragnarök could do to his surprise allies shot through his mind. A snarl cut over his face as he strained against the hands holding his shoulders. "You will not succeed in this. Your eggs will be found while you work to duplicate the drone."

"A few might. But you don't really think the eggs are how I plan to set the virus off, do you? I have it hidden much better than that."

"It's the ocean," Vincent said. "Holland, Tripoli, Venice. Every place he's drawn us to, except here and Riyadh, has been on a coastline. Even Memphis has the Mississippi River. He has the missing drums of virus locked down ready to empty into the water, and the ocean will carry it to every continent."

"Diving birds, circulating whales, shipping lines…" Pete said. "Especially the shipping lines. We first met this Collective in Rotterdam, busy with shipments from Libya."

"He has it on board ships somewhere," Vincent agreed, watching Mr. Black. "Probably that same Rotterdam line we first foun–" His voice cut off in a choke as the woman tightened her arm with a scowl. Black's head tipped, slowly, like a dog studying something it didn't quite understand.

"You are very good," Mr. Black's unnatural voice stated. "You surprise me by your penetration. I can see why you have been able to stop a little of the death we have tried to bring. But now you will be gone. The dark will win. And I will be immortal in history as the one no one could stop." His eyes turned to Simeon. Wide, burning eyes. "The dark always wins."

"Wrong." Simeon's word snapped through the night. He knelt on the cold concrete, four armored Collective looming over him, his hands bound behind him. But his face was still set in determined stone. "You can bring darkness. And, yes, it's easier to break than build. But no matter how much blackness you spread, there will always be light you can't touch. 'I am the Light of the World,' Jesus said, and His people work in this world. There will always be someone who shines brighter than you can kill. That you can't corrupt, and will never stop fighting back. Look at history, Black. Resistance fighters, martyrs, those marked in the books as heroes. Deepen the darkness and it only makes the points of light shine brighter."

The woman grunted and the red line on Vincent's neck became a thin stream. Black raised a finger and flicked it at her. She snapped her arm away with a little growl, swept up a blow torch resting under the building's overhang, and stomped away into the dark. Four eyes tracked her, knowing she was headed to crack open Perry, while the plane sat in a blackout, his usual careful security programming useless; as lifeless and helpless as a metal corpse. She went to collect a drone that could break the world in days. Mr. Black paced toward the silver disc. He reached into a pool of dark shadow beside it and drew out a small cooler. The lid squealed as he opened it. Mr. Black reached in and his black kid gloves came out again holding four syringes. He swept his mask off with his other hand. It dropped to the concrete with a clang. A smooth, tanned face met the moonlight, his features strangely still.

"Kirl would tell you the ones with the funding write the history books," Black said. "The winners name the heroes." His teeth flashed in an unnatural grin.

Half a world away, Aldrick Lefebvre stood behind his father's chair, his face pale as ash as he watched on his family's TV. Around him raucous cat calls and bravado reigned, most loudly declaring the whole scene an annoying setup, or some kind of promotional stunt, and throwing trash at the screen with loud orders to get back to normal programming. Aldrick just stared. Watching Mr. Black lift the needles. He twisted them to make the moonlight sparkle off the red liquid undulating inside. Enjoying the moment.

Aldrick felt hate for the man.

But much more than that, he felt the stars burning in his memory. He felt it with a physical tingling in his skin. The millions upon billions of stars he had watched as he rowed desperately through the darkest night he had seen in his urban life. His eyes went to the silver-haired old man his uncle worked for and Aldrick knew. His spine went a little straighter as he felt the wetness slowly gathering in his eyes. He would always be one of those points of light. For Uncle Guillaume's sake. For the God Uncle Guillaume served, Who sent angels in vests to save miserable boys caught by their enemies. In that moment, watching what might be the end of the civilized world he knew, Aldrick made the decision. He would burn in the dark, even if it ate him away to nothing but ash in the wind.

Across the ocean from the Lefebvres, Nakia sat in the tiny hospital room beside his brother. The last of his family on this side of earth lay in a drugged sleep. Darius neared the end of his long fight. Nakia stared at the small TV mounted in the corner. His eyes were dry as he watched. He didn't have the strength left to feel much at all. This Black nemesis spun the syringes in an unholy delight in the death he was about to bring. Nakia watched the eastern anti-terrorist-wonder twist in his captor's grip, a snarl rippling over his face. It would be pale and still soon, after those syringes. Nakia was thankful Darius was asleep and didn't know about all this happening a continent away. He would rest better thinking his little brother had someone to take care of him. Without knowing death claimed their ally too.

Death took so much.

But Life gave more. The Light of the World, the Bread of Life, the Door… Nakia knew the names of Christ. And in that moment he fell into them like the arms of a Father held out to comfort a broken child. A dry sob rent from him. But healing and growth rode with the sorrow in that hospital room. Some things can only be learned in rooms like that. And this wasn't Nakia's first time. When their father died, Nakia and Darius memorized Revelations twenty-one together. Nakia knew where the Door led. To a land with no sun and no moon, because the God of light filled the whole world. Burning every shred of darkness away.

A breath sucked into Nakia's lungs and his mouth set in a hard line as his fingers tightened in his brother's. Darius neared the end of the fight, and the beginning of unending life. Their strange, newfound ally looked like he would be joining the everlasting feast with Darius soon.

But Nakia's fight was just beginning.

Jack and Judy Leason watched Jack's computer screen in silence. There wasn't anything to say. They had helped find the one financing the business, and even stopped a war and the first outbreak of this virus. But it looked like when the Parabaloni tracked down the real one behind the Maeslant... Judy leaned into the comforting bulk of her husband. Jack slid his arm through hers and pulled her close, and they just watched.

Their thoughts moved to the last time they had seen that red, undulating liquid. Then the terror had nearly debilitated the couple. But this time they already had the Light pumping through their veins. Other people would need to hear His truth more than ever now.

"If this Black pulls it off, I'll be going back to paper and pens," the reporter commented. Judy squeezed his arm. Her voice came strong with approval.

"Them's fighting words, Jackie boy."

Colin was vaguely aware he was on his feet in his comfortable, palatial rooms. His phone shook in his hand as he stared at the unbelievable scene. Wasn't there anyone there to rush in and save the day? His knowledge of history whispered, *Not all days are saved.* He watched the moonlight sparkle off the red liquid and a choked gurgle came from him.

But even in that moment, in another detached part of himself, he saw the moonlight. It invaded the night and refused to let the darkness reign. And it never went out. That creepy, horrible Mr. Black turned the needles again, and the light sparkled off them. It made them shine. The moonlight made it almost beautiful.

The dark didn't win. There would always be light beyond it, light the dark couldn't touch.

Colin's eyes flew to the New Testament on his little table. It sat open to John 8, and verse 12 seemed to blaze off the page. Suddenly Jesus blazed brighter than any light and Colin choked again. He fell to his knees, joining those four brave men as he stared at his screen and shook.

He would kneel like them. To the One who said, *"Let there be light."* Colin would kneel, and he would rise to fight; a reflection of the burning Son that never went out.

In a living room in Tennessee, Walter's knuckles turned white as he gripped his chair. Why didn't someone do something?! Surely there were policemen there, someone… He glanced at his wife, aware of the strain it took to turn his head. She didn't even look at the screen, she stared at her father. Algernon Fitzkin sat with his elbows on his knees watching the scene in the Iowa zoo. His face was creased, as if he were trying to puzzle something out. He leaned closer, staring at the slim figure of the French sharpshooter, seemingly so limp and defeated. There it came again. A little flick of the finger, just an instant of movement barely caught on the video feed.

Algy's mouth shifted slowly into a little, terrifying smile.

Chapter 32

M r. Black spun the syringes. The moonlight caught the red liquid undulating inside and sent it sparkling. Pete felt a tremble run through the thick arm wrapped around his neck. He didn't think it was just because of the man's leopard-torn skin. If that virus once left its sterilized containers, it had the potential to change the world. Mr. Black turned his back on Simeon and his icy blue eyes landed on the Saudi. Pete had the uncomfortable urge to blurt out, "No, I will not speak the *Shahaadatayn*." He didn't like needles.

"Youngest first, I think," Black said. "You really shouldn't have tried to fight again, Lee. A good soldier knows when they're beaten." He took a step toward the thin Saudi kneeling on the concrete, held steady by three of Black's minions.

Simeon's thumb tapped his watch.

Floodlights clicked on through the zoo.

The motion light on the building blazed into life and pooled over Black.

Light shot through the dark night, straight through eyeballs adjusted for the dark. The Collective recoiled, startled and disoriented.

Four Parabaloni burst into motion. The ropes looped around their wrists seemed to unravel under the work of blades carefully pasted over their fingernails. Four Collective sailed over their captive's heads, smashed into each other with a resounding smack, and thudded into a pile on the concrete. A netting gun leapt from one of Simeon's vest pockets, and a padded net closed around the syringes in Mr. Black's hands. They ripped away from the villain and bounced harmlessly out of his range.

As the net fired, Vincent's fist came up with a sharp crack, and one of those holding him crumpled in a limp heap. Gigan's leg went out in a back kick that shattered one man's knee cap, and sent him toppling screaming into Pete's captors. Three of them went down like bowling-pins. A thin brown hand, weathered tan one, and a calloused freckled one shot out as their enemies fell and reclaimed their weapons. A burst of bullets spit from Floyd,

Clarice, and Adeela the Second. Bullets slammed into the neck line with perfect accuracy, into the tiny gap between armor and helmet. The enemy hit the ground and lay still. In ten seconds, only Mr. Black and the Parabaloni remained conscience in the Iowa zoo. Gigan rested Clarice against his shoulder as he stood up. He turned to Mr. Black.

"There, my creepy friend, you have miscalculated. We will always fight again."

Black's face rippled with dumbfounded fury. He leapt for the wall, one hand sweeping his rifle up.

"I assume the power's return is your work?" he said. His voice shook, just a little.

"You could say that," Vincent grinned at him.

"I will accept it," Jojo agreed over the team's hidden earbuds. She navigated the skitterer past the dumbfounded shadows at the power station, as they stared at their fried egg and the sudden return of power. Jojo couldn't help grinning at their shock as she watched over her feed. It took them long enough to notice. She had been in for fifteen minutes. It had only taken two minutes to set up a recording of the Egbert's pulse and take out the egg with Vincent's gadgets. Her skitterer had sat waiting to reset the power for ages. "You played the timing too close for comfort, Simeon! I would have preferred your order to start things before the needles came toward any of you."

"There's a certain dramatic flair that comes with the job," Vincent shrugged, though he and his team were the only ones who heard Jojo. His eyes flicked to Mr. Black. "Our plane has plenty of it built into him, too. Redhead doesn't have a chance at getting inside. You're not the only one who can plan ahead."

"How...? You did not have time to reach my egg or call in someone else, I didn't allow you that time!"

"Again you miscalculated," Pete answered, his half smile twisting his face. "There are more in this fight than just we four. And you gave us plenty of time to find out how you work and dissect what you would do next."

"So you knew I would not start my machine yet," Black said, and there was a definite shake to it. "You calculated I needed the infrastructure intact to let the Ragnaröks wreak death on the world. But now I have nothing to wait for."

His closed fist jerked the cord, his eyes blazing.

Black stumbled forward as the wire gave him no resistance. He held up the severed cord and stared at it. Black dropped to all fours to stare at his silver disc. Three perfect lines melted through it. The acid still steamed as it continued to melt. An inarticulate cry roared from Black and his finger slammed onto his rifle's trigger. Nothing happened.

"The clip is around here somewhere," Gigan commented, as Black scrabbled at his rifle. His blue eyes snapped at the Frenchman in disbelief. Gigan chuckled. "Oh come now, you didn't really think Sim would let you shoot us in the head while we waited to confirm where you actually put the virus. He had a reason for coming close enough to disarm you." Simeon's little pistol came down hard on Black's ear. The millions watching saw the old spy's hand land on his enemy's hair as he tumbled toward the puddle of acid leaking on the concrete. Simeon Lee pulled him away from the puddle.

A sharp crack rang as Sim's plunger bullet hit Black in the back of the neck. The man who would bring darkness on all the world sprawled in an ungainly heap.

"Dude, three perfect lines?" Vincent said, leaning over to stare at the machine. "How many acid balls did it take?"

"I used them all as carefully as possible," Gigan said. "That wasn't the hard bit, it was harder to get my captors to drag me into position. But they were susceptible enough to my prods if I seemed harmless. Why do you think I let you people do all the talking?" He shivered as he slapped Vincent's palm-sized spring gun into the inventor's hand. "I appreciate you wanting the sharpshooter to do the aiming. But next time if you want to use acid, you do it!"

"Sure, G, just so long as we don't have a vindictive madman we know will target me for Sim's sake," Vince laughed, and spun to the big boss. "Next time we do this, you get to be the sacrificial lamb."

"Fair," Simeon shrugged.

"Head's up, the wolf pack is curious about the noise," Pete said, his eyes on the trees. "And I think that is a bear strolling out of the woods."

"We are done putting on a fine show for the crowds," Gigan said, swinging Clarice's strap over his shoulder. He looked up at the cameras and waved, the laughter lines deep on his tired face. The millions watching wondered in awe what desperate mission had given him the magnificent black eye. "Come, let us go home and sleep. I could use it."

"Got to make a stop at the police station on the way," Vincent grinned.

Gigan's laugh rang around the zoo as Vincent flung an arm over Simeon's shoulders. They headed toward the gate, Pete taking point as they walked past the nesting birds. The beautiful strains of a Doxology in four-part harmony wafted out of the darkness as the Parabaloni scaled the fence and disappeared, headed for happier meetings.

Mr. Black and his Collective snored on beside the melted wreckage of his death-dealing machine.

Luther Kirl jerked up from staring over Jones's shoulder, a snarl curling over his face. The hymn still drifted from the cameras' feeds. Jones strained the sound equipment, trying to pick up one more note as it slowly drifted away. He wanted to hear more of it. He needed to hear more.

"At least one annoyance is out of my hair," Luther growled. "I'll deal with Vincent and his people on my own." Luther spun on his heel and stomped toward the door. Jones' jaw tightened. Fall saw the big man's fists ball. The geek had the burning desire to go hide under a rock somewhere. This had been the wrong job to take; sometimes the money wasn't worth it. He had laughed when his dad told him that before he left for this job. Fall shrank into his chair, wishing it would swallow him as he saw the fire growing in this big mercenary's eyes. Drat it, the money really wasn't worth this, he would have to apologize to his old man!

The wall of windows shattered. Fall screamed and dove under the chair. Two black drones whizzed in through the glass shards spraying into the room.

Luther felt claws grip his shoulders and jerk him back. It ripped his hand away from the doorknob and his heels kicked against the ground like a toddler having a fit. Wind rushed around him, and an inhuman buzz hummed in his ears. Out of the corner of his eye he caught his own dragging form on the screens, held by two black drones with rotors whirring in a blur, as another smaller drone videoed it and sent it over his own feed. Then the drones buzzed out the window, and he went with them.

A scream, high and piercing, rent from him as he looked past his kicking shoes to three hundred feet of empty air between himself and the wet London pavement.

"You didn't really think you were just walking out of this, did you?" a young, eastern, female voice drifted from the drones. She sounded amused. Luther had never been as terrified of anything as that humor in his own imminent death.

"Put me back," he gabbled in the drizzling rain. "Please. I can get you what you want!"

"What do I want, Luther Kirl?" the woman scoffed. The drizzle whipped into him as the drones shot past the streets.

"I'll let you in on our world-shaping. I can get you power, love, safety, a way to right all the wrongs," he gasped.

"I have the power of Christ's blood, and that comes with more love than your shriveled soul can imagine, enough to overflow into the righting of the world. Jesus is all I want, Kirl." The drones sped up and the wind pounded into him. His voice rose to a shriek, terror clawing through it.

"I can get you anything! Just don't kill me!" he yelled. Laughter melded with the drizzle and the wind, circling around his head in a nightmare.

"You just admitted to being one of the main causes of a plot to destroy the world! I don't have to kill you." He started to slow down and Kirl's eyes cracked open as he heard himself hyperventilating. The Thames ran on his left, a muddy gray expanse in the drizzle, and New Scotland Yard stood on the Victoria Embankment like a stalwart bobby just waiting for him. The drones zipped to the boxy building and brought Luther Kirl down gently on the flat roof in a limp, wet, shaking heap. "Delivery!" Jojo sang into the feed.

The TV went blank for a moment as the "special programming" ended. Just a black screen in the Aziz's new, spacious living room. It blinked to its pre-recorded program, and an Imman droned from the screen. The children's voices echoed through the house, exploring and claiming rooms and making a mess of the new white carpets. But they couldn't drown out the sound of that Imman droning on. Yousef straightened from where he leaned against the wall. He pulled his carving knife from his pocket and studied it for a moment, as the words of the prayer wrapped around him in a blanket of memories.

The knife sailed from his hand and slammed into the screen. Cracks spread in a sharp spiderweb. The picture flickered once, and then went black.

That knife cut through the last resistance. It cut through the pride and excuses holding him back. Through the guilt that had hung in Yousef's bones eating him away to a husk. His sister spoke the truth and he knew it. In that instant Yousef let himself believe what he had read in Jojo's Bible. And in that instant, Christ's power flowed over him in its cleansing fountain, flowing into every dark corner. Renewing, remaking, driving out the years of mourning in a sudden, beautiful whisper of, "I am with you...[65]" The Spider sucked it in, trembling at the knowledge of what he had just done.

Yousef's booming laugh echoed through the empty rooms of his new house.

Susie sat on the police receptionist's hard chair. She sat very still, staring at the blank screen after Jimmy[66] turned off the pre-

---

[65] Matthew 28:20

[66] Yes, I can call him by his first name, I've known him since he was five. Jimmy always preferred the lions, and I let him come with me and pet Horatio the First once when the vet had him sedated to trim the big cat's claws. He always

recorded weather report. Sarah flipped her pen nervously at the desk and Susie knew she was thinking about the right thing to say; Sarah used to do the same thing when she came for zoo field trips and someone asked her a question.

"They'll be able to rebuild your fence, Miss Quenton," Sarah said. "And I bet the vet can pull your gorilla through. You may have to hire more employees, your zoo is going to be famous after today."

"Oh horrors, I hope not!" Susie blinked, sitting up a little straighter and plunking her coffee cup on the desk. Jimmy grinned at her response. The door swung open and the stocky stranger stepped through. The police station grew suddenly still as every eye focused on him. He seemed oblivious to it. He only noticed Susie.

"Walk you home?" Simeon asked, soft and hopeful. Susie stood up, let the blanket fall off her shoulders, and handed it back to Sarah.

"I would be delighted. Thank you," she answered. Simeon held the door open and she strode out with her long gait, trained for eating up the miles as she made circuits around her animal pens. The door closed behind the classy, inimitable stranger and Jimmy and Sarah stared at each other.

"Miss Quenton has a man!" Sarah burst out. A raucous cheer broke from the local police force of Tuscaloosa, Iowa.

Outside, Susie felt the three young men close in behind them, shoving each other in the shoulder like roughhousing teenagers, teases and congratulations hurtling from them; just quiet enough it was hard to catch all the words. Simeon's face turned her way again, and she smiled in relief.

"Now you look like your picture!" Susie burst out. "Much better, I must say, I missed your normal face tonight." Simeon didn't try to hide his smile at the comment. "I take it you didn't want the millions watching to recognize you on the street, very clever. Do you think it worked?" Her eyes flitted behind her, then back

---

had a smile for me after that, no matter how old we both got. He's also quite good at catching my rabbit when she's being especially stubborn. Like the week she thought she was a gazelle and I gave up.

to Simeon. He acknowledged her silent question by slowing down. The boys took the offer and trotted up to join the party. "Do you think whatever you did worked?" Susie asked again.

"Just enough greasepaint and bite blocks to change facial structures and, hopefully, keep our real faces out of every database in the world," Gigan said. He heaved a long sigh. "All right, Simeon, I admit it, you were once again right. It is dangerous to give the bad guys even a starting point to find more about us. It lets them find our people."

"Your point valid too," Simeon shrugged. "Don't have to finish the cleanup now."

"There are enough people out there who know our name as the good guys to take that video footage seriously. Jojo already has the Iowa National Guard at the zoo, and people should actually look for the Egberts and virus," Vincent finished for Simeon. A grin stretched the inventor's face in two. "Which means we're done."

"The point to be decided is which valid point is more vital to our survival and the safety of our people," Pete put in. They all saw Simeon hesitate, and Susie chuckled.

"I'm afraid that's something of a moot point after tonight," she said. Gigan gave a little groan. Pete's hand shot out and rammed into Gigan's good shoulder, driving the Frenchman two steps to the left.

"So how many lemurs did you take out?" he grinned. Susie gave a little yelp. Gigan laughed and a string of French rattled at his partner's head.

"None," Simeon soothed, and Susie breathed again as she led the way onto her street.

"Don't worry the knight's maiden, Peter, it is not kind," Gigan finished his harangue in English.

"Why? She gave us all gray hairs tonight!" Pete objected. "But I am sorry about your tiger. If you want help procuring a new one, we know a guy."

"Hey Susie, tell him something nice about turtles, will you?" Vincent changed the subject, and Gigan and Simeon snorted back a laugh. Her smile turned brilliant, and Susie Quenton launched off, hurtling fun facts about turtles at Pete's head. He did his best imitation of pretending to be interested, as his work family laughed, and they all turned toward Susie's two-story family house.

✦

Jojo cut the feed from her drone. She looked at the café's TVs through the window of the private room she had claimed. The rest of the clientele milled around those screens mounted at the bar, watching in fascination. No one even glanced at the young Eastern girl with the laptop and gaming headphones. The screens cut back to their normal programming. Jojo didn't pay much attention to them. She wasn't quite finished yet.

Jojo hit the command sequence to bring her Luther-retrieving-drones home, dropped their joystick into her bag, and reached for the Ragnarök glove. She slid her fingers into the glove and looked out at the sleek red corvette sitting in the parking lot. The Ragnarök slowly pushed the trunk open and rose over the parking lot. Jojo took a moment to gently lower it on the trunk. She heard the click of the latch catching through her window, and then sent the drone rocketing into the cold winter air and zipping the thirty miles toward Susie Quenton's little town. She took a long, enjoyable sip of her chai latte as winter fields flashed by in a blur on her screen. Perry's dot showed in one corner of her laptop, blinking gently. Jojo slowed the Ragnarök and brought it in carefully to hover over their plane. She had used Heshman's skitterer to get the power back on about eight minutes ago. That redhaired lady should still be somewhere near the area. Jojo fed the Ragnarök a screenshot picture of the redhaired one, typed in a quick sequence of orders, and sat back with her chai as she watched it start to sweep. One pleasant sip, and her laptop gave a soft "ping."

A corner of her screen flashed up with the Ragnarök's video feed. A slim woman stood beside a jeep in a pretty neighborhood. A knife flashed in her hand, and Jojo watched as she expertly jimmied open the door.

"Not today, Red," Jojo murmured in a melodramatic voice. The drone swooped down and fired a quick blast from the cannon loaded with the Parabaloni's plunger bullets. Jojo watched two of them bounce off this lady's face. She tumbled to the side at the force of the blow, hit the asphalt street, and lay still in a heap. Jojo sent the drone rocketing up, above the clouds, above anywhere it could get into trouble. She hit the button for satellite mode, slid the glove off, dropped it into her bag, and sat back with her tea.

That seemed almost anticlimactic. Maybe she should have given the lady a chance to fight back or something. No, Jojo considered as she sent the lady's coordinates in a quick text to the captain in charge of cleaning up the mess at the zoo. She didn't need any more excitement in her life. She would happily take anticlimactic.

Jojo shut her laptop, slid it in her bag with the drones' controls, picked up her drink and boxes of pies, and headed for the door. She had a hard time holding back laughter as she watched the people staring wide-eyed at the television screens mounted in the café and listened to the buzz of startled speculation. Most of them thought it an elaborate hoax, of course, a way for the stations to get more viewers. But some pointed out the sudden bright light spotted miles away across the plains, just when the zoo's fence exploded. Not a single one of them had noticed her in the private room, speaking the words they heard spouted from a drone in a London drizzle.

This job could be really fun sometimes.

Maybe if she picked and chose what she did...

Jojo slid behind the corvette's wheel, dropped her chai into the cup holder, slid the pies on the passenger seat, and started to drive the thirty miles to Tuscaloosa. The streetlights dropped behind remarkably quickly, and rural scenes spread out in plains of moonlit winter fields. A hymn hummed from Jojo as she drove. This, right here, the end of a good mission with all her people safe and even happy, helping mop up the loose ends and bring order to the messy business of righting the world... This was what she enjoyed.

Although Sean had the real work of cleaning up after what they found in this business.

But then, he didn't *really* know what they did, or what was needed.

Maybe there should be someone in the gap. Between the hectic hard, hard work of meeting the darkness and smashing it, and the righting the world again after the smashing turned it upside down. Someone who knew the people on both ends. Knew the hardness of the smashing, and the work needed for the righting.

That would help Pete and the others too. If they knew someone who understood what really needed done was there, coordinating with all the funds and manpower needed to turn things right side up again. Someone who knew the faces too and could bring therapy and build new homes, and even do it all remotely if she felt like it, on her own time schedule…

Hm. This needed contemplated. Jojo drove and thought and prayed, and the miles sped quickly under the car's tires. She pulled to a proper stop in front of a large two-story old house and slid out with the pie boxes. The sun's beams began to invade the dark as a sliver of dawn showed on the horizon. Jojo strolled through the crisp cold air, only a little tainted by the acrid scent of smoke and large smelly animals, and paused with her hand raised to knock.

She could hear the laughter drifting out. Pete and Gigan and Vince, chattering and jawing at each other. Simeon's voice cut in occasionally, adding to the teases at the near misses and the hair-breath success. They called it "a debriefing." But it was really a jolly old party over all the bad things stopped by their hard work. They sounded so happy. This, right here, was where the four of them found their happy place. Together, alive, nursing battle wounds and telling old jokes and new teases over a job well done. Knowing they pushed back the darkness just a few feet more. A grin hovered on Jojo's face as she rapped on the door. They might be elite, sore, broken, and bruised from the fight. But these four men were made for this. And they fit it so well.

The door pulled open and homey warm light poured out around a thickset woman in a woolen sweater and a bright purple skirt. Her wispy brown hair poked out of a hastily done bun, and a hint of a fishy smell hung about her. But her smile blazed brighter than the light framing her. That smile felt like meeting Simeon for the first time, when he made all her fear and confusion at being loose in a foreign airport burn off like mist in the sun. It felt like sitting in a meadow with three young men and feeling home in a strange air.

The connection clicked into place as Jojo stood outside that door in Iowa. She knew why the email thread from two very different people had meshed like cogs in a beautiful machine. And why there was such joy radiating to the rafters of this old house at having won again. These souls rested in the love of the same Lord, Who had found them wherever they were, and carried them through every day. And that love overflowed to love the people around them. To these people, every single soul was a precious story, a fascinating thing to be cherished and helped and enjoyed. They cared so deeply about everyone around them. Jojo let herself fall into that caring as she stepped inside and gave this fish-smelling woman a hug.

Susie hugged her back. And it felt like meeting another aunt. It felt like kitchen conversations. It felt like pleasant memories and soft bedtimes. It felt like home. Because it carried all the love and safety of the best of home.

"Ah, here we are, all we were missing!" Susie Quenton said as she stepped back to let the young lady walk inside.

"Dessert!" four voices called out the inevitable tease.

"Sorry, I accidentally set you up for that one," Susie grinned at her, laughter creasing the natural lines beside her eyes and drawing Jojo into the joke.

Jojo felt a grin spreading through her as she walked over to join the Parabaloni and sat one pie in front of Pete and the other in the center of Susie's scratched, paint smeared table. The teases and chatter enfolded her, Susie's voice weaving among it in a natural rhythm. Jojo sank onto a wobbly seat, watched dawn's rays play over the pie box, and let herself enjoy.

Right here, right now, things were just right.

The End

Author Bio

Catherine Gruben Smith lives in the middle of Texas, which she begrudgingly admits is probably better than a magical tower. She grew up mostly in a dusty town in the southern New Mexican desert and will always carry the quirks. (Yes, New Mexico is a part of the United States, and no, she was not a missionary, and yes, you can drink the water.) It is her delight and privilege to be  a housewife, mother, and an Earl Gray connoisseur. Another of her constant activities is trying to keep her dogs from terrorizing the house and neighborhood with their determination to be always underfoot and hungry. (The work of a dog lover is never done.) She has always been fascinated by the written word, philosophical reasoning, and good stories of bravery and honor. When not writing, reading, chasing children or dogs, Catherine can be found board-gaming, baking, hiking, or possibly broad sword fighting with her older brother. If you want a fuller explanation of Catherine, go and read Psalm 30. The heart and purpose of her life can be found there, especially in the last two verses.

Catherine prays reading her books will help her readers find the urge to get up off the couch and serve. The Lord of all life calls us to the battlefield, to mop up the enemy after He has won the war. Don't sit on the side-lines. We have the tools to fix this broken world.

Where to find more information, or contact Catherine:
catherinegrubensmith.com
posttenebrasluxbooks.com
catherinegrubensmith@gmail.com

Books by Catherine Gruben Smith

Dreaded King Saga:
A Son Rises
Reign Falls
Knight Duty
Heir Raising
Splitting Heirs

Knight Jobs Series:
Wail of the Wyrm

Parabaloni:
The Parabaloni
The Slingshot Effect
As the Eagle Flies
Solitaire
Adele Angst
Blind Leader
Gathering Shadows
Black Out

Faerytales of Deweot:
How to Unmake a Dragon
Faery Wings and Pirate Things

Sojourners:
Ravens Ruins
Ravens Rescue
Ravens Return
Ravens Refuge
Ravens Raid
Ravens Rebirth